NEW BLOOD

NEW BLOOD

GAIL DAYTON

TOR®

paranormal romance

A TOM DOHERTY ASSOCIATES BOOK
NEW YORK

This is a work of fiction. All the characters, organizations, and events portrayed in this novel are either fictitious or are used fictitiously.

NEW BLOOD

Copyright © 2009 by Gail Dayton

All rights reserved.

A Tor Book
Published by Tom Doherty Associates, LLC
175 Fifth Avenue
New York, NY 10010

www.tor-forge.com

Tor® is a registered trademark of Tom Doherty Associates, LLC.

ISBN-13: 978-0-7653-6250-6
ISBN-10: 0-7653-6250-3

First Edition: March 2009

Printed in the United States of America

0 9 8 7 6 5 4 3 2 1

For the "big guys"—Richard, Andrew, Peter, and Christopher, gentlemen all. Can't wait to see what mountains you climb, oceans you swim, and dragons you slay . . .

Thanks again to C. E. Murphy for looking stuff up for me and showing me where to look it up. You're always looking out for me, woman. Thanks go to my agent, Elaine English, for sticking with it, even when I whined about that third revision, and to my editor, Heather Osborn, for recognizing genius (wink, wink). And always, thank you to Myles for putting up with me and worrying about me when I'm not writing. You're the best. I'll take another thirty-something years with you.

NEW BLOOD

1

H<small>E HAD BEEN</small> searching for a long time.

Just how long a time and just what it was he sought, Jax didn't know. But something, and a very long time.

There were a lot of things Jax didn't know. Many more things he wasn't certain of. Nor did he think he wanted to know them.

Now, Jax stood in the shelter of deep forest with Crow circling and cawing overhead, and knew he had finally found what he had been seeking over such an undetermined age. She—not it, for now he'd found her, he knew the object of his search was a woman—worked in a clearing of the forest, in a garden surrounding a tidy cottage.

She was tall and strong, the hoe she wielded biting deep into the earth as she fought encroachment by weeds. Her white-blond hair, the color of a ray of sunlight, was bound into a braid as thick as Jax's own bony wrist, and it fell past her shoulder to brush the herb plants where she labored. She wore a brown dress, woven of some sturdy fiber, simple shapes sewn together that clung to the womanly figure it covered.

A faint chill went through him. Without seeing her face, Jax knew she was a beautiful woman, and beautiful women made him uneasy. As did knowing things without understanding how he knew them. At this moment, though he stood motionless and unseen, blending into the shadows of the forest, inside his head Jax was rapidly descending into panic.

A tiny replica of himself ran screaming in circles, where no one could see or hear. Jax had no doubt whatsoever that this beautiful, terrifying woman meant something, and that same certainty told him he did not wish to know what that was.

Nor did he know what would happen next.

The woman straightened from her task and looked up, shading her eyes with a hand as she searched the sky for Crow. Jax faded deeper into the shadows, turning his face so its paleness would not catch her eye. His heart pounded, faster and harder than it had in as long as he could remember. Which wasn't saying much.

"I know you're in there."

The sound of a human voice—her voice—startled Jax into looking up. Had it been so long since he'd heard anyone speak? He couldn't remember.

She looked straight at him. How? And Lady—she was just as beautiful as he feared. Not young or dewy fresh, but the years and the knowledge made her stronger, more beautiful. Her skin was clear perfect sun-kissed gold, her mouth wide and generous, her chin stubborn, her jaw square, matching the strength in her arms. Her eyebrows flared like pale crow's wings over eyes so blue, it seemed a piece of the sky had been stolen.

Jax wanted to look away, but could not.

He felt like a maiden in one of the tales he couldn't remember hearing, mesmerized by the stare of a serpent. A dragon. But he was no maiden—he was fairly sure. And she was certainly—he hoped—no dragon.

"Did you hear me?" She raised her hoe, gripping it like a weapon. "I said, I know you are there. Come out."

He would leave. Go back into the forest and live as he had been. Solitary. Safe. His mind formed the intention, sent messages to his limbs to turn and walk away. Yet somehow he found himself walking forward into the sunlight, and he knew that his life had made still another of those fateful changes he could not recall. Nothing would ever be the same again.

Not for him. Not for her. Not, he feared, for the whole world.

AMANUSA SQUARED HER stance and lifted her hoe as the man walked out of the forest. She did not read danger in him, but she had not lived this many years without learning that pain and death often lurked behind an innocent face. And this man looked far from harmless.

He was big, taller than she, which was a rare thing in this corner of the Austrian Empire. Amanusa towered over most of her neighbors. This man was taller yet, broad-shouldered and rangy, with a loose-limbed stride as if he hadn't been fastened together quite tightly enough. The features of his long narrow face had that same rough, not-quite-finished appearance, but there seemed to be neither anger nor cruelty in them. Overall, he seemed . . . brown.

He wore a long brown leather overcoat, almost to his ankles, brown trousers, and a brown brocade waistcoat over a tan shirt. Even his silky neckcloth was a pale, creamy shade of brown. His thick hair glinted red in the sunlight, but despite the hints of russet, it was brown. Only his skin decried all the brown. He was pale, as if he had not seen the sun in a long time, even now, in high summer.

"Stop there," Amanusa ordered. She should have bade him stop sooner, farther away, but she could sense no harm in him.

The man stopped, showed empty hands, and she opened her senses wide, tried to read his mood. She found only confusion and . . . fear?

What would a man his size have to fear from a woman?

"Who are you?" she demanded. "What do you want?"

Slowly, keeping his blue-green gaze fastened upon hers and his open hands spread wide, the man went down to one knee. "I am called Jax," he said in a language Amanusa had not heard in far too long.

She fought back the memories that wanted to rush over her, memories of home and safety, and of terror. How had this man come so far from that place?

"Whether Jax is my true name or I have another, I do not know. Only Jax. As for what I want—"

A shiver passed over him. When he blinked, someone else knelt before Amanusa, looking out at her through coffee-brown eyes. A shiver whispered through Amanusa as well. There was magic working here. Inside the man.

"Greetings to you, blood sorceress." A different voice, bearing only the deep timbre of the man Jax, spoke through his mouth in the same foreign tongue.

Amanusa shuddered again with a sudden, deep chill.

"I left my search for an apprentice too late," the voice said. "I am taken up—but the magic would have swallowed me soon even so. I am left with binding my servant Jax to this task, of finding the next blood sorceress. And so he has.

"He can teach you what I have given him to teach. He can show you where to find the other things you will need to know. He will serve whatever needs you may have. He is not a bad servant. I do not know that he is a good servant, but he is not a bad one. Now he will serve you, perhaps better than he did me.

"Listen to the words I have given him. The blood magic must not be lost. I have seen terrible things coming, and the blood will be needed. Knowledge is all very well in its place, but some things are so terrible, so dire and awful, that only the magic borne in blood and bone and flesh can hold them back.

"I can only hope that Jax has surpassed his usual cork-brained efforts and found you quickly. There is much to learn and little time to learn it. Do not waste a single minute. Honor to you, blood sorceress."

As Amanusa watched horror-stricken, the man's eyes faded from brown to blue and his face slowly filled back up with himself. Jax stared at her a moment, blood beginning to trickle from his nose. Then his eyes rolled up in his head and he toppled over onto the comfrey.

IT WAS DAYLIGHT again, nearing noon. And still the man—Jax—lay motionless in her bed, scarce seeming to breathe. Amanusa checked one more time to be sure he did indeed breathe and propped hands on hips. What was she supposed to do with him?

When he had collapsed yesterday, she'd been sorely tempted to leave him where he fell. He'd frightened her, appearing out of nowhere like that. She could admit her fear to herself, even if she'd learned better than to let it show. But no matter the temptation, she couldn't have left him there. Not helpless as he was. It just wasn't in her to be so cold.

For one thing, he'd been bleeding. For another, there was that strange magic that had crawled out of some depth to possess his eyes and his voice. Amanusa shuddered. Poor man. For all his lean strength and height and handsome face, he had no power against the magic. Woman's magic, apparently.

A chill ran down Amanusa's back at the memory of that eerie voice. She made a warding sign in the air, then spit on the earth outside her door for extra protection. Women couldn't be magicians. Or sorceresses. Not here. Not in the Grand Principality of Transylvania, part of the Austrian Empire.

The Imperial Council of Magicians strictly enforced that rule, and Amanusa had no desire to bring them down upon her. She'd never seen their work, but she'd heard whispered tales of women left witless after the wizards' and conjurers' inquisition. As long as Amanusa stuck to small magics, the tiny spells allowed women, and denied her thirst for more, she would be safe. If this man and the magic that bound him called the council's attention to her . . .

She had to get rid of him and the temptation that was the knowledge he carried.

But that nosebleed concerned her, coming on top of powerful magic as it did. She had sworn to tend the sick and helpless. When he was helpless no longer, she would send him on his way. After he explained a few things. Such as why he'd addressed her as "blood sorceress".

A harsh caw brought Amanusa slowly around to see a crow walking through the open doorway of her cottage as though it were an invited guest. Amanusa tilted her head, watching it, and the crow cocked its head in seeming response, fixing her with one black beady eye. It cawed at her again, as if asking permission to be there. Amanusa wanted to laugh at herself for such fanciful notions, but couldn't quite.

She bowed, gesturing a welcome. "Do come in, Master Crow."

And with a flurry of black wings, it flew to perch at the head of her bed. Above the blue-green gaze of the man, Jax. The crow hopped down onto the blanket covering him and absently, the man raised a hand to stroke the ebony feathers of its breast, never taking his eyes off Amanusa.

"So, it wasn't a dream," he said in that same haunting language.

"You're speaking English." That wasn't what she meant to say.

His lips twitched in a tiny, hesitant smile that vanished. "So are you."

"Yes, but this is Transylvania. No one speaks English here."

"Except, apparently, you and me." He struggled to sit up, setting the crow to flapping until he stilled.

Amanusa quelled the urge to assist him. He was big. He was inside her home, in her bed, and she didn't know how ill he might yet be. He hadn't been armed, which eased some of her worries. At least he was still dressed, though now in shirt and trousers only, with all the buttons unfastened. After wrestling him into the house and the bed, she hadn't wanted to wrestle him out of his clothing.

He wasn't feverish. She'd found no open wounds or obvious injuries to cause his collapse. Nothing other than the magic. The bleeding had stopped soon after she got him inside.

"How did you get here?" she demanded. "What do you want? Where do you come from?"

Now that he was awake, the helplessness dropped away, transforming him into a dangerous creature, a man. Aggression was her best defense, she'd found, especially on her own ground. Fear made her angry, and she hid her trembling hands.

"England, apparently." He moved the crow gently aside and reached beneath the blanket to button his trousers. "How is it that you speak English?"

She shook her head. "My questions first. What do you want?"

Jax gave her a wary look as he brought his bare, bony feet out from under the blanket and set them on the plank floor. "What did I say?"

"A great deal of nonsense. How do you feel? Any dizziness? Nausea?" His caution made her brave and she dared to step closer and lift his eyelids, searching his eyes for any sign of head injury.

Things swam past in their depths. Brown flecks appeared in the cool blue and faded again.

Amanusa held her hand steady, refusing to flinch at the strangeness. She knew enough about magic that it didn't frighten her. She looked until she was satisfied she had seen all there was to see. Magic haunted this man, held him tight in its eerie grip. She took her hand from his face and stepped away.

"I didn't—" He swallowed. "Greet you as 'blood sorceress'?"

"Like I said, utter nonsense." Amanusa turned away to set the kettle on the hearth, kept her hands busy so they wouldn't shake. Kept her mind busy so it didn't shatter. She was no blood sorceress. Blood magic killed. It lived on blood and pain and death, and it ate the soul of its user. She would never be a sorceress. Ever. "If you know what you said, why did you ask?"

He rubbed a hand over his eyes and thrust it into his too-long hair, shoving it back out of his face. "I don't always—sometimes I remember things that didn't happen, and most times I don't remember things that did." He met her eyes when she looked back at him, his eyes haunted by ghosts of things un-recalled. "The magic . . . mixes things up."

"Are you a magician? A sorcerer or wizard?"

His bitter chuckle didn't escape, but Amanusa could sense it there, in his throat, and she wondered at his bitterness.

"No," he said. "No magician. Only a servant. Blood servant. Your servant now, lady."

He didn't stand. He slid from the bed straight to one knee, his head bowed. "I am yours. Command me."

"Oh for—" A tiny thrill of power sparked through her veins and Amanusa crushed it. She would not become what she hated simply because he would let her. She pushed aside the quiet whisper that said he might understand her fears, that he'd been where she was, that he might be there still. "Get up off the floor. That's my command. Sit. Answer my questions."

"As you will it." Jax returned to his seat on the edge of her bed. The crow hopped close and he stroked its feathers again, as if the action comforted him.

"Why did you call me 'blood sorceress'?" Amanusa measured tea into the pot.

"That is what you are."

"No." She shook her head emphatically. "I am not."

Jax only ducked his head without speaking. As if he didn't agree, but wouldn't contradict her.

"Why would you say such a thing?" Amanusa poured hot water over the tea leaves and hung the kettle back on its hook, moving it near the fire but not over it. She pretended the title didn't tempt her as much as horrify her. Think of the things she would know. The things she could do.

No. She wanted justice, not bloody vengeance. She wanted to set things right, stop the evil from ever happening again. But if in the process, those who'd done the evil paid for . . . No. She wouldn't let the wicked things done to her carry the same evil into her own heart.

"It's the truth." Now Jax met her eyes. "At the very least, you have the talent necessary to become a blood sorceress."

That was no comfort. Amanusa knew she isolated herself here in the forest, away from people. More so since her mentor, old Ilinca, had died. But that didn't mean her heart was cold and callous enough to work blood magic. Did it? It had been battered and broken, but surely it wasn't past mending.

"How did you get here? How did you find me?" She repeated the questions he hadn't answered as she smacked a pair of mugs down on the table, grateful for their sturdy construction. She shouldn't take her temper out on the crockery, even if the man and his words did upset her on so many levels. She peeked at the tea. Almost done.

"I walked from the station." The man fidgeted, as if he couldn't bear sitting still. "I should be serving you."

Amanusa waved away his protest. "The train station is fifty miles from here, in Nagy Szeben."

"I know."

"You walked."

"Yes." Jax took the mug of tea she handed him, wrapping his hands around it.

"Why? Why come here?" The things he'd said didn't make sense, didn't fit her understanding of the way the world worked, and she needed to understand, to know. Her thirst for knowledge had often caused her problems, but she couldn't stop it, not at this late date. Amanusa sweetened her tea with a dollop of honey and offered some to the man who'd invaded her home. "Where were you coming from?"

Jax frowned, not seeming to see her. "I was searching. I didn't know what I searched for until I found you, but . . . something drew me this way. The magic." He looked at her helplessly. "I think that before I came this way, I was in Russia. Or perhaps . . ." His forehead creased as he struggled to remember. "Bulgaria?"

"Do you want honey?"

He blinked, as if startled by the question. "Yes, please." He held his mug out and watched as she dripped the honey in. "Thank you."

She would not feel sorry for him. She had nothing to do with the magic that addled his mind, therefore his problems were not hers. She would feed him—he hadn't eaten since he collapsed yesterday afternoon, and who knew how long before that—and she would send him away. And she would feel safe again. "Do you feel well enough to eat?"

"I am fine." He took a bigger swallow of the tea. "The dizziness always passes off quickly once I wake."

"This has happened before?" Amanusa got out the bread she'd baked on Saturday and the cheese Danica had brought in payment for treating her boil and for the charm. The little charms Amanusa made were magic, yes, but not blood magic. Small things. Harmless. Helpful. Love charms, or charms against toothache or unwanted pregnancy. Magic too petty for the Inquisition to bother with. Women's magic.

"Aye." He frowned again as he puzzled things out. "I was Yvaine's blood servant. I remember she often used me in her magic." His frown cleared and he almost smiled. "I remember."

"I do not use people." Not even men. She wasn't like that. Not like them. She cut cheese and bread and set them on the table, adding a jar of berry jam. Her own work. "Come. Eat." She indicated a chair.

Jax hurried to set his mug on the table, his crow flapping its way out the door in protest against the disturbance. Jax held Amanusa's chair, seating her like some grand lady in some great house. It made her feel odd and she didn't like it. She was a hedge-witch with a lurid past. A scandal, not a lady.

"Sit down." She gestured at the chair again, irritated by the man's hesitation. "Stop hovering."

"My place—" He waved a vague hand toward the hearth. "I'm not—I should—"

"Sit," Amanusa ordered him. He was a guest in her house and she would treat him like one whether he wanted it or not. Whether she was comfortable with it—him—or not.

She didn't want to think about why her discomfort with Jax differed from the way she felt around all the other men who'd passed through her life. She wasn't afraid of him. Not anymore. Not exactly. More like afraid of what he brought with him, what he might mean. And she didn't want to think about it.

He sat, dropping into the chair as if his knees gave way. "Yes, my lady."

"Eat." She pointed imperiously at the food before taking some onto her plate and making a sandwich. Bread and cheese with blackberry jam might sound strange, but she liked it.

The meal passed in silence until most of the loaf was gone and half the cheese. She'd forgotten how much a big man could eat. She felt strangely pleased to be able to fill him up.

Jax swallowed his last bite and cleared his throat. "If I might ask, my lady—"

"Don't call me that. I'm no one's lady." She was who she was. Nothing more.

"Yes, my l—" He made an effort and swallowed the name.

"Ask." She was being rude and knew it. But she hadn't asked him to come, hadn't asked for the magic he'd brought. She wanted him to take himself and the temptation of magic—more, better magic— away again. Maybe if she was rude, he would.

He didn't fit into the pattern of her life with his manners and his offers to serve. She didn't know what to think about him or how she ought to feel, and she didn't like the confusion. She didn't like wanting things she couldn't have. She didn't like not being able to hold onto her fear around him. He was a man. She should be afraid, and she kept forgetting to be, and she didn't like it.

"How did you wind up here in this godforsaken part of the world?" he asked.

"God has not forsaken this place." Amanusa poured the last of the tea into her mug. "He has only forsaken me."

She found herself telling the story she hadn't told in so many years. "My parents were servants, my father the English valet to one of the under ministers at the British embassy in Vienna. My mother was Romanian, from the village down by the road, come to the capital to find work in a grand household. She found Papa too, or they found each other. So Papa remained in Vienna when the minister was recalled. We were happy until the great revolt."

"Eighteen forty-eight," Jax murmured, naming the year it had all happened; rebellion and revolution in virtually every country of Europe, ruthlessly crushed in most of them.

She ignored him. "I was a child then. We fled the trouble in the city, Mama, Papa, my brother Stefan, and me. I was eldest, almost twelve. Stefan was only six."

Why was she telling him this? She never talked about it, not even with old Ilinca. Was it the language? The English? "Mama brought us here, to her home. But the trouble followed us. Papa was killed. Many of the rebels who escaped the government came here to hide."

Amanusa gave a one-shouldered shrug, grateful she'd kept her voice calm for this much of the telling. Usually, just thinking of it brought tears, waking nightmares at the horrors in her memory. She didn't want to remember more, not now, not with him here. She skimmed over the rest of it. The worst of it. "Mama died. Stefan died. I did not. After a time, the old healer woman who had this cottage taught me all she knew—no one else would—and here I am."

"I am sorry for your loss." Jax met her gaze when she looked up, his blue-green eyes warm with sympathy.

She had to clear her throat. It was why she never spoke of this. It made her weak, and she could not afford weakness. She could not afford the sympathy he offered. She had to be strong. Strength was the only thing they respected.

"Thank you." The instant she said it, she wished she hadn't.

Amanusa jumped up and began clearing the table. Jax crossed to the doorway where his boots waited, stockings draped over their tops, and put them on. He disappeared out the open door.

Good. She wouldn't have the job of sending him away. Amanusa bustled around, content in her little world again. Until she heard the crack of ax on wood.

She dashed out of her cottage and around it, to the woodpile where the blasted man was placing another log to split. "What are you doing?"

Her cry startled him into dropping the ax, made him dance to avoid the falling blade. She was not amused. That was not a smile trying to get free, it was annoyance. She stomped to the woodpile and snatched up the ax. Who knew what he could do with such a weapon? "Did I say you could do this?"

"No, my l—" He flushed crimson. "No."

"I don't need you to cut my wood." Amanusa waved a hand at her woodpile, high as her own very tall head, angry with herself for not anticipating the danger. "Does it look like I need more cut? If I did, I'm perfectly capable of doing it myself. Do I look delicate to you?"

She shouldn't have said that either, for Jax slid his gaze along her, head to toe.

"You look magnificent," he said. "Strong and beautiful with skin so delicate a butterfly's kiss could bruise it."

Her suspicion ratcheted up at those lovely words, even as they made her melt inside. Did he really think she was magnificent? What did he want? Men who said pretty things always wanted something. But the instant Amanusa narrowed her eyes and firmed her lips, there he went again, back down to one knee.

"Pardon, mistress. I did not mean to offend." The nape of his neck, exposed between his shirt collar and the slight wave of his hair, looked so vulnerable.

"I'm no man's mistress," she snapped out, annoyed that she had to keep reminding herself of this man's threat. The word "mistress" triggered more anger than it deserved, but she couldn't stop it. "Mistress" was just one step above "whore," and she'd heard that word far too often.

"No, my—m—madame." Jax sounded horrified at the very idea, even as he stumbled over a way to address her.

"Call me by my name." Amanusa was losing patience. She just wished she knew whether she lost it with herself or with him. Surely him. Which was a lie. Hadn't she sworn never to lie to herself?

"I am to be allowed to know it?" He twitched, as if he wanted to look up at her but thought better of it.

Hadn't she told him her name? She'd been ruder than she realized, and it shamed her. "I am Amanusa Whitcomb. Miss Whitcomb."

"Yes, Miss."

She huffed a sigh. "Get up. I'm tired of you dropping to your knees all the time. Stand on your feet like a man."

"Yes, Miss Whitcomb." He stood, eyes still cast down. "But you should understand—I am not a man. I am a blood servant."

That was so patently ridiculous, Amanusa stopped

scolding herself for saying what she had and stared at him. Of course he was a man. How could he deny it? Granted, magic had swallowed up most of his mind.

Pity swelled, and Amanusa fought it down yet again. He wouldn't want her pity. Magic or not, he was still a man. She hefted the ax she held and marched around to the front door. After a moment, Jax followed, his crow fluttering from one side of the thatched roof to the other, as if to watch. Inside the cottage, Amanusa hid the ax under the bed—a bad hiding place, but she was in a hurry—and gathered up his clothes. When he came through the door, she bundled his waistcoat, cravat, and jacket into his arms and picked his long greatcoat up off the table.

"You should leave now," she said. "You've had a rest and a meal. You've delivered your message. I have no interest in ever learning blood magic, so I don't need a blood servant. You're free to go."

The man looked uncertain, almost fearful. Why?

"Let me at least repay you for the care and the meal," he said. "I have no coin—you saw that. If you do not need me to cut wood, surely there is something I can do. Carry water for your garden perhaps."

Amanusa eyed the bright blue bowl of the sky and the dry state of her garden. It was a long hike from the stream, and filled water buckets were heavy even with her shoulder yoke. And he had offered. Maybe he would spill all the water on the first trip and give up and go away. A fine gentleman like him wouldn't have the knack of handling the yoke.

As if he could sense her wavering, Jax laid his clothing on the table and stepped outside where the yoke and buckets lay against the cottage wall. Before she could actually say yes, he had disappeared down the path to the stream.

He didn't spill any of the water. Not from what Amanusa could tell. Jax handled the buckets like an expert. Like a man who had done this before. Like a servant. He had the garden watered in half the time it took her to do it. Then he rolled down his sleeves, put on his waistcoat and jacket, and tied his cravat. He tossed his greatcoat over one arm and took the bundle of food Amanusa had packed for him.

Food might help him bear his burden of magic. He had offered her no overt threat, had repaid the little she'd done for him. Food was the least she could do. A man needed to eat.

"Farewell, Miss Whitcomb." He bent in a graceful, flowing bow, like nothing she'd seen, even as a child in Vienna. "I wish you all the best in your life."

Amanusa gave him a fleeting smile—the only sort she had—and a nod, stifling the guilt trying to rise. "And to you the same."

She was not shoving him out of the nest too early. This was her nest, not his. He was not like her. He was dangerous. In more ways than one.

When he disappeared into the forest, Amanusa turned back into her cottage. The day was almost half gone and she needed to get working. She needed to make more love charms, as she was almost out. The silly girls who asked for them didn't know what they were asking, but Amanusa always put protective magic in them too. No harm would come to the girls who used them.

She wouldn't sell charms to men. If a man couldn't get a woman through his own charm—the kind without magic—he didn't deserve to have a woman. Her protective magic warded against any man using magic to seduce one of her clients against her will. At least she hoped it did. It was intended to.

A harsh cry alerted her to the crow's presence just before it flew through her door to land on her striped rug. Amanusa almost laughed. "Your friend has gone." She pointed at the forest. "If you hurry, you can catch him."

The crow cawed again. It fluttered to perch on the head of her bed and began to preen its feathers.

Amanusa wasn't the sort who needed company. She didn't mind being alone. Preferred it, in truth. The man's presence had been more of a nuisance than a pleasant change. She wasn't lying to herself. Exactly. But a crow—a crow didn't require attention, or conversation, or anything other than food, and even then, it could feed itself if need be.

If it preferred her company to the man's, she didn't blame it. The creature had taste and discernment. She wouldn't chase it off. "But you're not staying the night inside."

The bird stopped preening and looked at her, making a tiny sound as if in assent. Then it went back to its work.

Amanusa shook her head. Jax and his magic burden had made her go fanciful. She lit her lantern and closed her door on the setting sun. She had charms to make once dark fell.

2

THE NEXT MORNING, Amanusa pulled open her door, in a hurry to reach the jakes, and fell over something lying across her doorway. Large. Human—*male*.

Terror reached her first. She struck out, fists and feet, fighting to get free. But the man didn't grab, didn't clutch or slap or punch. He curled into a self-protective ball, and she recognized him, later than she should have.

"Jax!" She scooted free of him. "What are you doing there? Get away from my door."

He somehow got to his feet before she did, and lifted her to stand. "Sorry. Thought if I slept there—sorry, didn't mean to trip you up. Thought I'd be awake first. I suppose I was tired. Sorry."

"Why—? Never mind." Her need was urgent. She'd have it out with him when she came back.

But he was waiting just outside the outhouse when she emerged. Cursing the blush that burned her face, Amanusa shoved him out of her way.

He moved aside easily. Amanusa stomped past him to go inside and change out of her nightgown. Dear heaven, the man saw her in her nightgown, old and washed so thin it might as well be transparent. He would be impossible after this.

CROW CAME FLUTTERING down to land on his shoulder as Jax walked back to the cottage door. Automatically, his hand rose to stroke feathers and Jax had to smile. He should have known. When Crow stayed behind, Jax should have known then.

The door burst open before he reached it, and Miss Whitcomb stormed through, clothed again in her sad brown dress. "What are you doing here? I told you to go."

Jax started down to his knees before he remembered that *this* sorceress didn't like it. He bowed and held it. An angry woman was nothing to be trifled with, especially when she held blood magic.

"Well?" she demanded. "Why didn't you leave?"

"I tried." Jax bowed a little lower, hoping to appease her. "Four times I tried to leave, and each time, the path led me back here."

She made an angry noise in her throat and Jax flinched. She didn't seem to notice. "The path leads to the road which leads to the village where the highway leads to Nagy Szeben and the trains."

"I couldn't find it." Jax dared to raise up a bit and look at her. "The magic binds me to the blood sorceress. You."

She made another noise, a louder one, her hands clenching into fists. Jax held his ground with difficulty. When Yvaine had been this angry, he was safer on his knees. Yet this sorceress had struck out only when frightened, not in anger. Perhaps if he were more careful not to frighten her . . .

"I am *not* a blood sorceress and you are not my servant. You are leaving." She flung out her hand, pointing at the path to the village.

"Yes, Miss Whitcomb." He would try again. Maybe this time it would work. But he didn't think so.

Jax pulled out the bit of bread he'd saved from

supper and broke off a fat crumb for Crow. Who took it and flew off to perch on the thatched roof over Miss Whitcomb's door. Crow knew. Jax knew. They simply needed to convince Miss Whitcomb.

"Wait."

He turned, heart pounding, to see Miss Whitcomb disappear inside her house with a ripple of her loose, pale hair. Did she understand after all?

Jax followed, stopping in her doorway. She busied herself with something near the hearth. On the table between them lay rows of little bags made of leaves tied shut with string and . . . He picked up one of the charms and sniffed. Lavender inside, and rose, and *magic* to seal it. The lady had spent a busy night.

"Here." She thrust another napkin-wrapped bundle at him. "I know how much you men eat. Last night's remnants won't hold you through your journey."

"Thank you, my—Miss Whitcomb." Jax bowed, accepting the food in both hands. Kindness. From a sorceress. Who would have thought? Jax was grateful. He tucked the food in one greatcoat pocket as he drew out last night's napkin from the other and dropped it beside the charms. "I would repay your—"

"No need." She waved her hands at him, shooing him out the door. "Just go. You have a long trip."

He smiled. "Not so long, I fear. I am bound to the blood sorceress."

"Who isn't me."

Crow flapped his way down to her shoulder, startling her. But her hand rose to stroke the bird's glossy feathers.

"Think of it as payment for the bird." She sounded

desperate to be rid of him. Why? Why was she so afraid?

"Crow belongs to himself alone." Jax backed toward the path. How far would he get this time? "He chooses where he stays. I require no payment for him."

"His name is Crow?" Miss Whitcomb looked at the bird, so close to her, her eyes must have crossed. "Not Odin or Ragnar or something more impressive?"

Jax felt the laughter rumbling in his belly. He didn't let it out, but it was there. Twice in two days now. How long since that had last happened even once? Before Yvaine? He couldn't remember. "Odin's beasts were ravens, not crows. Crow is who and what he is. He has no need to impress. He may have another name, but that is his own, secret, crow-ish name. We have no need to know it."

The lady inclined her head. "Good-bye, Jax."

He bowed. It was not good-bye, but he did not know how to make her believe it.

AMANUSA HAD FINISHED breakfast but had scarcely gotten a stew on the hearth for dinner when she heard Crow's welcoming cry.

Welcoming? She didn't know how she could tell one caw from another, but this was no cry of alarm. Knowing who the creature greeted, Amanusa let go her temper as she stormed out to tell the man exactly what she thought.

Which brought her up short. She rarely let her temper loose on a man. The results were invariably painful. And yet her instinctive control did not work with this man. As if she had no fear of his reaction. Obviously, her instincts were off kilter.

Jax had stopped several yards down the path, still in the forest, as if afraid to come any closer. When he saw Amanusa striding toward him, he sighed, turned round, and started down the path away from the cottage again.

She lengthened her stride and caught up with him, taking hold of his elbow. "I will show you where the road is, so you do not mistake it."

"Thank you, Miss." After a stretch of quiet, with only the crunch of their feet on the earth and the twitter of birds overhead, he spoke again. "But it won't do any good. It's not the cottage I'm bound to. It's you. And you're with me. As long as I'm at your side, I can go anywhere. To India. Timbuktu. Nagy Szeben."

Amanusa snorted. She didn't believe him. She *couldn't* believe him. She was not a blood sorceress. And she didn't want any man hanging 'round. She didn't dare trust him, no matter what her instincts said. Or didn't say.

Another several minutes of walking and they reached the road. She pointed east. "There. That way to the village."

"Yes, Miss." Jax tipped an invisible hat and started off. Crow landed in a tree beside the road and cawed as if to ask where he went.

Amanusa shook off the fancy. Perhaps she had been alone a bit too long, to be imagining birds asking questions. But she liked her life that way. *More* could be dangerous. She crossed her arms and slipped into the forest, leaning a shoulder against Crow's tree, intending to watch the man until he was out of sight. Her drab clothes would hide her presence. If he stopped and returned, she wanted to see it, to be able to throw his lies in his face.

The man walked with a loose-jointed, ground-covering stride, head up to spy out his surroundings. He was a pleasure to watch. It was a pleasure to see any of God's well-made creatures do what they were made to do. He was a man, yes, but he had never hurt her. Not yet. And she'd be a fool to give him the opportunity. As she watched him, he seemed to walk straight into a ray of sunlight and disappear.

Amanusa blinked. She scrubbed her eyes and looked again, but the man, Jax, was gone and not around a bend in the road or over a hill. He'd simply—

He stepped out of the shadow, striding diligently back toward her. He still walked in that lovely head-up, alert fashion, but he didn't seem to see his surroundings, until Amanusa stepped out into the road in front of them.

He stopped, stared at her a moment, sighed, and turned as if to trudge back the other direction. But he hesitated before taking that first step. "How far did I get?"

"Not far. To that big patch of sunlight." She pointed.

"Did you see what happened?"

"Yes." She still didn't want to believe it, but she could not deny it. "You stepped into the sunlight."

"And?" Jax looked at her over his shoulder when she stopped talking.

She didn't want to say it, but when he looked at her like that, blue and brown swimming together in his eyes, she couldn't stop herself. "And when you stepped out again, you were walking toward me."

He turned his face back toward the village, but didn't take that first step. "Please do not make me try again. Please. Each time I try to leave, I am turned back sooner. If I keep trying—" He shuddered, eyes firmly on the distance. "Leave me just a few feet of space for my own."

Amanusa echoed his shudder. "What magic is this?"

"Blood magic." He turned those multicolored eyes on her. "*Your* magic."

"No," she whispered. *"No!"* Her sudden cry sent Crow skyward, shouting his alarm. She bolted, running down the path back to the haven of her cottage, the man running behind her, her fears chasing her.

She had enough sense left to skirt her garden when she reached the clearing. She ran inside her house and slammed the door shut, fully expecting that man to follow her in with his horrible accusations. But he didn't.

She could hear his harsh breathing through the door, but he stayed on the other side. The few feet of distance he asked for?

After a time, he rapped on the door. "Miss Whitcomb, are you all right?"

Amanusa shoved the kettle over the fire and tried to lose herself in the comforting ritual of tea making. But her hands shook so, she spilled tea all over the table. When she couldn't brush the leaves off the table into the pot, she made herself set the teapot gently and carefully down. She leaned against the table a moment, gripping it hard enough to turn her fingers white, until she got her breath under control. She wiped away the signs of weakness her tears had made, smoothed down her dress, then walked to the door and snatched it open.

Jax lifted himself off the wall beside the door where he had been leaning and pivoted to face her.

"I am *not* a blood sorceress," she cried. "I'm not like that. I care about other people's pain. I don't take pleasure in it. I don't steal children to take their blood. *I don't.*"

She screamed the last words, shaking and crying, halfway to hysterics. Or perhaps already plunged into their manic depths, for she didn't object when the man very carefully put his arms around her and drew her slowly in.

"Is that the trouble then?" He stroked a hand down over her hair as she surrendered and laid her head on his shoulder. He was just enough taller she could do it. She didn't have even the strength to scold herself for accepting the false comfort he offered. Just now, it didn't feel false.

"Of course you're not like that," he murmured. "If you were, you'd be conjuring, not working blood magic."

Amanusa pushed back and he let her go, easy as that. She swiped her hands across her cheeks and stiffened her spine. "What do you mean?"

"That bit about blood magic needing to steal blood from children—that's a bald-faced lie. Of course, the old sorceresses were some of the ones who spread it, but still, it's a lie." Asking permission with his eyes, Jax ducked through the door of her cottage and began brewing the tea she'd started, rescuing the spilled leaves with brisk, efficient motions.

Amanusa trailed back inside and crumpled into one of her sturdy chairs, content for the moment to let him wait on her. "Then where does the blood come from? I won't kill anyone for his blood—not even a condemned murderer."

Or so she told herself. She knew of a few she thought deserved death. But what if she was wrong?

"Good," he said. "The blood for sorcery comes from various places. The most important thing is that it be given willingly."

Willingly? But everyone *knew* . . .

Amanusa shook her head, trying to get it around this astounding new information. Jax was a blood servant, or so he claimed, and he had the magic to back it up. What reason would he have to lie?

He poured water over the tea and set it to steep, stirred the stew, and turned back to her. "What do you know about the great magics?"

She cleared her throat and sat up, straightening her thoughts as she did her body. "Only what everyone knows." She raised a skeptical eyebrow. "Whether that is rumor or truth, I don't know. They don't teach magic to girls in school, and I haven't been to a school since we left Vienna. Are you *sure*? Willingly?"

"Positive." He nodded, firm and certain. "Blood magic is not inherently evil. Nor are any of the others. What do you know about them?"

"There are four great magics: alchemy, conjury, wizardry, and blood sorcery." She ticked them off on her fingers. "Alchemy deals with the elements—earth, air, water, fire. Conjury is worked through spirits. Wizardry is herbal—plants and trees—and sorcery is done with blood."

"Essentially correct." He gave her a gentle smile. "These four magics are in the European tradition. Other places—Asia, Africa, the Americas—follow different traditions. I know little about them. And blood magic—sorcery—could more properly be called human magic, or perhaps body magic."

Amanusa frowned. "What do you mean?"

Instead of answering, Jax picked up one of the charms she had worked late into the night to finish. "How do you fasten these together?"

"With string. They're witch magic. Herbs, leaves, flower petals. *Small* magic."

"Small, yes." Jax tossed the charm into the air and caught it again, then opened his hand to show it to her. "Why didn't it come apart? The string is dislodged. Loose. But the charm is still intact. Why? *How?*"

"I—they always came apart until I started . . ." Amanusa paused, met the encouragement in his eyes before admitting her secret. "Until I licked the edges of the leaves. It seemed to hold them together."

"It does. The product of your body seals the charm shut and carries all the magic. There is no magic in these leaves, these petals. The magic is in your—" He pantomimed licking the leaf's edge. "Your saliva."

"But I learned these charms from Ilinca, the woman who lived here before. She was a witch. She made them all the time, and others, against straying husbands or rotting teeth."

"Do your charms work as well as hers? And how did she close them?" Jax tossed the charm to Amanusa who just managed to catch it. "Did she lick them shut?"

"No, she didn't lick . . ." Amanusa thought back, trying to remember. Now that she thought about it, Il-inca had warned her *against* licking the leaves. Other-wise Amanusa might never have tried it. But it worked. So she kept doing it. "And there are no more teeth in the barber's pail than before, so they work about as well." She bit her lip. "They didn't, before I started licking the edges."

"You see?" He handed her a mug of sweetened tea, asking silent permission before pouring one for him-self. He leaned against her cupboard, holding the mug in both hands. "You have some talent for wiz-ardry, perhaps, but for sorcery, for blood magic—you've worked it without knowing you are. Almost anything from the body can be used for magic. As long as it's willingly given. Why else would barbers be so fanatical about sweeping up their clippings to throw them on the fire? Hair and nail clippings work the weakest magic, because they're dead when they're cut, but they can be used."

"Then why is it called *blood* magic?"

"Because blood is the most powerful source of magic. Because its willing gift is the greatest sacri-fice."

"Oh." It made sense. It stood everything she thought she knew on its head, but it made sense.

"All blood has power." He held her eyes with the intent blue-brown gaze of his. "But the blood of the sorceress carries the most power. If any blood is spilled in creating magic, it will most often be *yours*. This is why blood sorceresses have always been rare, and why apprentices can be difficult to find."

Amanusa stared at him, her mind chewing on this

fresh news. Hadn't enough of her blood been spilled already?

Jax cleared his throat. "There is one thing that unwillingly spilled blood can do. The blood of a victim cries out for justice. At one time, a sorceress was a judge, and often executioner. This is the source of their reputation for ruthlessness. But it is never capricious or cruel for cruelty's sake. It is justice."

Justice. The word resonated through Amanusa's soul. Was it possible? Could she finally have justice for all the many wrongs done to her and her family? It was her desperate need for justice that held her here in this place, this forest. If she left, who would obtain justice for those she'd loved?

She shook away the longing. "Why do you always say 'sorceress'? Are there no blood sorcerers? No *men* working blood magic?"

"Men have tried." His mouth curved in a small, bitter smile. "But few men have proved capable of spilling their own blood time after time to work the magic. Every woman in the world gives up blood voluntarily every month of her adult life. Women are simply more attuned to this sort of magic, just as men seem to be more attuned to alchemy."

"So." Amanusa sorted her new knowledge. "Things willingly given from the body make magic. Blood and spit. Hair and nails." She worked her shoulders, trying to ease the discomfort riding her. Much of what she'd learned wasn't comfortable at all. "What if I don't want to be a blood sorceress?"

Jax opened his mouth and she waved him to silence.

"I know, I know. I'm already working blood

magic. But what if I don't want to learn any more of it? What if I don't want a blood servant? Why can't I just let you go?"

He didn't move a muscle, his expression didn't change, but Amanusa felt the difference in him, a sudden intensity as he watched her. "You would do this?" he said finally.

Amanusa could sense currents roiling beneath his calm appearance. He wanted to be set free. She nodded. "Tell me how."

Slowly he shook his head. "I do not know. Yvaine has books—Why would you wish to? I can see that I could be a great help to you, even if you have no wish to learn more magic."

Why indeed? "I suppose . . . it's like the blood. Do you serve willingly? If you stay only because you cannot leave, how is that different from—from stealing someone for his blood? It's not right."

He smiled. It held a tinge of sadness but it was more purely a smile than any he'd shown her. "I was bound willingly enough at the beginning. If I had not been willing, I could not have been bound."

"And now?"

"Now?" Jax shrugged. "It is what I am. Blood servant to the sorceress. I cannot remember any other life." He paused to meet her gaze. "You are not Yvaine. Already I know the difference. Yes, I serve you willingly."

"Until I can learn how to release you."

He set his mug on the cupboard and bowed. "If that is your wish, sorceress."

Amanusa scowled at him. Was he as agreeable as he seemed? Or would he turn on her the minute she relaxed her guard? *He'd seen her in her nightgown.* "You'll sleep outside."

"Of course, my—Miss Whitcomb." He bowed a little deeper.

"And you'll keep your hands and the rest of yourself to yourself." She was never doing *that* again. Ever.

Darkness overtook her suddenly, and pain. Her neck strained, twisting to turn her face away from the wet mouth, the teeth, the stinking, heaving male body crushing her. As quickly as the sensations swept over her, they departed again, leaving her shaken, shivering with sudden icy sweat sliding down her spine. She took a slow breath, hiding her shattered state. The memories would never be totally gone, but it had been a long time since one had possessed her like this.

"No, Miss." Jax tilted his head to look at her from his bow. He seemed to have noticed nothing. "Were you worried about that? About me . . . taking liberties?"

She couldn't deny it, despite her little, not-so-nonchalant shrug.

"You needn't." He straightened, blushing a little as he picked at the battered edges of her cupboard, keeping his eyes down. "That's part of the binding. I can't—" He coughed. "Have intercourse without permission of the sorceress. It's the magic. The . . . Well . . ." He trailed off.

"I . . . See." Amanusa's own blush burned. She ought to be more comfortable talking about this, given her past, but she wasn't. "Truly?"

"Truly. I am a—a eunuch, until permission is given."

Pity mixed with the relief rolling through Amanusa, knowing what she did about men and their affection for their private parts. Had the old sorceress suffered like she had? Amanusa didn't know, didn't want to ask. But the information reassured her. The man wouldn't have confessed such a thing if it weren't true.

She heaved a sigh and drank down the last of her tea. She needed to come up with a plan, but a plan for what? Did she want to learn this blood magic?

The promise of true justice, even the mere possibility of achieving it, pulled at Amanusa. And the hunger for knowledge, to *know* new things, burned deep inside her. She'd eagerly gobbled up everything old Ilinca had to teach her and begged for more, but Ilinca had none. She'd warned Amanusa against learning more, saying the Inquisition would notice a woman working any magic greater than these small spells and tiny charms, and they would pounce.

"What about the Magician's Council?" Amanusa asked. "Hasn't blood magic been banned? Will they even let a woman learn magic?"

"Blood magic isn't banned. Not officially." Jax shook his head slowly. "I think I would have heard and remembered if it were. It has merely been shunned. Avoided. Because it is women's magic. And because only the sorceresses know the truth of it."

"And women are banned from learning magic."

"They are?" Jax sounded surprised.

"Here, they are."

"Then we will go somewhere else. To Scotland. To Yvaine's tower. The English council doesn't bar women from magic." He frowned, as if trying to recall something difficult. "At any rate, there's nothing in the charter to prevent women from becoming members of the Magician's Council of England."

"The Hungarian council bans them, and I can't leave." Not until she obtained the justice she needed. The crushing grief and horrible anger that had gripped her when she swore that oath had eased. What held her now was as much stubbornness as anything. She *would* someday, somehow get justice for her murdered family, just as she'd promised.

Jax shrugged. He didn't seem at all interested in her reasons for refusing to leave. "Learn the magic. There's not many who'll dare cross a blood sorceress in her power. If they raise a fuss, we'll deal with it then."

Oh, she wanted to. Wanted it desperately. *It wasn't evil.* Who would have thought? It was just knowledge. Knowledge about magic she already practiced in small ways. And it was the *more* she'd craved for so long. Magic that held justice in its bleeding heart. She wanted it. But did she dare?

Jax offered her more tea, and when she turned him down, took her mug to the dishpan. He poured more tea for himself. "So," he said. "I thought I might begin with your roof. I noticed the thatching was a bit thin in a few—"

He broke off at a racket of caws from outside, Crow crying alarm. "Someone's coming. Not from the village. They're armed."

How did he know that from a crow's call? Amanusa's gut churned, though she was grateful for the warning. This time, they wouldn't take her by surprise.

Jax was patting around his waist as if looking for

weapons. He would get himself killed if he tried to fight—at least six of them always came together. *Dear God, how she hated them.*

Amanusa caught his arm. "They won't hurt me. Nor you, if I tell them not to. I think." She hoped.

"Who are they?"

"Outlaws. Anarchists. Revolutionaries. They hide in the mountains and plot freedom for Transylvania from the wicked Hapsburgs." Amanusa began gathering her tins of dried herbs and jars of salve, crushing the surge of fear and hate that made her hands tremble. *Don't let them see.*

"What do they want with you?"

"Healing. Doubtless they've got themselves into another fight trying to rob an imperial shipment of something or other and need patching up again. We have a bargain, the anarchists and I. I heal them when they need it, and they leave me alone the rest of the time."

"Will they be staying long?" Jax stood to the side of the open door, peeking out at intervals.

Amanusa paused, realizing she hadn't explained, then went back to her gathering. "They won't be staying at all. They don't come to me for healing. I go to them."

The realization struck her a fraction after it did Jax, for he already stared at her, horrified. "I cannot stay behind."

"How can—? They'll kill you." Amanusa tried to think.

Jax threw his greatcoat and jacket under Amanusa's bed and yanked the blanket off it. With a kitchen knife, he sawed a hole in the center and popped his head through it. "I'm your servant," he said. "I'm simple-minded. Treat me like I haven't the sense of a child and maybe they won't mind me coming along."

He scraped his expensive boots against the floor to scuff them up a bit more and scrubbed his hands through his hair to make it stand up as he let his face go slack. Dear Lord, the man suddenly *looked* like an idiot.

She stared at him in shock until the chink of metal outside reminded her of the situation. She plunged into her role. "I'll need a bag for myself, Jax. It's in the drawer under the wardrobe."

He bobbed his head and walked awkwardly to it. "Here?"

"Yes. Do hurry." Amanusa turned back to her medicines, carefully wrapping the heavy jars in rags so they wouldn't clink in their wooden case and perhaps break. *Do nothing to anger them.*

"I see you were expecting us." The outlaws' second-in-command ducked through her door and turned his deadly gaze on Jax. "Who's this?"

3

HEARING ROMANIAN AGAIN after two days of nothing but English was almost a shock. Amanusa slid her eyes toward Jax. She didn't want the outlaws to know she spoke English, but did Jax understand Romanian? Had the outlaws heard her give that order in English?

"He is my servant." She kept packing her box.

Would they accept this change? "His body is strong even if his mind is not."

"Where did you get him?" Teo walked to Jax, who cowered and drooled a bit as the second-in-command circled him. The other five stood at the door, blocking the light, but they stayed outside the cottage, thank God.

"I found him in the forest. Filthy, bleeding, and hungry. He's like a stray dog. I fed him, and now he won't go away." She set the last jar in her box, packing it tighter and heavier than usual because this time she wouldn't have to carry it herself. She braced her hands against the table a moment to steady her nerves.

When she looked up, Jax was pulling double handfuls of her undergarments from the wardrobe drawer and stuffing them into the carpetbag.

"Jax, no!" Amanusa leaped across the room, shoving Teo out of the way to grab her petticoats from her servant's hands. "*No.* I won't be needing these."

"No?" Teo's voice was dark, filled with heavy sensuality as he lifted her washed-thin nightgown from the bag with one finger. He laughed when Amanusa snatched it from him and shoved it back into the bag.

Teo caught Amanusa's elbow and spun her into his arms, crushing her tight as he ground his hips against her. Amanusa swallowed down her revulsion along with another surge of hate. Teo liked that she hated him, the pig.

She turned her face away as he licked a long, wet swath across her cheek, hanging onto her composure with her short-bitten nails. Dark things swirled in her mind, making her heart race. She thrust them ruthlessly away. She did not dare lose herself in memory now.

"You sure I can't tempt you to revisit old times?" he crooned.

Amanusa spoke in her sweetest voice. "Only if you want to wake with your balls shriveled to the size of peas and your bowels so loose they'll never close again."

Teo laughed as he let her quickly go, then laughed again, true laughter. "Look at your idiot. He wants to kill me."

The murderous hate in Jax's eyes sent alarm knifing through Amanusa. She wanted to learn magic from him, not bury him. "*Jax.* I need two dresses. The brown ones. And stockings. Get them *now.*"

Jax glared another moment at the outlaw, until Teo lifted his hand as if he meant to strike. Amanusa winced, but Teo only pretended to hit Jax and laughed when her servant pretended to cower in fear. Too much pretending. But it meant survival.

"He is loyal to me," Amanusa said. "Like a dog who has been kicked too many times and finally finds someone who does not."

"We have enough dogs at our camp." Teo glowered at Jax. "He stays behind."

Amanusa shrugged. "He will only follow. You may as well let him come. He can carry the medicines."

Teo scowled. "You always carry them."

"And I often run out because I cannot carry much weight. He is simple. He is obedient. What harm can he do?" Amanusa didn't truly want the responsibility of keeping Jax *and* herself alive and unharmed in the outlaw camp, but he could not stay behind.

She glanced up and saw Jax unbuttoning his trousers as if he meant to relieve himself in the corner of the room. One way to convince the outlaws of his missing good sense. Would it work?

"No!" she cried. "Jax, *no.*"

He turned, holding his trousers together, his expression vacantly wondering.

"Outside." Amanusa pointed at the door. "You know where you're supposed to do that. Go on."

The men backed from the door, laughing, as Jax hurried out, clutching at his trousers to keep them from falling.

Amanusa turned back to Teo. "You still think he will be a danger to you big brave outlaws?"

Chuckling, Teo waved his hands. "All right, all right. He can come. But you're in charge of him. Keep him out of trouble, or our bargain ends."

Amanusa turned away to hide her terror. Teo liked her fear too. Indifference would keep him away from her, and courage. "Only Dragos Szabo has the right to change our bargain."

"Maybe so. But I know Szabo and I know what he will say."

Hating that the man could see her hands shaking, Amanusa folded the dresses Jax had pulled from the wardrobe and laid them over her stockings in their careful rolls. Amanusa also knew the outlaw leader, far better than she liked, and she knew Teo was right. Neither she nor Jax could set a foot wrong in the camp if they wanted to stay alive.

"*Jax.* Come here." She went to the door and called. "Get the case." She gestured at the heavy wooden box on the table.

Jax picked it up and came back to take the carpet-bag from her. There was a little tug-of-war until she saw Teo's smirk and let go. Let the big strong silly man carry everything.

THE WALK TO the outlaws' camp took longer than she expected. Szabo had moved them deeper into the mountains since the last time they needed her. Jax stayed close, pretending to cower under Amanusa's protection, but she could sense him bristling every time one of the outlaws—especially Teo—came too near. It comforted her, and she didn't like that it did.

They stopped beside a stream near noon. Amanusa shared the food she'd packed with Jax. The outlaws wouldn't share theirs. She'd learned through uncomfortable experience. Their women, those at the camp, would feed her, but the men didn't care.

Sometime in midafternoon, they topped a ridge and descended into a tiny hidden valley filled with the rough-built shelters and ragged tents of the camp. Szabo came limping out to greet her, his black hair streaked with more gray than it had been two months ago. His shirt strained over a thick bandage around one shoulder and upper arm that showed through a bloody rip in his shirt. Szabo's scowl made her heart pound with fear, but Amanusa didn't dare let it show. Szabo respected courage, if little else.

"If Costel is not dead, it will be a miracle," the revolutionary chief growled. "Your insistence on living in that cottage wastes too much valuable time. You should be here, where you belong."

Then he noticed Jax. "Who is this? What do you

think you're doing, bringing strangers into my camp?"
His voice built to a powerful roar.

Amanusa refused to cower. "He is my servant and
he is simple-minded. I have already had this argument with Teo. I do not intend to have it with you.
Now will someone show me where you put Costel, or
do you intend to delay me further and let him die?"
She propped her fists on her hips and gave Szabo
glower for glower.

Finally the burly man took a step back and pointed.
"There."

"Thank you." She started down the path of well-
trod grass toward the indicated arbor.

"But if he dies," Szabo snarled, "we will renegoti-
ate this *bargain,* you and I."

Amanusa paused and half turned. "If you keep me
here," she said, her voice just loud enough to carry to
the chief, "I will kill you. Then where will your revolution be?"

"Go." Szabo threw his hand toward the hospital
shelter. "Just go. Keep Costel alive and maybe you
can live to see another day."

"Your threats are empty, old man." Amanusa
walked backward down the path. "If you kill me, who
will heal your hurts next time?"

Amanusa ducked into the shelter, her hands shaking with equal parts anger, hate, and fear. Only when
Jax swung the medicine box onto the small trunk beside the sickbed did Amanusa recall his presence.
She had been so focused on the confrontation with
Szabo, and Jax had done such a good job of making
himself seem small and harmless, she had forgotten
him.

The girl bathing Costel's forehead with a rag was new. She couldn't be much older than fifteen. She looked up, her eyes filled with fear—though whether with fear for Costel or herself, Amanusa didn't know. Some of the silly girls hereabouts thought the revolutionaries romantic and ran off with them willingly. Others had better sense, but wound up here anyway. Amanusa had.

"What is your name, child?" Amanusa opened Costel's shirt and grimaced. Belly bandage. A gut wound. That was rarely survivable, even had she been here the moment he was brought in.

"Miruna." The girl didn't sound any too willing to give up that information. "And I'm a woman, not a child."

"Of course you are," Amanusa murmured, her mind on the bandage she untied. Jax handed her a pair of scissors before she asked for them.

"You should have been here," Miruna accused. "His death is your fault."

Amanusa shot her a sharp look. One of those then, who fancied herself in love. "He's not dead yet," she snapped. "Now make yourself useful and fetch me some hot water."

Instead, the girl hovered as Amanusa lifted away the bloody bandage, exposing a small black-edged hole still seeping blood. Miruna moaned and began weeping loudly.

"Jax, get her out of here. And get me that hot water."

With a brisk nod, Jax picked the girl up by the arms, carried her outside the shelter, and set her down on her feet with a thump, hard enough that she stumbled. He crossed to the fire and used a corner of the blanket he wore to pick up the entire pot of steaming water and carry it back to Amanusa. She beckoned him closer.

"Help me turn him. I need to see if the bullet came out."

Jax nodded. He took hold of the injured man's shoulder and hip and rolled him onto his side. Costel groaned. Amanusa's breath sighed out in an almost-whistle. The bullet was out, but it had left a big, ugly hole in his lower back. Fear tried to freeze her. Better that the bullet was out, but what had it damaged on its way through?

"I don't know if I can save him," Amanusa whispered to Jax in English. "He's been shot in the gut. The damage—Even if I *had* been here . . ."

Jax placed a clean rag over the small wound on the injured man's stomach and turned him over to fully expose the exit wound. "Blood magic."

He met her gaze, the blue-green of his eyes fading until they were fully brown. Amanusa's spine prickled even before he spoke in that other voice.

"To heal wounds requires either blood or saliva. While blood is more efficacious, especially in the case of life-threatening injuries, it is also more risky, both to the patient and the sorceress. Saliva does not heal quickly, nor will it bring someone back from too near death. But it is effective in most cases and it prevents the putrefaction and fevers which often arise from wounds."

Jax paused, as if to ask what more she wished to know. It made Amanusa feel crawly inside. The old sorceress, Yvaine, had turned Jax into a living reference volume.

Did she want this magic? Nothing kept her from wanting to heal Costel. He had joined the outlaw band after she left them so he'd had no part in what had been done. And he seemed more the idealistic revolutionary sort than the opportunistic outlaw type. Miruna apparently liked him well enough. That in itself disposed Amanusa more kindly to him.

But the idea of *blood* magic still made her feel a bit crawly. And Jax—or Yvaine—said healing with blood could be risky. Not something she wanted to attempt on her first try.

. "How do I heal wounds with saliva?" Amanusa asked.

"First, expose the injury . . ."

Step by step, Jax's voice led her through the process. There was a great deal more to it than simply spitting on the wound, which seemed somehow more *wrong* than bleeding on it. She mixed the saliva with alcohol spirits—the potent home distillation of the area—and used that to clean the wound. She had words to say over it and somehow *felt* the medicine, or the magic or whatever it was, penetrate deep into the hole through Costel's gut.

It didn't seem quite sufficient, so she added a prayer for healing of unseen injuries. Then she got out her needle and thread and began stitching Costel's back together again. Three stitches in, Jax, who had been serving as candelabra in the shelter's gloom as well as textbook, crumpled slowly to the ground.

Shouting for Miruna or someone to come help, Amanusa abandoned her sewing. She scurried around the cot to grab up the candle and stamp out the smoldering grass and pine needles that floored the shelter.

"Is he dead?" Miruna whimpered, hovering at the door.

"No, he's not dead. He just fainted." Amanusa thrust the candle at her. "Take this. Relight it and bring it back. I need the light."

"I meant Costel. Is he dead?" Miruna took the candle, but didn't move.

"He's just fainted too. Now bring me my light." Amanusa dragged Jax to the edge of the shelter to get him out of the way and straightened him into a more comfortable position. Blood poured from his nose— had he hit it? He seemed all right otherwise, so she turned him onto his side so he wouldn't choke. Was it such a strain to be possessed by the magic? She would have to be more careful. Learn the magic some other way.

"What's wrong with him?" Miruna returned, shielding the candle flame with a hand, her eyes on Jax.

"He gets these falling fits." Amanusa positioned Miruna where she wanted her and picked up the needle again. "He was possessed by a powerful magician, and it cost him his wits. The power still rides him, and sometimes it does that. Sometimes, he says strange things, strange words too." That might help, if he slipped and spoke English where someone could hear.

On the other hand, these outlaws were a superstitious bunch. They might fear Jax rather than pity him. However, they were already half afraid of her . . .

"I have some magic myself." Amanusa took careful stitches in Costel's skin, piecing the ragged opening together as she made up her lie. She wasn't much good at lying, but this wasn't much of a lie. She did have magic. "The others may have told you. I have enough magic to control him, but if something should happen to me . . ." She shrugged. "Well, he's always been peaceful enough with me. I shouldn't worry about what else the magician might have left behind. Your camp conjurer might be able to handle him. Perhaps."

Szabo's pet conjurer—the only other person with any magical talent in the camp—had only a few spells, could call up only the newest, weakest of spirits. Even Szabo held him in contempt, while he indulged the man's vices to keep him conjuring for the rebel band. The man feared Amanusa and her herbs. They avoided each other for the most part.

After a time, Amanusa took the last stitch and cut the thread. She spread her wound ointment over the stitched injury and bandaged it. With Miruna's help, Amanusa got Costel turned again. She poured some of the magic-boosted spirits in the entry wound, murmuring the spell-words under her breath, in English as Jax had told them to her. This one took only a few stitches to close. Amanusa left Miruna to finish the cleaning and bandaging.

Walking out of the hospital shelter, Amanusa twisted from side to side, trying to ease some of the ache in her back.

"So?" Szabo popped out of nowhere, intending to startle, like he always did. It was his favorite game, sneaking up on people and making them jump. All the outlaws loved the game. For men with such violence and brutality in them, sometimes they behaved more like cruel children. She hated it, as she did everything else about this place.

This time, Amanusa won the game. She didn't jump. She shrugged. "He's still alive. Time will tell."

"If he dies—"

She dared to interrupt him. "He was likely dead the minute that bullet hit him in the belly, even if I had been here waiting for you. If he lives, it's *my* doing. But if he dies, Szabo, it's *your* fault. Yours for taking him out to get shot."

Szabo lifted his hand to strike. Amanusa didn't flinch. The outlaw chief wasn't as brutal as he liked to pretend. He never participated in his men's drunken revels and once—*once,* he had apologized to her. But he'd never stopped them either. She blamed him as much as she did the others.

"Do you want me to look at that arm?" She met his gaze evenly, and after a moment he dropped his raised fist.

"The leg bothers me more." He limped to a stump in front of the fire pit and sat heavily.

"What did you do to it?" Amanusa knelt and waited for him to pull his trouser leg up and his stocking down. She wouldn't touch any of the men more than necessary.

"I did nothing to it. It was that God-be-cursed—" He broke off to shout. "Gavril! Get that monster thing from the city. Maybe our witch will know what it is. God knows, our conjurer has no idea."

Amanusa wasn't anyone's witch. But she could be a sorceress if she wanted. She frowned at Szabo's leg. "Are you saying a *monster* bit you?"

"Bit? No. It *stabbed* me," he growled.

The calf was swollen and red, inflamed around an evil-looking wound. One entry, more like a puncture than a bite. Amanusa sighed. "And what did you do for it? Did you even use the ointment I left you?"

"I'm not an infant," the man growled, looking away.

"No. You're a man and therefore an idiot." Amanusa pressed hard on the wound, expelling the corruption the fool had let develop. She didn't at all mind hurting him.

Szabo grunted and jerked against the pain. He never bellowed, like some of his so-manly followers did. "Speaking of idiots, where is yours?"

She tipped her head toward the hospital shelter. "In there. He's—he has falling fits. He's sleeping one off." She wiped her hands on her bloody apron and stood. "I'm going to have to open this to get all that nastiness out. And you are going to use the ointment and stay off it for a few days."

"All right, all right," Szabo grumbled. "Damned nuisance."

"If you'd done what I told you when you got it, I wouldn't have to do this."

"*You* should have been here to tend it."

Amanusa gave him a hard look. "If I'd been here—if you made me stay here—I'd have taken it off at the knee, no one the wiser. You should know better than to threaten me, old man."

"How can a woman be so hard?" He shook his head. "I don't understand why you are so stubborn about this."

Amanusa stared at him until he looked up, met her gaze. "Yes," she said. "You do."

He flushed and looked away. "The others don't mind it. Not so much."

"Did you ever ask them?" Amanusa waited, but got no response. "I didn't think so."

A harsh clanking sound of metal on metal fractured the moment and Szabo turned away, seeming grateful for the interruption. Gavril, another one of Szabo's old comrades, Amanusa's old enemies, carried a strange object in his hands.

Made of a dark metal with a dull charcoal-gray sheen, it consisted of a melon-sized sphere suspended between two six-spoked stars, rather like rimless wheels. A pair of jointed telescoping arms dangled awkwardly from the center ball. The pointed one—sharp and edged, like a knife—still had rust-brown flakes of dried blood clinging to it.

"That thing stabbed you?" Amanusa quelled the horror whispering down her spine. "What is it?"

"You don't know?"

She could feel Szabo's suspicious gaze on her, but couldn't tear her attention from the—the thing in Gavril's hands. The shudder escaped her control. Even dead—inanimate, broken—it oozed *wrong* from every surface, contained *wrong* beneath that smooth-sheened skin. "I've never seen anything like it. Never imagined something like this could exist. Is it a windup toy?"

"We haven't found a key for winding, or a place to put a key. And if it is a toy, someone has a twisted sense of fun. It stabbed me."

How was that different from the cruel games his outlaws played?

Amanusa shook off her bitterness to focus on

the machine. "What did it do? Tell me what happened."

"It rolled down the street on those spokes," Szabo said. "Coming from the mines and the smelter near Nasdvar. You know where I mean."

She nodded. She'd never seen it, but others had told her, women whose men had gone to work in the mines, women who came to her for medicines to heal their men after they returned. The very air surrounding the place seemed to leach the life from anyone who ventured near. She wasn't surprised a place as *wrong* as that could produce something like this.

"It—it *saw* me. I swear it saw me, and this—" Szabo picked up the jointed limb without the knife and waggled it at Amanusa. Its tip was hollow. "This came squirting out of it and . . . it sniffed at me. I kicked it. Knocked it clear across the street, but before I could make the corner, it came rolling back, flying at me. Just before it reached me, this other thing—the sharp arm—came out of it and it stabbed me.

"So I kicked it again. Harder. It hit the side of the building and it died. I killed it." Szabo sounded just as satisfied over killing a machine as he did when he killed a man, an "enemy of the revolution."

Amanusa shuddered, this time at the pleasure in Szabo's voice. That was as *wrong* as the metal insect.

"Here. Take it." The outlaw chief plucked the thing from Gavril's hands and dumped it into Amanusa's before she could react. It felt as *wrong* as it looked, and she fought sudden, bitter nausea.

"Take it with you," Szabo said. "See if you can figure out what it is, how it works. Maybe we can use it against the government, eh?"

The machine was cold, colder than it ought to be, even if it had been kept in shadow, and slightly oily to the touch. And while heavy, it wasn't as heavy as it looked. The ball was probably hollow. Amanusa propped it against her stomach to take her hand away and wipe off the clinging, greasy feel, but that felt worse, threatened to steal her breath as well as empty her stomach. She let go of the central ball, holding it by two of the spokes, which helped.

She didn't want the thing, but better she had it than Szabo did. The metal bug might be dead, but it could still suck the life, the humanity out of those near it. These men had little enough humanity left them as it was.

Amanusa didn't know how she knew the machine could do such a thing, but she had no doubt of it. Perhaps her certainty was part of whatever made her a potential sorceress. Perhaps she had a sense of magic, like a sense of smell. Whatever this contraption was, it was not magic. It was . . . It was *anti*-magic. So, did that mean the place where it came from was too? Yet another whisper of horror scurried through her.

Szabo cleared his throat and she startled. She didn't have time to puzzle it all out now. Maybe Jax would know what it was.

"Let me go put this away." She hoisted the heavy machine, braced another spoke against her sleeve-covered forearm. "I'll get my supplies and be right back to take care of that leg. Then I'll look at your shoulder and treat the rest of your men."

At the hospital shelter, Amanusa propped the metal bug against one of the support poles—no one would make off with the nasty thing—and washed her hands enough times that the oily, awful feel went away. She checked on Costel, sleeping peacefully under Miruna's watchful eye, and on Jax. He seemed just as peaceful.

His nosebleed had stopped, so Amanusa took a moment to clean his face and bundle a clean rag under his head to get it off the bloody ground. Then she collected her biggest jar of wound salve and the other tools of her trade and went back out to conduct her open-air surgery.

JAX STILL HADN'T awakened by the time night fell. It would have worried Amanusa more, if he hadn't slept so long the last time Yvaine spoke with his voice. Miruna stubbornly refused to leave Costel's side. Amanusa didn't blame her. The camp wasn't safe without a protector. The hospital shelter protected Miruna now—none of the men dared break its neutrality.

Szabo had ordered Amanusa's tent set up. Part of her bargain was a tent to herself while she was here. Szabo ordered everyone to leave it, and her, alone, but she was her own protection more than he was. She had been since she'd made everyone so ill with her herbs and won her bargain. That had been six years ago. They were beginning to forget.

It was late. She wanted to retire to her tent. To hide in it. But she couldn't leave Jax lying at the edge of the hospital shelter. He might roll out. Or someone could decide "the edge" wasn't actually "in." Or—

Amanusa sighed. She had to be honest, at least with herself. She didn't want to leave Jax where he lay because she felt safer when he was near. Even if he was unconscious. She eyed the distance to the small tent set up near the tree line behind the shelter. Not much more than the distance she'd dragged him into her cabin. She could do this. It wouldn't hurt him any worse than he already was.

Crow gave his opinion from his perch atop the hospital arbor. He obviously agreed with her. Smiling at her fanciful thoughts, Amanusa rolled Jax onto his back so she could catch both hands and drag him. To her surprise, he mumbled something, then blinked as if trying to open his eyes.

"Jax, can you wake up?" Amanusa was careful to speak in Romanian, too aware of the curious girl watching. "You have to get up now. Just for a moment. You can't sleep here."

His eyes closed and opened again before they focused on her, but he turned to push at the ground, struggling to stand. Amanusa had to help him. He staggered and reeled like a drunk in a three-day stupor, but she got him to her tent. Bending to get him through the door flap ended with him collapsed on the ground, but he was inside.

Amanusa went back to the shelter for one of the canvas sheets they used to make stretchers. She laid it on the ground inside her tent and rolled Jax onto it. He would stay warmer with a layer between himself and the heat-stealing earth. She tucked his blanket-cloak more closely around him and retreated to the cot.

"Thank you." Jax spoke clearly and in English.

She thought about looking to see who might be near, might have heard, but she was too tired to care.

"For what?" she said in Romanian. But Jax didn't answer.

After a moment, she spoke again, in English. "You're welcome."

She took off her boots, unfastened the top few buttons of her dress, and lay down fully clothed, prepared for her usual sleepless night. She never slept well in the camp. It was too full of memories. And fear.

AMANUSA JERKED AWAKE in the black dark of deepest night. Her tent was empty. She was alone. "Jax?" she whispered softly, too afraid to make much sound.

She sat up, reaching blindly into the dark, fighting back the part of herself that wanted to panic. Jax was bound to her. He could not leave. But could he betray her? If she died, wouldn't that set him free?

Someone was moving outside her tent. *"Jax?"* she dared to whisper a little louder.

"Here." The low sound of his voice sent more relief than it should have rocketing through her. "Come. Give me a hand with this."

"With what?" Amanusa strained to see through the blackness inside the tent, hunting for her shoes with cold toes.

"Protection." Jax ducked inside, darkness against the light. Even at the quarter-moon, it was lighter outside than in. He moved across the tight space to the cot where she still sat.

"Take my hand," he said. "I haven't done this spell in so long, I don't trust myself to get it right. I don't know if I have the magic for it. But you do."

Amanusa groped in midair for his hand and it closed, warm and calloused, around her fingers.

"Come." He tugged gently and she followed him outside the tent, pausing only to grab a blanket from her cot for a cloak.

The moon's light bathed the world in a faint silver gleam, deepening the shadows under the nearby trees. It lit up Jax's face enough that Amanusa knew her pale blond hair had to be almost glowing. She pulled the gray blanket up over her head to hide it. Jax led her around the tent to a tangle of briars a few paces away and thrust his hand deep into their midst.

"What are you doing?" Amanusa grabbed his arm, pulled back his hand, now bleeding from a half-dozen scratches.

"Magic. My blood is enough for this. We don't need to bleed you. Walk with me. Gather in the magic." He raked the deepest scratch over a branch of the briars, smearing his blood along it. "East."

He led her in a circle around the tent, pausing at the south, the west, the north, to wipe his bloody hand on the grass, or a tree trunk, or a stone. Amanusa tried to gather magic, but had no idea what she was doing.

Finally he led her back to the entrance where he wiped away the last of the blood with a handkerchief and washed his hands in the basin Szabo always had set up outside her tent. One of the little amenities, like the cot, he kept hoping might tempt her to return. The deliberately ignorant fool.

"Do you feel the magic?" Jax murmured, urging her back into the tent.

Amanusa wasn't sure. She felt . . . something. Something she'd felt before, when she made the charms. Something *right*. Real, true, like the night itself had come to life. "I-I think so."

"Good. A smear of blood at the four directions, or in the four corners of a room, can be used for protection. I probably used more than necessary, but it's hard to control the amount when using briars to part the skin." He took both her hands in his. "Now, these are the words—"

"Wait." Amanusa squeezed his fingers. "I don't want Yvaine again. It's too hard on you. I want you conscious."

"This is magic I know." Jax squeezed gently back. "There was a time I cast this all on my own, without the sorceress to help. I only ask help now because it has been so long. These are the words." He wouldn't let her delay any longer. "By the mark of my body, I bind—"

"But it's not my body," Amanusa interrupted again, not ready yet for *real* blood magic. It felt strange, *intimate* somehow, standing in the dark so close to a man, his hands holding both of hers. She didn't like it.

And she did. His hands were warm. Comforting. His presence felt safe. Why? She ought to fear him. "It's *your* blood," she said, still trying to stall.

"My body is yours, Sorceress. I am blood servant to the blood sorceress. I am part of you. An extra arm." He shook her slightly. "Finish the spell. Can't you feel it gathering?"

She did. She could sense it now. Magic rose outside her tent. Power she could almost breathe in, almost grasp in her hands. Before, she'd known only faint, misty whispers trailing across her fingers, not smothering blankets of power like this.

"Finish it," Jax whispered. "Before it turns."

She could feel the power struggle against . . . something, and knew she had to bring it under control. The magic wasn't evil, but like fire, if it escaped, it could destroy much.

"By the mark of my body—" Amanusa felt the magic shiver at the sound of her voice.

"I bind protection around this place," Jax said.

Amanusa repeated the words and the magic danced, swirling in a happy pattern around the tent.

"By the blood of my blood, no harm shall come against me or mine, and peace shall dwell within this place."

As she spoke the last word, the magic pattern pulled tight and solid, the woven strands locking together. It left a faint shimmer in the air that Amanusa could just sense. A shimmer that promised safety.

She let go of Jax's hands and shivered. He touched her cheek. "You're freezing. Here—"

He urged her to sit on her cot, wrapping the other blanket around her shoulders. He tugged her unbuttoned shoes off as he knelt, and warmed her icy feet in their sleep-twisted stockings, sandwiching them between his hands and his muscular thighs. "Better?"

"Warmer," she admitted through teeth that no longer wanted quite so badly to chatter. She didn't know whether her shaking was due to the cold, or to the magic she'd just worked. Or to the man. It felt too strange to be cosseted this way. Too strange to be touching a man like this and not be afraid. She sat there, huddled in blankets with her feet on a man's thighs and wondered what to do next.

"I am sorry about your blanket." Jax rubbed her feet, apparently without thought.

"Blanket?" Amanusa pulled those over her shoulders closer.

"Cutting a hole in it. I thought my coat and jacket would give me away as something other than lackwit, but I didn't want to come in only my shirtsleeves."

"Blankets are easily replaced. It was quick thinking."

"I've played the idiot before."

She felt his shrug more than saw it as he dismissed the compliment. She knew she should pull away, tuck her feet under the blankets. She had no real reason to trust him. Except that she had slept.

In this place, surrounded by memories of horror, pain, and death, Amanusa had slept. Soundly. Uninterrupted until—until Jax left the tent. Something in her trusted him. Maybe even . . . *liked* him. And that disturbed her. Confused her.

"What happened this afternoon?" He held tight to her feet, almost clinging. "What did I say?"

"Nothing. Yvaine taught me to heal wounds." Amanusa's mouth twisted in an unseen smile. "Spit magic, not blood."

"You heard Yvaine?" Jax's voice held suppressed horror.

Amanusa didn't blame him, given what the woman had done to him, how tightly she had bound him so that even his manhood was not his own. "She spoke with your voice. It wasn't you speaking. The difference is . . . marked."

"And have you decided?" He spoke quietly, softer than before. "Will you learn the magic?"

4

Yes," AMANUSA SAID before she understood that she had indeed decided. The magic called to her. Whispered her name. "But not here. Not from Yvaine. This place is too dangerous for you to have any more fits. Even with the protection you just built. Unless it's something you can teach me on your own, like the spell we just did, I want no more lessons here."

"Yes, Miss." Jax dipped his head in his servant's bow. Amanusa could just see it. "I can teach you how to ride the blood, which is the beginning of justice." He paused. "I know you want justice. I can feel you crying out for it."

"Justice," she said. "Not revenge."

"Sometimes, it looks much the same."

She pulled her feet back and folded them under her. "Then teach me."

"Tomorrow." He moved back near the door. "It's not always a gentle ride. This night is too old. You need rest for tomorrow." He slid his tarpaulin nearer the tent opening and stood there, hunched over, until Amanusa lay down on her cot.

"How long will they keep you here?" He stretched across the doorway.

"Until Costel is out of danger. That's what Szabo

usually does." She wrapped herself tighter in her blankets.

"Will he live?"

"If the magic you taught me works like you said." She sighed. "It will be a miracle if he does. Belly wounds . . ."

"The magic will work." He fell silent.

Amanusa wanted to ask how he could be so sure, but decided she didn't want to hear the answer.

THE NEXT DAY was spent checking on Costel, changing Szabo's bandages and those of the others who'd let their minor injuries suppurate, and hunting the herbs that insisted on clinging to high mountain slopes rather than growing placidly in a garden plot. Jax made a bulky shadow, but Amanusa found herself grateful for his presence, and not only for his beast-of-burden talents.

After last night, she trusted Jax a bit more. Maybe more than a bit. He'd shed blood to keep her safe. Not much, but blood nonetheless. She'd inspected the scratch on his thumb in the morning's light and almost laughed at his sly request that she lick it whole again. She did lick her own thumb and rub it over his small injury. Even if she did not completely trust him—and she didn't—she trusted Jax more than she did anyone else in this hellhole.

As darkness deepened, Amanusa left Miruna to watch Costel through the night with instructions to spoon more broth and willow-bark tea into him if he woke again. She began to be cautiously optimistic that Costel would indeed survive his terrible belly wound. That did not explain the bubbles of tension that simmered along her nerves. She strolled with false casualness toward her tent.

"Amanusa," Teo bellowed. "You do not drink with us?"

"Not tonight, Teo," she called back and stepped through the magical perimeter surrounding the tent. It enfolded her lovingly as she passed through it, then solidified again into shimmering protection.

"You will make us think you don't love us." His teasing shout seemed to carry underlying threat.

"I love you all, Teo." She blew him a mocking kiss. "I just don't like you very much."

Jax eased up behind her, so close that his blanket-cloak brushed her hand. He stood straighter than his awkward madman's stance and Amanusa could feel the hostility simmering in him. Dear Lord, she did not need him starting anything tonight. Dead Yvaine hadn't turned him completely eunuch. He had a man's possessive jealousy.

"Go inside," she told him. "You're only making things worse."

He snarled, lip curling, eyes fastened on Szabo's second-in-command, but he obeyed her.

"Is that the secret?" Teo shouted. "You only fuck the feebleminded now? Half-men?"

Amanusa swallowed the hot-tempered retorts crowding her tongue. She had a hundred of them, a thousand, beginning with the size of brains compared to the size of—but she didn't dare use them. Even with the protection Jax had built for her.

She was tired of it. Tired of swallowing her temper and choosing every word. Tired of this place. Tired of this *life*.

And Jax waited inside the tent with something new. Fresh magic. Powerful. Different. Suddenly she wondered why she'd ever hesitated.

"Good night, Teo." She turned to walk the few paces to the tent's opening.

"Don't you walk away while I'm talking!" Teo's voice came closer, grew louder. "Come here, woman. I'm talking to you!"

Amanusa ducked inside, stomach churning, just as Szabo snapped out Teo's name. The outlaw fell silent, and after a moment she heard the crunch of footsteps walking away again.

Her knees crumpled and she reached out for . . . for . . . she didn't know. Something. Anything.

Jax caught her trembling hand. He helped her to the cot. He brought her a tin cup of tea, blowing on it to cool it before he handed it to her. He wrapped a blanket around her shoulders and knelt to unlace her shoes and ease them off.

"Thank you." She took a sip of the tea, huddling 'round its warmth. She didn't know why she should be so chilled; the night hadn't yet stolen away the day's warmth. "I feel so silly."

"That man means you harm." Jax set her stocking-clad feet on his thighs again and began to rub them warm. "It's natural to be afraid, especially since you have not had the magic to protect yourself. I don't know what he said, but I heard how he said it. We have work to do tonight."

Amanusa frowned as she sipped again. "I thought you understood Romanian."

He gave her a crooked smile, his rubbing changing from warmth-inducing to deep, penetrating kneading. Heaven. "I understand *you*. I can tell when you're speaking—Romanian, is it? But I don't understand them when they speak it. Helps with the simpleton role." He patted her toes as he set her second warmed, soothed foot back on his leg. "Finish up the tea and lie down. Better that way for your first ride, I think."

Now Amanusa was the obedient one as she drained her cup and handed it to Jax. He stretched his arm past the door flap to set it on the table outside while she stretched out on her back.

"There we go." He tucked the blankets close around her feet. "Arms out," he said. "At least for now."

"Explain what we're doing. What does it mean to 'ride the blood'?"

Crow walked into the tent and cocked his beady eye at them, as if checking to see what they were about, then turned and hopped out again, apparently satisfied. Jax chuckled as he sat on the ground near Amanusa's head, looping his long arms around his upthrust knees.

"Exactly what it sounds like," he said. "You will follow the blood—yours—" He pointed at her. "Inside the subject—me—" He turned his finger toward himself. "And ride it. It's one of the foundations of blood magic.

"When you ride, you can search out hidden thoughts, hidden illness—whatever you need to find. It's how the sorceress obtains justice. Secrets are impossible to keep when you ride another's blood. You can heal while riding the blood, though it's difficult and requires more blood from you."

He paused. "Death—the execution of justice—

requires only a tiny drop. Which is why I will take more from you than that."

"Why only a drop?"

Jax met her eyes a moment, before looking back at his loosely clasped hands. "Yvaine never explained it to me. That I can remember."

Amanusa shivered at the reminder of the magic he bore.

"But I think it's because the small amount allows the sorceress to maintain her distance. More blood means a closer binding."

"So how much did you take from Yvaine?"

He ducked his head between hunched shoulders. "Over the years? Seems like gallons, but I'm sure it wasn't so much."

"Will her magic interfere with this? With what we do now?"

"It shouldn't, or she would not have told me to do it." He unbuckled his belt. In another man it would make Amanusa run away in alarm. Now, she rolled onto her side and watched him.

"It was the last thing she told me, when I came to her before they burned her. 'Have her ride your blood,' she said. 'Soon as you can. Don't wait. Teach her to ride your blood.' Then she sent me away or they'd have burned me too."

His matter-of-fact tone sent more shivers crawling up Amanusa's back as he opened a hidden pocket in his belt and pulled out a small silver object and showed it to her.

It was flat, about as long as the tip of her forefinger at its sharp point, and twice as wide where it spread out at the base below. The chased metal was tarnished almost black at the base, but the point gleamed silver-white.

Jax rubbed at the tarnish. "I haven't had this out since Yvaine gave it to me. Haven't thought about it, to be honest, but it's good enough for tonight. I'll polish it later."

"What is it?"

"Yvaine's lancet." Jax began gently bending the broad, flat sides down, shaping them into a circle. "Now, it's yours."

Amanusa blew out a breath, wishing she could calm her nerves. She spoke lightly, to hide their state. "So far, Yvaine's bequeathed me a man and a lancet. What else?"

"Well, there's the tower." Jax concentrated on his task, glancing now and again at her hand trailing over the edge of the cot. "And the land that goes with it, of course. And the books—quite a lot of those. She had a fair bit of jewelry too. That should be all right. No one'll have gone into the tower. Then there's the bank accounts—"

"Wait, *wait.*" She caught Jax's arm to make him stop fiddling with the lancet thing and look at her. "I was joking."

"Oh." He shrugged. "I wasn't. All of Yvaine's possessions come to you, since she had no other heirs. Council law. Possessions—gold and jewelry and such—can be left to heirs of the body, if there are any. But in any case, a magician's workshop—Yvaine's tower—and all the magic items go to the magician's apprentice. You. In Yvaine's case, you get everything. The money and jewels, the books, the instruments—glassware, lancets, and such—and me."

"You're not a possession."

He winked at her. "No, I'm a magical item."

Amanusa huffed out a breath of laughter as Jax made a few more adjustments to the lancet. She could almost like this man, and how was that possible?

To be honest, she knew. He could make her laugh, even when she didn't particularly want to. He warmed her feet. He made her—somehow—feel safe. She didn't trust the liking any more than she trusted the man.

"There." A world of satisfaction swam in his voice. "May I have your hand?"

Bemused, she held it out.

"No, your other. You're right-handed. I want the right." Jax lifted her hand hanging off the cot. He slid the lancet over her forefinger and squeezed, tightening it a fraction more until it fit snugly. The broad flat section that had extended to either side of the instrument now curved around to hug her finger, while the sharp point extended beyond it to create an artificial claw.

Jax let her examine it. "You'll use your right hand as a source of blood eventually, but you'll want to take it most often from the left. Not because of any difference in the blood, but because many times, you won't want to impair the use of your right. There are other places to draw of course, but for small amounts, fingers work quickest and best."

The designs wrapped in silver around her finger included ancient words—Latin perhaps. She'd seen Latin written in churches, though not these words. They twined around tiny lilies and skulls. The whole of it sent shivers skittering through her. No wonder people feared sorcery if it could frighten even its practitioners.

"What do the words say?" She let him work the lancet off her finger.

"No idea." He sent her a crooked smile. "Might have known once but—" He lifted one broad bony shoulder. "We'll have to look it up together, when we get to those books. I'll draw the blood, all right? Until you learn how deep for how much."

"Yes, all right." Amanusa gave him her hand again, the correct one this time, her left.

Jax separated out her middle finger, the longest, and looked up at her with the lancet poised over her work-roughened fingertip. "Ready?"

Mutely, she nodded.

"Breathe in," he said. "Hold it an instant, then let it out. Focus on your body. Hear your heart beating your blood throughout. Feel me holding your hand, your finger. Feel the sensations in your finger, the air around it, the warmth inside it, the hand that touches it—"

As he said the word "touches," the sharp point of the lancet drove into the plump pad of her fingertip. Amanusa cried out, her hand jerking reflexively, but Jax held tight. Because she had been so focused on her finger, it hurt more.

"All right?" Jax watched her from beneath frowning brows. "Shall I stop?"

Amanusa bit her lip as she shook her head. The pain wasn't so much. She'd cut herself worse— nearly to the bone at least twice, and had the scars to show. It was just that she'd been concentrating so hard on her finger and its senses when he lanced it.

"These are the words." Jax squeezed her fingertip and blood welled up to glisten in a fat bead.

"Blood of my blood," she repeated the words he gave her. "Carry my soul safe with thee. Be with me. Answer me. Even as you journey without. My blood. My heart. My will."

Magic stirred. Deep inside her, something blossomed, opening to the magic's call. Warmth glowed through her and she followed its path through her body.

"Can you feel it?" Jax's voice came from very far away. "The magic?"

Amanusa started to nod, but she feared her head might wobble right off her neck. The warmth hadn't gone that way yet. She started to turn, to make sure her head was properly attached. But something pulled her the other way.

"Sorceress. *Miss Whitcomb.*"

That was Jax. Her servant. Her *man*servant. Amanusa blinked her eyes. Yes, there he was, his head floating in front of her. No, it was attached to his shoulders too. Something called, tugged at her.

"Do you feel the magic, sorceress?"

Carefully, Amanusa shaped her lips, pushed breath from her lungs. "Yes." A whisper.

"Follow it. Sweep it into the blood—this blood." He held up her hand and she saw the scarlet bead quivering on her finger, on the verge of trickling down its length.

"Yes-s-sss," she whispered. That was the call, the urge. The magic wanted to go into that droplet of blood. She let it go, giving way to the need, and she flowed through her body, down her arm, out her hand to the blood that adorned her finger.

"Pull back now." Jax quivered, his voice the tiniest bit shaky. "The magic is in the blood. It will answer your call. Pull back."

How? Amanusa wallowed in the glowing warmth. She hadn't felt anything so lovely in so long. Had she ever? Even the burn felt nice. It did burn a little—no, a lot. It *burned.*

She gasped, took a step back somehow, and as the cool air swept over her skin, she could think again.

"Sorceress—" Jax touched her cheek, lightly with just the barest tips of his fingers and she gasped again, jerking away.

Her skin felt raw, flayed from her body. The edges of—of what? Her soul? Her mind? Her *self*? All of those things together felt scorched. Seared by the magic's heat. It hurt, and at the same time, it felt good. Glorious. Warming all the frozen corners of her life.

"Are you well, sorceress?" Jax reached out again and she turned her face away.

"Well enough. Your touch hurts."

He spat some oath in a language she didn't know. "Magic burns. You should not have stayed with it so long. Didn't you hear me tell you to pull back?"

"Yes, but I didn't know how." She could speak properly again. It hurt a bit, talking. Everything hurt a bit.

Jax swore again. His hand holding hers jostled, and the fat drop of blood began to slide down her finger. He swore yet again when he saw it and tilted her hand to slow its path. "Do you want to stop? The magic is in the blood. It won't burn you now. But we can stop if you'd like."

"Can you feel it?"

"What? The magic?" The brown-flecked blue of his eyes searched hers. "When it went into the blood, I felt it then. Strong magic. Do you want to go on? I can tell you what to do, but I can't tell you *how* to do it. Perhaps we should wait."

Amanusa shook her head. A slight scorching was nothing next to the power she'd felt roll through her. "I managed to pull back. I can work out how to do the rest. I want to learn. Besides—" She wiggled her bloody finger. "Something tells me we shouldn't waste this."

He held motionless a moment longer, then he lifted her hand to his mouth. His gaze never leaving hers, he licked his tongue along the brief blood trail. Then he wrapped his mouth around her finger.

The wet heat of his mouth threatened to set the magic humming along her veins again. Or was this a different sort of warmth? This didn't burn. It quivered. And it soothed all her scorched places.

He stroked his tongue over the sensitive inner skin of her finger and sucked on it, gently at first, then harder and harder, drawing her tight inside herself. Slowly, he drew her finger out of his mouth, sucking all the while, and her nipples tightened into hard little peaks. But she wasn't cold. If anything, she was too hot.

"A little more," he said, still watching her. "For safety."

She couldn't move, couldn't speak, could only watch as he squeezed a bit more blood from her finger and curled his tongue around it, caressing long after the blood was gone. He trailed his tongue back down the length of her finger and probed the crease where it joined her hand. She shivered, whether from his touch or his gaze, she didn't know.

Jax sent his tongue swirling across her palm where blood had never touched and Amanusa let him, lost in the blue of his eyes and the shivery sensation of his teasing caress. With one last pulse of his tongue, he pressed a kiss to her palm, curving her hand around his face as if she caressed him in return.

He let her go. She could pull her hand back, but Amanusa hesitated. His cheek was warm, bristled with two day's growth of beard. Jax held absolutely motionless, his gaze fastened on her as she stroked her hand slowly up his jaw to touch the neat side whiskers in front of his ear, back down again, and away.

He shuddered and, finally, blinked. "Thank you," he whispered.

"For what?"

"For—" He shuddered. "For not being Yvaine."

"That's hardly any of my doing." She rubbed her hand along the blanket's rough wool to wipe away the sensations still tingling there as she brought it up to tuck beneath her cheek.

"But the *way* you are not Yvaine—I am grateful."

"Now what?" Amanusa wanted to wipe away all the other tingly sensations, but didn't want to scrub at her breasts with Jax there watching. What was wrong with her that she would feel so odd?

"A brief wait." Jax moved away from her in the deepening gloom inside the tent.

She watched him spread the tarp on the ground in

front of the door flap and lie down on it. "Why the wait?"

"Yvaine told me once that it is possible to ride the blood from the first moments, once the magic is safely contained. But those early moments tend to be disorienting. It is better to wait five or ten minutes for the blood to escape the stomach and find the veins. Once your blood has entered someone, it will answer you until you call it back."

"I see," Amanusa said, though she didn't. But she would. "Has it been long enough?"

"Not yet."

She rolled to her back, staring at the canvas over-head. After a time, she asked, "The protection around the tent—how does it work? Do people . . . run into a wall?"

"No." His smile showed in the deepening gloom, sounded in that one word. "If a person means you no harm, they can pass. If they intend harm however, it turns them aside. Sends them in a circle around us, or back the way they came. Or convinces them they didn't want to come here to begin with."

"Like you trying to leave my cottage?"

"Much like that, yes."

Amanusa fell silent again. She'd never been much good at waiting. She wasn't used to the thick dark-ness gathering in the tent, either. In her cottage, the fire's night-banked glow gave off enough light to see shadows. She could see almost nothing at all now, not even Crow's black shape as he rustled atop her medicine chest.

Her hands were clasped over her middle, she real-ized, her thumb rubbing over the tiny, lingering pain in her pierced fingertip. Not so much because it hurt, but the memory of Jax's mouth—she shivered and set the thought firmly aside.

"Are you ready?" His voice came floating out of the darkness, carried on the whisper of Crow's feathers.

"More than."

"Close your eyes—"

"Why?" Amanusa interrupted. "It's too dark to see anything. I see the same thing with them closed or open."

Jax chuckled. "Suit yourself then. These are your words: Blood of my blood, answer my call—"

She repeated them and went on, asking for vision, truth, understanding as she rode. Again she felt the magic rise. The slow warmth inside her spiraled out, reaching for part of herself that was somewhere else.

"Do you feel the magic?" Jax asked. "Your blood inside me?"

"Yes." Speaking was easier this time.

"Catch hold of it."

Amanusa didn't ask how. She doubted Jax knew. Instead she stretched toward that other warmth and the two pieces snapped together like the magnets she'd seen at local fairs. "I have it," she said when he didn't react.

"Good." He cleared his throat. "Now follow the magic inside and have a look 'round. Please don't interfere with anything—I took enough blood you should be able to tell if you inadvertently stop my heart or—or turn off my liver. But I'd rather you didn't."

"I shall be very careful." Amanusa saw her mental self tucking her hands in her pockets and the magic seemed to pull tighter. Now, how did she follow it inside?

The thought seemed to be sufficient, for she was moving, seeming to shrink, speeding along in a small warm space. Jax's veins? But how could she *look*—

Again, the thought sufficed. There was Jax's heart, pounding away, a bit frantically it seemed to her. She didn't know the other organs when she looked at them, their names or what they did, but they seemed to be working nicely together. Only the racing of his heart seemed worrisome.

Relax, she thought at him, afraid to touch anything even to soothe. *I won't hurt you.*

She didn't know if he heard her, but it seemed to help. His heartbeat slowed. She wandered through his body, looking at everything. He appeared to be an astonishingly healthy man. Not that she knew what to look for, precisely, but nothing looked *wrong*.

The magic showed her a clean red-orange glow in his legs and back. When she *looked* closer, she understood that she saw the ache of their past few days of climbing mountains, living rough, carrying the medicine case on his back. He was fine.

The magic could show her hidden thoughts, Jax had said. It could reveal a man's secrets. Amanusa turned from body to mind and the landscape changed.

She didn't know how she did it, she just made it happen. She saw Teo shouting at her and felt a fierce protectiveness so strong it startled her. Protection, not possession. Jax saw himself as *her* possession, not the other way 'round. His calm acceptance of it bothered her.

She could see flickers of the moment Jax took her blood and turned away. Her own reaction bothered her enough. She didn't want to know his. Instead, she went the other way, into the past. Beyond the moment Teo and his fellow rebels appeared, before the moment of their meeting when she towered terrible and beautiful over his kneeling form.

Terrible and beautiful? She wasn't—but she couldn't deny that to Jax she was, or had been at that moment.

Amanusa pushed on, sifting quickly through his wandering in the forest—for weeks, it appeared. There he was getting off the train in Nagy Szeben. Truth spoken about that. But when she tried to push further into his past, the memories began to crumble in her hands.

Amanusa couldn't get more than a flash of anything. *Why?*

She pulled back to look, moving somehow up as well as out. She saw a great, seething mass of—of *magic* squatting in the midst of his mind like some vast warty toad.

The magic that dead Yvaine had filled him with.

Was it just the textbook she'd turned him into, or was the binding part of it? Whichever it was, Amanusa didn't dare tinker with it. Not until she knew what she was doing.

Carefully, she withdrew from his thoughts, following the magic toward her own body until the two pieces parted with a faint *ping*.

Jax gasped. "Are you done?"

"For now. Until I know more." Possibilities and potential bloomed in her mind. "Teach me how to call the blood back to me."

"Yes, Miss." Quiet noises in the darkness told her he approached. "There is no need of it."

"I want to know how. I find—" She broke off. She didn't owe him an explanation. But she wanted to give him one. "The thought of being privy to someone's innermost thoughts any time I wish . . . disturbs me."

"Of course." He knelt beside her cot again. "You can use the lancet, but as the brier scratches from yesterday are not yet healed, they will do. These are the words."

Amanusa spoke the words he gave her and the metallic smell of blood rose again in the tent, bringing with it the tingle of magic. "Can you feel it?" she whispered. "The magic?"

"No." Jax knelt so close she could feel the faint puff of his breath on her cheek. "Now take the blood back to yourself."

She groped for his hand in the darkness, bumping his nose. He placed his hand in hers and she brought it to her mouth. Amanusa refused to put on a show like he had, merely swiping her tongue across the pad of his thumb. But he'd scratched more than just his thumb.

"Be sure you get it all." His voice sounded rough. "It can be dangerous to leave any behind."

He couldn't lie to her. He could perhaps fail to tell her everything, but he couldn't lie. She knew that from her journey inside him. Amanusa carefully licked clean all the bleeding scratches on his hand, reminding herself of a cat washing its kitten. Except Jax was no kitten. She thrust this thought away as well. The magic sighed, then folded away somewhere to sleep, like a banked fire, waiting to be stirred to life again.

She lay back on the cot, her mind whirling. Now, finally after all these years, she could know real magic.

And she could have justice.

5

THE NEXT MORNING, Jax woke with the sun, as usual, with an odd sensation thrumming through his insides, one that was not usual at all. It wasn't contentment, though that was present and distinctly unusual, but he could account for that.

Yvaine's command to find her apprentice no longer harried him. He'd found her, and the new sorceress was a much gentler mistress than Yvaine had ever been, even before the magic began to eat her. No, this peculiarity was something other.

Jax crept carefully out of the tent, putting on his "stupid" face, and rushed through his ablutions in the morning's chill, still pondering what felt so odd. The sensation wasn't unpleasant, he thought, as he carried the big kettle to the stream and filled it, Crow flying along to keep him company. The feeling hummed along his veins, whispering through his blood—

The blood. That was it. He carried Miss Whitcomb's

blood in his veins. No—she'd called her blood back. This was her magic he still carried.

He hauled the kettle back to camp and hung it on the hook over the fire he'd stirred up and rebuilt, then he stood over it, guarding it. The outlaws' women would steal the water for themselves before it was properly hot if he didn't stand watch. The men thought it was funny when he chased them off with animalistic roars and flapping arms. Jax didn't mind their laughter if it meant he could have plenty of hot water for Miss Whitcomb when she woke.

The magic burbled merrily through his veins, seeming almost to burst into song, now he'd recognized it for what it was. It poked into all his corners, polishing away all the dust and rust, putting things into proper order again. Jax shook himself, feeling the bindings settle into place, like harness around a plow horse after a winter's snooze in the barn.

Except he didn't feel much like a plow horse. This magic was different. He felt more as if—as if *armor* were fastening around him, like some knight's fine destrier being prepared for battle. Or . . . could it be possible? . . . as if he were the knight himself, arming in preparation for some noble quest.

Could this be how Miss Whitcomb saw him? Not as some living tool or a beast of burden, but as a—a man. A protector.

Jax scarcely dared think it. He knew the magic held the mark, the flavor of the one who wielded it. This was likely why Yvaine had wanted her apprentice to ride his blood as soon as possible, so that his binding could shift from the old master to the new. But such a change—

He had to remind himself to stoop and shuffle as he dipped the heated water into Miss Whitcomb's ewer. His spine kept wanting to straighten with . . . *pride.* He thought he'd forgotten how it felt, but here it came, creeping back again. Would this sorceress think it as dangerous as the last one had?

Jax carried the water into the tent and set it on the table he'd moved inside, Crow walking in behind him to caw a good-morning to his mistress. Jax left again to collect breakfast while Miss Whitcomb performed her own morning ablutions. When he returned with her porridge—he'd wolfed his own by the outlaws' fire to maintain his idiot's illusion—he began tidying the tiny canvas residence, rolling up his tarpaulin from the spot before the entrance.

As he bent to stow his bedroll out of the way beneath Miss Whitcomb's cot, he paused. The space was filled with rows of bottles and jars. All the things Miss Whitcomb had brought in her box of medicaments.

"Hand me another jar of the wound salve, will you?" She spoke from behind him.

"Certainly." Jax did as she asked. She *asked.* The thought made him smile and gave him the daring to ask. "Why is the salve under your cot and not in the box?"

"I needed the box for something else." She hesitated at the doorway, seeming to consider before reaching a decision. "Take a look and see if you know what it is."

"Yes, Miss Whitcomb." He bobbed his head and watched her go, Crow hopping behind her, begging for bread. Morning sick call would come after she saw to the man in the hospital shelter. He would have time to do her bidding and still be at her side when the sick and the malingering gathered.

Jax quickly finished tidying the small space and lifted the box onto the cot for a better look. Inside, he saw a bizarre metal contraption. The metal sheen of its central globe was pitted with a rusty-black corrosion, but despite its degraded appearance, the thing made his skin crawl.

Swallowing down revulsion, he reached past the rayed spokes on either side with care and touched it. Instantly, his finger burned like ice, then went numb. With a yelp, he jerked it back and popped it instinctively into his mouth. His lips and tongue went cold, then numb, and he yanked his finger out again.

Miss Whitcomb came bursting into the tent. "What happened?"

"I touched it." Somehow he managed to speak understandably, even with frozen lips and tongue. He frowned. "How did you know?"

"I felt it." Now she frowned. "I thought I called my blood back from you." She lifted his hand, studying the damaged finger.

It was blistered at the tip where he'd touched the metal monstrosity. White and dead-looking, then red and inflamed down to the first knuckle, and pale until it joined his hand where he could feel again.

"You did. It's the nagic." Jax tried again. "N-nagic." An "m" was apparently harder to say with numb lips than other sounds.

Miss Whitcomb turned his face toward her, squeezing his cheeks to purse his lips. "At least your lips don't look blistered. Let me see your tongue."

Obediently, he put it out to show her. Yvaine would never have bothered. It felt strange, having Miss Whitcomb look so intently at his mouth.

"I don't understand." She sank back on her heels, kneeling on the flattened grass flooring the tent. "How can I feel what you do? I called my blood back. And why did the machine thing freeze you? I touched it. I held it against my stomach. It made me queasy, but it didn't make blisters."

She raised up to flip the box closed and latch it. "Where's the lancet? I want to lock this thing away, put a protective seal around it."

"Here." Jax dragged her carpetbag from beneath the cot and found the lancet for her.

He marveled as, this time, the new sorceress lanced her own finger and spoke new words, changing those used to weave protection around their tent to ward against the evil of the thing in the box and hide it from the unwary.

"Now," she said. "Explain."

Jax blinked, eyelids fluttering without his conscious volition as he tried to find a way to do as she demanded. He felt magic welling up from the crumbled ruins of his memory to grip his thoughts.

"*No.*" Miss Whitcomb's nails dug into his arm, her hand gripped his face as she shook him. "I want answers from *Jax,* not Yvaine. I do not want to hear Yvaine speak. Not unless I ask for her knowledge specifically. Do you understand, you old besom?"

His blinking slowed as the surge of magic ebbed. He hiccuped, feeling light-headed and a bit fizzy in his belly region. "I nay not ve avle to exblain everything," he ventured.

"Tell me what you know, what you suspect, and we'll figure out the rest, as much as we can." She got off the grass to sit on the cot, patting the space beside her.

"Szabo's men will wonder what we do in here so long." Jax sat where she indicated, feeling strange at this semblance of equality between them. They were not equal.

"Let them wonder. They would wonder more at our conversation."

He dipped his head at the truth of her words.

"Why did I feel it when your hand was hurt?" She began her questioning.

"Nagic." The numbness was wearing off a bit, making his lips tingle and burn. "Vecause I an your vlood servant. The nagic-n-m-magic is different. I am vound to you."

He gasped as his finger began to burn fiercely. Miss Whitcomb's gasp echoed his. She captured his hand, enclosing his injured digit in the hollow between her palms, but when that didn't help, lifted it toward her mouth.

"*No.*" Jax jerked his hand free. "Zat's how ny nouth went numb."

"But it hurts."

"It shouldn't." He shook his head. "I mean, it shouldn't hurt you. I was vound closely to Yvaine and she never suffered like this. You should ve able to block the pain, if not the awareness. Gather your nagic, the nagic vetween us, the magic that binds me."

"It's not *my* magic. It's Yvaine's magic that binds you."

Did she still protest the truth—that she was already blood sorceress? Even after accepting the mantle and riding his blood?

"It's yours now," he said. "Your blood brought your magic to my bindings." His lips burned. Not as ferociously as his finger, but bad enough. Still, the fact that he could feel them made it easier to talk. He spoke faster, anxious to stop the pain Miss Whitcomb so obviously felt. She panted, her eyes wide with fear and pain.

"Do you have it?" He touched her arm with his uninjured hand to get her attention.

She nodded, swallowing hard. "I think so."

"Only part of the magic lets the pain through. Separate out that part and cut it off."

Jax watched her internal struggle play out in her eyes, in squints and gasps and tensing of this muscle or that, and he wished he could help her. He wished he understood the magic better so he could give more specific instructions. It was part of the binding, he knew, to care about his mistress's well being. But her kindness gave it something extra. He didn't want to cause her pain.

"I can't—cut it off," she panted finally. "But I think I can—" Her whole face and body screwed tight with effort and abruptly she relaxed, slumping against him, her head falling limp onto his shoulder.

Alarm skittered through Jax. "M-miss Whitcomb?"

"I'm fine, Jax." She stayed where she was another moment, a warm weight against his side, before pushing herself upright. "I couldn't cut the magic off, but I could squeeze it down so that almost nothing gets through. It hurts so much. How can you bear it?" Her eyes swam with compassionate tears.

Jax shrugged. His whole hand felt inflamed, throbbing agony with each beat of his heart. What else could he do but bear it?

His sorceress cupped his wounded finger again. He didn't think to stop her before she closed her hand around it. "Whatever happened to your finger, it's not spreading to me," she observed.

"Why not?" Jax opened her hand with his other, looking for burns, but it was pale and perfect—well, it was rough and callused with work, but perfect for her.

Miss Whitcomb shook her head. "I don't know."

This time, when she carried his finger to her mouth, he didn't jerk away, though he watched anxiously. She put out her tongue and touched just the pointed tip of it to the blister. It was the most erotic thing Jax had seen in—in as long as he couldn't remember, past the holes in his ruined mind. He was as certain of that as he was of the stirring in his long-dormant body, stirring he fought to stifle. She might feel it with him, and know he hadn't been precisely truthful about everything.

Yvaine hadn't quite rendered him eunuch. She hadn't minded his arousal. But it had been so long since anything had tempted Jax to such a state . . .

"No." Miss Whitcomb's voice broke into his thoughts, went shuddering through him. "My tongue doesn't feel affected either."

Jax slammed his eyes shut and squeezed them tight as she closed her mouth over the tip of his finger.

She'd done his thumb the same way last night when reclaiming her blood, but it had been different in the dark. Worse. And better. Being able to see her made it different. More arousing. Much more. Hugely, tremendously more.

"Am I hurting you?"

"No." Jax choked the word out, easing his damp finger from her grip. "On the contrary. It feels much better."

He opened his eyes to examine his injury. The blister looked the same size, but older. Almost ready to slough off the dead skin. He rubbed the dampness across his lips, easing the burn there. "Thank you."

"Why didn't it burn me?" she asked, turning on the cot to face him more fully, folding one foot beneath her.

"I don't know. You said the thing made you queasy?"

She nodded, looking thoughtful. "The outlaws seemed to handle it without it affecting them at all. But it did. The thing sucked at their life . . ." She frowned, an adorable crease forming between her brows. "No. That sounds as if it fed on their life energy and it didn't. It . . . ate away their life. Killed them by inches, like—like floodwaters on a riverbank, cutting the earth away. But a river carries the earth downstream to deposit elsewhere. That thing . . . destroyed what it touched. More like fire consumes. But slowly."

She looked up at Jax. "Does that make any sense at all to you?"

"The burn felt more like ice than fire." He couldn't think what else to say. "You should let Yvaine speak. I don't remember things." And it frustrated him.

"No. Not here." Miss Whitcomb was thinking again, chewing on her lower lip as she frowned. "It's too dangerous to have you out of commission. The thing was . . . anti-life. And anti-magic as well. The opposite of magic. But . . . *I'm* the sorceress, aren't I? I'm the one with the magic."

"You're the one with the power," Jax said, beginning to make a bit more sense of it. "I'm little more than a bag of bones tied together with magical strings. Your strings. It's your power in the magic that binds me."

"So it was . . . trying to burn the magic out of you?" She gave him a worried look. "I agree that we want to—to clip your strings, but I don't think this is the proper way to do it."

"Nor I."

"Oi!" A shout came from outside the tent in the language Miss Whitcomb said was Romanian, a rush of irritated words.

"Maybe you need to learn a little patience, Nicu," she shouted back, rolling her eyes at Jax, sharing her opinion. "I'll be there when I'm ready."

More words followed, along with raucous and probably lewd laughter. Jax could understand the intent, if not the words. He wanted to go out and pound a few heads. But there were many more heads than a few out there, and if he got pounded back, or knifed, or shot, he couldn't look out for Miss Whitcomb.

She grabbed him by the hand and hauled him out of the tent behind her, displaying his still-inflamed finger to the shouters. "My servant burned himself," she said. "I was treating *his* injury."

Teo, the brute who'd led the party that dragged Miss Whitcomb to the camp, shouted something.

"But *I* care," she retorted. "Jax is *my* servant, and I most certainly do care more about him than about you. About *any* of you. Now, if you want me to treat your scratches, get back over to the hospital and line up. I'm not treating a rowdy mob."

Teo reached for her, but Miss Whitcomb skipped out of his reach. One of the others shoved him back, talking fast in a joking tone, apparently hoping to keep the thug from taking offense. Jax could feel her trembling through her grip on his arm, but nothing showed where anyone else could see it. Gradually, the outlaws faded away and she let go of him.

Instantly, Jax took her elbow to provide support. She could stand on her own against these outlaws, he had no doubt. But with him here, she didn't have to.

THAT DAY PASSED much as the days before and each one that came after. Costel continued to improve. It was evident to Amanusa that he would live, but Szabo refused to believe her. In truth, he probably did believe, but he refused to let her go until Costel walked out of the hospital tent under his own power. He was sitting up in bed, taking small steps while leaning heavily on Miruna to collapse in a camp chair. And with every improvement in Costel's health seemed to come a corresponding deterioration in the mood of the camp.

Not because of Costel's health, but because of Teo's inability to break Amanusa's will. He could batter himself against it until the end of time, but she would never give in, and with every failure, his mood grew blacker. And when Teo was in a black mood, everyone suffered.

"Why don't you just give in and give him what he wants?" Szabo asked one afternoon when Teo went snarling and stomping away yet again.

"Because he wants me broken and whimpering at his feet," she said calmly, picking up the no-longer-clean laundry Teo had dashed from her hands. "And that will never happen. Ever."

"He will kill you."

Amanusa shrugged. "Then he kills me. He will not break me."

She could sense Jax stiffen behind her in denial. His reaction made it harder for her to accept her fate calmly, as she always had before, because she felt his rebellion.

"He will kill your idiot first," Szabo growled. "Have a care for him if not for yourself."

Amanusa had to force another shrug, this time through her own pangs of denial. Her own life she could risk as she liked. It was not so easy to treat another's life as unimportant. But Szabo—and the rest of them—could not be allowed to know it. "Then our bargain is broken and you have no healer. This is your problem to solve, old man."

She turned away and marched back to the stream to rewash the clothing, leaving the bandit leader muttering to himself.

"A woman should not be so strong!" he shouted after her.

"A man should be strong enough not to fear a woman's strength," Jax muttered, startling a laugh from Amanusa.

"When did you become so wise?" she asked,

shooting him a teasing glance from beneath her lashes.

Jax gave her a crooked smile in return, after first checking to be sure no one was near. "After a very long and painful education." He winked, then his face lost all its humor. "This place is becoming too dangerous."

"*Teo* is becoming too dangerous."

He took the laundry from her hands and knelt beside the frigid mountain stream. He kept insisting on actually doing a servant's job. But this time . . .

"Let me do that," Amanusa said. "You stand watch. I don't trust that man not to come after me when he thinks no one is looking."

This time, Jax gave up the task without argument. Doubtless he too thought Teo might ambush them. "We must leave."

"I can't. Not until Szabo says I may."

"No, I mean *leave*. Go to England, to Scotland and Yvaine's tower. Szabo has no power there."

Leave Transylvania? Leave her cottage and . . . "I can't."

"Why not?" Jax sounded at his wit's end. "Your friends will understand. We can replace whatever—"

Amanusa shook her head, swallowing down the churning in her stomach. "It's not—I haven't got any friends. Not true ones. I—"

"What?" he snapped. "What could possibly be more important than your life?"

"Justice."

The word seemed to echo in the forest, against the mountain walls beyond the trees. It sent Crow fluttering up from his pecking at the ground to land in a tree. He cawed a question.

"Or maybe revenge. I don't know." Amanusa pulled Jax's shirt from the water before she scrubbed a hole through it. She poured the emotion crashing through her into the effort of wringing it dry. "These people hurt me. They *owe* me. I won't leave until I collect what they owe. I swore it, Jax. I will have justice for the wrongs they've done me."

She looked up at him, standing tall and stalwart above her on the bank and called his eyes to her by the force of her will. "Teach me this magic, Jax. Teach me justice. Tonight."

Slowly he nodded, holding her gaze. "If you wish it of me, I will. But know this. It is a powerful magic, one that requires great strength of will to control."

"Do you believe I have the strength?"

"Yes," he said. "If you have the will to use it."

"I have it." She did. She truly did not want revenge, but justice. She understood the difference. She wouldn't let old grief get in the way.

"Then I will teach you."

"Tonight," Amanusa said. "In case Yvaine needs to speak."

THE GLORIES OF Paris opened up before the pearly, mist-shrouded glow of the dawning sun, spreading a sumptuous feast before the eyes of any awake at this hour to see. The working people of the city, those not already hard at their labors, paused for a breath to see what the city offered up. Others, stumbling home after a night's sinning, knew only that the sky lightened, and scurried like roaches for the darkness.

A few, who had been striving all night for answers

to seemingly unsolvable puzzles, welcomed the dawn's light as a possible end to their struggle. The battle was far from won, but weary warriors deserved—required—a little rest before they could rise again to fight on.

A quartet of these paladins paused on the doorstep of the anonymous building around the corner from the Bourse to take in the sky's pastel glow.

"Get what rest you can, gentlemen." The senior of the party settled his top hat in place on his balding head and passed a hand over the luxuriant mustachios decorating his face, smoothing any stray hairs back into place. "We'll go hard at it again this afternoon."

"You lads may be going hard at it," the neat, slender man said as he began a glide down the steps of the building. "I, however, do not intend to waste my first visit to Paris in not seeing Paris. I will be . . . in Paris." He flourished his walking stick as he bowed.

"You can't, Grey," the older man protested. "You're magister of the English conjurers. We need you at the meeting."

"Whyever for?" Grey waited while the others descended to join him in the street.

"To represent the conjurers!"

"Relax, Billy." The stocky man in the bowler hat, whose expensive suit strained across his shoulders, moved between the two men. "If 'e don't want to come, an' you make 'im, 'e'll just kick 'is 'eels and sulk and be no use to anybody. Not that he's much good to anybody now."

Grey crossed his eyes and stuck his tongue out at

the well-dressed Cockney, who rolled his eyes but ignored him otherwise.

"Sir William, *no.*" The fourth man in the party spoke up. "If England's conjurer fails to attend, we'll be blamed if this conclave fails—and I can't see how it can succeed against such a foe. We face nothing less than death itself."

"Oh, don't be so dramatic, Nigel." Sir William adjusted his frock coat on his angular frame, a stork settling ruffled feathers. "Henry is right. Grey *will* be worthless. He's rarely anything else," he muttered, loud enough to be heard. Grey grinned.

"But—" Sir William lifted an admonishing finger. "I expect you to use this . . . *expedition* to sweep the rubbish from that indolent brain of yours and usher in some fresh ideas. Ideas which I expect to hear promptly."

The younger man, who wasn't quite so young as he seemed at first exposure, gave the group a cheeky salute and sauntered off down the street in the general direction of the river.

"He'll be drunk as Dick's cat when he returns." Nigel, who towered over even Sir William's considerable height, but otherwise possessed few distinguishing features, watched Grey's departure with an expression that hovered somewhere between disapproval and envy.

"Won't affect him none," Henry said, shifting his shoulders until the seams of his coat threatened to burst. "Just like stayin' up all night arguin' didn't bother 'im. 'E's fresh as a daisy, that one. I expect 'e will come back drunk, with 'alf a dozen new ideas to take to the conclave."

Sir William eyed the powerfully built man with a sour expression. "Henry Tomlinson, I swear you abandon your grammar and drop your H's just to annoy me. I *know* you've been educated better than that."

Henry grinned. "It's why I call you Billy, too."

"I am past being annoyed by that." Sir William assembled his dignity. "Come. Let *us* return to the hotel and get some sleep. The meetings will begin promptly at half of three."

"Actually—" Henry fell into step beside the other men. "I thought I might take another look at the dead patch here in Paris. There's metal left in 'em. Earth, water, fire. My elements. I know I've studied the patches in London an' Manchester an' such, but maybe this one's different. Or maybe it's the same. I dunno. I want to look again. Seems to me the more we know, the better."

"Yes, all right." Sir William nodded, thinking as he walked. "But don't venture into the zone itself. Not unless you take someone with you. Someone without magic. One of the serv—"

"Sir." A small woman in a modest gray walking dress, her hair tucked away beneath her bonnet, blocked their path.

"Oh, for—" Sir William broke off in exasperation. "What are you doing in Paris, Elinor? Go home. I am not going to take you as my apprentice."

"Then I shall apply to one of the other master wizards." Her chin tipped up, firmed with determination. "Someone will have the vision to accept what I can do."

"Here? The continental councils are even more

conservative than we are in England. Give it up. You will never be accepted to the Magician's Council. No woman will." He pushed past her, the other men following suit. "Go home where you belong."

"I will never give up," she called after them. "You need me. England needs women on its council. The world needs women among their magicians."

"Go *home,* Elinor," Sir William bellowed without turning around. He shook his head wearily. "That woman will be the death of me," he muttered. "I wish I'd never taught her anything. I never thought she'd be serious about it."

"She's your daughter?" Henry raised a brow in surprise.

"Goddaughter. Distant cousin, or niece of some sort. Parents are good people, though her mother's a bit of a radical. Female education and all that."

"Women." Nigel's feet slapped the pavement. "Why can't they just keep to their place?"

"Don't they realize?" Sir William's frown deepened. "Magic is dangerous."

"Life is dangerous," Henry said slowly. "How many women die in childbirth every year?"

Both the other men frowned. As wizards, they would know intimately just how dangerous a woman's life could be.

"It bothers me," Henry went on. "Not havin' any blood sorcerers."

"And a good thing we don't, if you ask me," Nigel put in.

"I didn't," Henry muttered.

"Perhaps you're right," Sir William said. "But the issue is moot. When Yvaine died without having taken an apprentice, the magic was lost. We have the books, but they do us no good."

"It should remain lost, as far as I'm concerned," Nigel said.

"Why? Because it's women's magic?" Henry leaned forward to glare past Sir William at the other man as they walked. "What's wrong with that?"

"It's evil magic. Hence its affinity for women. Women are the weaker sex. A woman is inherently less able—"

Henry snorted, turning away. "What about Yvaine's workshop? Maybe there's something there wot can 'elp us with the books. Ain't anybody looked inside it?"

"No one knows where to look," Sir William said. "There were rumors, years ago, that Yvaine had a tower somewhere over the border in Scotland, but no one knew where. We did look, but those were turbulent years. Dangerous for all magicians."

"Others besides magicians searched." Nigel gave the others a significant look. "Criminals. Murderers. Thugs. Those who wanted the power, or the gold."

"For all our looking, no one's ever been able to find it. I believe the tower is a myth, spread by fools who know no better." Sir William shook himself and looked around, his expression determinedly cheerful. "What pleasant avenues Paris has. Broad enough for three carriages to pass with ease."

"You can thank Napoleon Junior." Henry's voice held cynicism. "Since the 'Forty-eight, those years back, he's been tearin' down the city and rebuildin' the streets too wide to be barricaded."

"Damned proletarian," Nigel muttered at Henry.

"Bloody bourgeois," Henry muttered back.

"Boys, boys." Sir William sighed. "A truce, if you will. We have larger problems to solve. The world is dying in patches. We magicians are the only ones who might be able to do anything about it. And so far, we've no idea what that might be."

6

"THEY BELIEVE WE are lovers," Jax said when he followed Amanusa into the tent that night, before the sky had grown completely dark. "Strange, twisted lovers."

"Let them think what they like. We know what is truth." Amanusa took out the pins holding her braid to her head and let it fall down her back, massaging her sore scalp. She didn't wear her hair loose in this place. She didn't know why her hair made these men act like idiots, but it did, so she pinned it up.

"I should sleep outside the tent." Jax got his bedroll from beneath her cot. "Teo would cause less trouble that way."

"Perhaps if you had slept outside from the first. But if you changed now, he would think I tossed you out to let him in." She was tired of this conversation. Jax brought it up every night. She flicked a hand at the dying patch of grass just by the tent flap and he spread the tarp in his spot.

"Tell me about the justice magic," she said, unable to wait any longer. "Tell me what you know first, Jax, then call Yvaine."

"As you will it, my sorceress." Jax sat crosslegged on his mat and rested his hands on his knees.

Amanusa did not like it when he called her that, but he was her servant, and she was a sorceress. According to Jax, at any rate. She did not feel much like one.

"The magic requires the blood of the sorceress," he began. "A few drops are enough to search dozens of people for the truth. If you have some of the blood of the victim—dried on a cloth, perhaps—it can add much to the magic, but it is not absolutely necessary."

The instruction went on, late into the night. Amanusa had to light a second candle as she wrote furiously in the notebook she always carried for her medical observations, trying to get everything down. After the first time, she tried not to ask Yvaine to repeat anything, for it made Jax stutter and twitch. Asking him—her—them to slow down didn't seem to bother him-them, so she was able to keep up better once she figured that out.

Finally, Jax's eyes—brown at the moment—rolled up into his head and he crumpled to his side. Amanusa sprang up to stretch him out on his pallet. She turned him onto his side when he coughed up a bloody spray.

Was it Yvaine's old, used-up blood he expelled when he collapsed like this? Would he be ready to act by morning, or would he still be unconscious?

She blew out her candle and crawled beneath her own blankets. She wouldn't sleep, not for ages yet, with all the new knowledge crawling around in her mind. But she would try anyway.

"Good night, witch-woman," Teo's voice called out from the main camp, sending a shiver skittering down her spine.

Tomorrow. She would use the magic tomorrow. She would have her justice, and then she would leave this hated place. If not for her thirst for justice, she'd have left long ago.

Now she had the chance for everything she'd ever dreamed. Justice first, then she could grasp the bright world of magic Jax offered.

DESPITE HIS COLLAPSE, Jax was up before her, crawling into the tent with the ewer and basin of hot water when she woke.

"I want to do it today," Amanusa said before he got out again. "I want you to take the blood and put it in the porridge pot, and in the tea kettle. Those who don't eat porridge drink tea, and those who don't drink tea . . ."

"Yes, Miss Whitcomb." Jax waited, bent over in the doorway.

"Can you do it without anyone noticing?"

"Of course. Yvaine often had me deliver the blood to the vessel."

"Don't stand there blocking the light," she snapped, irritated for no reason and annoyed because of it. "Come in or go out, but don't stand in the doorway."

"Of course, Miss Whitcomb." He left the tent.

"No, come back."

Obedient as always, he returned and waited for her command. Amanusa wished she knew what to ask of him.

"You think I'm wrong, don't you?" She didn't know she was going to say it until the words were out. "You don't think I should do it."

"What I think doesn't matter."

"Yes. Yes, it does. I want to know. Why do you think I shouldn't have my justice?"

"I don't think that! Not at all. You deserve justice for what they've done. Of course you do." Jax went to his knees beside her cot and caught her hand. "But . . . magic is a wild thing, easy to stir up and difficult to control. *This* magic is wilder than most and I am afraid for you. I worry that you are not strong enough yet to control it."

"You said you think I have the strength."

"I know I said it, and I believe it." His smile was crooked, his eyes clear and pure blue-green. "But I can't help worrying."

A chuckle escaped Amanusa. "Try not to. I'm worrying enough for both of us."

"Then I shall have faith. Give me the blood to carry." He held out his hand, palm up.

Instantly, Amanusa sobered. She reached into her pocket for the cloth she'd kept with her over the last dozen years. "Get the scissors from my kit."

She spread the stained, stiffened rag over her lap and took the sharp, narrow scissors from Jax. "This spot," she said as she snipped a few threads from it to fall into her servant's hand, "holds my mother's blood, wiped from her brow after they beat her. And this—" More threads fell. "This, my brother coughed into the handkerchief when he was broken inside. Blood of my blood. Blood of victims crying out for justice."

Amanusa thrust her forefinger into the opening of the lancet laid ready beside her and plunged the point deep into the pad of her left thumb. She welcomed the pain as it mingled somehow with the unhealed grief of her loss. She stirred it into the magic that rose with the welling blood and let it drip onto the threads in Jax's palm. Two drops, three, then four, and the wound began to seal shut. She squeezed out one more, then pressed her forefinger over the puncture.

A harsh caw startled her, brought her head jerking around to see Crow hopping up onto the little table. He cocked his head and turned a bright, beady eye on their activity. His presence somehow reassured Amanusa.

Jax laid a small strip of thin paper over the blood in his hand. It soaked the blood up almost instantly. He blew on it, drying it somewhat, then divided it carefully in two. "When I drop it in," he said, "it will dissolve so quickly no one will see it."

"Boiling won't hurt it? Won't weaken the magic?" Amanusa tried not to worry, but it was difficult. Even under Crow's watchful eye.

"It's magic." His smile was gentle, reassuring.

"Where did you get the paper? What is it?"

"Rice paper. Very absorbent. I always keep a few strips handy. Never know when you might need it." He pulled another strip from his waistcoat pocket to show her, then put it back. "I'd better go tend to this." He held up his squares of blood-soaked paper. "And let you tend to your washing up."

With that, he ducked out of the tent.

Amanusa didn't want to wash. She wanted to dog

his every step. But she didn't dare hover. The outlaws didn't like her coming near their food, even if they were beginning to forget what she'd done to them the last time.

She washed quickly and hurried into her plain brown dress, then crossed to the hospital tent to check on Costel's progress while watching Jax's.

He stood at the fire where breakfast cooked. Had he already tossed in the papers? Amanusa watched as closely as she dared, but saw nothing. Since she was supposed to see nothing, matters ought to be going as they should. Her nerves were still on edge.

Finally, Jax came shuffling back with her bowl of porridge and cup of tea.

"Is it in there?" Amanusa took the dishes from him, not sure how she felt about breakfasting on the bespelled food.

"No. The blood went in after I dipped out your food."

Amanusa took a bite. It had no magic in it, according to Jax, but she could detect a faint hum of magic. "I can taste it. The magic. Or, I taste something."

Jax cocked his head. "Truly? There is no blood, I swear it. Could you be . . ." He gestured, as if scooping something toward himself. "Gathering it?"

Amanusa shook her head. "No. Just eating breakfast. But I sense the magic even so. It . . . makes my teeth hum."

"Interesting."

"Why?" Now she was worried. Just a bit.

He smiled as he shook his head. "Nothing to fret over. Yvaine couldn't sense magic that way. Not unless she was actually gathering the magic to judge. I think that you, as a beginner, are more powerful than Yvaine ever was." His smile changed, went wry, wise. "As I said. Interesting."

Footsteps neared, Miruna returning from washing her dishes and Costel's in the stream. Jax rearranged his features into dullness and stared off into the distance. Amanusa sighed and finished her boring meal. No more interesting conversations until nightfall. Of course, she intended to trigger the magic before then, so maybe she wouldn't have to wait. But other things needed to be done first.

"Jax." She handed him her empty bowl and cup, raising her voice to an ordinary volume. "After you do the dishes, fetch the medicines I'll need for sick call." She moved closer, laying a hand on his arm to hold him as she gave quieter instruction. "Be ready to go. I want to take the box with the machine. Anything else can be replaced, but the machine should go with us."

"Yes, Miss." Jax bobbed his head.

She was tidying away after sick call when Jax entered the hospital tent. He met her gaze briefly with a subtle nod, and hunched over to shuffle out again, in the direction of the fire. Everything was ready for their departure.

"For once, I have caught you alone." Teo's voice preceded his grip on her arm by mere seconds.

"What are you doing?" Amanusa cursed her distraction as she tried to free herself. "This is the hospital tent. It's off limits."

"Off limits to who? Not to me."

Frantic, Amanusa searched her surroundings for

help—Szabo, Jax, anyone who might . . . Gavril held Jax prisoner, a knife at his throat. Szabo was nowhere to be seen—the coward. The *liar*.

He had set this up deliberately, hoping to keep her in the camp. He'd taken himself off so he could claim later to have known nothing about what Teo planned. The *cheat*.

"I will kill you," Amanusa snarled. "I will kill you first, and then I will kill Szabo."

Teo laughed. "Who will be killing who? I think you are in no position to be making threats, pretty one."

He slammed his fist into Amanusa's face. Jax roared. She could feel him fighting to break free of Gavril's grip, feel the bodies pile onto him, the blades prick his skin. Blood welled.

"No," she cried. "Jax, don't fight them! I will handle this." She licked the blood from her split and swelling lip, fighting down the terror that pushed at the edges of her mind. She was a sorceress now. He would not rape her. Not this time.

Teo hit her again. "You will handle me? See how you handle *this*." He grabbed his crotch, thrusting his ugly arousal at her. "I knew he was no idiot. I knew you would not take such a man to your bed. I saw you talking to him. I *heard* him. And I showed Szabo how you made a fool of him."

Amanusa spat at him, bloody foam spattering his face and neck. "Blood of my blood," she cried.

At her words, a scouring wind of magic swept the camp, springing from nowhere, from the blood everyone had ingested.

Teo shuddered and looked around, his eyes rolling

in all directions, whites showing. "What was that? What are you doing?"

"Blood of your victims!" Amanusa's voice echoed with the power she gathered in.

Teo raised his hand, clenched it into a fist.

Amanusa laughed. "Do it! Hit me again. Give me more blood for my magic."

Only then did he release her and back away, horror coating every line of his face and body. "Who are you? *What* are you?"

"I am Amanusa." She spread her arms wide, exulting in the torrent of magic pouring through her. "I am the blood sorceress, and I call for *justice*!"

She heard Jax cry out in the instant before she burst into a thousand bits—or perhaps only half a hundred. However many had tasted the blood in the food. She saw through scores of eyes, screamed with a multitude of throats, weighed the beating of myriad throats.

Cruelty after cruelty displayed itself to her, and through her to everyone in the magic, from petty bullying to horrible scenes of torture. The agonies of her mother, her brother, herself—pain she had locked away long ago—replayed. The indignity, humiliation, and desperate helplessness felt once again as real and vivid as when it happened. She relived all of it in moments, as if she had endured all of it herself.

She screamed, hundreds of voices echoing her pain, living it with her. She had to make it stop, had to make them pay. Had to make sure they could never hurt anyone ever again.

"Blood of my blood," she whispered again through swollen lips. "Justice . . ."

The screaming stopped. A few whimpers sounded before the magic slammed into her like a sledgehammer blow, and everything went black.

DEAR GOD IN heaven, what had his sorceress done? Jax struggled from beneath the pile of limp bodies and staggered to his sorceress where he dropped to his knees. Her pulse still throbbed in her neck, thank God. What had she been thinking, to let the magic run free like that?

The quiet, after all the screaming, sent a chill up his spine. Were they all dead?

Jax reached across Miss Whitcomb to Teo's ankle for the pulse behind the bone. He was dead, to no one's surprise. So, Jax suspected, were those who'd held him prisoner, taken him to the ground when he'd fought. If they were so wicked as to be willing to take part in this assault on his sorceress, their pasts were likely black with similar sins. Sins for which such wild magic would claim repayment.

A feminine moan sounded from the other side of the hospital tent's shelter. Miruna lived. Apparently the magic hadn't taken too much offense at her minor cruelties. If her Costel hadn't survived, though . . .

Jax needed to get his sorceress out of this place. He crawled to his feet and heaved her up over his shoulder, grunting at the effort. His new mistress was not the small woman his old one was. He didn't mind in the least.

Still, he was grateful he'd hidden the warded machine box some distance across the stream, on the way to her cottage. Everything else would have to be abandoned if he had to carry both the box and Miss Whitcomb out of the mountains.

He wished he knew a more direct route to the railhead, so they wouldn't have to return to the cottage. The outlaws—if any survived—would look there first. Perhaps Miss Whitcomb would wake soon. He doubted it, though. That had been powerful magic whistling past his ears. Good thing he'd eaten his breakfast before he bespelled the porridge pot.

Jax had collected the box with its frightening contents and shouldered his sorceress's unconscious body again when the first wails rose quavering from the camp. Faded by distance, the cries bounced around the mountainsides and shivered down his spine. Blood sorcery had earned its fearful reputation this day.

Some of sorcery's reputation was indeed well deserved, but the righteous had no need to fear it. Murderers and other criminals would now once again tremble in fear, as they should. He only hoped Miss Whitcomb had not paid too high a price.

He hurried down the mountain as fast as his burdens would allow. Not nearly fast enough, he feared. Miss Whitcomb's continued unconsciousness worried him. She could not possibly be comfortable, tossed over his shoulder with her arms dangling down his back. But she did not wake.

Every step felt as if his spine compressed another fraction. He'd be several inches shorter by the bottom of the mountain at this rate. And his left arm, the one carrying the converted medicine case, would be several inches longer. For the rest of his life, he'd lean to one side as he walked.

Smiling at his own foolishness, Jax eyed the sun's

position. Noon was long past. His stomach screamed its unhappiness at his neglect. He wasn't nearly far enough down the mountain to suit him, and Miss Whitcomb still hadn't woken up.

Watching the sky instead of his step, Jax put a foot wrong, and the rocks rolled, sending him skidding. He dropped the box, trusting the machine to its latches and the lady's magic, and grabbed for Miss Whitcomb, desperate to keep her from hitting the rocks face first. Down they slid, and rolled, and tumbled, the case crashing alongside, Jax taking the worst of it, he hoped, with his arms wrapped round his sorceress's head.

Finally, he got his feet pointed downhill long enough to dig them in and bring them to a slow, unsteady halt. For a few minutes, he lay there with Miss Whitcomb draped across his body while he fought for air. He could feel her breath warm against his neck, so he hadn't killed her. He realized then that he could feel most of Miss Whitcomb warm against most of him, including that recently awakened unruly part that she feared.

Jax shifted, sliding his hips from beneath hers, taking care they didn't go tumbling downhill again. Surveying their surroundings, he saw a somewhat level spot to the right, anchored by a gray, lichenspotted boulder. Now, if he could only reach it with Miss Whitcomb in tow.

He took another moment to relish the feel of his mistress's lithe body in his arms, her cheek resting soft against his. She was never so close or pliant when awake. He liked her strength. But he liked her this way too. Except for the unconscious bit. He didn't like that at all. He wished she would wake up.

With a deep breath, and a pause to dig his heels deeper into the porous earth, Jax stood, Miss Whitcomb draped over his arms. Testing each step, he bore her to the boulder's shelter and laid her gently in the deep-piled leaves of countless years past. He brushed her hair out of her face—she'd lost most of her hairpins in that tumble, if she hadn't lost them before—and studied the scrapes and bruises he found. Only some of them were new from the fall. The scrapes, mostly.

Jax spit on a corner of his blanket-cloak and dabbed at the blood seeping from the rawest scrape. Her poor face. He wished for cold water and clean rags to tend it for her. Might as well wish for the moon, or the magic to heal her, for all the good his wishing did. He went after a spot of dirt and she moaned, pushing his hand away.

Jax did not jump up to dance a jig, no matter how much he wanted to. "Miss Whitcomb?" He smoothed her hair behind her ear again, where the breeze had disturbed it. "Miss Whitcomb, can you hear me? Can you wake?"

She didn't respond. He didn't want to hurt her again, but he wanted her awake. That much magic that much out of control . . .

Gently, he shook her. "Miss Whitcomb. *Amanusa.*"

"What?" The word was half moan, half plaintive whine.

"Time to wake up, my dear." Jax cringed when he heard himself say it, dreading her reaction. But maybe she didn't hear it. "Amanusa, wake up."

She screwed her face into an adorable grimace. "Don't want to. Head hurts. Sun's too bright."

Jax shaded her eyes with his hand. "I'm sorry your head hurts, but we must leave Transylvania before what's left of Szabo's outlaws catches up with us. So you must wake up."

She lifted one eyelid to squint at him. "Oh. It's you."

"I'm afraid so." He gave her a little smile. "Other than your head and your battered face, how do you feel? Do you think you can walk?"

Amanusa—Miss Whitcomb groaned her way up to a sitting position, swiveling to lean against the big rock at her back. "I'll have to, won't I?" She squinted at their surroundings, shading her own eyes. "Where are we?"

"Just over half the distance back to your cottage. I would have cut cross country to the railhead at Nagy Szeben, but I didn't know the way."

"I don't either. And I want some things from my house if we have time to get them. What happened? How did we get here?" Her eyes narrowed with suspicion rather than sunlight. "Did you carry me?"

"How else do you suppose I got you here?" Jax shocked himself with the retort. But he was tired of her endless suspicion and knew by now that she wouldn't punish him for impudence. "As for what happened— you let loose a bloody great pile of wild magic without putting any controls on it, is what you did. And when it finished punishing everybody it thought needed punishing, it smacked back into you. Hard.

"What did you think you were doing?" he demanded, his hours of worry overwhelming him. "You can't let magic go like that without putting any controls on it, without edging it round with commands and limits. You just threw it out there and let it do whatever its heart desired. Except magic doesn't have a heart. It doesn't care who called it. It could have killed you just as easily as it killed everybody else."

She stared up at him, eyes wide and filled to the brim with tears, her lower lip caught between her teeth. Oh dear. He couldn't cope with tears.

"Don't cry, Miss Whitcomb." Jax shoved a hand back through his too-long mop of hair, wishing he dared take her into his arms again. "Please don't. I—"

"Amanusa." She interrupted him with a touch on his arm. "Anyone who's shared a tent with me for five weeks and carried me halfway down a mountain has to know me well enough to use my given name."

The smile crept up on him and pounced. "Amanusa." He nodded, trying to hide just how pleased the privilege made him.

She was biting her lip again, looking frightened. "Did it truly kill *everyone*?"

"No." Jax looked over his shoulder for signs of pursuit. "Not everyone. Teo's dead, and that Gavril chap—"

"*Good.*" Amanusa nodded with satisfaction, and winced, raising a hand to her head.

Jax knew how much it must hurt and wished he could help. Maybe if she knew the rest. "But there's others that lived. Most of the women. A few of the men, maybe. I didn't take the time to check. The ones it didn't kill got knocked back right smart. I was more concerned with getting you out of there before they began to recover. And Szabo wasn't there, re-member?"

"Let's hope he hasn't come back yet." Her tone soured. "He wouldn't want to be back until everything was over."

"The bastard." Jax didn't usually hold grudges—he couldn't remember anything well enough. This one he could. A man couldn't keep his hands clean by doing as Szabo did.

"Jax—" Amanusa was searching the mountain's slope. "Did you get that machine? Or did you have to leave it behind?"

"No, it's here somewhere. I dropped it when I fell." He stood and looked uphill, where he remembered seeing it last. It was several yards farther down, wedged between two close-growing birches. "There it is. I'll get it."

A scramble up, a slide back down, and he presented the still-latched case to his sorceress. "Your magic warded it well."

She shook it, listening to the clank inside. "Do you suppose the tumble broke anything?"

"I don't know. Nor do I care to find out."

"Me neither." Amanusa handed the box back to him, then held her hand out for an assist. She must truly feel bad, for she usually refused help. "Let's get moving. Sun's flying westerly."

Jax pulled her up and steadied her on her feet. "As you will, Miss Whitcomb."

She gave him a stern look. "Who?"

His smile felt shy. "Amanusa."

He gestured for her to take the lead, and with cautious steps, she did.

7

IN PARIS, AT that very moment, a barrel-chested man in a black bowler hat and brown tweed suit stood at the center of a wide boulevard. Behind him, a breeze off the Seine rustled the leaves of the chestnut trees planted along the sidewalks, filling the air with green scents of summer overlaying the dank, familiar smells of river and city. Before him, the trees reached barren, brittle limbs to the sky in a silent, futile plea for help. Even the bark had sloughed off, leaving the wood dead and gray, like driftwood still anchored in soil.

Henry Tomlinson, who preferred to be called Harry, scowled as he studied the barren terrain before him. "Dalcourt, how big did you say this dead zone was?" he asked, without turning to look at his companion.

"Five of the city's blocks." The Frenchman was a fraction shorter than Harry and far leaner, dressed in dapper black and white. "It has grown at a rate of perhaps a meter each fortnight."

"How big is a meter?" Harry muttered.

Dalcourt held up his hands to illustrate.

"About a yard then." Harry nodded. He put up his own hands, palms out as if feeling for a barrier. "When—?"

"The first *endroit de la mort* appeared—pardon, I spoke wrong—it became *noticeable* approximately a year ago. The *conseil* is certain that it existed for far longer, but was too small to notice, too small to kill." Dalcourt watched the Englishman intently. "What are you doing? Can you sense the *endroit*?"

"Not here." Harry propped his hands on his hips and scowled. "Not on the edges, but when I'm farther in, yeah. Any magician can."

"You are *un alchemiste, n'est-ce pas?*"

"Yeah. Which means I can pick up on the magic inherent in things, in stone and brick and dirt. There's magic in the air too." He stabbed a finger at the dead zone in front of him. "But not in there, there ain't. It's all dead." He paused. "There's not anybody livin' in there anymore, right?"

"We evacuated the buildings." Dalcourt shrugged, that quintessentially French gesture. "A few died, four I think, at the beginning, when *l'endroit* was yet very small. The first were old, dead in their beds, not unexpectedly. It was not until the child died, the third to die, that anyone began to suspect mischief. He was a sturdy child, twelve years old, strong and healthy—no reason for him to be dead."

Harry's face was grim as he nodded. "Yeah. It went like that in London too, and Manchester. We went looking for magic and found nothing. Absolutely nothin' at all. And others died before we figured out *that* was what killed 'em."

Dalcourt scowled. "But we have not been able to keep everyone out. Many avoid it because they think it is cursed. Others do not believe in curses. They think their little spells will save them. There are always those—thieves, or the desperate—who will go into these places for shelter or to see what they can steal. And the young and foolhardy dare each other to brave what frightens them. Some of them die. Two last month."

The two men stared morosely at the dead trees

lining the dead street another long moment before Dalcourt spoke again.

"The *Conseil Française* thanks you for sharing your discovery before any more people died. We cannot force fools to give up their foolishness." He paused. "I thank you, personally."

Harry gave a brisk nod. "No worry."

"No. The worry is how to stop it before it destroys us all."

"Right." Harry looked Dalcourt in the eye. "You're a clerk, right? A bureaucrat with the city. Not a magician."

Dalcourt stiffened slightly. "That is correct, Monsieur."

"Terrific. That's exactly what I need." Harry took a deep breath of air, swinging his arms as he stared deep into the dead zone. "I'm going in there. If I get into trouble, I'm countin' on you to come pull me out. You're not attuned to magic, so it won't affect you like it does me, right? I won't go out of your sight. You wait here, and watch. If I keel over, you come in and drag me out. Understand? I swear you'll be fine. It won't hurt you, not goin' in for just that long. Will you do it?"

Dalcourt drew himself to attention and nodded in almost a salute. "*D'accord.* I will do it. You can rely on me."

Harry gave him a return salute. "All right then."

He took several more deep breaths and blew them out again, facing the dead trees. "All right, then," he repeated. One more breath and he stepped forward, into the dead zone. *L'endroit de la mort.*

He strode forward normally, past the first pair of

trees in their sidewalk spaces, but his face began to pale and his breath came quicker, in shallow gasps.

"Monsieur?" Dalcourt called.

Harry pushed onward, beginning to stumble on the pitted, crumbly paving. He veered toward one of the elegant buildings and examined its surface. The stone facing was discolored and eroding as well, the magic and the life stripped from it. A faint skittering sound echoed along the empty avenue and Harry's head jerked up.

"There—" he called out. "Did you hear that?"

"Non, monsieur. I heard nothing."

Leaning against the wall, Harry struggled to breathe without sound, listening intently. The noise grew louder, took on a metallic tone. Harry bent, looked down the barred stairway to a lower-level entrance, and saw a hole through the building's foundation. A hole big enough for a large dog to pass through—something bloodhound-sized.

"Wot in blazes—?" Harry wiped clammy sweat from his face and searched for the gate giving access through the black iron fence. The metal wasn't corroding. It was devoid of magic, but it wasn't dead or dying, like the stone.

The gate was locked, but that wouldn't stop Harry. He'd learned many useful things during a childhood in the Seven Dials. By the time he had the gate open, the skittering had become clanking, and he needed the support of the iron railing to remain upright. He took a deep breath and was seized by a coughing fit.

When it passed, he wiped his streaming eyes and opened them onto a horror coming through the hole below. Made of bits of metal turned from other purposes—plates off a furnace, spoons bent and flat-tened, riveted to melted tea trays—it resembled a nightmare insect more than anything, with multiple legs. And multiple stingers—sharpened knives bris-tled from oddly jointed arms.

Harry scrambled back, letting the gate clang shut. Deprived of his support, he fell to the ground, scoot-ing backward like a crab on hands and feet.

"Monsieur Tomlinson!" Dalcourt dashed into the dead zone, intent on rescue.

"No, stay back!" Harry waved him off as he rolled to his knees and convulsed in another fit of coughing.

Dalcourt ignored him, lifting the bigger man to his feet in a burst of fear-powered strength as the metal creature reached the top of the stairs and clanged into the fence railing.

"Should've found a bigger clerk," Harry mumbled, trying to stand on his own. "Bigger'n me, any road."

"I am big enough," Dalcourt retorted. "And there is none more determined. My family lived next to the house where Louis Martine—the child—died. *Ma mère* was frail for months after we moved away."

The monstrous machine cut through the fence rail-ings faster than Harry and Dalcourt could stagger away, using some sort of saw—clippers combined with a fierce heat. It broke through just as Harry tripped over a pit in the paving and fell to his knees, taking Dalcourt with him. The thing clanked toward them, its mode of travel awkward, ominous, and re-lentless, until abruptly, it froze.

Harry's head lifted. He sniffed. "Smell that?"

Dalcourt sniffed as he continued his fight to get

Harry upright again. "It is only the river. It stinks as always."

"It's *life*." Harry planted both hands on the stones beneath his knees. The paving had been cut and minimally shaped, but otherwise the stones were the same substance they'd been when pulled from the earth. "There's magic in these stones. Not much, but it's there. And I could swear it wasn't there ten minutes ago. *Two* minutes ago."

He dragged in a deep breath and paused, as if waiting for another bout of coughing to strike. It didn't. Finally, he allowed the slender clerk to drag him to his feet.

"And look," Harry said, pointing. "That monstrosity—it's retreating. It can't come where there's magic."

The creature was indeed sidling slowly back to its stairwell, scraping step by multilegged step, as if being driven back.

Abruptly, Harry shouted with laughter, snatching off his hat and tossing it high in the air. "They've done it, Dalcourt," he cried. "The council—one of the magicians—*somebody* 'as figured out how to stop this bloody mess from spreadin', how to drive it back. It's over! Nothing left but the cleanin' up."

Dalcourt stared warily, hopefully at the other man. "Do you mean it? Can it be so?"

"Course I mean it. What else can it be? Feel." Harry grabbed the Frenchman's hand and slapped it against the stone flower box at the curb. "There's magic there. A minute ago there wasn't. Now there is."

He plunged his hands deep into the soil in the box

and brought them up again. Dry, sandy grains clung to his skin like glitter, nothing like loamy topsoil, but no longer the dead ashy stuff that had filled it moments before.

"I will have to take your word for it, Monsieur." Dalcourt felt his way along the stone briefly before giving up. "I have no sensitivity to magic. I am also tone deaf."

Harry clapped Dalcourt on the shoulder, leaving a perfect sand-colored handprint on the black twill suiting. "Come on, man, let's go find out 'ow they did it. An' call me 'Arry."

"*Oui*, 'Arry. And I am Armand."

"Pleased to know you."

The two men shook hands. Harry slung an arm around Armand's shoulder as they marched back up the boulevard. "An' thanks for the rescue. I 'ate to think 'ow that thing might've cut through me, if it caught me."

"It is, as you say, no worry, 'Arry. I am pleased to be of service."

AT HER COTTAGE inherited from old Ilinca, Amanusa collected the few bits that held memories of her lost family. The lace collar her mother had knitted. Her brother's cap. Her father's shaving cup and razor. They retrieved Jax's frock coat and overcoat from beneath her bed. He looked much more elegantly turned out than she when he put them on, despite his now-grimy shirt.

It didn't matter. Stationmasters didn't care what you wore if you had money for a ticket, and Jax assured her their supply was ample. She piled everything she wanted to take on the blanket without holes, and tied it into a bundle which Jax threw over his shoulder. He refused to let her carry anything, saying that until he ran out of arms and his back filled up, the burdens were his.

Just after sunset, they were on the road bound for the railhead at Nagy Szeben. They stopped when the full moon was at its zenith to catch a few hours of sleep. Amanusa slept. Jax stood watch. He slept when they caught a ride with a market-bound farmer and his aromatic wagonload of onions the next morning. The next night, they both slept, figuring it far enough from the mountain hideout. But when they reached the town, they discovered rumors ran on faster feet than theirs.

The sun was just tucking itself behind the mountain peaks when they reached the outskirts of Nagy Szeben, though Amanusa was certain it had been at least an eternity since noon and the last of their hurriedly collected foodstuff. But they hadn't quite got into town proper when she gasped and ducked into the shadowed gap between two houses. Crow fluttered into a tree nearby and cawed a query.

Jax took another moment to realize where she'd gone and to follow. She grabbed his sleeve and pulled him out of sight beside her.

"What's wr—"

She cut him off with a hiss, then whispered *"Look,"* and pointed.

There, stalking down the center of the rutted dirt street as if he owned it and all he surveyed, was an *Inquisitor.* Which meant that though he might not actually own the street, he could do as he liked with it.

He could enter any building, destroy any property, slaughter any animal, arrest any person, all in his quest to root out illicit magic.

"Who is he?" Jax whispered back, catching at least a bit of her urgency.

"An Inquisitor." Amanusa wanted to shake him for his ignorance. Didn't he know anything?

"How do you know?"

"Look at him. He's all in black, even his shirt and neck cloth. And he's got the red badge on his coat. *And* a cockade in his hat."

It was the bright red-feathered badge stuck jauntily to the brim of his shiny top hat that made Amanusa's blood run cold. It meant the man was Inquisitor Plenipotentiary, a leader among the howling pack.

"That doesn't mean he's necessarily looking for you. If you behave suspiciously, they will suspect you. Act as if you have nothing to hide and they will see an honest citizen." He scrutinized her from head to foot and glanced down at himself, then handed her the blanket-wrapped bundle. "I am afraid we can do nothing about the bruises on your face, and until I can tap your funds, we can't do anything about your clothing. I recommend we trade roles. No one looks at servants. I will keep everyone looking at me, and no one will notice you."

"B-but-you don't speak Romanian." Amanusa liked the idea of hiding behind Jax so much, there had to be something wrong with it. It was, at the least, cowardice.

Jax grinned at her. "All the better. I'll be the mad Englishman on a world tour, with a local to translate for me."

"But if I'm supposed to translate, won't that make me noticed?"

"Hmm—you're right. So you'll be mute. Just carry the bundle, follow my lead, and we'll breeze right past the nasty chap."

Jax stepped out of the shadows and made a show of studying the flowers planted around the house in an attempt to brighten its raw, unpainted wood construction.

"*Lilium variegata*," he said in a plummy voice. "Not that you understand, of course. Don't know why I'm bothering. Education just rolls off a woman, you know. Like water off ducks. Useless. Well, I suppose some of it might soak in. Women do read, after all. But the *things* they read . . ."

He nattered on about the various flora they encountered as they continued down the road, disparaging the value of female education and making up Latin nomenclature. Amanusa knew he made it up because she knew some of the proper names. Jax sauntered past the deadly blade that was the Inquisitor. Amanusa kept to his shadow.

"*Halt.*" The Inquisitor's voice sent horror racing down Amanusa's spine and back up again.

Jax ignored him, strolling on as if he hadn't a thing to fear. Or as if he didn't understand Romanian.

"You!" The Inquisitor took two strides and caught Jax's arm, hauling him around. "I said *stop.*"

"I say—" Jax removed his arm from the other man's grip. "There's no need to accost me like that. You only had to speak civilly to me. Talk sense, my good man. You can't possibly expect me to speak the sort of gibberish the locals go in for."

Amanusa had to stifle a sudden urge to giggle. It diluted her terror, but made it more difficult to play the stolid, beaten-down peasant.

The Inquisitor tried again, speaking another language. One Amanusa didn't know. French, perhaps. It sounded rather nasal. Then he tried German, which Amanusa understood, and Hungarian, which she didn't.

"Look, it's no use speaking anything but English," Jax said, putting on impatience. "Another sort of gibberish is still just gibberish. You'll have to speak a proper language if you want to talk to me. Now if you'll excuse me?" He touched his forehead in a substitute for tipping the hat he didn't have and turned to walk away.

"You—" The black-clad menace pointed at Jax, driven to hand-gestures as well. "Come." He beckoned, then made walking feet of his fingers. "With me." The Inquisitor pushed Jax ahead of him.

Amanusa trailed behind as they marched down the street, Jax being propelled with the occasional shove. Crow followed too, a silent black presence flying from tree to tree, lamppost to lamppost along their path.

The Inquisitor marched along, ignoring Jax's endless flow of words. The tone of Jax's speech sounded as if he protested his detention, but the words were instructions for Amanusa, telling her how and where she should run.

She wanted to. Desperately. She longed to run away and hide until the danger was past. But she feared the danger would never be past, not as long as she remained near the mountains where Dragos Szabo—and the Inquisition—could find her.

Nor could she abandon Jax. He had given her the tools to achieve the justice she'd hungered for for so long. And when the magic had blown up in her face, due to her own mistakes, he'd rescued her. He had carried her for miles on his back. Leaving him in the hands of the Inquisition would turn her into the person she'd sworn never to become. The kind of person everyone believed a sorceress to be.

Besides, she was certain the Inquisitor knew exactly where she was, and if she didn't come along, he would make certain she did. In ways she wouldn't like.

Their little processional drew attention, gathering folks along the edges of the streets and on the sidewalks when sidewalks appeared, but they followed only with their eyes. Amanusa could read in all those watching eyes the relief that it was not them marching to the center of town under control of the Inquisitor Plenipotentiary. She was just glad that most everyone's eyes focused on Jax in his splendid leather overcoat and scuffed kneeboots, skimming over her modest self with her bruised face and shapeless, drab, brown dress.

The Inquisitor took them to the center of town and marched them up the steps of the brand new city hall with its high, pointed towers, into a plain room at the back. A rawboned boy—surely he could not be so old as twenty—with an Inquisitor's patch on the sleeve of his uniform coat, jerked to his feet from the small table against one wall where he'd been industriously writing, surprised by their entry.

"Go and get Captain Janos," the Chief Inquisitor snarled. "The man speaks English, I believe."

"Yes, Inquisitor Kazaryk." The boy bobbed his head and hurried off, tripping over two chairs and a table leg before he got out the door, leaving his superior muttering darkly about "hinterlands," "idiot apprentices," "allocation of manpower" and other things Amanusa couldn't quite make out.

Then they waited. Inquisitor Kazaryk entertained himself by looking over the reports the apprentice had been writing. Jax paced, tossing out the occasional protest as if he thought he needed to keep his hand in, and scowling darkly at Amanusa every time he passed her. Amanusa stood in a corner near the door and tried to think herself small and unnoticeable.

She didn't get any smaller, but she thought she might be getting somewhere with the "unnoticeable" part, for when the youth returned with Captain Janos, a man just as lean, dark, and intense as Kazaryk, but taller, the pair of them scarcely glanced at her.

"I need your translation skills, Captain," Kazaryk stated. "This man speaks only English, and while I speak five languages besides, of course, Romanian and Hungarian, I do not speak English. I am told that you do."

The captain clicked his heels and gave a little bow, studying Jax with frank curiosity. "Do you suspect him of conspiring with the anarchists?"

"I do not care." Kazaryk ground the words out between his teeth. "I am not hunting for anarchists. They are all dead, save for a few stragglers and women—"

"Dragos Szabo escaped."

Kazaryk ignored the interruption. "I am after the

criminal magician who murdered them! Who knows where she has gone? Who knows what harm she might be doing, who she might be killing right this minute? The power she obtained from so many deaths—"

The deaths hadn't given any power at all, Amanusa thought, staying absolutely still in her corner. It made her nervous, the Inquisitor thinking that. What might the idea make him do?

"Yes, of course, Inquisitor," Janos was saying with another, more respectful bow.

The Inquisitor gestured at Jax. "Now, if you would be so good, please ask this . . . *gentleman* . . . to be seated, and to identify himself and explain his reason for being in this town."

Jax sat in the hard, spindle-backed chair Kazaryk placed in the center of the room. He planted his feet spread wide, hands on his thighs with elbows out, taking possession of the space in as arrogant a fashion as possible. He displayed nothing but confidence and disdain for the others' petty concerns.

Under questioning, Jax spun fables out of nothing, telling stories of workshops and weavers in towns with names too foreign for him to pronounce, much less recall. He had no business cards or paperwork from these places because none of their products or proposals had appealed, and he'd tossed everything away. Of course he couldn't remember the names of the men he'd met—they all had ridiculous, outlandish names like Kazaryk and Janos. Nothing sensible like Tottenham or Burke.

His answers to their questions remained just plausible enough to be believable and just vague enough to keep them from tripping him up with details. Amanusa marveled at his ability to keep it all straight.

"What else do you want to ask?" Janos asked Kazaryk, dropping wearily into another chair.

It was late. Amanusa didn't know how late, but very. She was hungrier than she'd been when they reached town. Her feet hurt and her knees ached and she wanted to sit down. On the floor in her corner would do nicely, but she was afraid that any motion would bring the predators in the room whirling to pounce on her. She tightened and relaxed her sore muscles, hoping for relief, but it didn't help much.

"I begin to believe he is exactly what he appears," Janos went on. "A stupid, arrogant English businessman who sees only what is beneath his nose, and then only if it is of personal interest to him."

Jax looked tired, but less so than the two officials. His days' beard gave his jaw a ruddy shadow. The Hungarians just looked dirty, with their black beards growing in.

Kazaryk the Inquisitor smoothed finger and thumb across his luxuriant oiled mustache. "Perhaps. Perhaps not. I am not convinced to let him go. Not until every stone has been overturned. To search for magic, one must use magic."

He pulled a pocket watch from his waistcoat and flicked it open to check the time. He snapped it shut with a satisfied nod. "It lacks only ten minutes to midnight. Just enough time to prepare."

8

PREPARE FOR WHAT? Amanusa could see her alarm echoed in the tiny jerk of the military captain's head as Kazaryk called his apprentice back into the nearly empty room. Jax appeared just as relaxed and arrogant as before, but the taut flex of his hands where they rested on his knees betrayed his worry.

The apprentice bustled around, moving the remaining chairs to the far corners of the room, and sliding the table out from under a window. Then he proceeded to chalk a large pentagram with a circle around it on the floor at the end of the room nearest the door, another circle around Jax's chair, and various runes and sigils Amanusa didn't know in other places. He ignored Amanusa and the converted medicine case completely, as if they were invisible, or additional furniture.

They hadn't opened the wooden box, or even asked what it contained, although the contents of Jax's pockets lay spread on the table no longer under the window—three crystalline rocks, two lengths of string, a small pearl-sided pocket knife, an empty wallet, a ragged handkerchief, and five coins—two Bulgarian, two Russian, one Turkish. Perhaps, being the sorceress, her "I'm not really here" thoughts were turning the officers' attention aside. If it was a spell, she shouldn't have left Jax out of it. She should have thought of it sooner.

The boy chalked one last symbol over the window

where the table had been, and hurried to join Kazaryk and Janos in the pentagram, too near Amanusa for her comfort. She took the chance provided by their movement to slide down the wall until she crouched cowering in the corner. Jax finally appeared apprehensive as he sat in his chair in the center of its chalk circle.

Kazaryk began to chant what sounded to Amanusa like nonsense words, but could have been Latin. Maybe with some Turkish mixed in. Or Greek. She looked up at Jax and found him looking back at her. Their gazes locked, held for a long moment, then he closed his eyes and let his head fall back. Amanusa hid her face behind her updrawn knees and wrapped her arms around her head.

She wished she'd been able to wrap some protective magic around the both of them, but there hadn't been time. And she didn't know any protective magic. She knew healing spells for after the harm was done, and she knew warding spells to keep people out, turn away their attention. She knew nothing that would protect from physical harm. Did blood magic even have those sorts of spells?

And if she had the spells and used them, could the Inquisitor conjure up some way to sniff them out? She'd thought from the first that the man was a conjurer. This confirmed it. Most conjurers couldn't work magic 'til after midnight. Or so Amanusa had been taught.

She could be as wrong about that as she'd been about sorcery. But since the Inquisitor waited until the clock in the tower across the square began to chime the hour before beginning his spell, she figured that much was truth.

Most Inquisitors were conjurers. She wasn't sure why. Perhaps because the spirits they controlled could snoop and spy into hidden places. Or because the time they spent communing with and controlling spirits separated them from ordinary human emotions. Kazaryk was as cold and emotionless a specimen as she'd ever seen. But that might be because he was an Inquisitor, not because he was a conjurer. He was the first magician she'd met with any real power. Szabo's pet conjurer didn't count.

Amanusa felt a faint presence, a whisper of *magic* across her thoughts. She clamped her arms tighter around herself, squeezing her eyes shut and whispering, "Don't see me, don't see me," over and over again, too quietly for Janos, Kazaryk, or his apprentice to hear. She hoped.

Kazaryk cried out in surprise and triumph. Alarmed, Amanusa cracked an eye open and peered out beneath her left elbow. A bright blue glow wrapped around Jax, intensifying like a halo around his head . . . and at his groin. Amanusa felt a blush rising. Thank goodness no one was looking at her. The box containing the machine creature also glowed, but an amber gold rather than blue, and not nearly as bright.

Did the different colors denote different spells, or the different person who had worked them? Amanusa assumed the blue glowed brighter in those areas of Jax's body because that was where the binding affected him most—in his mind where Yvaine had deposited her storehouse of knowledge, and in his manhood where she'd stolen it away.

The Inquisitor suddenly slumped against his apprentice, panting and sweating as if he'd just pushed a boulder up a very steep hill. The apprentice appeared to be expecting it, for he was braced and ready to catch the older man.

"What does it m-mean?" Janos stammered, staring in obvious awe and more than a little fear. "That glow?"

"Fetch the master a chair!" the apprentice snapped.

The captain hesitated, looking warily around the room. The nearest chair was just out of reach, outside the pentagram where the three men were crowded together.

"The spirit is gone," the boy said scornfully. "A chair!"

"The glow," Kazaryk gasped out when the chair had been brought and he was lowered into it, "means that the man and the wooden case have both been bespelled."

Amanusa unwrapped herself enough to examine her own definitely not-glowing hands and arms. Why didn't she glow too? Because she was the worker of the spells and not the one bespelled? Or because conjury and sorcery didn't mix? Maybe the conjurer's spirit-servant wasn't powerful enough to see past her warding thoughts.

"It is obvious now," Kazaryk was saying, no longer gasping, though his voice was still weak. "The case had to have been bespelled, or we would already have searched it. Ask him what is in it."

"Nothing you'd be interested in." Jax set his jaw when he replied to the captain's translation. "Machinery."

"Open it." Kazaryk flicked a finger at the box.

Captain Janos was the one who moved, still rolling

his eyes as if searching for spirits. He paused before touching the box. "Will the glow—?"

"It is harmless. Merely a visual marking of magical workings inside this room. And look. Already it fades." With the help of his apprentice, Kazaryk sat up straighter. "Open it."

Jax glowered when Janos knelt beside it. "That's private property," he said. "*My* property."

Janos ignored him as he flipped the latch and took hold of the handle to lift the lid. The whole box came off the floor. Janos pried at the lid, then hit it and tried again. The case refused to open.

Amanusa was impressed with herself. She'd had no idea her spell would work so well.

Janos got the apprentice to come hold the bottom while he tugged at the lid. The box remained shut.

"Never mind." Kazaryk waved a hand. "Obviously, the spell is sealing it shut. Order the Englishman to unlock it."

"Can't," Jax said, folding his arms. "Had a magician seal it. I won't be able to open it 'til I have another magician break the seal. Which I won't do 'til I'm back home safe in England."

Kazaryk sighed when Janos translated Jax's defiance. "Very well. I'll simply have to open it myself. But not tonight. Lock him up—"

"On what charges?" Janos dared interrupt to ask.

The Inquisitor looked at him as if he'd lost his mind.

Janos flushed. "The man is *English*," he protested. "You have no idea how much trouble their embassy can make if we don't have some plausible excuse for detaining one of their citizens."

"Then arrest him for smuggling and for working prohibited magic. That ought to satisfy them." Kazaryk waved to his apprentice who came to lift him from the chair.

"What magic *is* prohibited?" Janos asked, as if wondering how much worse it might be than what he'd witnessed tonight.

"Whatever the Inquisition says is prohibited." Kazaryk leaned heavily on the apprentice as he limped from the room.

Janos thought for a minute, then made a "that makes sense" face as he went out the door, leaving a pair of guards standing in the hall. Maybe they truly had forgotten Amanusa's presence.

She dropped her bundle and scurried past Jax to the window at the far end of the room, and peered out. No escape that way. Two more soldiers stood guard, one directly beneath the window.

"Here." Jax was on his feet, whipping his belt from the belt loops.

"We can't get out this way," Amanusa hissed, not wanting anyone to hear her and remember her presence, if they'd forgotten it. "Guards."

"Take it and go." He held the belt out to her. "The information to access the bank account is in the pocket where I kept the lancet. Walk out the door. Don't worry about me. I'll be fine. Just get the money and take a train for Calais. Or Paris. Paris is better. You can disappear in Paris if they decide to follow you."

"I'm not leaving you," Amanusa insisted, refusing to examine the reasons why she was so adamant. "I need you." He had all the sorcery locked away in his head. That was it.

"You need to stay alive. You're more important than I am." Jax seized her hand and put the belt in it. *"Go."*

She glared up at him several more long moments, but he was as stubborn as she. "All right, I will."

Because it had finally occurred to her that she could more easily get him out if she were free, than locked up in here with him. Amanusa buckled the belt around her waist where the brown of the leather lost itself in the brown of her dress and sagged to drape loosely over her hips. She shouldered her brown blanket bundle, and turned back when Jax spoke her name.

"Amanusa." He smiled at her, voice warm and gentle as his smile, warming her inside where she'd never known she was cold. "As a favor to me, when you buy a dress—make it any color but brown."

The smile stole sneakily onto her face, a bit at a time, as if her mouth had trouble remembering how. "I will," she said. "Brown is *your* color. I'll come show you, tomorrow."

"What? No, wait—" Jax began his protest, but she didn't wait to hear it. She was out the door, shutting it behind her, with only a glance from the soldiers guarding it.

Amanusa kept her pace deliberate, remembering what Jax had said. If she behaved as if she belonged, people would see what she wanted them to see.

So far in their adventures together, Jax had pretended to two different roles, neither of which put him in a good light. He'd taught her magic and saved her life. For a woman determined to stand on her own feet and live her own life without depending on a man for anything, she'd been doing a poor job of it these last several weeks. Now it was time to do as she claimed she wanted and make pudding for the proof, as it were. It was her turn to rescue Jax.

She just had to figure out how to do it. As she started across the oddly busy square in front of city hall, Amanusa felt an odd tug. A stir in her blood, in her magic. And she remembered that Jax hadn't been able to leave her. They'd been together for so long now—which hadn't actually been all that long, save that they'd been side by side every minute of the day *and* night, so that it seemed she'd known him forever. Long enough she'd almost forgotten how it all began.

Could she leave city hall? She tried it, walking slowly across the square toward the bank on the far corner. The tug intensified. It was uncomfortable, but not painful. Did it feel the same to Jax? She didn't want to hurt him. She stopped beside the small round fountain in the center of the open space and *reached* for the magic her blood had left inside Jax. It felt stretched thin, straining between them. Would it break?

Amanusa didn't think so. The magic seemed incredibly strong. But there wasn't much for her to catch hold of. Maybe she shouldn't have called her blood back from him. Since she had, however . . . She tried feeding more magic into the binding between them. She still felt stretched out. Pulled in one direction. Toward Jax.

Amanusa looked up at the night sky, at the sliver of a waxing moon surrounded by all the stars. Then she looked at the square around her, at the soldiers walking their quiet patrols, meeting now and again to exchange a few words, perhaps a joke. The train station to her right showed dim light around its edges. Trains would only pass through on their way to Istanbul or Vienna at this hour of the night. They wouldn't stop.

Farmers and peddlers were bringing carts into the square even at this hour, to be ready for market day in the morning. Most parked their carts in their favored spot and crawled beneath to sleep for a few hours, until time to rise and set up their displays. The soldiers wouldn't notice another body sleeping in the square.

Obeying the pull, Amanusa walked back to city hall, having to skirt only one eager merchant who'd arrived since she'd crossed in the other direction. In the corner beside the grand stairway to the front doors, she curled up, tucked her bundle beneath her head, and closed her eyes. Crow gave a "there you are" caw as he fluttered down to strut a moment on the paving before flying up to perch on the roof edge. Now that she knew where Crow was, her worry about Jax and her nonexistent plan to free him kept her awake. Mostly though, it was the simple absence of Jax that disturbed her.

She thrust the thought aside. First thing tomorrow, before she did anything else, she would go to the bank. Once she had money, everything else would fall into place. Maybe she could bribe the Inquisitor, if all else failed.

A laugh snorted its derisive way out her nose at the thought. *Bribe an Inquisitor.* She'd have better luck trying to seduce one of the Sultan's eunuchs.

Inquisitors were about power, not money. But maybe she could bribe Captain Janos.

JAX HAD WONDERED whether the Inquisitor would leave him all night in city hall. He would much rather they had, despite its lack of a cot or other amenities. That room was at least dry and free of stinks, unlike the dank, mildewed cell to which a squadron of soldiers escorted him. It did have a cot, but the blanket on it was damp, and the cell's previous occupants had left behind pungent aromas Jax didn't care to identify, as well as a large variety of wildlife which all thought Englishmen quite tasty.

The jail cell was also farther away from wherever Amanusa had settled for the night, which gave him a pounding headache. He'd hoped the distance might magic him out of the cell, the way it had turned him around on the road, but no such luck. He comforted himself with the reminder that she had to wait until morning to get to the bank for money to catch a train. He hoped the pain wouldn't get too much worse when she left town.

Considering everything, Jax was actually pleased to finally be collected and returned to city hall for further interrogation, especially since they'd left him kicking his heels and nursing his terrible headache all morning and much of the afternoon. He wasn't thrilled, however, when they sat him back in the chair and this time tied him down.

Apparently, it had taken all day for the Inquisition chap to winkle the box open. Or smash it to bits. Jax wasn't sure which. The box was nowhere to be seen, and large splinters of wood lay scattered near the walls. Inquisitor Kazaryk did look pale and sweaty. Either way, the nasty bit of machinery sat on a table in the center of the room.

It looked even nastier than the last time Jax had seen it, when Amanusa put it in the box. Not more wicked, but more disgusting. The dull sheen of its surface was almost entirely gone, covered with pits and scaly corrosion, as if someone had poured acid on it. The edges of some of the arm segments were eroding away.

It didn't upset Jax any to see the thing in such poor state, except that the deterioration would make it that much harder to figure out what it.was, and why and how it had done what it did when Jax touched it. Of course, all of that assumed that he and the object would be liberated from the hands of the Hungarian Inquisition.

Jax very much feared that was Amanusa's intention. His headache had worsened fairly early in the morning, and he'd rejoiced. Until it improved dramatically a few hours later, according to the chiming of the city clock. In the hours since, the pain had waxed and waned, as Amanusa apparently went here and there around town, doing whatever it was she thought so necessary to do. Why didn't she just get on the train and go? He didn't need rescuing. The fear of what could happen to her if she didn't go hurt him far worse than any headache.

The Inquisitor spoke, crackling his knuckles inside the black leather gloves he wore, his voice laden with cruel intent. A chill slid up Jax's spine, though he couldn't understand a word the man said.

"What is this thing?" Captain Janos tried to echo

the other man's sinister tone, and very nearly succeeded. "You are very much in trouble, *Úr Angol,* Mister English. It is forbidden to transport harmful magical devices through the Austrian Empire."

"I don't know what that thing is," Jax retorted. "I can tell you what it's *not.* It's not magical. It's not in the least bit magical. In fact, it's *anti*-magic. That's why I'm taking it back to England. So a decent scientist can examine it and learn what it is."

Janos spun on his heel, toward Jax, putting the momentum of the spin behind the fist he slammed into Jax's face. "Who are you?" he demanded. "What are you doing in Transylvania? Where did you find that evil thing?"

Jax spat out the blood collecting in his mouth, wishing he had the power to use it. But if his sorceress came back, it would be there for her to use. A bit of it got on the Hungarian. Good. "My name is Albert King," he said. "I am in Transylvania on business, and I bought the machine in the mountains. In a town with mines and smelters. I don't know the name of the town."

"Lies." Captain Janos hit him again. "What is your name? Where did you meet the anarchists?"

"My name is Albert King." Jax tried to spit the blood as far as Inquisitor Kazaryk, where he hovered in the background, but failed. "And I don't know anything about any anarchists."

Janos's fist drew back again, but Kazaryk lifted a hand, murmured something. The captain let his fist fall. Then when Jax relaxed, Janos punched him in the gut.

"We want to be sure you can talk," the captain said

with a cold leer. "Tell us what you know about this abomination."

"The man who sold it to me said . . ." Jax gasped out the tale Dragos Szabo had told them in the mountains. His head hurt from the blows to his face. So much that he couldn't tell whether Amanusa came near or drew farther away. He hoped desperately that she'd caught the train for Paris. Or Budapest. Or anywhere—Vienna. Moscow. Madrid.

He couldn't bear the thought of Amanusa in the hands of these villains. Her sex would evoke no mercy. Even he with his faulty memory knew how ruthlessly the Inquisition in this part of the world— from the Baltic to the Caspian and beyond—crushed any female with aspirations to practice magic. And his sorceress had gone far beyond aspiration.

"Who was the magician you hired to seal the box?" Janos asked between blows. "Where did you find her?"

"Wasn't a woman," Jax groaned. "Old man. Found him down the valley from where I bought it."

"Old—" Janos said after conferring with the Inquisitor. "White-haired?"

Why did that matter? "I don't rememb—"

Apparently the Inquisition did not approve of faulty memories, for Janos cut off Jax's reply with another blow to the face. Jax got to spit blood again.

"I-I suppose. Yes. Yes, I remember now. He had white hair. He had whiskers. Mustaches and side whiskers. They were white."

"Think carefully, *Angol férfi*, Englishman—" Janos said. "Could this magician have been a woman? A tall, mannish woman?"

"Not with all those whiskers, he couldn't."

Jax paid the price for his impudence. When Captain Janos tired of bruising his knuckles on Jax's ribs, he paused to catch his breath and confer with Inquisitor Kazaryk. Jax fought for his own breath and had to spit out more blood. It was getting everywhere.

"Why do you do that?" Janos demanded suddenly. "Spit your blood? Do you think it possesses some power to save you?"

"Of course it does. Everyone knows the blood of innocents will rise up and cry out for justice. I am innocent."

"Pah!" Kazaryk's scowl blackened when Janos translated Jax's retort.

"The blood magic is lost." Janos translated Kazaryk's words. "It was lost when the last evil sorceress died, hundreds of years ago. It is nothing more than superstition, without power."

"Maybe." Jax's mind whirled. He'd been hunting Yvaine's apprentice a long time, but *hundreds* of years? Could so much time have passed? "But maybe not. What if you're wrong? What if sorcery is real? What if it was never lost? What if every drop of innocent blood you've shed is only waiting for the proper time to reach for justice?"

Janos hit Jax again, this time so hard it knocked the chair over, Jax with it. Fear fed the blow. Jax could see it in the man's eyes. And he hadn't bothered to check with Kazaryk first.

Captain Janos opened the door, snapped some order to the soldiers standing guard outside. They slung their rifles over their shoulders, came into the room, and lifted Jax and the chair upright again, then went back where they came from and shut the door. Janos flexed his hand, working out stiffness, or perhaps pain. Jax hoped it hurt to hit him so hard. He hoped Amanusa was on the blasted train. But he was very afraid she was not.

"LOOK." HARRY TOMLINSON stood once more on the boulevard where four days ago the dead zone had receded.

This time, he stood with a veritable horde of men in black frock coats and shiny top hats. It had taken the conclave of magicians' councils this long to be argued into coming out and actually seeing what had happened.

Old Billy—Sir William—had refused to believe it when Harry first reported the news. The conclave hadn't discovered anything new, hadn't worked any magic at all, so obviously Harry was mistaken in what he thought he observed. The head of the Magician's Council of England had refused to report any such nonsense to the conclave.

Harry had to resort to buttonholing other alchemists and dragging them to the site two and three at a time, along with a Frenchman of some flavor to confirm that yes, *l'endroit de la mort* had indeed extended this far. Then he got them to verify for themselves that magic and life had been restored to this once-dead stretch. The tiny sprouting of weeds in the flower boxes inspired him to haul a wizard or two out to see, and finally the whole conclave had decided to come and have a look for themselves.

"The limit—the boundary of the dead zone—was here, right?" Harry indicated the previous location of the place where the magic had stopped. "You French, you know that. It was here."

The chairman of the French Magician's Council consulted with his clerks, looked at a series of maps and charts, studied the buildings around them, and sent an apprentice off to pace the distance from the corner behind them.

"*Oui,*" he said finally. "That is correct. I thought perhaps the measurements were wrong, but *non.* This is where *l'endroit de la mort* began as of this past Monday morning."

"All right then." Harry beckoned them forward, advancing some ten yards down the street to the point where the weeds began to lose their struggle for life. He opened his mouth to speak, then paused and cocked his head as if listening.

"Do you 'ear that?" He lifted his head and stared intently into the dead zone as a faint noise of metal scraping and clanking on stone grew quickly louder, coming from inside the zone where nothing living existed.

Others heard it too, their exclamatory wondering what it might be drowning out the sound only for a moment. As the things creating the noise hove into view, creeping up areaway stairs, bursting open rotten doors and rattling down the street, the magicians fell silent. Their faces took on expressions of horror, fear, curiosity, or a melange of all three, depending on their natures.

"What are those things?" someone whispered, as if afraid the metal creatures might hear.

"Dunno." Harry glared at the horrific machines. "That's somethin' else we got to find out. I don't imagine they're any too 'appy—if a machine like that can be 'appy—to have their territory shrink like it did. 'Cause *now,* the boundary is here. Some of the other alchemists went all the way 'round this patch, and it's the same on all sides. The dead zone's been pushed back about eight meters, according to your folks' measure, all the way 'round."

"How is this possible?" The president of the conclave—it was Prussia's turn this term—chewed on his blond mustache.

"That's what I want to know." Harry propped his hands on his hips, glaring at the no-magic. "And what else I want to know is: If we didn't do it, who— or what—did?"

9

AMANUSA GAZED INTO the mirror at the dress-maker's shop, unable to recognize the woman she saw. The eyes—the eyes were her own, and the sharp angle of her jaw. The rest . . .

When Amanusa had removed the many-times-folded paper from Jax's belt that morning, the bank's name written there hadn't been in London, as she feared. A London bank might arouse the interest of the Inquisition. The account with Yvaine's name on it was at a bank in Geneva, Switzerland.

The local banker was suspicious at first of a bedrag-gled woman in a grimy brown dress asking to draw funds from a foreign bank. But she spoke perfect Ro-manian as well as Viennese German, and told a story about being set upon by bandits in the mountains. Everyone knew bandits were thick in the mountains. Soldiers had come all the way from Budapest to hunt them down.

After the banker received a return wire from the Geneva bank with the amount of funds available to draw upon, he suddenly transformed into her smiling, fawning, exceedingly voluble servant. Amanusa withdrew a thousand Austrian marks, which made scarcely a dent in the million or so pounds sterling in the account. She wasn't sure how much that many numbers amounted to.

The banker was happy to refer her to the best hotel, the best dress shop, the best restaurants in the town. He hoped she hadn't suffered too much in the bandit attack, and wasn't she lucky to be alive? Much luckier than the bandits who had been massacred in a mysterious, sorcerous slaughter by a villainously wicked witch.

Amanusa let the horror show on her face. The banker would expect her to be horrified as he regaled her with tales of fountaining blood and bodies lying without a mark on them. Though how one could get blood fountains and unmarked bodies both at once, Amanusa didn't know, and wasn't about to ask. She did ask about the witch. So she could know her and run if she saw her.

The sinister creature who'd committed the horrific crime—even though the victims were all outlaws and anarchists and doubtless deserved their fate, but not in such a terrible manner—was a giantess, apparently. She stood at least seven feet tall, with snow-white hair that stood out from her head in a wild tangle, eyes that burned the color of blood, and talons that could claw a man's tongue from his mouth.

Shuddering with fear and horror that she could be seen in such a way, Amanusa encouraged the exaggeration. The less human this witch seemed to be, the less likely anyone would look at her. Amanusa couldn't do anything about her height, but she wasn't anywhere near seven feet tall. At least three inches under six, in fact. The rest, she could disguise.

And so she had rented a hotel room, paying in advance for a week, and she had ordered a bath. Crow complained outside the closed window, but a crow strolling about in a hotel room would be remembered, so she ignored his raucous complaints.

She inquired from the hotel staff about hairdressers who might also know about discreet face paint. The bruises left by the bandit attack were so disfiguring. Thank heaven the swelling had gone down.

Amanusa's own natural pale blond was too close to the snow-white of the wild tales circulating, so that would change. While the henna rinse was soaking into her hair, Amanusa was measured for a new dress.

Now, in the early evening, she examined herself in the mirror while the seamstress fussed about, trimming stray threads and encouraging the skirt to fall properly over the hoops and starched petticoats. The hairdresser adjusted a few of the curls that had been tortured into Amanusa's straight hair.

The bright scarlet of the dress actually toned down the shocking red of her hair, which perhaps was only shocking because she wasn't used to it. The scoop neck of the blouse allowed the wide vee of the jacket collar to display all the creamy cleavage she had. More than she'd suspected, once the maid and the dressmaker's assistants had laced her into the whaleboned corseting.

Atop her frizz of curls perched a delicacy of a hat produced by the dressmaker in case Madame might like the finishing touch. Makeup hid the green and blue of the bruises on her semitransparent skin, and made her appear a little brassy, a little not-quite-proper. Which was all to the good, because it made her look less like Amanusa.

She paid for the dress and the shoes and the hat and the parasol and the undergarments and the night-clothes and the carpetbag. She paid for the rushed alterations and the coiffure and the makeup and the manicure, then she added generous tips for everyone, including the dressmaker's three assistants.

When everyone was gone, she looked at herself in the mirror once again and took as deep a breath as she could manage in the blasted corset. *Magic hour.*

Time to go forth and do battle like some primped and painted paladin to free her—not her servant. Jax was more than that. Her liege man, if she wanted to continue the imagery. Loyalty like his deserved loyalty in return.

So, she would rescue him from the Inquisition. She didn't know exactly *how* she would do it, but they'd muddled along all right this far. Something would come to her. Amanusa had great hopes for the "don't see me" magic.

She used it to leave the hotel with its onion-shaped

towers and gilt-painted lobby and crossed the square to city hall. Crow cawed at her from overhead, so he could see her, but she didn't think anyone else did.

The bustle of the market was winding down in the late summer evening, only the food stalls left open to cater to the merchants and farmers packing up their wares. Amanusa paused to buy meat pirogies in case Jax was hungry. She was too keyed up to eat herself. Her working spell meant she had to simply take the pies and leave the coins. She didn't dare let the magic go for fear she might not be able to do it again.

A few people bumped into her as she strode through the square. They stopped to stare, obviously startled by her presence. She assumed therefore that actual physical contact broke the magic, because those people were forced to notice her presence. After that, she kept her distance from everyone as much as she could.

Just inside city hall, she left the carpetbag and napkin-wrapped pies in an out-of-the-way corner, hiding them with magic. Then she breezed through the warren of offices in the gloomy, after-hours city hall to the room where Jax was being held. The room she'd escaped from last night.

The soldiers guarding it stood to either side of the door, making it easy for her to walk right in. As she shut the door behind her, she dropped her magic. Everyone in the room froze motionless while they stared at her and she stared back.

In the center of the room, Inquisitor Kazaryk and Captain Janos stood over Jax who sat naked, bound to a straight-backed chair, his face and upper body bloody and bruised. Off to one side, the infernal machine sat on a table. Something twisted inside her to see Jax so hurt. Something else thumped at seeing him unclothed. She ignored both thumping and twisting. *First, get him free.*

Jax's blood had spattered both Janos and Kazaryk, the captain more liberally than the conjurer, for the military man had obviously been the one beating their victim. They had made some attempt to clean it up, but the blood of the innocent was still there, crying out to her. Amanusa reached out with insubstantial hands and gathered in the power it offered.

All three men stared in astonishment, even Jax who lifted his poor battered face to goggle at her. She knew the instant he recognized her, for his swollen eyes widened in shock—as much as they could—and his puffy mouth dropped open.

"Gentlemen." Amanusa decided on English as her language of choice at the last minute. She simpered as best she could, and gave a little curtsy to offer better opportunity for the Hungarians to look down her décolletage.

"Imagine my surprise," she said. "I come to this rustic little town to meet my husband on his business trip, and I am told you are holding him in custody. Whatever for?"

She pretended to notice Jax for the first time. Perhaps if they thought her stupid, they would suspect her less. "Oh, hello, darling. There you are." She squinched her face into an idiotic frown. "Where are your clothes? Aren't you cold?"

Jax matched her casual air, despite his inability to

speak clearly, given the state of his mouth. "I'm sorry? Have we met?"

Janos apparently recovered from his shock. "Who are you? What are you doing here? How did you get in?" Spittle flew from his mouth as he wound up.

Amanusa curtsied again and held out a hand as if expecting it to be kissed. She'd watched the grand ladies and gentlemen when she was little. She knew how the upper classes acted. "It is a pleasure to meet you." She actually got that lie out of her mouth, more or less smoothly. "I told you. I've come for my husband. As for how I got in—I simply walked in the door."

Janos swore under his breath and stomped to the door, muttering about dereliction of duty, courts martial, and fool women who didn't know how to keep their noses out of men's business. He stopped when Kazaryk held up a hand.

"Keep her here," the Inquisitor said, his voice sending a chill through Amanusa's spine that threatened to crumble it.

But the corset wouldn't let her crumble, helped her stiffen her spine and her resolve. What marvelous armor it was.

"Perhaps she knows the things we wish to know." Kazaryk paced. "She hasn't sense enough to consider whether her man wants us to know them. And if she knows nothing, perhaps a threat to her will convince him to admit what he has so far refused."

Kazaryk clasped his hands behind his back and stared at her. Amanusa gazed blandly back. Her decade-long contest of wills with Szabo and his anarchists gave her the experience she needed now. *Silly,* she reminded herself. She didn't need to be aloof as she had been in camp. She threw another simper at him.

"He claims not to know her," Janos ventured.

"Of course he does. He would not want his wife falling into our hands. But even if he speaks the truth—which I doubt, because if she is not his wife, why would she brave this room? But if she is not, he is English. They are sentimental about women. A threat to her would still be useful." Kazaryk pursed his lips. "Ask her about the machine."

Amanusa continued to gather in the power that rose as blood oozed from Jax's lip. Janos asked the Inquisitor's question and Amanusa realized she had no idea what Jax might already have told them. Would it matter? They were hoping she might tell them different things. Would they believe her more? She didn't know the best way to respond. *Silly,* she thought again.

"What machine?" She gave them a blank look, then turned as if just noticing the metal creature on its table. What had caused it to deteriorate so quickly? "This?" She made a disgusted face. "I have no idea what it is. Where did it come from?"

"Your husband had it in a locked case," Janos said. "Locked and then sealed by magic. Where did he get it?"

"Ask her about the spell on the man himself," Kazaryk interjected. Janos did so.

The lie she'd told the outlaws would do. "I told you not to quarrel with that magician in Ankara, or İstanbul or wherever it was," Amanusa scolded Jax. "You see what his spell has done to you? Made you all grouchy and hot-tempered and stubborn, and now look where you are!" She pouted at him. "I should never have let you wander off into the mountains alone."

Was that going too far? Or just far enough? The captain looked disdainful, so perhaps she'd found the right balance.

"What was this magician's name?" Kazaryk asked and Janos echoed.

"Oh heavens, I don't know. Mustafa Mumbletypeg. It could have been Ali Baba for all I know. He certainly seemed to have forty thieves in his employ." Amanusa took a few flouncing steps toward Jax, stopping when Kazaryk's scowl deepened.

"You were in Bucharest for how long?"

Now they were trying to trick her. It didn't matter. She and Jax would be out of this makeshift torture chamber and on their way to Paris soon. Amanusa now held enough magic power to take out those forty thieves—or two torturers and a handful of guards. If she knew the spell to do it. These men hadn't swallowed any blood, so the same spell that worked on Teo wouldn't work here, would it? Would sorcery work better on conjurers than his conjury had worked on her?

"Six weeks." She plucked the answer from thin air. "I was in Bucharest six weeks." Which was approximately how long it had been—give or take a few days she'd lost track of—since Jax had stumbled out of the forest into her life.

"And so—" Janos's sinister pacing brought him closer to her. "You know nothing of the magician who put the seal on the case holding the machine? A woman, perhaps? A crone?"

The giggle bubbled out of Amanusa, escaping the churning cauldron of hysteria in her gut. "Women can't be magicians, silly." She got her eyelashes to flutter after a fashion. Then the perfect solution to— to *everything* hit her. She was surprised she didn't stagger with the impact.

She simpered at Jax. "Didn't you tell them, darling?"

Jax's eyes widened, and he shook his head in a tiny signal. Which Kazaryk of course caught. He pounced. Exactly as Amanusa intended.

"Didn't he tell us what?"

"You are *so* clever, Bertie. I don't know why you insist on keeping it such a secret. I'd wager there's no one else in the world who can do what you can." She looked at Kazaryk, who was so obviously in command, even a dim woman could catch on. "He did it himself, he did."

Jax widened his eyes even more. Or he tried. His eyebrows went up. Amanusa knew he was furious with her. Kazaryk apparently took it as dismay that she'd spilled Jax's secret.

Amanusa gave her liege man a bland look, then blinked her eyes slowly, once, hoping he'd catch on soon. "Well, you did," she said. "You took my blood to make the spell."

Now Kazaryk's and Janos's eyes went wide with shock and horror, while Jax adjusted his expression for blandness. He was so crimson and swollen with bruises, so scarlet with blood that any expression was difficult to see.

"Of course . . ." Kazaryk hissed, evil satisfaction rising on his face.

"B-but if he's a blood magic sorcerer," Janos stammered, "why has he not acted before now?"

"Because all of the blood spilled has been his own, you idiot."

"Blood of innocents," Amanusa said.

"No use denying it any longer. Blood of the innocent," Jax agreed, throwing the first words of a spell out for her to catch. He began adding the other words of the spell. "Blood of the helpless, crying out for justice—"

The Inquisitor and his tool began to back away, the conjurer's eyes rolling from side to side, as if he could see the magic build in power with every word Jax spoke. Amanusa didn't know the spell, but Jax did. Jax couldn't control the magic, but Amanusa could. Her lips moved, repeating it silently.

She blocked the path to the door, sealing it against the men with a swipe of her shoe, smearing the blood she'd stepped in on the door's bottom edge. The locking spell took only a moment, a brief whispered word in the midst of the justice spell Jax was building for her.

He was careful with it, confining it to this room, to those who had actually spilled innocent blood or caused the spilling of it. Amanusa fed power into the words until she could feel it throb around her, ready to burst. Janos was already whimpering.

"Blood of my blood," Jax called out, his voice strong without shouting. "Answer my call. Do my will."

The two men screamed as their bodies convulsed, bruises blossoming on their skin. They fell to the floor, into the blood spattered there, and their screams rose in pitch. The Inquisitor's pain seemed magnitudes greater than Janos's suffering, and the captain suffered greatly. Amanusa asked Jax about it as she crouched to untie his hands, ignoring the shouts and pounding on the door.

"Because I didn't confine the spell to justice for *my* innocent blood alone," Jax said, bending to free his ankles. "Find my clothes, will you? They should be in here somewhere."

Amanusa blushed—he seemed more a man and less a victim with his hands free—and hurried to obey. His clothing had been piled in a corner behind him. The lining was ripped from his frock coat, but all else was wearable.

"I myself am not so very innocent, after all," Jax went on. "So I made my blood stand for all the innocent blood these men have shed. Their own blood knows what they have done. And that is why Kazaryk suffers more than Janos. Captain Janos is merely a brute. Kazaryk is a torturer. He enjoys the pain of others."

Jax had his shirt and trousers on but not fastened. He refused to let Amanusa assist him, so she took his ruined frock coat and spread it over the corroded machine-thing, rolling it up inside. She tucked up the tails, folded down the collar, and tied the sleeves together to make a handle to carry it. Even wrapped, she didn't know how far she could carry the nauseating thing. She had to poke one of the dangling metal arms back inside, but finally she had a more-or-less tidy bundle.

"You're taking it with us?" Jax hissed with pain as he buttoned the last button on his trousers. "Hasn't it caused enough trouble?"

"That's why I'm bringing it. I don't want it to cause any more trouble here. I want to turn it over to someone who will actually examine it to see what it is and how it came into being, and that won't happen here. The Hungarian council is too busy 'following tradition' and tracking down unfortunate woods witches to bother with real danger."

Amanusa used Jax's blood spattered on his coat to seal a protection around it. It wasn't as strong as her warding around the box, but she thought it would hold the bundle together and keep the machine's magic-killing aura from hurting Ja—anyone.

"Sounds like the guards have brought a battering ram." Jax draped his long leather coat over his shoulders.

"Then it's time to let them in." Amanusa touched her thumb to the blood on his cheek and dabbed it behind her ear where it wouldn't show, if they did happen to get noticed. She spoke the words triggering the "don't-see-me" spell and released the magic seal on the door.

The soldiers in the hall slammed their makeshift battering ram into the door which splintered, and they stumbled into the room. Their cries of alarm and shouts for assistance layered under the screams of the condemned, and in the roar of noise and confusion, Amanusa and Jax slipped out of the room and out of city hall, picking up the carpetbag on their way out the front door.

She tried to help Jax across the square, but his torso was far more tender than his limbs. He could walk, and it hurt him when she put her arm round him. She confined herself to hovering.

As they climbed the platform to the train station,

Amanusa gradually released the magic hiding herself, so she wouldn't seem to appear out of nowhere. Keeping Jax close at her side so no one would stumble over him, she produced the tickets the boot boy had purchased for her that morning. It was last call for the last train of the day out of Nagy Szeben. The tickets secured them the last private compartment on the train. Overnight to Budapest, arriving just after noon. Surely the Inquisition wouldn't be able to organize a pursuit so quickly. Kazaryk wouldn't be capable of conjuring at midday. She doubted he would be capable of speech.

At the last moment, Crow swooped in through the open compartment window and took a perch on the overhead luggage rack with a mutter. Amanusa gazed out the window as the train puffed out of the station, watching the expanding uproar of the search for the escaped prisoners sweeping around city hall, catching up more and more of the passersby in its turmoil and confusion.

When the train was well away from town, she had the porter bring a basin of hot water so she could clean Jax up and tend his injuries. Just looking at him made her throat close up and her temper flare. They had hurt him and he was *hers*.

After she finished her cleanup, she took one look at Jax's tightly closed fists and shallow panting and pulled her lancet from her pocket. She punctured a finger, waited for the blood to well up, and touched his cheek with the two smallest fingers of her lancet-hand, brushing gingerly against his swollen lower lip with her thumb. "Open."

He obeyed instantly, watching her through slitted eyes as she slid her little finger into his mouth.

"I need to see how badly you're hurt," she said. "I don't like you hurting."

Jax rolled his tongue over her finger, once more turning the taking of her blood into a sensual event. Amanusa burned, and she wasn't sure it was all magic. She felt peculiar, even after she swept all the heat and all the magic into the droplet of blood. She pulled back, both physically and magically.

"If I might—" Jax caught her eye a moment before dipping his head in a seated bow. "I ask that you leave me my thoughts. They are too ugly for your eyes and ears."

Amanusa gave a bitter laugh. "I doubt they could be uglier than mine. But yes, of course I will leave your thoughts to you alone. Everyone should have the right to be private in his own mind."

His crooked, lumpy smile made her heart twist. How could he be so grateful for something so small?

While she waited for the blood to work its way into his bloodstream, Amanusa busied herself with bespelling the outrageously expensive train-supplied vodka into her healing potion. She'd done it enough times at the camp that while it required focus, it didn't require much time. Then she got out the pirogies she'd bought and offered them to Jax. He was grateful for the food, but insisted on sharing with Amanusa.

With her stomach knotted up so, she wasn't very hungry, but she took a pie. Jax wouldn't eat if she didn't at least pretend to. Something else disturbed her peace. Something other than Jax's injuries. She spoke his name. "Jax?"

"Yes, my sor—Amanusa?" He pushed himself straighter.

"At the outlaws' camp, when I lost control of the magic—how did I lose it? Why? What did I do wrong?" She stared hard at him. "I don't want to hear from Yvaine. You're in no shape to endure a visit from her, so if you feel her coming on, stop."

He nodded, his mouth attempting a smile. "I believe that your magic controls hers now, especially with your blood in my veins again. Amanusa is my sorceress, no longer Yvaine. So when you say Yvaine shall not rise, she does not."

"All right then. Yvaine shall not rise tonight." Amanusa sat back in her corner. "So where did I go wrong? Were there words I didn't speak?"

10

"MANY OF THEM."

Amanusa couldn't see the teasing twinkle in Jax's swollen-shut eyes, but she could hear it in his voice. She rolled her eyes at him.

"This evening, you used the words I spoke in the room to work the magic that freed us. Do you remember them?" He stared at the pie in his hand, then took a careful bite. He didn't speak again until after he swallowed. "When you call for justice, you must set limits. You have to say, 'Justice for this crime and no other.' Tell it *which* crimes it is judging."

"But doesn't the blood of the victims, the blood used in the spell, create those limits?"

"It can. But in the camp, *you* were one of those victims, and you are the sorceress. When you released the magic, you called merely for justice, which allowed the magic free rein to do what it willed. Words have power, but you have to use them."

"Just ordinary words? The conjurer used . . . strange words. Latin, or Egyptian. Something I didn't know."

"For sorcery, ordinary words suffice. Yvaine experimented, using the old Latin and using only English, and the magic worked just the same. Better, actually, because the sorceress can enforce her will better if she knows what she's saying. You can also cry payment short of death, and tell the magic where to go when it is done. You forgot that as well, in the camp."

Amanusa blinked at him. "Where can it go, besides into me?"

Jax sighed, shaking his head. "Did you not listen at all to the instructions Yvaine gave you? Or to the words of my spell tonight? The spell *you* used?"

"I was a trifle busy trying to hold onto the magic. They'd spilled so damn much of your blood, I had enough magic for the whole town."

"Yes, well . . ." He took a deep breath. "The magic will *want* to go back into you. You're its . . . lodestar, perhaps. Its natural gathering place. And often, you'd be wise to let it return to you. But that much magic— you know what happened in the camp. If you need to conserve magic, or let it build, you're better off shunting the magic into me."

"Oh yes, I could have carried you so easily down the mountain."

"It's unlikely the magic would have knocked me unconscious. First, because I'm larger than you. And

I am—when I said that I was a magical instrument bequeathed by Yvaine to her apprentice, it wasn't a metaphor. A large portion of the magic worked on me, magic that transformed me into her blood servant, made it possible for you to use me to store excess magic."

"Why would I want to do that?" Amanusa didn't like the idea of using a man—*Jax*—as a coal bin, or an oil tank.

"Some spells require more magic than you can contain in your own body. Though you, with your height, can contain more than Yvaine, who was quite small. I am given to understand that a wizard's familiar works in much the same manner."

"Familiars are animals, not human beings." She shook her head. She would learn about those "larger" spells later. Maybe. "But if the magic doesn't return to me, or to you, where does it go? Where should it go?"

"To rest. To peace. Especially if you are using blood from the dead, from a murdered victim. You should send it to find peace with the soul it belongs to. A murder victim's blood doesn't seek justice on those who did it no harm, but it still burns hotter than other blood, other magic." He paused, his head lying against the high back of the seat, his legs sprawled wide.

"Your blood has reached my veins," he murmured. "Already it eases the pain. I did not expect that."

"Good. I don't like the idea of you in pain." Amanusa moved to sit directly in front of Jax, dusting off spilled crumbs from her uneaten pie.

"You said that." Jax lifted his head and peered at

her. "When you gave me your blood, you said it. Not as part of a spell. You just said it." He pulled the rest of himself up to sit straight, staring at her. "The words alone were enough to focus your intent and create a spell."

The way Jax stared made Amanusa uncomfortable. "Then I suppose what you said is true. The magic works better when the sorceress understands what she's saying."

"It also means you'd better be very careful of what you *do* say, when you're bleeding. Or I am."

Dear Lord in heaven, he was right. Who knew what she might do? "Then it's a good thing I'm not particularly chatty, isn't it? I'll keep my mouth shut when I bleed myself." She summoned up a smile, felt it trickle onto her face. "Let's see what's happening inside you, shall we?"

She gathered the magic, spoke the words he'd given her, and *reached* for the magic inside Jax. His internal organs were as battered and bruised as his outsides, or nearly so. The blows had to go through skin and muscle to reach his inside parts, but the organs were more delicate. Amanusa wished she knew more about the body and how it worked so she could understand what she saw. The magic told her there was damage, but nothing that would not heal on its own. She hoped the magic was right. Jax's pain made her chest ache.

"Ease his pain so he can sleep," she whispered. "Assist his body in healing these injuries so that he is sooner whole." She feared doing more. Feared even that might be too much.

When she pulled back into herself, Amanusa felt

drained of what little energy she had left. Jax lay sprawled on the seat, his battered face utterly relaxed for the first time since—since ever, she realized. The entire time she'd known him, he'd always had some worry or other weighing him down, wearing it on his face.

Amanusa put a "don't look" spell on Crow when the porter came in to make up the beds. Neither she nor Jax had eaten much, so she used the scraps to keep the bird quiet. Falling crumbs seemed to puzzle the porter a time or two, but he brushed them aside and completed his task. They would get a good night's sleep, and they would be in Budapest in time for lunch tomorrow.

Not far from the Paris Bourse, magicians in clumps and trickles wound their way up the stairs into a boring red brick building. A woman scurried alongside one of the men, talking earnestly, her navy blue skirts bobbing at the speed of her pace.

"You *must* accept me as your apprentice, Mr. Mikkelsen," Elinor Tavis said. "You have seen the magic I am already able to work without benefit of training. How can you deny me the opportunity to learn?"

"I *must* do no such thing, Miss Tavis," the tall, thin Norwegian replied. "Yes, you show astonishing ability, but surely you can see how impossible it is. You are a lovely young unmarried woman. My wife would not understand—"

"I would explain it to her. I would tell her that I have absolutely no romantic interest—"

"She would not care." Mikkelsen interrupted her

in return. "It is not *your* interest that would concern her."

"Mister Mikkelsen!" Elinor recoiled.

"No, no. I love my wife. I am not interested in straying. And my wife knows this. But the gossip— no one *else* would believe any woman could be interested in magic to the exclusion of everything else. And the gossip would wound her. No, Miss Tavis. It is impossible." He headed up the stairs, leaving Elinor behind on the cobbles.

"But—how am I to learn?" she cried after him in despair.

"Poor thing," Harry Tomlinson said as he brushed past her.

"Don't tell me you think the man should have said yes?" Nigel Cranshaw sounded utterly appalled, climbing the steps alongside Harry and Grey Carteret, the conjurer of their delegation.

"Why not?" Harry pushed open the door and they entered the clamor of the lobby outside the Great Hall where the conclave was meeting.

The lobby soared two stories and stretched across the entire front of the building, paved in black-and-white diamond-patterned marble, lit by sunlight slanting through the rows of second-story windows to reflect off the mirrors lining the opposite side. Just now, it smelled overwhelmingly of the cigar smoke twisting its way through the rays of light.

"Because, dare I say, she's a woman?" Grey sounded as if he didn't particularly care either way, save for the entertainment value of a quarrel. He handed his hat into the cloakroom as they passed it, and the others followed suit.

"So?" Harry led the way through the knots of talking, gesticulating men. "If she can do the magic, why shouldn't she learn?"

"Because she's a woman!" Nigel exclaimed. "It's unnatural. Women's constitutions are simply not made to—"

"Bollocks," Harry interrupted. "I been lookin' at the old books, tryin' to find some cure for these dead zones. Back then, back when there weren't any dead zones, there were all kinds of women magicians. The charter says the council will accept and train *any* candidate with the talent for magic. How else did I get to be a magician?"

"Point to Harry," Grey said cheerfully.

Nigel sneered. "But you're a man. The charter says nothing about accepting female apprentices."

"It says nothing about the sex of apprentices at all. It just says '*any*'. Seems to me 'any' means '*any*'."

Nigel stared at Harry in horror. "You'll destroy civilization as we know it."

Harry's expression went hard and grim. "No." He stabbed a finger in the direction of the river. "Those dead zones are the death of civilization. And if we don't figure out how to stop 'em, they'll keep growin' until there's nothin' left at all. All the magic'll be gone, and so will everything else. An' if takin' on a few female wizards'll 'elp stop those damned death traps, I'm all for it."

"Take her as *your* apprentice then," Nigel snapped, "because I never will. Nor will any other wizard I know." He stalked away.

Grey watched him go, a speculative expression on his face.

Harry swore and ran a hand through his short-cropped hair. "I would," he said, "if I thought she could learn alchemy."

"They're afraid," Grey said, his voice unnaturally serious. "Wizardry is female magic. They're afraid they'll be surpassed if women begin taking it up again."

"What they ought to be afraid of is those dead zones."

"True, true." Grey looked around. "Let's go in and claim a seat and hear what the investigators have learned."

They'd learned a great deal, as it turned out. President Gathmann reported that dead zones all over Europe had decreased in size. The farther east the zone, the more the decrease. Of course, the farther east their inquiries ran, the more difficult it was for their investigators to travel to inspect the zones, and the fewer telegraph lines existed to send requests for information.

Conjurer's communication spells were working, but they occasionally took more time than a telegraph. Especially when the conjurer at the other end of the spell had less talent. Or wasn't listening. The conclave hoped for a report from Moscow and St. Petersburg by the next day, but so far none of their questions had turned up reports of new magic being worked.

The Hungarians were also slow in responding. The telegram had reached the council offices for the kingdom of Hungary in Budapest, but the staff there reported that all the magicians in the whole of the Austrian Empire had been called out to deal with some sort of crisis in Transylvania. The conjurers certainly weren't paying any attention to visiting spirits. Gathmann wondered whether the crisis could have something to do with the changes in the dead zones, but no one had any way of knowing, and no one knew when the magicians might report in.

WITH EVERY HOUR past their train's scheduled arrival in Budapest, as day faded into night, Jax's worry grew. Because with every hour that ticked away toward midnight, the Inquisition's conjurers grew stronger and their magic more powerful. Trains in Transylvania and Hungary were notorious for their failure to stick to schedule, but this seemed worse than usual. Was it deliberate? The possibilities felt ominous.

"Perhaps we should get off the train," he suggested for what seemed the sixty-dozenth time. "The Inquisition won't expect us to arrive on foot."

"They don't know for certain we're arriving by train either. Or if we are, which train." Amanusa began ticking items off on her fingers. "They can't know for sure we're coming to Budapest. We might have gone the other way, into Romania or Bulgaria. To Greece, maybe. They'll have to inspect every train coming into every station. They can't have that many Inquisitors."

"Process of elimination would have them focusing on Budapest," Jax retorted. "The Hungarian Inquisition *can't* look for us in Romania, since it's part of the Ottoman Empire, not the Austrian—"

"They can watch at the border."

He ignored her interruption. "And given where

they know we were, in Nagy Szeben, and that the last train out that day was bound for Budapest, it's only logical they look for us to arrive *here*. We should leave the train. Should have left it hours ago."

"But we didn't," Amanusa said. "We have to be almost to Budapest by now. Where do you suggest we get off?"

"It stops for water and coal. We could get off then."

"And maybe it won't stop again before we get there. Maybe they'll think we ran back into the mountains. Maybe they're looking for us there."

"Amanusa." He sighed at her. "They think we're both English. Where would we run but back to England? We need to get off the train."

She sighed back at him, turning away to brush her fingers down Crow's feathers where he sat at the window. The bird opened an eye and complained, fluttering to the luggage rack over Jax's head to take himself out of human reach.

"Jax? I think it's too late to get off the train." She pointed out the window where lights shone in the deep dark.

He blew out the lamp flame and the landscape outside the train became immediately more visible. Buildings. Large and close together. They had reached Budapest. He stood to look out the window, to see how much time they might still have, what they might be able to do.

The buildings they passed were great warehouses with dedicated rail sidings for freight, and rows of cheap, tightly packed houses. They were still on the outskirts of the city then, the visible lights shining outside taverns and along the street around the businesses. They had a little time. Perhaps they could—

Pain lashed through his whole body at once, sending him crashing to the floor. Above him, on the seat, Amanusa writhed. Did the same agony touch her?

Jax didn't have breath for screams. He had to see what was wrong with his sorceress. *God,* he hurt. Worse than all the blows the captain had inflicted put together. He struggled to get his knees under him, to pull himself off the compartment floor.

Amanusa whimpered, the sound slicing through his physical pain. Jax caught her hand, by sheer luck, he was sure, since neither of them seemed to have control over their limbs.

"Are you all right?" Amanusa gasped out the question before he could.

"Are you?" He couldn't answer for himself until he knew.

"It burns," she whimpered.

Memory locked in, Yvaine feeding him the information instead of taking him over to give it directly to Amanusa, since Amanusa had forbidden that. Yvaine was nothing if not adaptable. "Magic assault," he croaked. "It's an attack on your magic. Take my other hand."

"Why?" Always the questions, the resistance to touching him. But she did it, and the pain lessened a little more.

"Too much magic can do as much damage as too little. Push it into me."

"Doesn't it burn you?" Another argument.

"Just *do it,*" Jax snapped out. But still she held back. Stubborn woman. "I'm equipped to hold it, remember? I told you this. Now give me the damned magic!"

She did as she was told, finally, shoving the excess magic into him, layering it in the channels along his bones. It made him a little dizzy—he hadn't held so much magic in more years than he wanted to remember—but it also eased the pain. Had they stripped him when they flooded her?

"It still hurts," she whimpered when the magic stopped flowing. "Why does it still hurt? I got rid of all the extra."

"Because the—the nerves, the vessels—whatever it is you use to hold the magic, were forced. Like wrenching a joint out of place. You can put it back, but it still hurts."

"How could they do it? Not, 'how could they be so cruel' but *how*—each type of magic is different, right? I can't use a spirit, or the elements or plants—"

"Well, you *could,* if you had the spells and materials. An ability to use magic is an ability to use magic, of any sort, though most magicians *lean* one direction or another. But—" Jax struggled for the words to explain what he meant. "In a magic assault, the damage is greater by forcing magic on you that is not your own inclination."

The train jerked as it slowed. Amanusa startled, and hissed at the pain caused by the motion. Jax used her hands to pull himself off the floor, retaining possession of them as he sat beside her.

"What do we do now?" Amanusa's forehead brought out its little worried crease. "How can we fight back if we don't even know who they are?"

We. He liked the sound of that. "There *is* a warding magic, a strong protective magic that can hold almost any solitary attack at bay." He was hesitant about mentioning it to her, however. Especially since he hadn't mentioned it at the beginning, when he'd explained the truth about blood magic.

"What? What is it? How do I do it? How much blood does it take?"

"None." Jax gave her a wary look. How would she react when he told her? "It's sex magic."

"What?" Amanusa recoiled, snatching her hands from his. "You're lying. There's no such thing as sex magic."

Jax stood, backed to the door to give her the room she seemed to need. He wished now he hadn't put out the lamp, so he could see her expression. So she could see his. "I'm not. Sex magic is part of blood magic. It's another part of the reason blood magic has been so reviled, and it is very real. Ask Yvaine, if you don't believe me."

At his mention of her name, Jax became aware of moisture in his nose and reached for his handkerchief. The droplet of Yvaine's blood that had held the information she'd given him about the magic assault was finding its way out.

"Why didn't you say anything about this before? Why keep it a secret?"

"Because I'd barely got you to listen to the truth about blood magic, and because it was clear you were afraid of me, and of anything to do with men and sex. I didn't want to frighten you any worse than you already were. I thought I could wait to tell you about sex magic until later, until you trusted me a bit."

She frowned. "Why are you bleeding? I said I didn't want to hear from Yvaine until we were safe."

"You didn't, did you?" He dabbed away the blood, folded the handkerchief, and put it carefully away to be properly disposed of later. "Yvaine slipped a bit of knowledge into my head for me to give you, that's all. Not enough to cause a problem."

"What kind of sex does this magic require?" Suspicion rode her words.

His fault. She had trusted him. Now she did not. He would have to start again from the beginning to rebuild her trust. If it were at all possible.

"Any kind," he said. "Even a kiss will work magic if there's true desire behind it."

She bit her lip again. She would gnaw it away entirely if she kept it up, but Jax didn't have the right to ask her to stop. "I don't know if I can," she said in a small voice.

"All right." Jax nodded and regretted it immediately. The acute pain of the attack had faded, but it still hovered just behind his awareness, ready to pounce at any unwary motion, like a nod. "Here's what we'll—"

"Shouldn't we at least try?" Her voice shrank even smaller, but it poured through Jax's ears and reverberated inside his head. Could trust still linger?

What was she thinking? Hadn't she been angry just a moment ago? Her about-face bewildered Jax. He kept very still, afraid to react in any way for fear of alarming her again. "Are you sure? We can find another way if you'd rather."

"Will this other way protect us as well?"

He had to give her truth. Even if it weren't part of the binding, he would not lie to this sorceress. "No. But it is your decision, not mine. I am only your servant."

"No." She started to shake her head, winced, and stopped. "You're my—my liegeman. We are a team, you and I. Jax and Amanusa. And that is how we will win, because they think they face only one."

A flood of astonished pleasure rushed through him. Jax could not hide his grin, one he was sure looked exceeding silly. She valued him that much. She *trusted* him that much. Still. He hadn't destroyed it with his silence. "Amanusa and Jax," he said, for something to say. "You are still the sorceress."

"Yes, but Jax is short and simple and Amanusa is such a mouthful of sounds. Jax fits better in front, leaving my name to trail endlessly behind." She winked at him. "Besides, isn't that where a liege man belongs? In front with the shield for me to hide behind?"

Jax laid his hand over his heart and bowed low. "And that is where I shall always be. Shielding you from those who mean you harm, whether scouting ahead or watching your back."

Amanusa cleared her throat, looking out the window at the passing city. The buildings were more imposing now and better lit as they neared the train station. "About that kiss . . ."

Now Jax had to clear his throat. "Are you sure?"

He'd never kissed anyone who didn't want him to kiss them. Not that he could remember at any rate. How did one manage it? Should they stand? Sit? Should he wait for her? If he did, he could be waiting all night. He knew fear motivated her reluctance, so what would frighten her least?

Jax sat. It made him closer to her size and hopefully less intimidating. "I am your loyal supporter," he said quietly. "I will never, ever, *ever* do anything to harm you. Even if I could, I wouldn't. But if I frighten you, remember, your blood flows in my veins. All you have to do is grasp hold of it and you can stop my heart."

"I don't want to stop your heart!" Amanusa sounded alarmed. "Can't I just stop your muscles?"

"Yes, but it requires more control over the magic." He smiled. "I suppose I'll simply have to not frighten you. We don't have to do this, you know."

The train jerked and Amanusa lurched, almost falling to the floor. Jax caught her by the arms and she met his eyes, searching them through the darkness in the compartment.

"Yes," she said, "we do. If I am going to be a blood sorceress, I can't be afraid of half the magic I can do."

That explained her quick turnaround, that and her trust in him. It humbled him. "We don't have to do it now," Jax amended. "You've only just learned that there is magic in sex. Take some time to swallow the concept."

"I think I've got to gulp it down." Her worry crease appeared in her forehead. "I'm afraid that if I don't do it now, it will be harder to do the next time, and I will keep backing away from it until it's too late, until I'm locked up tight in a cage of fear. And I won't let those—those bastards do this to me. I won't let them win."

11

HOW MAGNIFICENT SHE WAS. How strong and courageous—everything a sorceress should be.

"All right, then." Moving as slowly as the creeping of the train would let him—they had to be almost upon the station—Jax lifted his hand to her cheek, brushing her satin skin with his fingertips. Heart pounding, he lowered his face to hers, watching her eyes for the flare of panic.

As he neared, her face filling his vision, she squeezed her eyes shut. Out of fear? Or did she feel the same intensity that pounded through him? That this was almost too much to bear.

A breath away from her lips, he paused, wanting the final decision to be hers. He could smell woman, and soap, and the faint scent of forest. His heart pounded faster.

Her eyes flicked open and her bright sky-colored eyes gazed into his. "I'm not afraid," she whispered in wonder. "But there's no desire either. Didn't you say there should be desire?"

Only one of them had to feel desire, and Jax felt enough to light all of Budapest into one great conflagration. His body hardened and burned to possess her. But if he told her, it would spoil her fragile trust in him, and he'd already come too near to destroying it.

He turned sideways on the seat, bringing a knee up between them to hide his aroused state and to maintain a safe distance between them. All the while, he kept his mouth hovering just above hers.

"Fondness," he murmured, inspiration striking. "Fondness will do. We do at least *like* each other, do we not? God knows, I adore you for pulling me out of the hands of the Inquisition."

A breath of silent laughter puffed across his lips. "And I am indeed fond of you for carrying me down the mountain away from Szabo's camp."

"I am cut to the quick," Jax breathed. "See how my adoration is repaid with mere fondness." If he kept things light, perhaps he could keep her fear at bay.

His whole body quivered with the effort of holding himself in place, a fraction from her lips, without touching them. The echo of the magic assault trembled just behind his weary muscles, threatening to return if he lost the least bit of control.

But Amanusa's breathless giggle made it all worthwhile. She was not given to much laughter, and if he could grant it—especially in this moment, fraught with the weight of so much that had gone before—he would give her whatever he could.

"Hush your nonsense," she whispered, "and kiss me."

Her order released him from his self-imposed confinement, and he realized they were kissing. He hadn't moved, or didn't think he had, but his lips melted into hers, savoring their soft warmth, their sweet intoxicating taste. Wine that bypassed his head to shoot straight into his veins.

His fingertips slid along her cheek until he cupped her face in his hand, the touch of her skin filling his palm and all of his fingers, a complete handful of Amanusa. Then her fingers brushed his cheek, her hand cupped his face in an echo of his own touch, and Jax thought the top of his head would explode with joy.

"I feel it," Amanusa whispered against his mouth. "I feel the magic gathering."

Of course she did. He hadn't touched a woman, much less kissed one in . . . far longer than he could, or wanted, to remember. His desire had no bounds. Only his actions were under his control.

"Collect it." Jax wanted to kiss her again, kiss her more. Their lips still brushed as they spoke, and he wasn't about to pull away before she did. "How much is there? Enough?"

"I don't know. Some. How much is enough?" The sweep of her lips over his would drive him mad.

"More would be better." He did not feel guilty at all. Yes, he wanted more kisses, but more magic would indeed be better.

"All right." Amanusa's easy acquiescence surprised him.

He thought it might perhaps have surprised her too, but he didn't have time or sense for thinking just now. Amanusa was kissing him. She was curving her fingers around the top of his ears and playing with the dratted curls he could never keep cut. If Amanusa liked playing in them, he'd let them be.

Her mouth parted and Jax caught his breath as he

let his own mouth open. Did she know what she did? Did she intend it? Jax sent his hand up into her hair. It was still braided, coiled and pinned to her head, and he wished he could take it down, run his fingers through it. But there wasn't time, and who knew if she would ever let him kiss her again?

She might call him her liege man, but he was in truth her servant. She didn't have to collect the sex magic herself. She could send him out to do it for her. And despite the wonder and joy spinning through him at the delight of kissing Amanusa, he would go and gladly, if a quick rutting in a back alley would keep her safe.

All on its own, Jax's tongue crept past his teeth, heading for escape. He brought it back twice. Amanusa might have parted her lips, but she showed no signs of wanting more. Jax slanted his head, changing the angle of the kiss, drawing more sweetness from her, and his tongue took advantage of his distraction. Before he could stop it, it licked out of his mouth and across the plump fullness of Amanusa's lower lip.

She jerked away to stare at him in shock as the train came to a complete halt and the conductor called their arrival in Budapest, only twelve hours and twenty-three minutes late.

"Are you all right?" He had to ask, to be sure he hadn't frightened her, hadn't put her completely off kissing forever after, whether she kissed him or someone else.

"Yes. Fine." She paused, her eyes shifting to watch something Jax couldn't see. "And you're right. There's more magic. More *is* better."

"Good. Now gather it in. Take some of the magic you gave me from the attack, if you can make it mix properly." He felt magic leave him, getting dizzy all over again. "Here are the words you need."

Similar to the warding magic they'd laid around the tent in the outlaw camp, this spell carried protection against magic as well as physical harm, and could be laid around their persons. The power of the kiss should last through the rest of the night. Perhaps longer. It was only a kiss, but there had been a great hoard of desire behind it.

Outside, the station was waking to the bustle surrounding the late-night arrival of their train. Porters creaked their sleepy way toward the baggage cars and the first-class compartments. Folk in the second- and third-class cars were already disembarking. Less comfort in their accommodations made them ready to get out and stretch.

Amanusa spoke the last of the words Jax gave her and felt the magic close around her like a comforting blanket. Did it cover Jax too? She reached for his arm, to check, and put her hand through the magic shield. As she touched him, she felt the magic soak in, settling into his skin. Another magician might be able to tell magic had been worked here, but she didn't think he could know who had worked it, or what had been done.

She looked out the window at the sleepy activity and saw soldiers spread out along the edge of the station's platform. Near the military officer stood a cluster of men yawning and knuckling sleep from their eyes.

"Look." She pointed them out to Jax who was

pulling the machine case from the overhead luggage rack.

"Inquisitors." He sounded as grim as she felt.

Crow fluttered to the floor in front of the door to the train corridor and squawked at her, like a dog asking to be let out. With a mental shrug, and without moving from her seat, Amanusa leaned to open the compartment door and watched him walk out into the empty hallway. Everyone in the first-class compartments was using the doors on the other side to exit the train. Crow walked and hopped his way down the corridor, heading off to do who knew what.

"Amanusa." Jax called her attention back to the view outside the window. "Look at that Inquisitor's badge."

She scooted along the seat, as much as her modest crinoline would allow, and looked. Terror yanked her away from the window, then made her feeble. Her hands had no strength to grab hold of Jax's coat, or his sleeve, or anything to pull him into the compartment's shadows, out of sight. Her voice stuck in her throat, unable to call out, to warn him.

"Do you see it?" He turned, and when he saw her terror, he dropped to one knee and caught hold of her hand, which hid him from view. "Amanusa, what's wrong?"

"K-k—" She could only stutter as fear paralyzed her. Why was she so afraid? She'd beaten the fear once. Beaten him. But here he was again. She smothered the panic with sheer determination. "Kazaryk," she whispered. "The Inquisitor Plenipotentiary. He's *here*."

"Are you sure?" Jax lifted himself smoothly onto the opposite seat, away from the window, and looked out. "Where?"

She kept her hand close to her body as she pointed. "With the army officer, giving commands."

"Then that likely explains— Look at that Inquisitor's badge. The one just outside there." Jax tipped his head to indicate the young man nearest their first-class carriage.

The man yawned, his top hat canted at an odd angle. The red Inquisitor's badge pinned to his coat . . . was *pinned* to his coat. With a long hat pin. It curled up at the bottom.

"He's not a regular Inquisitor." Hope breathed into Amanusa, then leached away again. "Has Kazaryk called out all the magicians in Hungary and appointed them Inquisitors? Could he be so frightened of me?"

Something else occurred to her. "How did he get here before us? I've heard some conjurers can have their familiar spirits carry them great distances at the speed of a thought. But *Úr* Kazaryk did not seem such a powerful magician to me. Was I wrong?" Did they need to fear worse attacks?

"This train is over twelve hours late," Jax reminded her. "Fast horses on a more direct route could possibly have beaten us here. It is possible the train was deliberately delayed."

"Why didn't they just take us off the train when it made one of its endless stops?"

"I imagine it took some time to assemble and appoint all these Inquisitors. Budapest is a more convenient assembly point. They would have wanted an overwhelming force to face you. They are frightened of you, remember? You left Kazaryk writhing on the floor in pain."

But Kazaryk didn't know Amanusa had worked the magic. Jax had pretended to do it. She wouldn't remind him, though. He would probably want her to go on alone, and she refused to even think it. Still, she wondered if that deception might cause them trouble later.

"If the magic hurt him so badly, how could he endure such a ride?" Amanusa rubbed her arms. She was so cold, but she didn't think another shawl would help.

"Fear can motivate great feats of endurance."

"But I'm nothing to be afraid of."

He jerked his head around to look at her, only his eyes showing a reaction to the pain it caused. "Yes, Amanusa. You are. You are a blood sorceress. You are judgment upon the wicked and justice for the helpless. You are everything they have ever feared in their entire smug, selfish lives."

"Oh." Amanusa didn't want people to be afraid of her. Unless they'd done something wrong. She didn't like bullies. Or murderers, or, well . . . If people did what they ought, they had no reason to fear her.

Which was exactly what the Inquisition said. If a person hadn't done anything wrong, they had nothing to fear. But "wrong" tended to be whatever the Inquisition said it was. And their justice depended on whether you could pay for it.

No, she wasn't like the Inquisition. Jax was right. They *should* fear her. Because they were wicked and unjust and there were more of them than there was of her. She had to get to that tower in Scotland and learn all there was to know about being a blood sorceress, until she was powerful enough to take them on, all the wicked and unjust people. And she would take apprentices, so that she wouldn't be the only sorceress against all the wickedness in the world. And—

And first they had to get off this train and out of Budapest. Out of the Austrian Empire.

She invoked the "don't-see-me" magic. Not enough to make them virtually invisible, but enough to avoid notice. To make them seem unimportant. Not the people the Inquisitors wanted. She let Jax help her onto the platform.

The sleepy Inquisitor stood a few feet away. He stared at them, long enough that Amanusa began to fear he could see through her spell. Then Crow burst from the railway carriage two cars up with a flutter of black feathers and a raucous cry.

The station exploded with shouts and screaming and a few blasts from soldiers' rifles before their officers got them stopped. All of the soldiers and most of the Inquisitors—including Kazaryk—dashed across the platform and shoved through the crowd to swarm the distant car. Crow flapped his way into the girders of the station's roof where he made a black spot amongst all the white and gray pigeons.

Jax and Amanusa watched the excitement for a few moments—everyone else was and they wanted to blend in—before making their weary way to the row of waiting cabs with all the other weary debarking passengers. Amanusa did her best to appear merely tired, rather than wiped clean and smashed flat.

"Clever, clever Crow," she said when they were safely shut into the carriage, their trunk tied on behind.

"Must have known we needed the distraction." Jax rapped on the carriage ceiling with his knuckles and the cab started off. "I'm concerned that the spell that hit us set off some kind of alarm with the Inquisition. It could well have been targeted specifically for sorcerers."

"We probably shouldn't take the train out of Budapest, then. Would we have to tap the bank account again to purchase a carriage and horses?" She frowned, trying to piece Jax's reasoning together. "How could they target the spell for a sorceress, if there hasn't been one since Yvaine died? They had your blood, of course, but wouldn't using it to target you be blood magic?"

"Since I wasn't there for the making of the spell, I do not know, but it's possible—the spell could have been blended of conjury and alchemy and wizardry and told 'Any magic that is not *this*—attack it.' Words focus the magic, if you'll recall, so there are any number of ways it could have been done."

His voice was as calm and precise as always, but Amanusa could hear the undercurrent of frustration and annoyance. "Apologies." She patted his arm where he sat beside her. "I should know better than to ask questions you couldn't possibly know answers for. But you know so much more about the great magics than I, I'll take even your guesses."

"As long as you realize they *are* guesses, and do not rely on them as fact." Jax removed his arm from her touch to part the curtains and peer out at the street. "As for further transportation—Budapest is on the Danube. I suggest we take a boat."

"But—" Amanusa's heart pounded faster, not quite panic, but alarm, perhaps. "Wouldn't that take us to Vienna? Didn't we talk about going directly into the German states, to Dresden? Out of the Empire altogether."

"I consulted a map the conductor was kind enough to share with me while on the train. To go directly north to Prussia, or to Dresden in Saxony, we would have to travel as far through Hungary as we would going due east to Vienna and Bavaria beyond. And the country to the north is far more rural. Two English, or any foreigners, would be as noticeable as—as a crow among pigeons."

So he had seen Crow in the rafters as well. Amanusa nodded for him to go on.

"A river cruise on the Danube is a popular holiday for all sorts of foreigners. We can be lost in the crowds. And we will get to the western coast and England that much more quickly. Besides—" He shrugged ruefully. "The river traffic cannot be any slower than Hungarian trains. Especially if the authorities are deliberately delaying the trains."

"Very well." Amanusa nodded, using the motion to keep herself awake. "You've convinced me. We'll take a boat to Vienna and decide there how to go next."

"Back on the train, likely. Austrian trains run more efficiently than Hungarian."

"What odd things you can remember." If she went riding on his blood again, to poke around inside his head, what would she find this time? She wouldn't do it, of course. Jax deserved to keep his head to himself. But she was curious.

"Think how bizarre it is for me." He smiled at her. "All sorts of peculiar bits keep popping up from nowhere, and I have no idea how I know them."

"We should probably try to change our appearance again." Amanusa tried to think of everything they needed to do. "The women who dyed my hair in Nagy Szeben said it would wash out in three or four washings. Maybe if I go back to blond—"

The carriage clattered to a halt. Jax had asked for a hotel away from the train station, claiming his wife's frailty couldn't take the noise. Moments later, they were installed in a comfortable room and Jax was making up a pallet on the floor.

Amanusa thought for a brief moment about trying to convince him to take the bed. He'd been hurt by the magic assault and was still hurting from the beating as well. She could tell by the careful way he moved. But he was so stubborn, she knew she wouldn't win. And she was so tired, she fell asleep in her chemise before she got her stockings off.

THEY WERE OFF in the morning. Amanusa's face burned like fire at the realization that Jax must have removed them. Thank heaven he wasn't there to see her blush. He wasn't anywhere in the room. She blushed all the harder for being grateful he'd been magically gelded by Yvaine. And felt horribly guilty for it, both for Yvaine's cruelty and her own gratitude.

It was only at that moment that Amanusa realized *why* Yvaine had gelded him. Jax said he needed permission for—for *that*. Her vision went dark. She smelled rank sweat, but before the memory of hairy, naked, heaving flesh could sweep over her, she reached for the magic and it burned the images away.

She grasped for other images, other bits of sensation. Soft lips over her own. Jax's lips, caressing hers in her first real kiss. The outlaws had—had taken her, but they had never kissed her. A man kissed his sweetheart. He didn't kiss a whore, and that was what they'd made of her. But Jax had kissed her.

Though they had never spoken of her early time in the outlaw camp, Amanusa knew Jax knew about everything. And still he had kissed her. Sweetly. Reverently, and yet with a fierceness that had touched some deep-down ferocity inside her and pulled the magic forth. His hand cupping her face had made her feel safe and protected, and when he'd thrust his other hand into her hair to grip her head and hold her still for his kiss, she had somehow sensed the iron control he maintained over himself.

It allowed her to let go. To release her fears and her own control and relax into his, because she trusted him to contain whatever she let loose. Sensation and emotion and magic went racketing all over the place so that she scarcely knew what she felt, whether physically or internally. She knew only that she *felt*.

If a mere kiss could feel that way, no wonder it created magic. And no wonder Yvaine did not want Jax doing—*that*—if it would not benefit her and her magic. Amanusa knew enough about the last sorceress to be confident of that. The old besom.

Amanusa hopped out of bed and rushed into her clothes. On the dresser, near her father's razor which Jax had been using, she found a note written in a strong, slashing hand. "I've gone to book passage and do some shopping. Back soon. Stay in the room."

She ordered up breakfast and hot water, and used her time waiting to wash the henna rinse out of her hair.

When Jax returned, his arms piled with packages, she was staring at herself in the mirror, struggling not to scream.

"What's wrong?" he asked as he crossed to the window to peer out. Crow cawed back at him.

"Look at my hair," she wailed, throwing her hands up. "It's *pink*!"

"It isn't *very* pink." He tried, but he was obviously unequal to the task of dealing with a woman upset over the state of her hair. "Just the tiniest bit pink— perhaps if you wash it again?"

"I've washed it six times. If it hasn't come out after six washings, I doubt it's going to come out at all." She wanted to rip her hair right out of her head. She would do it too—if being bald wouldn't make her even more noticeable than being pink.

"Come and see what I've bought," he said, carefully changing the subject. He paused a moment. "Maybe it won't look so pink after it dries."

If she weren't so angry over her horrid pink hair, she would laugh at Jax's attempts to be helpful and soothe her, without turning her wrath on him. "We can only hope," she grumbled, not feeling any happier, but the excess anger had bled off and she didn't feel quite so ready to explode.

The new purchases did much to improve her mood. So did the fact that her hair did look less pink when it dried, and even less so in her new dress. She still tucked as much of it under her new bonnet as she could when they left the hotel, Crow sulking in the cage Jax had bought for him.

On the way to the river docks, they saw a makeshift Inquisitor, backed by a quartet of soldiers, march up the steps into one of the grand, downtown hotels. A shiver ran through Amanusa as she realized they were getting out just in time. The attack must have signaled to the Inquisition that a sorceress had arrived in Budapest.

She saw another Inquisitor strolling down the street ahead of them, pretending to idle along while watching the traffic intently. They were searching for her.

Where was Kazaryk? Coordinating the search in some official building while nursing his saddle sores, she hoped. She didn't see him here.

She touched Jax, *feeling* for the protective blanket of magic around him. It was easier to *feel* for it on him than fumble to find it around herself. She found only the faintest remnants of the spell clinging to him. It couldn't be enough to hide them.

She needed to reinforce the spell, which meant she needed more of the sex magic. It still bothered her a little, that she had so easily accepted Jax's word that sex created magic in the same way blood did. She felt vaguely as if she should have protested more, should have refused to believe him. Except that Jax had never lied to her, ever.

Besides, it made absolute sense. Sorcery was *body*

magic, worked with more than just blood. If blood and spit could work magic, why not a man's seed? Blood was shed the first time a woman had sex, and blood was shed when she gave birth. Blood and sex went together, like rope and pulleys.

"Jax, kiss me."

12

JAX DIDN'T HESITATE. Didn't try to argue or delay, as Amanusa would have. Because it was an order and he was bound to obey? Or because he was a man and hoped for more than a kiss? It didn't matter. She didn't have to learn the rest of the sex magic today.

He braced one hand on the seat between them, touched her face with the other, and kissed her. Amanusa waited for the magic to bloom, but could gather only the faintest of trickles. It wasn't working.

Jax broke away, cupping her face between his hands as he drew back to look at her. "You're too distracted."

"There's an Inquisitor right outside," she hissed at him. "They're all over the city, looking for us. And the protection spell is fading. I'm not distracted at all. I am totally focused on the magic."

"Not on the kiss. You can't work this kind of magic when you're focused on something else. Your attention has to be on what you're doing. On the kiss. The . . . sex." He rubbed his thumb across her lower lip and she reached out to push it away.

He caught her hand in his, leaving his other still touching her face as he brought her hand up to rub its back across the faint roughness of his cheek. "Do you honestly want me to kiss you, Amanusa? Because if you truly want to learn how to work the magic of desire, you have to let go of everything going on up here—" He tapped her forehead. "And *feel* what your body is doing."

"I—" She shivered. The Inquisitors were just outside. How could she forget them? They made her too nervous. Or maybe it was Jax who made her nervous. She trusted him. She *did*. She just—

Jax released her and peered out through the open window. "I don't see any more Inquisitors. The attack last night surely can't be duplicated any time soon, and we've changed our appearance. We should be safe enough."

"For now, maybe." Amanusa just couldn't concentrate on kissing Jax, knowing Kazaryk was out there searching, but she was determined to learn how to do this new magic properly. "What about later? What about on the river? Or when we come into Vienna? What if they set up another ambush there?"

"I can gather the magic for you." Jax stared at the floor between his boots. "With your permission, of course." Two patches of red stained his cheeks as he stared determinedly straight ahead.

"My . . . permission?" Amanusa didn't think she liked where this was going. But then he'd told her about "permission" at the very beginning. She just hadn't wanted to think about it.

"To—" He cleared his throat. "Participate in intercourse. With someone else. You don't have to take part in the—"

"Sex."

"Right." He cleared his throat again, his eyes flicking around the inside of the carriage, in every direction but hers. "The magic is automatically gathered and stored inside me—like that you gave me after the assault. You don't have to be present, or even nearby."

This bothered her. Not the idea of sex creating magic, but the thought of sending Jax out to—to whore himself for her. The whole topic of sex disturbed her. Given her history, it shouldn't, but it did. "I just, I—" She struggled for words to explain without being unforgivably crude, or embarrassing herself, or him. "It makes me feel like, like a procurer. Sending you out to, to—"

He interrupted with a curse. "It's just sex, Amanusa. We have to be able to talk about it. People do it all the time and nobody gets hurt. It's not murder. It's not even rape. There's always somebody willing for a quick tumble, and most of the time, they don't want money for it. They do it because it feels good—for the woman too, if it's done right. And I know how to do it right, because usually there's more magic that way. If everyone involved enjoys it."

Amanusa's face burned so hot, she couldn't believe it didn't light the carriage interior with its glow. Jax was right. She had to get over this embarrassment. Enough to at least talk to him about the magic. About sex. She couldn't live this way. She was a *sorceress*.

The carriage pulled to a halt and Jax looked out. "We're here."

The smell of damp and of green fermenting things confirmed his announcement. Amanusa put a hand on his elbow to delay him a moment. "Let me think and we can talk again about what to do. We *will* talk."

He held her gaze a moment, then gave her a solemn nod and hopped out of the carriage to direct the unloading of their trunk, and the box he'd bought for the machine, and Crow in his cage, before helping her down.

The riverboat was neat and streamlined, with a small paddle wheel in the back. Their tiny cabin had two bunks against the wall and barely enough room for Amanusa's skirts in what remained. They saw their luggage stored in the cabin and returned to stroll on the aft promenade while the boat's crew cast off from the dock. No Inquisitors appeared, before or after the riverboat turned out into the current and chuffed away up river, leaving Budapest and Kazaryk behind. She hoped.

When they retired to their minuscule cabin that night, Amanusa hadn't yet thought enough to have that promised conversation with Jax. Everything was mixed up with the horrors of her past, and what had happened since Jax walked out of the forest and into her life.

What she thought about things was tangled up in how she felt about things, and how she thought she *ought* to think and feel, until she didn't know what was up and what was down. Left and right had departed long ago and she wasn't any too sure about inside or outside. Several days passed with that muddle churning inside her while Hungary and then Austria drifted by on either side of the boat.

"The captain says we'll be reaching Vienna tomorrow." Jax leaned down to murmur in Amanusa's ear as the gentlemen joined the ladies in the salon after dinner one evening.

"I know. I have ears." Guilt instantly consumed Amanusa. She'd been in a nasty mood since they got on this silly boat, and she'd been taking it out on Jax, who deserved far better. Especially since he never responded in kind.

"I'm sorry." She laid her hand on his arm as he straightened, hoping he understood that she truly was sorry. "You're too good to me, putting up with my moods."

His smile touched his lips, glinted in his eyes. "You have much to be moody about." He came around the settee and offered his arm. "Walk with me?"

She smiled back, grateful for the forgiveness. "Of course."

Jax took her out onto the promenade where the creak of the stern paddle wheel and the splash of the water would hide their conversation from the other passengers. "The only reason I mentioned Vienna—if I am going to call magic for your protection, it should be tonight. Madame Villet—"

He named the widow who Amanusa suspected had never been married, with her brazen manner and not-quite-respectable fashion. "She has indicated a willingness for me to visit her cabin." Jax paused by the rail, staring out at the deep blue of the midsummer twilight. "But I must have your permission in order to do what is necessary."

Amanusa's insides churned furiously, both her mind and her stomach. Her fingers dug into Jax's forearm.

"I will not hurt her, Amanusa." He covered her

hands with his other and the assurance of his touch allowed her to relax her grip. "I promise that Madame Villet will exper—"

"But you're *mine*." The words popped out of her mouth so quickly, her hands couldn't clap themselves over it fast enough to keep them inside. Oh dear heaven, that couldn't be what had her so mixed up about all this, could it? Some kind of possessive feeling she had for Jax? She didn't want to own him. She *didn't*.

Jax held motionless a moment longer, then slowly turned to stare at her, the blue-green of his eyes—no brown flecks at all—shining in the stern lamps. "What did you say?"

She couldn't say it again. Couldn't believe she'd said it the first time. She shook her head at him, eyes wide, hands still clasped over her mouth.

"I *am* yours, Amanusa," he said so quietly she could scarcely hear him over the splashing of the water. "It is because I am yours, because I am bound to you with magic, that I am able to call this magic for you—"

"But I don't want you to." The words came out muffled, squeezing past her hands.

Gently, Jax peeled her hands from her mouth and held them in his. "What?"

She was better than this. *Braver* than this. She had faced down Szabo and his outlaws for six years. Somehow, that had not been as difficult or as frightening as this, as explaining—or even understanding—how she truly felt about—about *things*.

She summoned up all her courage. "I don't want you to."

Jax had to bend his head closer to hear her. When he heard, he shook it, looking up at her again. "Amanusa, if magicians in Vienna have set up another ambush, you *need* the protection this will provide you."

"I know. I just—I can't—" She twisted her hands so that she held his hands too, and tightened her grip in frustration at her inability to explain things to either one of them. "When I think about—about you, doing that. With her. With anyone—"

She had to rub a hand over her knotted stomach. "It makes me sick. Not because of what you're doing. I know it's not rape and I know you can make her like it, and that's what makes me so sick, because you're *mine*. You're *my* Jax. *Mine.*"

She was clutching the hand she still held to her chest, staring up at him, trying to find her way through to understanding. "Because it's not 'just' sex. Sex is more important than that.

"It has to be. How else could a simple kiss call up so much magic? Why else would—would what happened to me have me so afraid of sex for so many years? I think sex touches more than just your body, Jax. I think it touches your soul. And I do not want that woman to lay one red-painted fingernail on your soul."

Jax stared at Amanusa a very long moment while she blinked back tears. Strong emotion of any kind brought them on, and she hated it, because the outlaws had always seen her tears as their victory. Somehow, she didn't mind so much exposing her weakness, her emotions to Jax.

He swallowed visibly. "I—" He had to stop and

clear his throat. "I would like very much to kiss you right now."

Amanusa's lips curved in a faint smile. "I think I would like that. I would like that very much."

He lowered his head, she lifted hers, and their lips touched. He let go of her hand and she laid it on his chest over the strong, swift thumping of his heart. His hand rose to cup her face, hold her in place while he took possession of her mouth.

This time, when his tongue swept over her lower lip, she didn't startle or pull away. She opened her mouth and let him in, let him rub over her tongue and invite her to join in the sensual play. Jax's kisses felt new and fresh. Untainted, and therefore all the more precious.

He had an arm around her back, she realized, holding her up, holding her against him while his other thumb stroked along the pulse in her neck. They kissed another moment, mouths melding, tongues teasing, until he drew away into a series of kisses across her cheek toward her ear. Then he wrapped her in his arms, laid his cheek atop her head and simply held her.

And magic bloomed all around them.

Amanusa had only to gather it in and give it focus in the warding spell. "Did you kiss me to call up magic?" she asked idly as the shield nestled in around them.

"I kissed you because I wanted to. But the magic is a nice bonus." Jax turned his head to rest his other cheek on her head. "Did you kiss me for the magic? It's all right if you did. I don't mind."

"I kissed you because I wanted to." Amanusa liked

being held safe in the circle of Jax's arms. He seemed to like holding her. Her arms were squeezed between them, in the way, so she moved one of them and put it around Jax, over his frock coat, and realized that holding him was quite as nice as being held. She liked the broad solid feel of him in her arms.

"We are not private here," Jax murmured as she laid her head on his shoulder.

"I know." She sighed. "Perhaps that is why I'm not afraid. Because I know this can't go too far as long as we're out here."

"You know I will never do anything you don't want. If kisses are all you ever want from me, I will be happy with kisses."

"Liar."

His laughter rumbled through her, shook against her cheek. "There is no hurry. This spell will last long enough to get us through Vienna, and if it doesn't, there are always more kisses."

Amanusa's lip curved between her teeth and she captured it. Her old fears—the fears she was determined to defeat—were not her only reasons to hesitate. There were old promises as well. Promises made to her mother, and to herself.

"Jax?"

"Yes, my sorceress?" he said when she didn't go on.

"Will you marry me?"

Jax went so very still, she might have thought him made of wood or stone, rather than flesh and blood, save for the suddenly speeding beat of his heart under her hand.

"I know I am not the sort of wife a man dreams

of." She had to fill the stretched silence with something besides the splash of the paddle wheel and the
thump of his pulse. "I'm too tall and too pale and
not at all dainty. I'm old. Twenty-seven. I'm not
untouched—but you know that. And then there is that
whole sorceress-servant-binding matter. But if we do
get you free of the binding, and if you don't want to
be bound any other way—being divorced is no more
of a scandal than being a sorceress."

Jax still didn't react in any way. She wasn't sure he
breathed. His heart still beat, though, and his arms
still held her, so he hadn't fainted or died of shock.

Amanusa pulled back to look at him, to read what
she could in his face. But it held absolutely nothing.
Even his eyes were impossible to read. "What do you
think?" She had to know.

He blinked and seemed to come alive. "Amanusa,
I—I don't know what to say." He slid his hands
from her shoulders down her arms to her elbows.
That reassured her, that he kept his hold. "I—it's
not necessary."

"Actually, it is." She set both her hands on his
chest, on the gold brocade waistcoat that looked so
well on him. She savored the feel of the lean muscle
beneath. That wasn't wrong, was it? "I promised my
mother. I promised *myself,* back when I left the outlaw camp and went to live on my own in the cottage,
I promised that I would never have sex with another
man unless he was my husband."

She bit her lip, the tiny pain helping her deal with
the things hidden in memory. "I knew no man would
ever want to marry me, so I was safe." She adjusted his
collar which didn't need adjusting. "I see I was right."

"Amanusa." Jax captured her hands, held them over his heart. "It's not that I wouldn't be delighted to be honored in such a way. But I am your servant. I am not your equal. You should find someone who is. Someone you can love."

She couldn't meet his eyes, not after exposing herself this way. She lifted a shoulder and let it fall in a listless shrug. "I don't think I can love. I don't know that I want to." She pulled a hand from his grasp and fussed with his collar and tie again. "I trust you, though. That's more important to me than love. Besides, we've been traveling as husband and wife. Why not make it true?"

Jax took a deep breath and let it sigh out through his nose. "I don't see any need to decide things now. Let's get to Scotland, to the tower. If you still want to marry, once things are sorted, then ask me again."

It had been hard enough to ask him once, and he wanted her to do it *again*? No wonder women made the men do it. "If I ask you again, will you say yes?"

A smile quivered at his lips. "Yes, Amanusa. I will." He held up his hand to stop whatever she might have intended to say. "But you can't ask again until we reach Scotland."

She narrowed her eyes at him. "I don't want to wait until Scotland. Vienna. I'll wait until Vienna."

His smile had become a grin. "That anxious to possess my lily-white flesh, are you?"

She couldn't help laughing as she shoved herself out of his arms. "You're such a joker. I'm laughing so hard. Ha. Ha."

"You did laugh. I heard it." His smile faded from his mouth, but kept up residence in his eyes. "Paris then. When we reach Paris, if you still want it, you can ask me there. But I don't want you to take such a drastic step for fear of the Inquisition. I want you to do it for the right reasons. Or at least because of your promise to your mother."

"You don't think that's the right reason?"

He touched her cheek lightly with a fingertip. "There are many reasons to marry, Amanusa, most of them good and sensible. But only one is right."

She understood what he was trying to say, but she didn't agree. When Jax offered his arm, she took it and strolled with him along the port side walkway back to their cabin. It was settled—as far as she was concerned, anyway.

The next morning, when they were still ten or so miles out of Vienna, Amanusa lured Jax to their cabin for a kiss and a reinforcement of the protective magic spell. This time, perhaps because she felt safe in the cabin, she was able to focus on the kiss, rather than her fears. She was all too aware that it was *Jax* kissing her. It was Jax who captured her face between his hands, Jax who opened himself for her tongue's timid exploration, Jax who whispered lovely things she couldn't remember after the magic swelled. Jax made the magic possible.

Vienna was stuffed full of Inquisitors, both the regularly employed and recently drafted types. Not one of them took a second look at either Amanusa or Jax. If the Inquisition had set up a magical ambush around the city, they sailed right through it unnoticed and untouched.

Kazaryk must have remained in Budapest. Surely he had. Hungary was part of the Austrian Empire, but the Hungarian Inquisition—any Hungarian institution—was not considered the equal of its corresponding Austrian organization. Perhaps the Austrians thought Kazaryk's news a product of hysteria. Amanusa could only hope.

Her hair had lost the last of the pink tint by this time, and Jax's bruises had healed, except for a bit of yellow discoloration under his eyes. They didn't look like anyone the Inquisition might be looking for. So they exited the boat, caught a cab straight to the station, and boarded the first train bound for Paris.

In PARIS, HARRY Tomlinson stood at the edge of the dead zone, scowling at a few inches of wilted weeds. "It's growing again," he snarled.

"So I see." Grey Carteret poked at the dying greenery with his walking stick, careful not to put any of his person over the boundary. "Damn."

Then he shrugged, as if realizing his foul word didn't fit his care-for-nothing persona. "Easy come, easy go."

"If I thought you meant that, I'd knock your block off." Harry propped his fists on his hips. "Why can't they figure out what made it shrink? If we knew why it happened to start with, we'd know how to do it again. An' wot about those machines? Are they doin' this? What do they 'ave to do with—with anything?"

Grey shook his head. "Maybe it's the woman. Miss Tavis. Maybe she's working the magic."

Harry lifted his head and turned it to stare at Grey, long enough to make the conjurer fidget. "I know you said that just to stir me up. But I'm thinkin' you might be right. I'm thinkin' I might just go look Miss Elinor

Tavis up, an' if she ain't got a wizard to apprentice her yet, I'll offer. She can study wizardry if she don't take to alchemy."

Grey's air of ennui faded into a fierce grin. "Oh, that will stir up fireworks. Sir Billy won't like that at all. A mongrel out of Seven Dials spending time alone with his goddaughter." He laughed. "Oh, what a show it will be."

"Her maid can sit in on lessons." Harry scowled more. "It's not like I'm interested in *her*. Just—can she do magic? Can she stop these dead patches?"

The other man still chortled in slightly malicious glee. "You know that. I know that. And likely Miss Tavis knows it, too. She's not exactly a diamond of the ton. But Harry, nobody will *care*. The gossip will be too delicious to bother with the truth."

"I don't give a flying goose-and-duck for gossip." The alchemist stalked away from the dead and dying street. "An' if Miss Tavis really wants to learn, neither will she."

"Wait, where are you going?" Grey followed, covering ground quickly while seeming merely to stroll.

"To find Miss Tavis. No use wastin' time."

"What makes you think she'll agree? She wants to be a wizard, not an alchemist. You can't share wizard's guild secrets with her."

"Maybe not. Maybe we can figure out a way 'round that later. Maybe she won't agree to it. But it's a chance I'm offerin'. An' if she's smart, if the *magic* is wot she really wants, she'll take it."

THE TRAIN CHUGGED its way along the banks of the Danube through eastern Austria toward the Kingdom of Bavaria. Amanusa passed some of the time with sleeping, and with coaxing Crow back into his cage for porter's visits, but mostly she spent it learning magic from Jax. On the train, with the threat of the Imperial Inquisition rapidly retreating, she allowed Yvaine to emerge and dictate information, which Amanusa wrote down in the notebooks Jax produced for her.

Later, when Jax recovered from his fainting spell and bloody nose, she practiced it. Amanusa hoped that if she could leach all of Yvaine's old blood from him, he would be easier to free from Yvaine's old bindings.

There was a bit of a kerfuffle at the Bavarian border. They had to hide Crow and his cage with a bit of "don't-look" magic. Crow wasn't happy about being in the cage. Amanusa threatened to tie his beak closed if he didn't stop complaining. She was only mildly shocked when the bird seemed to understand and kept quiet during the "special exit customs" inspection.

The lone Inquisitor at the border was young and untried. It didn't take much magic to shield themselves from his inquiry. A bare hour after the halt, the train puffed on its way again. It wasn't until after they crossed from Bavaria into the Kingdom of Wurtemburg that things began to go wrong again.

13

THE TRAIN HAD just started up again after its stop in Stuttgart. Crow flew back in through the window after his brief constitutional, and Amanusa called the porter in to make up Jax's bed early. He'd been feeling ill all evening, looking far paler than usual—a pasty-gray sort of pale, rather than his healthy pinkish-pale—and it worried her. She sat up beside him for a while, to be sure he didn't get any worse.

Once they got out of the city into the countryside again, he seemed to improve. His face gained color and he breathed a bit easier in his restless sleep. Amanusa had her own bed made up and got in, determined to get some sleep. If Jax did get worse, she would need to be rested to help him. He was hers. It was her responsibility to look after him.

Crow's cawing woke her. She'd been trapped in a dream, at a party filled with glittering society, while her stomach churned violently and she had nowhere to escape to be sick. But when she woke, the nausea remained. It had shaped her dream.

Amanusa flipped onto her back, which made her stomach roll up to her throat and back down again. Where was the basin? Could she find it in time? Crow fluttered onto her bed and pecked at her hand with a harsh caw. She pushed him away as she curled onto her side around her aching belly. Crow came back and pecked her again, then flew across to perch on Jax's shoulder where he lay on his side facing her. Crow cawed at her.

"Leave me alone," she moaned. "I feel terrible."

The nasty bird refused, returning to her bed for another peck and caw before flying back to caw at Jax.

"Leave poor Jax alone too. Whatever ailment he's given me, he's had it longer." Amanusa opened her eyes to peer at Jax in the dim moonlight filtering through sooty windows.

Crow pecked at the hand lying on the pillow beside Jax's face. Jax didn't stir.

He should have. Crow's sharp beak *hurt*.

"Jax?" Amanusa rolled to the edge of her bunk, reaching across the narrow aisle to brush her fingers down his arm. That wouldn't wake him if the bird peck hadn't.

She sat up, holding her head so it wouldn't fall off, hoping her stomach would stay where it belonged. "Jax, wake up."

She shook him hard, but he didn't wake. He toppled limply from his side to his back, like a broken doll. Like a corpse.

"Jax!" She snatched up his hand, forgetting her nausea and aching head.

He took a gasping breath, coughed, and breathed in again. Dear heaven, hadn't he been breathing?

Alarmed, Amanusa crawled across to his bunk, pushing him against the compartment wall to make room for her, maintaining her grip on his hand. She brushed his hair back and laid her hand on his forehead. He felt cool, not feverish. Chilled.

Seemingly satisfied, Crow hopped off the bunk onto the top of his cage and began to preen his feathers.

"Thank you, Crow." Amanusa's gratitude was heartfelt.

She let go of Jax to drag the blanket off her bunk and the nausea slammed into her afresh. It had gone away when she touched him, but when she let go . . . She wrapped her hand around his again. Jax's chest rose as he drew in another breath. Did he breathe only when she touched him? She didn't want to test the theory.

Maintaining her grip on Jax, Amanusa spread her blanket over his. Doing the job mostly one-handed made it more difficult, but she needed to get him warm without letting go. She needed him to wake up.

Amanusa lay down atop the blankets in the tiny space at the edge of his bunk and laid her hand along his face. "Jax?"

She tucked his hand against her cheek and held it there as she slid her other hand down to the strong column of his neck. "Jax, I need you to wake up and tell me what this is. Is it Inquisitors again? Could they have followed us out of Austria?"

She shook him, more gently than her fear wanted. *"Jax."*

" 'M'nusa." Her name was slurred, but he said it. "Cold."

"I know. I'm trying to warm you."

He shivered—more of a shudder, really—and Amanusa snuggled closer, knees bumping his. "Talk to me, Jax."

She pushed his hair back off his forehead, and it flopped back down as she put her arm around him, over the blankets, trying to rub warmth back into him. Air whistled in his chest, a wheezy sound, as if he couldn't drag enough in.

"Jax!" She cupped his cheek, touched his throat, and the wheezing stopped.

Skin-to-skin. If she touched his bare skin with her bare hand, he could breathe.

Amanusa's fears stared her in the face. Either she trusted Jax or she didn't. Either she was afraid, or she wasn't. So.

She did, and she wasn't. Or wasn't very much. Jax was sick. He couldn't breathe without her naked skin against his. Right now, her hand in his, her hand on his face was enough to keep him breathing. But what if he got worse?

Was she willing to do whatever became necessary to keep him alive?

Amanusa stroked her hand down his face, studying its rough-edged structure, the full lips, deep-set eyes, strong blade of a nose, the high, broad forehead. Some might say he was a handsome man. Amanusa was a poor judge of such things. But they didn't matter. Handsome or homely, he was hers. He would not die if she could help it.

She lifted the blankets she'd been lying on and slipped under them. Next to Jax. Her bare toes brushed his shins and recoiled. But of course his legs would be bare, just like hers. He didn't sleep in his trousers. He did have on a nightshirt. His sleeping attire didn't matter. Getting him warm and breathing properly did.

She crawled over him and slid into the space next to the wall. Hiking up her nightgown, she snuggled her naked thighs up behind Jax's hard, hairy ones. She unfastened the top few buttons of his nightshirt and dragged the sleeve of her gown to the elbow, then slid her arm inside his nightshirt so that her bare forearm lay across his equally bare chest.

Unlike the bearlike outlaws she'd known, Jax had

only a faint sprinkling of hair on his chest. She'd seen before, in the torture room, when he'd been completely unclothed. Perhaps the lack of hair would help increase the contact between them. She flattened her hand just over his heart, trying for the most contact without removing any more clothing. Surely this would be enough.

It was some time before his shivering stopped and he began to breathe easier. Amanusa was drifting into sleep, her hand gone limp on his chest, when Jax tensed. His whole body went suddenly board stiff and it brought her out of her comfortable drowse, especially when his hand closed over hers.

"Jax? How do you feel?" She raised onto an elbow to see him.

"Ama—nusa?" He broke her name into pieces with his bewilderment. "Why are you—? What happened?" He started to lift her hand from his chest.

"No." Amanusa held him tight. "You stopped breathing. Something's made you sick. Made both of us sick. As long as we're touching, you breathe and my stomach stays where it should be. Is this—could it be Inquisitors?"

"I . . . don't know." He laid his hand over hers on his chest, as if holding it in place, and fell silent.

Amanusa could almost feel him thinking. "Jax?" She nudged his back with her chin when he took so long to answer that she started to fall asleep again.

"Yvaine doesn't remember any magic attack like this, not with the cold *and* the suffocation." He stroked his fingers over the back of her hand as if he didn't realize he was doing it. Or as if he hoped she would think he didn't. "And you're nauseated?"

"Yes."

"Then no, we don't think this is Inquisitors."

"Yvaine—talks to you?" She didn't like it. The old witch had given him away. He belonged to Amanusa now.

"It's more like I have access to the knowledge she stuffed inside me. She talks to you. But she lets me remember."

Amanusa dragged her lower arm out from beneath herself and tunneled her fingers into his hair to grip the back of his skull. "I want her out of here," she growled. "If she's dead, she ought to *be* dead."

"She is dead." Jax's smile sounded in his voice though Amanusa couldn't see it. "It's only memories I carry."

"Memories in her blood." She shook her head to clear it. Yvaine's tainted legacy wasn't a priority now. "So if it's not a magical attack, what is it?"

"I didn't say it wasn't a magical attack. Merely that it wasn't likely to be Inquisitors."

"Then what—?"

"It does seem to be an attack on magic. Something bent on destroying the magic that holds me together, keeps me alive." He turned his head to look over his shoulder, but couldn't turn quite enough to see her.

Amanusa scratched her short nails across his chest as she drew them together, then rubbed her fingertips along the same path as she spread them out again while she tried to remember when it was he'd said it before. She repeated his words twice before she could. "The machine. Did the machine make you feel this way? When you touched it? It made me queasy."

Jax twisted, trying to look at her again, still without success. "It was more intense, more localized, but . . . the feeling is similar."

"Can you see out the window?" Amanusa rummaged through memory again, hunting this time for Szabo's description of the place where he'd found the strange, now-dead machine.

Jax struggled onto an elbow, Amanusa rising with him to maintain the skin-to-skin contact. She couldn't see past his broad shoulders until she rose higher than he.

Dawnlight cast its pale gray illumination over a desolate landscape. The train traveled slowly through a maze of smoking factories and slum-like boardinghouses. The few trees visible were desolate skeletons, bare of leaves in the height of summer. A stream of gaunt, hollow-eyed workers trudged through the gloom toward the factories, providing the only living element in the scene. The smell of smoke and burnt metal filtered through the window, shut tight against the train's own smoke and cinders. The smell still got through.

"Whatever made the machine—" Amanusa urged Jax back down on the bunk, staring out the window a few moments more. "It's out there. There is no magic out there, except for those poor people. And . . ."

She shuddered, wondering how she felt it, but certain she did. "They're dying. Everything else is already dead, and they're next."

"Can you see an end to it ahead?" Jax asked. "Trees with leaves? Something green?"

Amanusa shifted and stretched, craning her neck to see as far as she could without having to leave the bunk and stick her head out the window. She wouldn't abandon Jax. "Not as far as I can see. It's all gray and black and brown. No green."

"Damn."

She couldn't help chuckling. "You put it so eloquently. And precisely." She lay back down behind him, snuggling in close. "So, do you think that's it? That some giant machine is attacking us?"

"Attacking us personally?" Jax craned his neck to look over his shoulder yet again.

"I hate this," he announced. "Not being able to see you when I talk to you." He twisted in the bunk, bringing his shoulders flat. They were so wide he almost tipped off into the narrow aisle between. He caught and braced himself with a hand on the other bunk, his unbuttoned nightshirt twisted half off his torso. "There." He looked up at her. "That's better.

Amanusa didn't think so. With him looking at her, there was no escaping just how close he was, or how almost-naked. They were pressed tight against each other from shoulder to toe. Amanusa fought the urge to panic, to fight her way free from the close confinement.

This was Jax. She had an urge to squeeze her eyes shut and hide from him, but didn't know if that would make the panicky feeling better. It might make it worse, make it possible to forget that *this was Jax.* She kept her eyes fastened on his, her hand and forearm plastered across his chest, and the fear smashed as flat as she could keep it.

She sat on it like some monster under the rug. It kept lurching under her, keeping her off balance, trying to break free. She refused to let it. She would *not* be afraid of Jax. What had they been discussing?

The magic illness. "It doesn't feel personal. Or much like an attack." She tried to think, to analyze what had happened, and maintain her gaze on Jax's face. "It came on gradually. More like—like a poison."

He frowned in thought and his eyes narrowed, focusing inward, giving Amanusa a bit of relief from his attention. "I'm not sure that's right," he said slowly. "It's not something added. It's something taken away. Like in a vacuum bottle." His gaze flicked up and speared into her. "There's no magic at all out there?"

"Yes. What's a vacuum bottle?"

"A bottle from which all the air has been removed. I've seen them in alchemists' laboratories. Creatures die without air."

"There are people out there, but—" Amanusa followed his thinking. "But they're dying. Because . . . it's a magic vacuum? A life vacuum."

"And because there is no magic, I cannot breathe without your touch. My thanks." Jax lifted her hand from his chest to bring it to his lips for a kiss, and began to wheeze before he got it halfway there.

Alarmed, Amanusa slapped her arm back down, yanking her sleeve higher to get more skin touching his. If she was frightened *for* him, she wasn't nearly so frightened *of* him. And she wasn't truly afraid of him. It was habit. Reflex. The automatic reaction that "large, half-naked man" meant "danger." But this man did not.

"Gratitude is well and good." She tried for a light tone. "But not at the expense of breathing."

"Breathe. Right." His smile hid fear behind it. "Are you all right? Don't drain yourself to keep me alive."

Amanusa blinked. The thought had never occurred to her. Was that what was happening? Was it even possible? "I don't feel drained," she said slowly, testing each word for truth. "I feel fine. Whole. Full of energy. Because I'm the sorceress?"

Worry swelled on a flood tide inside her. "Am I draining you?" She rose onto her elbow to peer down into his eyes. "How do you feel?"

"A bit tired, but perfectly well, as long as—" He gestured at her arm braced along his bare chest. "You know."

"Hmm." Amanusa lay down again, wriggling to fit herself into the gap between Jax and the wall. He had to grab for the opposite bunk to keep himself in place. "So. I'm the sorceress. My blood has power. Right?"

Jax gave an encouraging noise and a vague nod.

"And you're my servant. Your blood has power too, but not as much as mine."

"Any power I have comes from you."

"Yes, all right, but it's there." She was getting a bit tired of his self-effacing attitude. "The power is there. And . . . when we touch, I can tap it? Your power . . . feeds my power, which feeds back into you?"

Jax looked thoughtful. "It could be."

"So we're not draining each other, we're powering each other. Like a, a—what are those things called? That store sparks?"

"Electrical cells. But they can be drained."

"Probably we can too. I'm sure we'll need to eat and sleep to fuel our bodies. But this magic vacuum can't last forever. Can it?" She lifted her head and looked at Jax, worry rising again. She had never in her life been west of Vienna, and not out of the Carpathian mountains in fifteen years. She had no idea what the rest of Europe might be like.

"No, I'm sure it can't." He brushed a strand of hair from her face and tucked it behind her ear.

"Then we can last. We'll tell the porter we've fallen ill—it's the truth—and have our meals sent in, and we'll get through it. We're stronger together than we are apart."

At that, Jax smiled, a true, bright smile that lit up his face. "So we are," he said. "So we are."

Amanusa laid her head down again and squirmed, trying to find a comfortable position. Jax shifted to give her a bit more room and almost fell off the bunk again. His elbow, squashed up between them, poked her in the ribs. She leaned back, but that just changed the rib his elbow jabbed into. Maybe if she rotated, letting it poke into each of her ribs in turn, the discomfort could be spread out.

"Here." Jax slid his arm from beneath her and wrapped it around her shoulders. Her head now rested in the hollow of his shoulder and he held her tucked against his side. "Better?"

Much. They fit together this way. It bothered Amanusa. She wasn't afraid of him. They were partners, but it felt as if he were protecting her. Shielding her. No one had ever done that for her, not since her mother died. It felt strange. It felt . . . vulnerable. Like she needed his protection.

Maybe she did. If it was her job to protect Jax, to keep him alive, shouldn't she accept that he might think it his job to protect her? Shouldn't she be willing to accept that protection?

But depending on someone else made her weak. Didn't it?

She'd said that she and Jax were partners, but did she really mean it? In the past, she'd had no one she could depend on. She had to count on herself and only herself, because there was no one else. Not after Mama died. Ilinca was old and unable to help, even had she wanted to. But now, Amanusa had Jax.

It wasn't just that they were stronger as a team. Having Jax at her side made her stronger in herself. His belief in her made her believe in herself. His presence made her . . . kinder. Gentler. Softer. Which terrified her, because it had never been safe to be kind or gentle or soft before. And yet . . .

All this thinking made her head hurt. She yawned and snuggled in closer to Jax's warmth, finding the best spot for her aching head. She brought a knee up, but it clunked into Jax's, so she straightened it again. Knees and shins were such bony things. As she drifted off to sleep, she felt Jax press his cheek to her hair and—did he kiss her forehead? Or was that a dream-memory of Papa from so long ago?

"MR. TOMLINSON." ELINOR TAVIS nodded to the man as they passed in the heavily gilded hotel lobby.

"Miss Tavis." Harry Tomlinson stretched a hand toward her, but stopped before he actually caught her arm. "I've been looking for you. Might I have a word?"

The Cockney hovered beneath his carefully pronounced English. He gestured to a small sitting area set against the far wall, a pair of shieldback chairs with a spindly table between, beyond the cluster of businessmen talking loudly in the lobby's center.

Eyebrows rising with curiosity, Elinor gave a slight smile of agreement, a tiny nod, and laid her fingertips lightly on the tweed-clad arm he offered. He seated her on the white velvet-upholstered chair and began to speak as he took the other. Elinor's eyebrows climbed even higher in surprise as she listened. They talked, their heads drawing closer together, like a pair of conspirators. Or lovers.

They'd been conversing for several minutes when Sir William Stanwyck came through the heavy glass doors from the street. He was halfway across the lobby toward the stairs before he saw the couple. Elinor's gray-blue walking dress and Harry's dun-brown tweed did not attract notice, but Sir William saw them. Several emotions chased across his face—outrage, annoyance, frustration, exhaustion—before he seemed to settle on curiosity, and strolled across the lobby toward them.

"Afternoon, Tomlinson," he said in his hearty voice. "Elinor, my dear."

"Good afternoon, Cousin William." Elinor rose to clasp her godfather's hand.

Harry stood with her, on his best manners, and gave a quick nod of greeting to the older wizard. "Sir."

"And what might you two be discussing so intently, hiding here in the corner, hmm?" Sir William tried to keep a jovial tone, but it grated at the end.

"In the corner?" Harry looked in either direction,

the Cockney sliding back into his diction. "Corner's over there. An' over there. We're not in the corner, an' we're not 'iding. We're 'aving a conversation right out in the open."

"What about?" Sir William gave up any pretense of friendliness, his eyes and voice going flinty hard.

"Not that it's any of your business, sir," Elinor said quickly enough to forestall any retort from Harry. "After all, I am well over twenty-one and free to associate with whomever I please. And you are neither my father nor my guardian. But I do not mind telling you. Mr. Tomlinson has just done me the great honor of asking me to become his apprentice."

14

SIR WILLIAM HAD been puffing up, swelling larger and redder in the face with every word, until the last unexpected one. "His *apprentice*?" He shook his head as if to clear it.

"That's right." Harry turned a crooked smile on the older man. "Wot? You thought I arst her for me wife? Not that she ain't a sweet armful of a woman, but I know better'n to 'ope she'd accept me there. She's not a woman what wants marriage. She'd be married by now if she did. It's the magic she wants. An' if nobody else is willin' to offer it, I will."

"Take it back!" Sir William thundered.

"No, sir, I won't." Harry folded his arms across his burly chest, accent fading. "I made the offer. It's her choice to take it or not."

"You're an alchemist," the wizard blustered. "Women can't learn alchemy."

"Prob'ly not. But there's nothing in the charter says I have to teach her alchemy. It only says 'Masters shall take apprentices to teach them the workings of *magic*.' It don't say what kind o' magic. It don't say alchemists 'ave to teach alchemy or only wizards can teach wizardry. That's the way it's worked out 'cause it's what's easiest. But there's no rule says it has to be so."

"I forbid it. I forbid it absolutely." Sir William was so wrought up, spittle flew from his lips.

"You cannot," Elinor said calmly, tugging her gloves on. "Again, you are neither my father, nor my guardian."

"I'll write to him, by God. I'll tell him what nonsense—"

"Cousin William." Elinor laid her hand on his arm in an attempt to calm. "My father is not an autocrat. He does not believe in 'forbidding' his children. Nor does my mother. Browbeating with guilt, perhaps, if sweet reason does not suffice, but not 'forbidding.' No letter will change him. He will say 'Whatever Elinor thinks is right.' You know he will."

"Bloody idiot," Sir William muttered, before his eyes narrowed and his expression hardened again. "I might be merely your godfather, Elinor, not your father, worse luck. But I *am* head of the Magician's Council of England. And in that office, I can and do forbid it."

Harry was shaking his head. "No, you can't. That's in the charter too. The council has no authority over a master magician's choice of apprentice. An' it says the council *shall* educate all persons found with the ability to work magic. *Persons,* Billy. Not men. Last I looked, women were persons. Women were part of the council when the charter was written. I think it's past time they were members again."

Harry unfolded his arms and turned toward Elinor. "I made the offer. I ain't—I won't take it back. It's up to Miss Tavis whether she accepts or not. It's between her an' me an' no one else. Not you, not the English Council, or the whole International Conclave. It's *her* choice."

Harry took her hand, holding her gaze a moment before bowing over it and heading for the stairs.

"Well!" Sir William glowered after him briefly, before turning to his goddaughter. "Elinor, you can't possibly be considering—"

"Why not?" She cut him off. "Why the bloody hell not?"

He recoiled, both at her profanity and her vehemence.

"He's right, you know," she went on. "Magic is the only thing I have ever wanted, since I was a little girl. Since I discovered that I could make Mama's flowers open. And if that man is the only chance I am going to have to get the only thing I want, then nothing— do you understand me, Sir William? *Nothing and no one* will keep me from grabbing hold of that chance with both hands and holding on tight."

"Elinor." Her name was a groan in the older man's voice.

Sorrow swept across her face before it vanished behind determination as she tugged at her gloves. "I am sorry I cannot be what you think I ought,

Godfather, but we can all only be what and who we are. And I haven't actually accepted him yet. I need to think."

She checked her image in the mirror behind her. "Shopping is good for thinking." She turned and smiled brightly at Sir William. "And this *is* Paris, after all."

THE TRAIN FROM Vienna chugged deeper and deeper into the magic vacuum on its way to Paris. It would pass through regions of countryside where some magic returned and Jax could breathe, but those moments of respite came farther between as they neared the branching of the line between Karlsruhe and Rastatt, with Strasbourg and France beyond. Each time they plunged back into the magic-free areas, the vacuum was more pure than the last.

By the end, Amanusa had her nightgown torn down the back to expose skin all the way to her waist. Jax sat behind her, his only concession to modesty the nightshirt wrapped round his hips as he draped his mostly naked body over her.

They'd ripped the sleeves from her gown so she'd have something left to hold it up while he aligned his bare arms alongside hers. Her skirt was hiked up, baring her legs to rest atop his. The exposure had mortified her at first, but Jax was so matter-of-fact about it that she eventually relaxed. Then later, when he kept losing consciousness and sliding down the wall wheezing, she'd been so frightened for him that she hadn't time for embarrassment.

When the train finally crossed the Rhine into France and then chugged out of the vacuum region near the river, she fell asleep, exhausted. Jax woke before she did, and had dressed, tended to Crow, and cleaned up the compartment as much as possible with Amanusa lying unconscious on one of the bunks. His actions eliminated any "waking up in bed together" awkwardness, for which Amanusa was grateful. And yet, she couldn't help being a bit disgruntled as well.

They were almost in Paris, where Jax had promised to marry her if she asked him again. Where he'd promised to teach her the sex magic, after they were married. Wouldn't it be easier to get through that morning-after, if they'd already managed to get through this one?

Jax was behaving as if he'd never pressed his strong naked chest to her equally naked back. As if he had no idea what her bare legs might look like—or even if she had legs under her skirts. And she was an idiot for caring what he thought. Amanusa buttoned herself into her Budapest clothes and strolled with him to the dining car for breakfast.

They traveled through two more minor vacuum areas, where hand-holding sufficed to keep them feeling well, and they were in Paris in time for a late breakfast the next morning. Jax opened the compartment window to let Crow fly free. He would find them later. He always did. Then it was time to disembark, exchange tickets for luggage, locate a cab and a decent hotel.

It took Jax a few moments to realize he understood the shouting in the streets. He could speak French. Of course. He'd learned it when he was young and had traveled . . . he couldn't remember.

But he did understand the newsboy's cry about a grand reception given last night at Tuileries Palace by Emperor Napoleon III in honor of the magicians gathered for the International Conclave meeting in Paris.

He handed Amanusa into the cab and called to the boy, who scurried over with a paper and scowled as he waited for Jax to find a few sous amongst all the marks and pfennigs in his pocket. The conductor had been happy to change several marks into francs, at the exorbitant on-the-train rate.

"What is it?" Amanusa asked when Jax settled into the cab opposite her and flipped open the paper.

"The conclave is meeting in Paris."

"Yes?"

"The conclave." He set aside his impatience and pulled himself out of the newspaper to explain. She couldn't help not knowing. "Magicians in every country have a council."

Amanusa nodded.

"The conclave is the council of national councils. Representatives from all the councils—usually the head of the national council and the magister of every guild—meet together to discuss matters of importance to all magicians. Somewhat like the Congress of Vienna, but larger and much, much older. The conclave has existed since the Caesars."

"And the Congress of Vienna is . . . ?"

"Was. It was the meeting of governments after Napoleon's defeat, to decide what to do about France."

"Ah."

Jax shot a quick look at his sorceress, but she didn't seem angry, or even annoyed by his impatience and didactic tone. He smiled at her, hoping to keep her un-annoyed. "Usually the conclave meets every four years to show off new discoveries in magic study, hash over silly differences in national charters, and quarrel. This time, it appears they've called an emergency session, only two years after the last, to discuss those vacuums. They're calling them *l'endroits de la mort.* Dead zones."

Amanusa shifted position, her eyes flicking to the spell-shut machine case beneath Jax's seat. "Do you think we should give them the machine? Is that why you're so interested in this conclave?"

"Probably. I'm sure they'll want to see it. But that's not why *we* are interested." He shook out the paper and re-folded it. "Remember, I said all of the national councils send representatives. This includes the British council. Since Yvaine was a member of the British council, your claim to your inheritance as her apprentice must go through them."

"Oh. Dear." Now she bit her lip. Jax truly wished she wouldn't do that. She sighed. "I knew becoming blood sorceress wouldn't be as easy as you made it sound."

"My apologies." He had to smile at her. "But first, you already are a sorceress, and second, the British council is different from the Hungarian. It might not be easy to claim your proper place, but it should not be life-threatening.

"And—" he went on with what had occurred to him the minute he'd heard the news. "It could be easier to convince the representatives in Paris to confirm your status and your inheritance before we have to tackle the entire council. We might even be able to avoid having to take them all on, if we can get the head to approve your petition here."

"I see." Amanusa nodded, quickly following his reasoning. Her cleverness was one of the things he liked so well about her.

Jax shut that line of thought down. He was her servant. It did not matter what he liked, or whether he liked her at all. His opinion had no bearing on anything. In fact, he shouldn't *have* opinions. Ideas, yes. Especially if they benefited her. But no opinions.

"So where do we begin?" Amanusa sat back in her seat.

"At the hotel where the British delegation is staying, I should think." Jax rapped on the roof, and when the cab driver opened the window, he asked whether the man knew where *l'Anglais magique* were staying. He did, of course, and it turned out to be the same hotel Jax had already given as their destination. Coincidence? Or memory?

It didn't matter. They were in Paris. Out of Hungary. Out of the Austrian Empire and the reach of the Hungarian Inquisition. They were in reach of Scotland and home, and they could take a few days—or weeks—in Paris to ensure the secure possession of that home.

"Now what?" his sorceress prodded.

Jax looked up at her, clothed in deep green with a simple, unadorned bonnet. She was lovely, and not at all sorceress-like. "We shop. If we want these magicians to accept you as a blood sorceress and fellow magician, you must look the part. Your dress is the wrong color."

Amanusa's lips quirked in a smile. "Ah. I need red."

He shook his head. "Red is the alchemist's color—or one of them. They wear red, blue, or gray. Wizards' robes are green or brown. Conjurers wear black."

She was frowning now. "Blood is red. If a sorceress doesn't wear red, what color does she wear?"

"White."

THAT AFTERNOON, JAX sent a note requesting an audience with all the members of the British delegation three days hence, concerning a matter of utmost importance. Then he dragged Amanusa out to the dress shops, which were exactly where he somehow remembered them being.

Crow appeared at the hotel window late the next day and squawked to be let in and petted, but he disappeared again after only an hour or so. Apparently he had much business, of one crowish sort or another, in the city.

The dressmaker was delighted with the coin showered upon her establishment for the rush job. So were the milliner, the glover, and the shoemaker, who blinked at the order for walking shoes in snow-white calf leather. Jax also bought white satin slippers for their meeting.

"I'll never keep them clean," Amanusa complained as they walked down the hotel corridor to the private parlor where the meeting had been arranged. "Not slippers or shoes. With my hoops, no one will ever see them. Such an impractical color."

She stopped to look at herself in one of the massive mirrors spaced along the hallway. Her fingertips brushed the white feathers of her hat sweeping along her cheek. "Why white? You never did say."

Jax took a deep breath, counseling himself to have patience. Arriving late could be interpreted as having more power, rather than being inconsiderate. "So that any spilled blood can easily be seen. Blood is precious, not to be wasted. It shows on white so it can be retrieved."

"Oh." She looked at him in the mirror. "Why didn't you tell me before?"

Why indeed? Because he'd enjoyed being in charge of things for once in his possibly-far-too-long life? "Because you didn't ask before." He was the servant. Nothing more. Nothing else. Blood servant to his sorceress.

Amanusa blinked at her reflection. "I suppose I didn't."

"Shall we go?" Jax gestured down the hallway. He would rather arrive on time.

Amanusa looped her arm through Jax's, putting herself at his side rather than in the lead, where he knew she should be. "I'm a little nervous."

"Understandable." He scarcely got the word out before she laughed.

"No. That's a lie," she said. "I'm very nervous. You know what everyone thinks of blood magic, of sorcery. And here I come, presenting myself as the new, the one and only sorceress and practitioner of blood magic. What if they decide to burn me like they did Yvaine?"

"I wouldn't let that happen." Jax's hands tightened into fists as he drew Amanusa closer.

"You couldn't help Yvaine."

"She wouldn't let me." And her fate hadn't mattered so much to him. "She was old, and tired. The magic had hollowed her out over all the years. And it wasn't council magicians who burned her. It was a mob of civilians."

"How old was she?"

They'd reached the parlor. Jax didn't have to plumb the gaps in his faulty memory. "Remember. You are the sorceress. You hold the magic. You call the power. Don't let them intimidate you. I am your servant. I'll speak for you. You have better things to do than dealing with such mundane matters."

"Do you mean I have no idea how things are supposed to be done, or that I don't know how to deal with other magicians who aren't trying to kill me?"

Jax winked at her, trying to lighten her mood—though he was surely as nervous as she. "Both."

He knocked on the door, and when the sharp *"Come,"* rapped out, he opened it and bowed his sorceress into the room.

She swept inside, looking so beautiful, so delicate and powerful and magnificent, that he thought for an instant his heart might burst. It didn't, of course, but it felt too full to hold everything he wanted to put in it. *Would* she ask him to marry again? She hadn't so far. Did he want her to? But this was not the time to consider the matter.

Jax closed the door and surveyed the space as he stepped to the center of the private parlor. Four men rose to their feet at Amanusa's entrance. The tall gray-haired man with the mustache as massive as his head was bald was undoubtedly their leader. The three younger men—a taller, thinner blond; a shorter, dapper dark-haired gentleman, and a burly man with sandy-brown hair and rough edges not quite knocked off—Jax identified as the representatives for the wizards, the conjurers, and the alchemists, respectively. He didn't know how he knew, but he was certain of the identification. The head of the council was a wizard as well.

"Gentlemen." Jax bowed and stepped to one side as he spoke. "May I present to you Miss Amanusa Whitcomb, blood sorceress and apprentice to Yvaine of Braedun."

"Good God!" exploded from the older gentleman.

"Preposterous," sputtered the blond wizard as he crossed himself.

The stocky alchemist stared silently, intently at Amanusa.

"*Goody.*" The splendidly dressed conjurer leaned against the mantel and folded his arms as if preparing to watch a show.

"Get out." The younger wizard hurried forward, hands out to catch hold of Jax and his sorceress and propel them from the room. "How dare you? How *dare* you bring this, this whore of Babylon to—"

"'Old on there, Nigel." The alchemist caught the wizard's coattail and stopped him cold, though the wizard—Nigel—struggled. "No need to be callin' names and insultin' ladies." The alchemist's voice carried the unmistakable accents of London's East End.

"She's no lady! And he's spouting lies," Nigel shouted. "Nothing but lies. Yvaine of Braedun was burned at the stake outside Yorkminster Cathedral in 1642. This woman cannot possibly be her apprentice."

Ice ran through Jax, from the base of his skull to the end of his spine, and shot out to his extremities. He suppressed the shudder. He didn't know what year this was exactly, but he knew it was 1860-something. More than two hundred years after Yvaine's death. It didn't matter. It was still the truth.

"We're dealing with magic here, Mr. Cranshaw." The council head seemed to have recovered his composure. "It would behoove us to step carefully before we declare anything impossible."

The other wizard stopped struggling, but the alchemist kept his grip anyway. Jax approved.

The older man performed introductions, then looked pointedly at Jax, who swept into a low bow, one hundreds of years out of fashion.

"I, gentleman, am Jax, who was blood servant to Yvaine and set upon the task of finding her successor, whom I now serve."

"You expect us to believe you're two hundred thirty years old?" Cranshaw protested.

"Older'n that," Tomlinson the alchemist said. "If 'e was just two hundred thirty, he'd've been a babe in arms serving Yvaine, wouldn't he? I'd say he's two hundred sixty, at least."

Jax wanted to turn around and look at Amanusa, see how she was taking all these revelations. Better than he was, he hoped. His stomach felt twisted into knots. No wonder he couldn't remember things. He had more to remember than any human mind could store. Though he did remember more now than he had when he'd found her.

"In truth," he said, "I am closer to three hundred and sixty years old, for I served Yvaine almost a century before her death. And she was old when I was bound as her servant."

"Don't be ridiculous." Cranshaw jerked himself free of the alchemist and flopped into a chair in an act of deliberate rudeness. "You have no proof. No proof of any of this."

"Proof's in the magic," Tomlinson said.

Sir William shook his head. "He could be telling the truth."

"You cannot possibly believe any of this preposterous claptrap—" Cranshaw began, sitting up in his chair.

"There is a portrait." Sir William ignored the other wizard's outburst. "There are always portraits of current council members in the great hall, as you know. The old ones are not destroyed, simply moved into storage, or into other places in the council buildings. There is a picture of Yvaine in the library, where the books on sorcery are shelved."

"Yeah, that's right." Tomlinson nodded. "I've seen it. You seen it too, ain't you, Grey?"

The conjurer raised one bored eyebrow. "What, pray tell, does a portrait of the last sorceress have to do with the current conundrum?"

"Because Yvaine isn't the only person in the portrait." Sir William spoke ponderously, almost ominously. "The portrait has a brass plaque on it, dating it to 1557, the year Yvaine bound a blood servant upon the death of her previous one, when she was already more than a century old, so that he could be identified by council members."

"I remember." Tomlinson looked hard at Jax. "Bloody hell, it's *him*. That's the man in the painting."

"You are out of your bloody be-damned minds!" Cranshaw exploded from his chair. "This impostor might resemble the man in that painting, but he is not the same man. He cannot possibly be. The man in the painting died. He died, and has been dead for over two hundred years, set free from the abomination of serving that female."

Amanusa edged behind Jax, as if for protection. Good. Then she seemed to realize what she'd done and stepped back out. Jax moved to keep her shielded at his back.

"This is a plot cooked up by these two to get their hands on Yvaine's gold," Cranshaw ranted on. "They recognized the resemblance and—"

"How?" Tomlinson interrupted. "How could they recognize it? Nobody gets into the council library except students of the council school, magicians recognized by the council, and their apprentices. I ain't—I have never seen either one of these two anywhere on council grounds."

"Yvaine's blood servant is dead," Cranshaw insisted. "He was killed in the fire when the witch was arrested. You've studied the same history I did. The servant was struck down and left behind in the house when it was burned. *He died.*"

"No, I didn't."

Amanusa's skirts pushed at Jax's ankles when she moved closer to him. He hated these hooped monstrosities and the distance they imposed. Did she come closer for reassurance, or to offer it? Jax took whatever he could get.

Even Cranshaw fell silent at Jax's words, though more arguments were visibly building up behind the wizard's eyes. Jax dragged the memories out of the abyss where they'd fallen. "I was struck down, yes. But I didn't die. I wasn't in the house when it burned. I lost my senses for a few moments only. They'd shut me in my lady's dressing room to burn, but it had a small window. I had to dislocate my shoulder to get out, but once I got my shoulders through, the rest of me slithered out behind."

Amanusa's tiny whimper should have been too quiet for him to hear, but it cut straight through him. Was she distressed on his behalf? The shoulder had hurt like the very devil when he'd done it, but better that than burning.

"I went to liberate Yvaine. Instead, she gave me her knowledge and sent me forth to find her successor. Because of the lies told about sorcery and the women who practice it, I have been this many years at the task. But it has ended. Amanusa Whitcomb is successor to Yvaine."

"No one has ever told lies about sorcery. It is all truth," Cranshaw sputtered. "Blood magic is spawned by the devil. It relies on pain and death and torture for its power."

"How do you know?" Amanusa's voice startled everyone.

15

JAX TRIED TO interpose himself when Amanusa stepped out from behind him, but she caught his arm and pinched it in a silent *no*. He eased to one side, keeping himself closer to Cranshaw's threat.

Amanusa shared her attention among all four men. "How do you know where blood magic gets its power?" She arrowed her gaze at the younger wizard. "Have you ever used blood magic?"

"No, of course not—" Cranshaw sputtered.

"Then how do you know?"

"Everyone knows that—"

"Oh?" Amanusa cocked her head. Jax tried to watch her without taking too much of his attention from the men. "Just as everyone knows that all spirits called by conjurers are from the devil? Just as everyone knows all alchemists are greedy, and all wizards steal babies and trade them to the fairies in exchange for magic?"

"Myth." Cranshaw dismissed her with a wave of his hand. "Fabrications of fearful minds that—"

"Then why is it impossible to believe that what 'everyone knows' about sorcery might also be the fabrication of a fearful mind? If blood magic draws its power from death, why can only women—who bear the life of each new generation—practice it? Doesn't new life come in blood and pain? Pain willingly borne, blood willingly shed by those who bring forth life?"

"Whore! Abomination!" Cranshaw was almost

frothing at the mouth. The other magicians stared at him with various expressions of disgust, worry, and amusement. Jax watched him for the first sign of attack.

"Good Gad, Cranshaw, there's no need for histrionics." Sir William frowned at the younger wizard. "Get hold of yourself, man. We don't know anything about blood magic or where the power comes from. That knowledge died with Yvaine. The witch burnings took more than enough of our numbers. It wasn't just Yvaine who fell. Plenty of conjurers and wizards went up in smoke as well. We do not want to start that nonsense up again."

"Why don't you know anything?" Amanusa sailed a bit farther into the room, Jax doing his best to stay ahead of her. "Didn't you say you had books of sorcery in your library? Doesn't anyone read them?"

"I thought you said you were Yvaine's apprentice," Cranshaw said scornfully.

"Only a magician with a talent for sorcery can open 'em." Tomlinson ignored the wizard. "An' there 'asn't been any since Yvaine. We been lookin', but apparently not in the right places. Where did 'e find you? Yvaine's servant, I mean."

"Jax is *my* servant now."

Jax liked the way she said that. Quick. Possessive.

"Abomination," Cranshaw muttered. "No man should serve a witch." Everyone ignored him.

"I was born in Vienna to an English father and Romanian mother," Amanusa continued. "After the 'Forty-eight, I lived in Transylvania, where Jax found me."

"What magic can you do?" Tomlinson offered her

a seat on one of the armless ladies' chairs near the high wingback chairs where the men had been sitting.

Cranshaw burst out again. "You cannot possibly be considering—"

"Shut up, Nigel," Tomlinson said.

Jax took the opportunity to assist his sorceress into the seat. It took a moment to adjust the hoops. Amanusa had been practicing, but neither of them had much experience with the things and they were blasted hard to sit with. Women's fashions made no sense.

"I have a solid knowledge of the workings of sorcery and can work a number of varieties of spells with it," she said when everyone was seated—Cranshaw sprawled again, sulking. Jax stood properly at her elbow. "I can heal serious wounds. I can cast illusions and protective shields, against physical intrusion as well as magical attack. And I can answer the cry of innocent blood for justice."

"You don't believe—"

"*Shut up,* Nigel." It was the conjurer, Carteret, who said it this time.

In the commotion created by that little disagreement, Amanusa whispered the words to turn their eyes away from Jax, and he felt the magic prickle against his skin. They'd agreed that the invisibility spell would be the best for their purposes, since it was unlikely anyone would agree to be injured for her to heal, and they had no innocents handy needing justice. Before leaving their room, Jax had tucked a smear of his own blood in his hairline for Amanusa to call. Better his blood than hers. He didn't like seeing her skin pierced.

"I admit," Amanusa said when Cranshaw had subsided again, "that my control is not yet perfect, especially when dealing with the blood of innocents shed in horrific crimes. But I am improving with every day that passes."

"Can you demonstrate, Miss . . . Whitcomb, is it?" Sir William gave her a frosty smile.

Amanusa smiled sweetly back at him. Jax shivered at the ice beneath its surface. "I already am, sir. Do you see my servant, Jax, in this room?"

"You have no servant," Cranshaw snapped. "What is this nonsense?"

Tomlinson frowned. Carteret's eyebrows climbed his forehead. "I seem to recall—" the conjurer drawled. "Wasn't there someone—?"

"A man came in with 'er," Tomlinson said. "'E introduced her, said she was a blood sorceress an' then 'e . . ."

Sir William leaned forward, squinting at the place where Jax stood. Jax moved to Amanusa's other side, but the older gentleman's eyes did not track him.

"I see 'im." Tomlinson pointed straight at Jax. "There. I saw 'im move."

"You're barking mad." Cranshaw sprawled again. "She never had a servant."

Sir William frowned, following Tomlinson's finger toward Jax's new position. "Are you sure?"

"Sure I'm sure. He's there." Tomlinson narrowed his eyes, peering through his lashes. "He's kind o' shivery-shiny. Like mirrors an' chameleon-colors mixed together. He's hard to see, but he's there."

"Yes." Carteret squinted at Jax. "I can see him now."

Amanusa snipped the spell with a flick of her fingers and Jax returned to visibility.

"I thought you were a stronger magician than that, Nigel," Carteret drawled, leaning back in his chair. "You completely forgot the man's existence."

The blond wizard flushed red, all the way to his thinning scalp. "Smoke and mirrors," he snarled, but his denial felt weak to Jax.

Tomlinson sniffed. "Don't smell no smoke. Not even from the fireplace. An' I don't see any mirrors. I vote we admit 'er to the council."

"Absolutely not!" Cranshaw exploded with venom once more.

Jax moved aside, away from the barrier of his sorceress's hoops, ready for potential attack.

"Apart from the issue of blood sorcery—which is not so easily set aside as you might suppose," Cranshaw was saying. "There is the inescapable fact of her sex. She is a woman!"

"Yeah. So?" Tomlinson seemed unconcerned.

"The practice of magic is not a feminine pursuit. Women cannot be, *must* not be, admitted to the council. They have no place in the Council Hall."

"Women helped build that precious Council Hall of yours," Tomlinson retorted. "They were part and parcel of the council from the day it was started until so many were burnt in the witch hunts that killed Yvaine. Same history you was quotin' just now, Nigel. The council agreed not to take women as apprentices for a while. 'Til it was safe for 'em. 'Til they weren't so likely to be burnt."

The Cockney alchemist looked from one man to the next, intent on his audience. "I ain't 'eard of anybody bein' burned as a witch lately, 'ave you? Not in a 'undred years or better. I think it's past time we brought 'em back. We need women's magic. I think we need more than just one sorceress, but if she's all we got, I think we'd be idiots to turn her aside."

"She is evil," Cranshaw hissed.

"Oh for—" Tomlinson shut his teeth on oaths even Jax could see wanted out.

"Control yourself, man," Sir William snapped. "You cannot go about making such accusations without any proof, on the basis of mere prejudice."

"Are you all mad? She practices blood sorcery. Blood sorcery is evil, therefore *she* is evil."

"Who says?" Tomlinson took up Amanusa's cause. Jax wished he knew why. Because he believed in her? Or because he thought it would give him the chance to bed her? Jax stifled the incipient jealousy he had no right to feel. An alchemist was a far better match for a sorceress.

"Why would raising magic through blood be any more or less evil than conjuring spirits of the dead?" Tomlinson demanded. "Magic's magic. It's all in how it's used as to whether it's evil or not. Why d'you think we got Inquisitors and Briganti and Massileans and such? To catch the folk wot use it wrong. Sayin' it's evil just 'cause of the kind of magic it is, is the same thinkin' that got Yvaine and all those wizards and conjurers killed along with 'er."

"Where does the blood come from?" Cranshaw's eyes showed white all around, his voice hoarse with terror.

"Women bleed every month, Mr. Cranshaw,"

Amanusa said, matter-of-factly. "Does that frighten you? Is that evil?"

Cranshaw blanched. Sir William looked shocked. Carteret grinned and Tomlinson burst out laughing. Jax smothered his own grin. He had been gone from polite society a long time, but he was fairly certain such things weren't discussed in mixed company even in these modern days.

Amanusa didn't back down. "I realize it is most indelicate of me to speak of such things with men present, but I have it on good authority that this is why women have their affinity for blood magic. More than that, I cannot say. There are things held secret by your own disciplines to be known only to those who practice those arts."

"By God," Tomlinson murmured, staring at Cranshaw. "I think you might be right. I think the man is afraid of women."

"Preposterous." Cranshaw flung himself to his feet. "I will not stay and listen to any more of this lunacy. I am unalterably opposed to the admission of this or any other woman to the ranks of magicians. I vote nay, and I will never cease my opposition."

He stormed from the room, the other occupants carefully not watching him go, staring mostly at the carpet until the door boomed shut behind him.

"Well, I vote aye," Tomlinson said then, into the quiet. "That's one for and one against. Makes you the tiebreaker, Grey. What do you say?"

As everyone's eyes turned to the aristocratic conjurer, his air of languid ennui dropped slowly away until he sat straight in his chair, the hard planes of his narrow face making him seem almost a different man entirely. "I also say aye. Admit her.

"I agree with Harry," Carteret went on. "Until we know what caused these dead zones and how to stop them, how to restore life to them, we cannot afford to exclude any possibility. Sorcery has been lost for two hundred years. Who knows how long the dead zones have been growing to become what they are today? Perhaps it was the loss of sorcery that enabled them to grow."

Jax scarcely dared hope as all eyes turned to Sir William. As head of the council, he didn't vote except to break a tie, but he could still affect decisions, especially decisions like this, made outside a full council session.

"I don't know." Sir William took a deep breath and puffed it out again, setting his mustache to fluttering. "Two to one. But Cranshaw has a point. Not about sorcery being inherently evil, but about plunging recklessly into things. Until we can return to England and compare this man with the painting, until the full council can meet to approve membership, we must be cautious."

Tomlinson leaned forward, propping an elbow on his expensively clad knee. "Billy—Sir William—we *need* the magic. 'Ere we been moanin' an' groanin' for fifty years or better 'cause we lost sorcery, 'cause there ain't been no sorceress for so long, an' now we got one come to us out of nowhere, out of the wilds of the east, and *you don't know*?" His voice rose to a near roar.

"Was it all just words?" Tomlinson dropped his volume again, this time to a near whisper. "As long as there was no chance of anybody turnin' up who could do it, you could go ahead an' wish for it, but now she's here, you changed your mind? Are you that afraid of change, Billy?"

Sir William wouldn't meet the alchemist's eyes, staring stubbornly at the carpet.

"Or is it that if you admit Miss Whitcomb, it'll be that much harder to argue against your goddaughter learning magic?" Tomlinson said gently. "It's poor thinking, either way."

Jax silently cursed fate. If they'd got caught up in the midst of a domestic quarrel, it couldn't help their cause.

Sir William pursed his lips, pressed them together, worked his jaw, all the while staring between his boots. "Provisional," he said finally. "Miss Whitcomb is granted provisional membership in the Council of Magicians for Great Britain, awaiting confirmation by the plenary council, and proof of her apprentice-ship to Yvaine of Braedun."

He stood and raked his gaze across the others. "As Yvaine was a member of the council, we cannot deny membership to her apprentice. If Miss Whit-comb is indeed Yvaine's apprentice. Which has not yet been proven to my satisfaction. If she is found to be otherwise, then her petition to join will of course be denied."

Sir William left the room and Tomlinson jumped to his feet, cursing, followed promptly by an apology for his language. "If he thinks he'll get around me that way, he's wrong. I'll take both of you as my ap-prentices if I 'ave to."

"Oh, no fair, Harry," Carteret protested, putting on his air of boredom again as he returned to his slouch.

"You can't have all the lady magicians as your apprentices."

"Stubble it, Grey," Tomlinson snarled. "It's about magic an' nothin' else, an' you know it." He pulled a pocket watch from his waistcoat pocket and flipped it open. "Afternoon session of the conclave's set to start up at three. We got just enough time to corner Sir Billy and convince him to present Miss Whitcomb to the lot of 'em."

Carteret's face slowly filled with an unholy glee. "Oh goody," he drawled. "Fireworks."

Sir William reluctantly agreed to accompany them and present Amanusa to the conclave. The potential restoration of sorcery was a matter of vital interest to the group. Nigel Cranshaw was nowhere to be found, which made more than Jax wonder what he might be doing.

The session had already started when the party arrived at the French *Chambre de Conseil,* their council hall where the conclave was meeting. As Tomlinson held the door for Amanusa, an usher leaped halfway across the lobby to throw himself into the breach and bar her way.

"Magicians only, *monsieur,*" he gasped, hands raised as if to block even Amanusa's sight of the proceedings.

"This is a magician," Tomlinson said. "Miss Amanusa Whitcomb. Sorceress. Practitioner of—"

"La sorcellerie du sang," Carteret filled in. *"Elle est une sorcire."*

The man blanched, but stood his ground. *"Impossible."*

"She is a member of the British council. You're required to admit all members of a national council, aren't you?" Tomlinson insisted.

Throughout the lobby, and even in the back of the hall itself, heads were turning, people—men—stopping what they were doing to watch the goings on. Amanusa wanted to shrink away, to hide and quiver and say, "Never mind. It's too much bother." So much notice had always been dangerous. She wanted to cower—but she wouldn't. She couldn't.

Jax had said it. She was a blood sorceress. She couldn't unlearn the knowledge she'd been given. Nor did she want to. She wanted to learn more. She wanted to use this power to prevent others from suffering as she had—or to give them justice if all else failed.

Mr. Tomlinson seemed to think her magic could help in the magicians' fight against the magical vacuum, the dead zones. She already knew her magic could help the weak and powerless find justice. She refused to throw it all away because it was proving difficult to reach her goal. She had survived the outlaw camp. She had beaten them. She could survive this. And she would win.

"Magicians only," the usher was saying yet again.

"An' I'm tellin' you, she is a magician." Tomlinson was equally stubborn.

"Enough of this." Sir William finally stepped up and identified himself. "Stand aside, man. Now. This is a matter for magicians."

As she passed through the door, Jax faded back as if to remain outside the chamber. Amanusa grabbed his hand and hauled him along behind her. They hadn't been separated for more than a few moments of time since his imprisonment and torture in Nagy Szeben. She would not be separated from him now, not in the midst of this crowd of powerful, potentially hostile men.

Tomlinson was on her side. Possibly Carteret as well, but she couldn't expect him to lift a finger in her defense if things went badly wrong. She wanted Jax. She could count on Jax.

No one challenged his admission to the council hall. Only hers.

Amanusa wrapped her hands around Jax's arm, taking comfort in its strength, insisting on his escort at her side when he would have walked behind. As they advanced down the aisle toward the front and the only place where chairs had been placed widely enough to accommodate her skirts, shocked silence rippled across the Great Hall, spreading from the point of her impact.

She held her head high, putting all the composure she possessed into her steps. She was Amanusa Whitcomb, blood sorceress. If they insisted on fearing what she could do, then *let them be afraid.*

The man at the podium, up on the dais, tried at first to carry on as if nothing were happening. It seemed he didn't quite know what to do, whether to stop or continue. On the heels of the first stunned silence, a babble of conversation rose as those who could not see demanded to know what was going on, and those who could see began to discuss what it meant. Those on the platform gathered, conferred, and as the volume of voices rose, a few beginning to shout, a blond man wearing a red velvet stole and a gold cord draped around his neck seized the gavel from the man who held it. He began pounding on the podium, shouting at the crowd in German, demanding quiet.

That didn't help much, so he shouted in German-accented French, then in English, and in French again. It took several minutes for the noise to subside, the blond man banging his gavel the entire time. When it was mostly quiet, someone shouted once more. In French, this time.

Amanusa looked up at Jax, who understood her silent question and translated. "He wants to know why a woman has been permitted to enter these sacred walls."

She could understand Jax, whatever language he spoke, just as he could understand her, but everyone else had to speak English, Romanian, or German.

"Here." Tomlinson nudged her and held his hand out. "Take this. I got another."

Curious, Amanusa turned her hand palm up. The alchemist dropped a pebble into it and suddenly, she could understand everything being said. She turned surprised eyes up to him.

"Translation stone," Tomlinson murmured. "Specialty of alchemy. Stick it in your pocket an' you'll do fine."

"Thank you, sir." Amanusa tucked the small stone away just as the German with the gavel turned to glare at Amanusa from beneath beetled brows and demanded to know the meaning of this.

Sir William straightened to his full, considerable height, and stepped forward, addressing the presiding officer, turned so the whole chamber could hear him as well. "This young woman is here to represent the sorcerers of Great Britain."

Immediately the chamber exploded once more into cacophony, and the blond at the podium started pounding again. It didn't take quite so long this time to quiet everyone.

Sir William continued when he could. "Miss Amanusa Whitcomb has demonstrated an aptitude and a knowledge of sorcery sufficient for admission to the British Magician's Council—"

Amanusa raised an eyebrow at that. She supposed the older wizard might not want to air all their private doings before the conclave, showing a united front, and all that.

"As a member of a duly-constituted national council," Sir William went on, "she is therefore required to be admitted to this conclave, particularly as she is the only delegate for sorcery from any nation at the moment, and particularly since the challenge we face, of these *endroits de la mort* is so great as to call for all four of the great magics practiced by our predecessors."

Once more the council hall erupted into chaos. The president didn't try to restore order. He sent a group of stout fellows in striped sashes to collect the English delegation, gathered up the gentlemen on the dais, and left the chamber.

Amanusa clung tightly to Jax's arm as they were escorted through a door near the dais and the warren of corridors behind it to a room set up with a large table ringed by chairs. The men from the platform were already there.

"What have you been hiding from us?" The German pounced the instant Sir William came through the door. "It was agreed. Any council that rediscovered any knowledge of sorcery would immediately inform the other councils. And you have learned enough to have your own sorceress? This is not acceptable. How dare you keep this hidden? How dare you—"

"We haven't hidden anything," Sir William roared back in the face of the German's outrage.

"There it is!" The blond threw an accusatory hand in Amanusa's direction. "There is what you have hidden, the knowledge you have refused to share."

"Gentlemen." Amanusa had to put a touch of power into her voice to get their attention. "Flinging accusations before you know the facts accomplishes nothing, Herr—?"

"Gathmann." He clicked his heels into a precise military bow, a slight flush staining his cheeks, doubtless because she'd reminded him of proper manners. "Georg Gathmann. Alchemist. Praetor of the Prussian Magician's Council and therefore president of the conclave for this term."

He introduced the others with him, officers of the governing board, from the United States, Russia, Egypt, Sweden, and France. There were other governors, from India and Brazil, but they hadn't been able to travel to Paris in time for this emergency session of the conclave.

Niceties out of the way, Gathmann turned on Sir William again. "How have I been 'flinging accusations,' sir? What feeble explanation can you offer for this?"

"Only that we are just now bringing Miss Whitcomb's existence to the attention of the conclave because we first learned of her existence no more than an hour ago."

Gathmann looked taken aback by the news. "You have not been secretly educating her in your hidden tower?"

"That hidden tower is a myth," Sir William retorted. "It does not exist—"

"Actually, it does," Jax interjected. "At least, I believe it still does. It should. Yvaine laid quite a lot of protection around it before we left that last time. It should still be exactly as she left it."

"And how would you know where that is?" Suspicion and fear rode every line of Gathmann's lanky frame. "Where is it?"

"In Scotland," Jax said. "In the remote Highlands. I know because I was Yvaine's blood servant. When she died, I was sent to find Yvaine's successor, and finally, I have."

Amanusa hoped they didn't get into another discussion-slash-argument of whether or not it was possible for Jax to be three hundred years old. She hadn't yet wrapped her mind around the idea, but his age wasn't relevant at the moment.

"Gentlemen," she spoke up again, hoping to divert them from Jax. "The issue here is the magic. *Sorcery.* Are you going to lose it again simply because you're afraid of it?"

"I am afraid of nothing!" Gathmann announced.

"Why are you not sorcerer?" the Russian conjurer demanded of Jax. "Were apprentice. Why not sorcerer?"

"I was Yvaine's servant, not her apprentice," Jax said. "Her blood servant, bound to her by magic."

"What are you now?" the Russian said. "Yvaine is dead."

"I am Miss Whitcomb's—"

"Betrothed." Amanusa got the word in quickly. She didn't want Jax shunted to the edges, or even pushed out of the room. He *was* her betrothed. Essentially. He'd promised to marry her when they got to Paris, if she asked him again. That was betrothed enough for Amanusa. "We are engaged to be married."

16

EVERYONE STARED. MOST of them gave Jax pitying looks. Mr. Tomlinson's expression was neutral. Mr. Carteret blinked, then grinned and extended his hand.

"Felicitations, my dear." He bowed over her hand, then shook Jax's.

Tomlinson followed suit, looking as if he had much he wanted to say, but wouldn't for now. No one else congratulated them, or even looked congratulatory.

"But—" Gathmann said, "if you haven't been educating her in some secret school, where did she come from?"

"Transylvania." Amanusa rather enjoyed shocking them all again. "I came to the British council because I am Yvaine's successor and her membership was in Britain. And because the Austrian Empire is even less amenable to sorcery and female magicians than you are. Especially in Transylvania and Hungary."

The way the conclave officers stared seemed to hold more than surprise at her origins, more meaning, more portent, more—

"You came to Paris through Hungary?" Gathmann asked.

"Why?" Tomlinson spoke up. "What's been happening?"

"Our investigators finally reached Vienna and Budapest, and have been able to send word back to us here. No one was available in the national offices to answer our questions because all of the magicians in the Austrian Empire were called out to hunt down a dangerous criminal." Gathmann's gaze fastened on Amanusa at those words and tried to bore inside her head.

She refused to let him in. The man was an alchemist. Only blood magic could see inside another's heart and mind. "If it is a crime to be female and practice magic—and it *is* illegal in Hungary—then I suppose I am indeed a criminal."

Amanusa let go of Jax, hoping he'd spoken truly when he said the white made her look delicate and ethereal. She held out her hands, wrists together as if already bound. "Do you agree? Am I evil? Should I be locked away and punished? Then do it. Arrest me."

It was Sir William who cleared his throat, who looked away as if embarrassed. "I'm sure that won't be necessary."

"The reports claimed this criminal magician left a trail of death and destruction." Gathmann didn't back down.

Amanusa lowered her hands and raised an eyebrow. "Is defending oneself from attack considered a crime now?"

"If that attack comes from duly-constituted authority, yes."

"And if they had succeeded in destroying me, would you have scolded *them* for hiding evidence of sorcery's return? Or would you have ever known of it?"

Gathmann frowned as he opened his mouth for a retort, but apparently could find nothing to say.

"If you ask me," Tomlinson said, ignoring the fact that no one *had* asked him, "the criminals are the ones who were hunting her down. Simply practicing magic shouldn't be a crime, no matter who's doing the practicing. The only crime is what's done with the magic. And any councils that have laws saying this person or that can't have magic should be told to change their laws or get out of the conclave."

"This is not acceptable!" The Egyptian governor jumped to his feet. "The laws of the—"

"We are not here to discuss changing national charters." Gathmann cut him off. "This conclave is strictly for the purpose of finding ways to deal with the dead zones."

"About that—" Tomlinson strolled farther into the room and propped a hip on the polished wood of the table. His accent slipped back toward Cockney as he stopped paying such close attention to it. "The dead zones shrank four weeks ago, exactly. Twenty-eight days back. We 'aven't been able to find any magic anybody worked that could've caused that change."

Amanusa shrank toward Jax under the intensity of the look Tomlinson turned on her. The warmth of Jax's hand settling in the small of her back gave her back her confidence.

"Wot I want to know is this—" Tomlinson's eyes bored into Amanusa much more effectively than Herr Gathmann's had. She'd thought the English alchemist an ally. "Did Miss Whitcomb work any magic that might account for the dead zones shrinkin' that day?"

"Twenty-eight days past?" Amanusa looked up at Jax. She'd lost track of time while they'd traveled. "We've been four days in Paris. How long on the train from Vienna?"

Together they counted up the days until they reached the day they had left the outlaws' camp.

"I worked blood magic that day," she said. "I answered the call of innocent blood for justice."

"A great working?" Tomlinson asked. "Powerful magic?"

So powerful it had escaped her control and come close to destroying her, along with those who'd been judged and condemned for their crimes. But she wasn't telling them that. "Yes. It was the first time I had done such powerful magic."

"Have you done it since?"

"Like that?" Amanusa shook her head. "No. I have done justice magic. Innocent blood was spilled and I used it in our defense. But it was not so great a working. Fewer crimes, fewer criminals."

"You say your enemies are the criminals." Gathmann sounded scornful. "Criminals always claim innocence. Always blame the law for being in the wrong, abusing its power. It is *the law.*"

Amanusa turned her head to stare at the Prussian, using her gaze as he tried to use his earlier. She was more successful, for Gathmann flushed and looked away. "The law can be used to protect the people from those with power and wealth, or it can be used as a bludgeon against the powerless. Surely, in the years since Yvaine's death, when sorcery was lost to you, the magician's councils have not forgotten that innocent blood will cry out for justice, and that only sorcery can hear that cry."

Most of the others could not meet her eyes either. The American governor, a brash young man with a gray alchemist's stole over his shoulders, was one of the few who did. "Yeah, I've heard that. I've also been told that blood doesn't lie. That true too?"

Amanusa inclined her head. "It is. Blood carries only truth."

The Egyptian's eyes narrowed as he glared at her. "But the sorceress—being a woman and therefore weak—she can lie."

Gathmann cut him off. "We are not getting into that debate."

Tomlinson spoke up again. "Seems to me the important thing here is that the first time Miss Whitcomb cut loose with powerful sorcery is also the first time these dead zones ever shrank instead o' growin'. Seems obvious to me that shows 'ow much we need the sorcery she can work. Don't matter 'ow offended you are by the idea of a female doin' magic. Be offended all you want. But don't you dare say we don't need 'er. And don't you dare say she can't be what she already is. She *is* a sorceress."

"If you bunch don't want her working magic here

in the Old World," the American said, "we'll take her in America. Her and her fella. We're not so stuck in the old ways of doing things."

"Miss Whitcomb is a member of the British Magician's Council," Sir William said stiffly.

Amanusa thought it was rather dog-in-the-mangerish of him. He didn't particularly want her, but he didn't want any of the others to have her or her magic either.

While all the men stood about scowling at her, Jax leaned forward to murmur in Amanusa's ear, reminding her of the machine they'd lugged all the way from the rebel camp.

"Speaking of the dead zones . . ." Amanusa reluctantly called their attention back her way. "We have a machine, a thing that moved on its own and attacked a man, that we think came from one of these dead zones. We brought it with us, sealed in a case. I can handle it, but Jax cannot. If you have scholars—"

"Yes, excellent. This is excellent news." Gathmann rubbed his hands in apparent delight. "We did not know about such machines until Herr Tomlinson encountered one that day, the day of the shrinking. We have seen them ourselves. Our magicians have been trying to catch one ever since, without much luck."

"We will be happy to turn it over—"

"I'll take you," Tomlinson offered. "The blokes in the laboratory'll want to quiz you about it. About everything, I reckon."

"No decision has been made about admission to the conclave," the Russian conjurer said.

"If she is a member of the British council, any decision before the conclave regarding admission is moot," Gathmann said. "She is a British magician, therefore she is recognized by the conclave."

"Egypt will never recognize a woman—"

"Egypt does not have to," Gathmann said. "Nor does Hungary or Transylvania or Turkey or anyone who does not wish to recognize her. But Egypt is not the conclave."

"Bloody good thing, too," Tomlinson muttered.

Amanusa wondered if Sir William would reveal her provisional status, but he remained silent.

"Very well." Gathmann came to attention. "Let us return to the *Chambre de Conseil* for the announcement to the conclave. However, I think we should keep this news among magicians only. The public might not take well to knowing that blood sorcery is once more among us. We do not want to upset them."

When they went back into the council hall, Gathmann insisted Jax wait in the lobby, since he had admitted he was no magician. Then the Prussian made Amanusa climb the platform with him and the other governors for the announcement. She felt vulnerable standing on the dais with all those men staring at her, without Jax at her side. But at a distance, she could sense Jax's supportive presence. It helped.

Herr Gathmann's announcement that Amanusa was accepted by the conclave as a sorcery-practicing magician caused an uproar in the chamber. Several of the delegates attempted to walk out of the proceeding, but the Praetor-President had stationed burly ushers at every door to prevent it. When the shouting finally quieted, he explained his reasoning and his request to keep the news from the general populace.

"This is a matter that concerns magicians, and magicians alone," he bellowed over the residual noise. "Only we know what is truly at stake here, and only we know the truth about sorcery."

"Evil!" someone screeched from the back. "Spawned by Satan!"

Amanusa wondered if it might be the English wizard, Mr. Cranshaw, but the room was too tumultuous and the voice too strained for her to be sure.

"It is *magic*!" Gathmann shouted back. "And it is not a matter for the uninitiated."

Amanusa hadn't actually been initiated either. She wondered what initiation might entail.

"Do you swear?" Gathmann called out.

Amanusa felt magic rising, magic tasting of earth and of green growing things, and of a sharpness that had to be conjury, and she wondered whether she ought to—or could—add in the coppery blood-taste of sorcery. Then again, they weren't used to even the idea of sorcery. Best not to confront them with its reality yet.

"*Swear.*" Gathmann's voice rode the magic, reaching every corner of the dark, wood-paneled chamber. "Swear that you will keep this knowledge, magician's business, to magicians alone. Swear that you will reveal it only to those who have a right to know."

Amanusa winced. He shouldn't have added that last bit. Some might use it as a loophole to tell whomever they pleased, because they "have a right to know." Perhaps Gathmann intended it. Perhaps he wanted non-magicians to know, wanted to incite a riot and get rid of her that way. But they were already swearing, locking the oaths in with magic to prevent betrayal.

Maybe Gathmann was only bad with words, rather than malicious. Or perhaps he was stupid, which was as troublesome. Amanusa wished she knew. Maybe she could sneak a bit of magic into his tea. . . .

"Miss Whitcomb?" Tomlinson stood at the edge of the dais, bouncing on his toes. "You ready to fetch that machine o' yours? The lads'll be gobsmacked to see it."

And Jax would be waiting for her in the lobby. "Yes." She hurried down the steps, remembering to bob a farewell curtsy to the governors at the last minute.

Tomlinson plowed a path through the throngs in the aisle. Amanusa's hoops jostled her this way and that as she tried to keep up with him, as those he'd moved aside pressed in again to slake their curiosity or vent their outrage. "Oh!"

A pair of particularly persistent men coming at her from either side managed to crack one of her hoops. Tomlinson whirled, grabbed the nearest by his jacket, and flung him aside. "Leave off!" he roared. "She's a lady!"

"She's a sorceress!" someone shouted back.

The crowd around her felt more curious than threatening, but there was enough menace to it that fear skittered up Amanusa's spine. *Never let them see it.*

She tossed her head, hoping to draw attention to her clever feathered cap as she drew off one of her gloves and slipped her bare hand into her pocket. The pocket where she kept her sorcerer's lancet.

"Yes." She pitched her voice where it would carry. "I am a sorceress. And so, even if you do not believe I deserve the courtesies usually rendered to a member of my sex, do I not at least deserve respect? Respect for the magic I wield? For the magic in blood?"

She raised her hand, finding a spot of light to reflect off the polished silver tip of the lancet on her forefinger. She curled her fingers, making them graceful, with only a hint of claw, save for the one with the lancet. That one she used to point at the men crowding her. As she pointed, they backed away. "I will demand compensation from the conclave for the damage to my wardrobe," she said. "But from you, I demand respect."

Amanusa looked pointedly at the men standing in the aisle, in her way, trying her best to imitate Inquisitor Kazaryk's intimidating, imperious glare. She must have copied it well, or perhaps it was the lancet on her finger that she flicked from side to side, gesturing for a clear path, for they melted away. She gathered her sagging skirts in both hands and swept forward, hurrying in hopes that no one would change his mind before she reached Jax.

He was at the door, helping the ushers clear the way, holding back the magicians who had come through the lobby wanting a look at her, a piece of her. She smiled and nodded, shook the hands of those who seemed less aggressive, and finally the lobby began to clear. Amanusa took a deep breath in relief.

Jax smiled his faint smile and patted her hand as he tucked it in the crook of his arm. "Enthusiasm can be exhausting."

"I do think I've had all the enthusiasm I can take for a while." She strolled with Jax toward the door. "But we still have to deliver that machine to Mr. Tomlinson's 'lads.' And answer their questions."

"More enthusiasm," he said gloomily.

Amanusa laughed. She was still laughing as they emerged from the building into the afternoon sunshine where the English delegates waited on the steps. As she descended with Jax to join them, holding up her broken hoop with one hand, a smallish woman in dark green came rushing up the other way.

"Uncle Billy—Sir William, is it true?" The woman came to a panting halt, hoops swaying, on the step below the group of men. "I heard you admitted a woman to the council as a magician."

She spotted Amanusa coming down the steps and darted around the men. "Are you the one? The magician?" Her somewhat plain face was alight with excitement, alive with eagerness, and the glow made her pretty, if not outright beautiful.

Amanusa had to smile at her. "I am Amanusa Whitcomb. This is my fiancé Jax. I am the new—" She broke off, looking at the busy street below. "I am a magician, yes."

"Provisional status," Sir William harrumphed. "Pending confirmation of her apprenticeship to Yvaine of Braedun."

"Yvaine . . ." The young woman's mouth dropped open, then the light in her eyes returned, fiercer than before, and she seized Amanusa's hand, the skirt falling to drag on the stairs. "This is marvelous. To have the return of—"

"We're keeping that bit quiet just now, Miss Tavis,"

Tomlinson interrupted, controlling his accent. "To keep from alarming the civilians."

"Miss Whitcomb." Sir William couldn't have been any stiffer if he had a fence post sewn up the back of his coat. "Mr. . . . Jax, forgive my goddaughter for her shocking lack of manners. This is Miss Elinor Tavis. Who should not be in Paris at all."

"Are you a magician, Miss Tavis?" Amanusa could sense a faint aura coming through the hands that squeezed hers. "Let me guess—a wizard?"

"She is not—" Sir William began.

"How did you—" Miss Tavis blurted.

"I've asked Miss Tavis as my apprentice." Mr. Tomlinson was the only one who got all the way through his sentence.

So this was the one. Amanusa should have guessed, but she'd forgotten the woman's name almost as soon as Tomlinson had mentioned it. "It is a true pleasure to meet you, Miss Tavis." Amanusa squeezed the other woman's hands in return and beamed a smile at her.

"Please, call me Elinor." With another squeeze, Elinor released Amanusa, allowing her to gather her wounded skirts.

They walked side by side all the way back to the hotel, talking magic. The men trailed silently behind. Elinor might have come up to their suite with them, so thirsty was she to talk about magic, but Mr. Tomlinson asked her to remain behind to "discuss a certain matter." Amanusa assumed he meant to have an answer to the apprenticeship question, but she wouldn't pry. Not unless she didn't hear anything without asking.

The machine was still in its case. Or it should be. Amanusa hadn't looked since she shut it in the new case. The locks hadn't been opened and the seals hadn't been touched. It still felt heavy when she lifted it, enough so that Jax scolded when he took it from her.

Amanusa changed out of her white dress. She felt like a beacon in it, calling all her enemies to her. Besides, her hoop had to be repaired. The simple navy blue dress she put on had a narrower silhouette, needing no hoops. It would be much easier to walk in. Or to ride in the hired carriage awaiting them.

It was a large carriage, big enough for Amanusa, Jax, and Mr. Tomlinson, as well as Elinor who still wanted to talk magic, and Mr. Carteret who seemed to hope for mayhem and rioting, at least in small amounts.

"Well?" Amanusa looked brightly from Elinor, squeezed on one side of her, to Mr. Tomlinson, squeezed in almost as tightly between Jax and Mr. Carteret on the opposite seat. It was a large carriage, but perhaps not quite large enough. "Did you give Mr. Tomlinson your answer, Elinor?"

"One would think you had proposed marriage, Harry, the way everyone's going on about it." Mr. Carteret seemed to enjoy risking his life, given the way he kept provoking people.

"Shut up, Grey," Tomlinson growled.

Elinor blushed, but it didn't stop her speaking. "Oh no, Mr. Carteret. This is of far, far more import than mere marriage. Which is why I have been so careful with my answer." She shot a look at the alchemist from beneath her lashes. "And I have told Mr. Tomlinson that I would be honored to serve as his apprentice."

The man in question cleared his throat. "We'll make it official when we get back to London. And call me Harry. All of you. I'm no 'Mister.' Leastways not with friends." He gave Carteret a sour look. "An' whatever Grey here is."

"Neutral acquaintance, old chap." Carteret clapped Harry on the shoulder, or tried to. He wasn't entirely successful in the close confines of the carriage. "Or at least, non-enemies. And I shall ask everyone to call me Grey. After all, Miss Whitcomb's gentleman friend has but one name, so it's only fair—"

"I have more." Jax's voice sounded hard. Hard and ruthless and utterly un-Jax-like. Amanusa whipped her eyes in his direction to stare.

"I have a complete set of names." His eyes glittered and his sharp cheekbones seemed somehow sharper, his jaw more angular. His mouth had changed too, become firmer, hard in some way, though his lips were still as full and soft-looking as when he'd kissed her. "I am John Christian Alvanleigh Greyson, fourth earl of Leaford."

"Jax?" Amanusa tightened trembling fingers together. He was an *earl*? And she was the daughter of a valet and a parlor maid. No wonder he argued against marrying her.

"Th' Devil Earl 'imself—" Harry Tomlinson whispered.

Grey Carteret burst out laughing. Everyone glared at him. Save for Jax, who stared straight ahead at nothing, as if glaring were beneath his dignity. As if everything were beneath his dignity, including the company. Especially Amanusa, who sat directly across from him.

Amanusa straightened in the seat and Jax—the earl of Leaford—shot her an anguished glance, there and gone again when he went back to his staring over her head.

"Oh, Uncle George will be apoplectic," Grey wheezed, wiping his streaming eyes. "He's twelfth earl of Leaford. Only he can't be, can he, since the fourth one's still alive. M'mother was a Greyson. Hence the name: Greyson Carteret." He gestured at himself, as if introducing himself afresh. Perhaps he was.

"So, Uncle Jax—" Grey grinned like a maniac at his newly discovered relation. "Obviously you didn't make a deal with the devil . . ."

Jax blinked, then turned bleak eyes on the conjurer. "No," he said. "I made a deal with Yvaine, who was not the devil. But it still cost me everything I possessed."

"Even your soul?" Elinor asked in the kind of fascinated horror that made people gather at train wrecks and house fires.

Jax's eyes warmed, though Amanusa was sure she was the only one able to recognize it. "No, not my soul—though for a time I wondered. But my memories. I did not know any name other than Jax until a short time ago."

He turned his hard look on Grey Carteret. "And you will not inform your uncle George, or anyone else, of who I am. I am no longer that man, have not been for centuries. I only wanted a name. My own name. There are any number of Greysons in the world. We do not have to be related."

"Oh, but I like the idea," Grey drawled. "Though I suppose if you insist on secrecy, you will have to be Cousin Jax, rather than Uncle, since Mama has all of her siblings numbered."

"I could be Alvanleigh." Jax raised an eyebrow as he considered.

Why did he want another name? Because Amanusa had claimed him as her fiancé? Was this his way of trying to maneuver out of it? Or did he want a name to give her when they married? She was afraid to hope.

"Amanusa Alvanleigh," she mused. "That is quite a mouthful. Amanusa Greyson is much simpler."

"Then Greyson it shall have to be," Grey Carteret said. "And you shall just have to put up with me as your shirttail relative."

"Are you certain?" Jax looked at Amanusa, his old Jax-look back. Amanusa discovered that she'd rather liked the new Jax-look, and missed it now it was gone. He sat forward and slid his hand over hers and it was all right again.

"I am not at all certain I wish to put up with your relations." Amanusa made her voice tart and teasing. "But since I have none at all to claim as my own, I suppose any family is better than none. We can always invite him to visit and smother him in his sleep if he proves too annoying."

Grey burst out laughing. "Mama is always making that same threat. M'brothers just threaten to shoot me."

"Too bad they never carried it out," Harry grumbled.

Conversation faded as the carriage rumbled on for a considerable length of time. Finally it rattled to a halt and Harry peered out the window. "Yeah, we're here."

He opened the door and climbed out, the other men following. Jax let Harry hand Elinor out, but stepped in to assist Amanusa's exit. As if making his claim on her clear. Amanusa rather liked that. He might be a once-upon-a-time earl, but she was a sorceress. Surely that balanced things out. She wouldn't insist he marry her if he truly did not want to, but she did not want to marry anyone else. And she had other things to fret about now.

Amanusa laid her hand in the crook of Jax's arm. He hefted the case holding the machine, which had traveled in the luggage boot, and followed Harry and Elinor into the building, Grey bringing up the rear. The building was the only substantial construction in the area, solid brick rising three stories in the air amidst ramshackle warehouses lining a different part of the Seine than Amanusa had so far seen.

"The city wouldn't let us work near the *Chambre*," Harry said as they mounted the stairs inside the building. "On account o' th' smells. An' the occasional boom. Same reason why the French council wouldn't let us have a laboratory in their chateau. The conclave had to buy this building because no one would lease us space. Can't lease out the rest of the space neither. Either. Except maybe to other magicians."

He tapped on a wall as they passed. "Might make

good personal workshop space. For those that don't need more privacy." Harry seemed to be making an effort to control his accent and correct his grammar.

At the top of the building, Harry opened the door into a large open space broken by columns and tables holding all the accoutrements of all the great magics. Save for sorcery, of course. Men sat and stood around the tables, mixing, peering, sniffing, tapping—working magic.

17

"WE GOT A MACHINE," Harry called out, and a dozen heads popped up to stare.

One of the men cheered and the others joined in as they quickly gathered around the table where Jax set the case. "Where did you get it?" asked a short, balding man with black hair that stood out in tufts over his ears. "When?"

"Someone gave it to me," Amanusa said. "In Transylvania, about three months ago."

All eyes turned on Amanusa. The intense scrutiny was a bit unnerving, but she detected no hostility in it.

"What are you about, Harry?" another man demanded, this one tall, dark, and Latin-looking. "Bringing women to this place. It is not safe."

" 'S'okay. This one's my apprentice. Miss Elinor Tavis." Harry tugged Elinor forward and she bobbed her head at them. "She's studying wizardry, not alchemy, because no wizard would apprentice her.

Mikkelsen." He scowled at another tall man, this one slender and blond.

"I could not, Tomlinson," Mikkelsen retorted. "You are a single man and more able to than I."

"Yeah, well—" Harry kept scowling. "Teach 'er wot you can while we're 'ere."

"She does not need much teaching. She is quite accomplished in the magic already." Mikkelsen bowed to Elinor, who was blushing again. "I will, however, be happy to share what I know."

"Guild stuff, Stein."

"*Ja, ja.* I said I would do it."

Amanusa watched them, trying to read the nuances and failing. It was none of her business.

"And who is this beautiful lady?" The Latin fellow had somehow captured Amanusa's hand while she wasn't looking and was bowing over it, pressing his lips to it. He started to turn it over, as if to kiss her palm, and she snatched it back, wrapping both her hands securely around Jax's arm.

"This, gentlemen—" Harry raised his voice, filled it with portent. "This is the new sorceress. Amanusa Whitcomb. Blood magic is with us again."

Silence fell as everyone stared at her. Then someone—perhaps the same man who'd done it before—cheered, and they all burst out in huzzahs.

Amanusa flinched at the first shout. When she realized the shouting was friendly—delighted, in fact— her throat tightened with tears. This was the first positive reaction to the news of her magic that she'd received, and it caught her off guard. Hostility, rejection she was used to. Acceptance—delight—was something new.

"Back away, Tonio." The balding man with the fluffy hair shoved the Latin man out of his way and pulled the machine case in front of him. "Let's see what they've brought us." He flipped the latches on the case, but couldn't open it.

"Oh. Sorry." Amanusa squeezed through to the table, pulling off her "proper lady" gloves as she did. "I'd forgotten. I had to seal it up. The machine was quite harmful to my . . . my fiancé, and I had to wrap magic around it to keep it from hurting him."

"Fiancé?" Tonio, who apparently fancied himself a great lover, looked disappointed for half a moment. Then he moved closer to Elinor and smiled at her.

"Jax Greyson." Jax offered his hand to the man examining the machine. "I am also Amanusa's blood servant, as I was for Yvaine before her. Which means I'm held together with magic. That machine doesn't like magic."

"Pyotr Strelitsky." The alchemist shook Jax's hand, never taking his eyes off the case and what Amanusa did to it.

"Blood of my blood," she murmured under her breath where no one could hear. She caught hold of the magic with something that wasn't her hand, but could be manipulated the same way. She pulled the magic tight as she licked her thumb and rubbed it over the smears of blood on the three unhinged sides.

"Your task is done," she whispered, and felt the seals dissolve. The magic dissipated.

Amanusa flipped the top open and winced at what she saw inside. Several of the spokes were corroded almost completely away, and the central shell had holes eaten through it to expose complicated inner workings, which also showed signs of corrosion. She pulled it out of the box, blackened bits flaking away as she did.

"Apparently," she said, "magic dislikes it as much as it dislikes magic. It seems my protective warding caused it some damage."

"This is good to know. So we know that magic does have an effect on these things, on the dead zones. It is not immune." Strelitsky took the machine from her and held it at eye level to inspect it. But he had only a moment or two to peer into its insides before his eyes rolled up in his head and he collapsed.

The machine clunked to the floor, magicians skittering out of its way as it rolled lopsidedly off a few feet. Tonio dropped to his knees beside the felled alchemist and ripped the man's shirt open to put his ear to Strelitsky's chest and listen. "He is still alive."

Tonio straightened and pointed at one of the gathered men. "Pascal, get the bag. Now."

The very young man ran to do as he was told. One of the other magicians shoved the machine farther out of the way with the toe of his shoe and Elinor picked it up by a spoke and set it back on the table.

"Can I help?" Amanusa hovered near the wizard as he rummaged through the colored glass bottles in the case his apprentice brought.

"We want to keep him alive," Tonio muttered, preoccupied. "Not kill him."

Amanusa recoiled at the verbal blow, though she quickly understood it came from ignorance rather than malice. "Blood magic has its healing arts," she said evenly as the wizard marked Strelitsky's bare, hairy chest with herbal oils. "May I add my magic to your dosing?"

Tonio looked up at her, his gaze sharp enough to bore holes, all trace of the Latin lover gone. "His heart scarcely beats. I do not know if I can strengthen it. I do not know if I can get my 'dosing' down him. If you believe you can help him, and you swear to do no harm, then by all means." He gestured with the blue bottle in his hand. "Join me."

"Measure your medicine." Amanusa knelt on the other side of Strelitsky. "I will administer the dose."

It was awkward lancing a finger one-handed inside her pocket. The power residing in the sorcerer's blood had been a guild secret of sorcery since it began. Amanusa understood why, once Jax pointed it out to her. If others knew the true source of the magic, they could be tempted to appropriate that power by appropriating the sorcerer's blood.

And while innocent blood cried out for justice, if the sorceress was dead and all her blood spilled out through the gash in her throat, she couldn't work magic with her own innocent blood. Ignorant and greedy people too often couldn't resist killing the goose for the gold.

These men could perhaps be trusted, but all the great magics had secrets held within their own guilds. This was the greatest secret of sorcery. Amanusa would keep it.

Tonio handed her the tiny cup with his potion in it. Amanusa smeared a generous drop of blood along the lip of the cup where the medicine would sweep it up as she poured it into Strelitsky's mouth. Much of it dribbled out again, but enough slid down his throat in a choked, reflexive swallow.

As she held her magic quiescent, waiting for the proper moment, she could sense the magic Tonio had brewed into his potion. It was different from her workings, the magic instilled when the potion was created rather than at the moment of its use.

"Do you draw no blood?" the wizard asked, checking Strelitsky's feeble pulse again.

"All the blood I need is inside Mr. Strelitsky," Amanusa said with complete honesty. "And that is where it will stay for now. When it is time, I will take only a very little. A drop. No more."

The alchemist's color was improving, from pasty to pale. The potion was working. Time for Amanusa to go to work as well. She woke her magic inside the odd little man. It was dim and blurred, hard to see, and uncomfortable. Nothing like the crystal clarity and sense of belonging she had when wandering through Jax's bloodstream.

Images from Strelitsky's memories kept impinging on Amanusa's awareness. Plump-cheeked little girls and an equally plump-cheeked wife. Cluttered workrooms. Spell formulas. Amanusa shoved them aside as best she could, trying to keep them out of the way without harming them. He would need those spells again, and losing any memory of one's family was a tragedy. She didn't need to sift his memory. Amanusa's purpose was purely physical.

The potion was a stimulant, something to give Strelitsky back the strength and energy the machine had stolen. Amanusa linked with Tonio's magic, adding life magic to life magic. Then she willed the magic to show her Strelitsky's heart.

It stuttered, lacking any rhythm, as if it had forgotten how to beat. Amanusa pulled up the magic—the wizard's and her own—and listened for the beating of her own heart. She called it into the magic—carefully, for she'd learned to heed Jax's warnings—and shared it with the stricken alchemist. Strelitsky's heart began to beat more soundly, but it needed more.

Her own heart faltered for a moment and she heard a faint, faraway cry. Her name? She was cold, so cold. So tired.

Then warmth surrounded her, seeping into the cold. Strength followed, settling in behind her, beneath her, supports holding her up. Another heart beat with hers, the rhythmic *thump-thump* singing to her of life and of possibilities.

She drank it in and shared it out again, calling up those memories she'd pushed away, giving Mr. Strelitsky back his own possibilities. The magic in the wizard's potion swirled around her, enhancing what she did, adding the warmth of sun-kissed leaves, the stubbornness of roots digging deep into the soil. The alchemist's heart seemed to listen and remember, slowly echoing the rhythm Amanusa shared, stronger and stronger with every beat.

Carefully, Amanusa withdrew, ready to jump in again if the weakened heart faltered, but it continued to beat steadily. Back in her own body again, her eyes fluttered open. Jax knelt behind her. She seemed to have collapsed into him. Onto him. Both.

She reached for the lancet in her pocket, but couldn't seem to make her arms—or anything else—move. Jax understood her intent and brought the lancet out for her.

"Over his heart?" He held the lancet poised over Strelitsky, waiting for her assent.

Her voice didn't want to work either, but she managed to force a yes-shaped sound from it. Jax scored Mr. Strelitsky's chest and Amanusa called back the blood she'd sent into the alchemist. Jax used the side of the lancet's tip to scoop up the droplets of blood that oozed from the tiny wound and brought them to Amanusa's lips.

It seemed a bit barbaric to lick up the blood under the fascinated and slightly horrified gazes of the other magicians. Amanusa did it anyway. This was sorcery. If it was barbaric, so be it. Perhaps the world needed to be a little less civilized.

Only when she had licked up the last traces of the blood—her own, but none of them knew that—did Tonio the wizard reach across their patient to check Amanusa's pulse. Of course he'd been monitoring Strelitsky in the interim, but he still waited until the barbarity was done to check on her well-being. "How do you feel, Miss Whitcomb?"

Twining her fingers with Jax's, Amanusa found voice enough to answer. "Weary, but improving."

Tonio rose higher on his knees, asking permission before lifting her eyelids to peer into her eyes. "I did not realize a sorceress shared her own life essence in a healing, or I would not have permitted it."

"I didn't share my 'essence.' I shared—" Amanusa looked up at Jax for inspiration, an aid to recall what he and Yvaine had told her on the long train trip. "Knowledge is perhaps the best way to put it. Your magic gave back much of the strength he lost, but his heart needed to be shown how to beat properly again."

She sighed, pressing her palm flat against Jax's palm, increasing the contact. "Instead, he almost made my heart forget what it knew. Fortunately, Jax was here to help me."

She twisted in his embrace to look him in the eye. "And I promise I will not try new magic without you ever again."

The new Jax, the one with the hard edges and stern eyes, looked back at her. "Swear it. Never again."

A little thrill went through her at his tone. She raised a hand in pledge. "I swear."

"Do you mean to say this was your first time to attempt such healing?" Tonio demanded, aghast.

Embarrassed by the admission, Amanusa bit her lip as she nodded. "There has to be a first time sometime, and I *did* help him. I've practiced on Jax dozens of times. Maybe hundreds. He's healthy as a horse, but that means I know what the internal organs should look like and how they're supposed to work."

She paused to look up at all the appalled magicians staring back at her. "It isn't as if I have a master sorcerer to stand over my shoulder watching everything I do. I'm the only one there is right now, and yes, I'm still learning. Sorry if that offends you, but I'm all there is. And I do have Jax."

"What I've been wantin' to know—" Harry Tomlinson spoke up, "is just what part a blood servant plays in sorcery. How does he help you? Why do you need one?"

She struggled to stand, feeling very much at a disadvantage sitting sprawled on the floor while most of the others stood over her. Jax rose, helping her to her feet as he did. Holding tight to his hand clasped with hers, Amanusa put her other over the hand he'd set at her waist, keeping it there.

At that moment, the fallen warrior in this bizarre fight against the dead zones and their creatures groaned, his eyelids fluttering. Tonio organized a litter party to bear Strelitsky to one of the cots set up for magicians who needed to rest before plunging back into the fray. "Wait for my return," the wizard ordered. "I want to hear our sorcerer's answers."

"I want to hear too," Strelitsky complained in a feeble voice. "What will I hear?"

"We could come with you . . ." Amanusa looked to Tonio for permission. She didn't want to interfere with Strelitsky's recovery.

Tonio checked his patient's pulse, peered at his eyes, and did several other tests Amanusa didn't recognize before agreeing to the plan. The bearers gathered Strelitsky up and everyone trooped off to the back of the room.

Elinor moved up to walk alongside Amanusa and Jax. "Antonio Rosato is one of the most famous wizards in Europe. He is also a medical doctor," she murmured.

"Why aren't you apprenticed to him instead of Harry?"

"Because one of the things he is famous for is the number of his love affairs. He has left broken hearts scattered in his wake from St. Petersburg to St. Lo." Elinor's voice held more amusement than condemnation, but both were there. "I am sure he would gladly take me as apprentice, but I would learn absolutely nothing, for *Dottore* Rosato would spend all his time attempting to seduce me, and when he tired of the attempt—or tired of me after success, since

I am only human after all and he is a very handsome man—"

"Is he?" Amanusa shot Tonio a second glance. "I hadn't noticed."

"You wouldn't. But when it ended badly, I would be tossed out on my ear without a reputation, without the knowledge I want, and without any entree into the circle of magicians. With Mr. Tomlinson as my master, I will at least have knowledge, through access to the council library, as recompense for my reputation's loss. For all that he sprang from the gutters of Seven Dials, Harry Tomlinson is an honorable man in his own fashion."

Amanusa had thought so as well. She was glad to have her judgment confirmed by so sensible a woman as Elinor seemed.

When Dr. Rosato had his patient settled as comfortably as possible on a camp cot, all eyes returned to Amanusa once again.

"We're not askin' for guild secrets, mind," Harry said. "But seein' as we ain't—haven't had any sorcery around for so long, we're all a mite curious. So, how does a blood servant help you?"

"I am bound to my sorceress by blood and magic." Jax spoke up before Amanusa had a chance to open her mouth. He didn't know what she might say, how much she might reveal. They would accept his word. He was the servant, after all. "I am her magical reflection, if you will, able to reflect her power back into her. A source of strength, much like a familiar."

"A source of blood?" one of the younger men asked.

"Of course. But since I am apparently over three hundred years old, it is obviously not fatal." Jax's smile had sharp edges. He wouldn't give away the deep secrets, but sharing a bit more of the truth about blood magic could keep the hounds of hate and fear from her. He hoped. "Whatever service my sorceress requires of me, I provide. I am proud to serve this sorceress."

"But blood servant isn't the same as a footman or a . . . a valet," Amanusa said, her graceful long-fingered hands tightening around his. "And it's more than a familiar's relationship—as I understand familiars. I know less about other magics than I do about sorcery. Jax is a man, a human being, so of course the relationship is far different than that with an animal familiar."

She frowned, her "thinking crease" forming between her brows. He wanted to smooth it away. "Mirror—reflecting magic back into me—yes, that's part of it, but I believe the proper word is *partner.* He is my partner in the magic."

Jax stood, stunned motionless by Amanusa's words. She'd said it before, but he still found it difficult to believe it was what she truly thought. When her blood, her magic had begun to replace Yvaine's in his bindings, he had noticed the difference, but he had been afraid to hope.

"Jax cannot gather the magic, or use it in spells, but I can use his words to create the spell. It was his strength, his heart that kept mine beating just now. When we traveled through the magical vacuums on the train through Baden, we kept each other alive. It is—"

"Wait." Harry held up a hand. "Magical vacuum— do you mean a dead zone?"

"Yes. We didn't know what it was properly called, but that was what it felt like to us, so—"

"You came on the train *through*—what route did you come?" Harry led them to a huge map of Europe pinned on the wall.

Other maps were there, of Asia, North and South America, Africa. The maps had pencil hatchings laid over different areas, delineating the dead zones already identified. Jax traced their route on the map from Vienna to Paris, through the center of one of the largest zones.

"And you survived the crossing?" Harry sounded incredulous.

"Together, yes. We had to be close—touching— but—"

"It affected me worse than it did Amanusa," Jax interrupted. "It is possible she would have survived the crossing on her own." She was so strong, in so many ways.

"I don't think so. I didn't stop breathing, but I got very ill . . ."

"And you were able to pick up that machine." Harry looked back across the laboratory to the table where the corroded machine sat. "You held it as long as Pyotr, but he collapsed an' you didn't."

"Pyotr is an alchemist," Tonio said. "You're the one, Harry, who postulated that our ability to withstand the dead zones is related to the type of magic we practice. Your theory has seemed to hold true in our experimentation so far."

"Yeah, yeah." Harry nodded his head, lost in

thought. "Alchemists go down first, then conjurers, then wizards. And sorcerers last?"

"So perhaps the ability to withstand the malevolence of the machine is similar?"

"Miss Tavis picked it up and put it back on the table." Grey Carteret spoke for the first time since entering the lab. "Perhaps it is women who have the greatest resistance."

Jax's free hand curled into a fist. He'd like to cure the man of his delight in stirring up mischief.

"She *is* a wizard," Amanusa said. "Perhaps other wizards can handle it."

"Or perhaps it's just that I'm wearing gloves." Elinor held up her hands to show her thin kidskin gloves.

"Pyotr wasn't," Harry said. "Were you, Amanusa? When you pulled it out o' the box?"

"No, but I've touched it before. It makes me nauseous, but little else."

"What about you, Jax?" Harry asked. "What happened when you touched it?"

"I did not lose consciousness. I touched it only an instant. My fingers froze, went utterly numb, and when I touched my mouth with them, it froze and blistered as well. The machine was in much better condition, however, when I touched it. No corrosion or visible damage to it."

"Hmm."

Several other magicians echoed Harry's "hmm." They all trooped back over to stand around the table and stare at the battered machine. Pyotr complained from his cot, where Tonio's apprentice Pascal sat on him to keep him in the bunk.

"Only one thing for it," Grey said, after a long moment of staring. "One of you other wizards needs to pick it up."

He didn't wait for them to try, however, but grasped one of the dangling arms with a gloved hand and lifted it off the table. He held it only a moment before passing it over to one of the wizards, looking a bit pale.

The wizard took hold of a pair of spokes with his bare hands. "Not too bad," he said. "I can feel a bit of a chill in my hands, a bit of dizziness."

Tonio grasped the man's wrist, checking something medical. Jax held his breath, admiring the man's bravery as he shifted his grip to the central sphere.

"Don't push this so far you need Amanusa to bring you back," Jax said. "She can't do it again." He wouldn't allow— He was the servant. It wasn't his place to allow or permit. But . . . was it a fiancé's place? A partner's place?

"No." The test wizard was gasping for breath when he released the machine to thump back onto the table, but he seemed in reasonably good health. "Freddie, you try it with gloves."

A third wizard had already retrieved his gloves from inside his hat and was pulling them on. He was able to handle the machine a much longer time. After five minutes, he showed very little ill result, and the others were pulling out pocket watches to time him.

Amanusa was getting bored. Jax could read the signs in the way she began to shift from one foot to the other and let her gaze wander over the other cluttered tables in the room.

"Do you have any other questions for us?" Jax drew Harry aside to ask. Better one man than the whole horde of them.

"Not right now. Not that I can think of. The lads'll want to be tinkerin' with it for some time yet. Why?"

"I'd like to take Amanusa back to the hotel. Feed her dinner. Let her rest."

"I'm not a child to be tended." Amanusa joined them.

"No, you're a woman and a sorcerer who's been through a long, trying day and hasn't had any dinner." Jax knew Amanusa enjoyed gentle teasing, but he still couldn't help feeling as if he took his life in his hands whenever he contradicted her in the least. "And you're bored."

She sighed. "True. I am bored."

"We can't 'ave that, can we? A bored magician is a dangerous magician, ain't that right, Grey?"

"That was *not* my fault." Grey's voice came wafting from the back where he'd gone to lie down on one of the cots. Apparently the machine had affected him more than he'd let on. "Monkeys are very clever on their own."

"Why don't you take Elinor back with you?"

"No." Elinor was protesting almost before Harry completed his suggestion. "If I am your apprentice, I need to stay with you while you are working magic."

"We might be here all night," Harry warned. "And Amanusa's leaving."

"Nevertheless." The glint in Elinor's eye could almost be called martial, if it wasn't devilish. "If one of these gentlemen is so overcome by my feminine charms as to make untoward advances, I know I can count on you and Mr. Carteret to rescue me."

"I'll be one of the ones advancing," Grey called, causing two of the apprentices and at least one magician to blush.

"An' I'll be blackin' both your eyes," Harry retorted. "Maybe you ought to take Grey back with you."

Grey groaned. "No. I can't endure lurching across town in a carriage with this head. They're perfectly capable of getting themselves back to the hotel on their own. Let the betrothed couple have a bit of time alone, you anti-romantic."

"'Ave it your way." Harry shrugged. "But if I strangles ya, I strangles ya."

18

JAX ESCORTED AMANUSA out the door while the "discussion" continued. If they waited for formal farewells, they'd be waiting all night. The magicians he remembered hadn't been much for formality. Apparently they hadn't changed a great deal in the passing centuries.

The hired carriage waited in the street, the driver dozing on his box. He was most agreeable to the idea of taking them back to their hotel and returning to wait for the others. Jax had spent plenty of time kicking his heels, waiting for magicians to finish some business or other. Magicians also tended to get a bit testy if they were inconvenienced. The driver would be paid for his time, so he didn't object.

"Do we have to dine at the hotel?" Amanusa asked as they passed the train station, nearing their destination. "We've eaten every meal there."

"Of course not. We can dine anywhere you like." Jax smiled. She was easy to please, and he liked pleasing her. Something of a new experience for him. "What would you prefer?"

"That's just it. I don't know. I've never been to Paris before and since we arrived, I've seen dress shops, the hotel, and the conclave chamber. I don't know what I would prefer. I don't know where the best food is served or what—"

Jax rapped on the roof of the carriage with his stick and after a moment, the driver drew the horses to a halt. Jax assisted Amanusa to alight on the elegant street, glittering with lights, angry with himself. He should have realized she would be curious, interested to see the city famed for its culture and cuisine.

"It's not so very late in the evening," he said as the carriage rattled off. He tucked her hand in the crook of his arm and led her to the sidewalk. "We could still catch a performance of the theater after dinner, if you like."

"Oh." Amanusa's hold on his arm tightened. "But that would run very late, wouldn't it? The day already feels like it's been endless. Perhaps another night." She looked down at her skirts. "And I'm not dressed to dine anywhere *too* elegant."

Jax smiled down at her. "You would grace the halls of the emperor himself, were you wearing rags. But I would not have you uncomfortable." He escorted her through the doors of precisely the sort of

establishment she seemed to want—excellent food
without too many jewels adorning the patrons.

Dinner was delicious and Amanusa lively and an-
imated, talking of the people they'd met at the laboratory and making guesses as to the experiments
being conducted at the various tables. Jax sat back
and watched her run on, encouraging her with the
occasional comment or question, while his mind
ticked over other things. Did she really mean what
she'd said? Fiancé was one thing. Partner was another. Did she truly think of him—her blood
servant—as a partner?

Her mood seemed to be turning pensive as she
spooned up her crème brûlée. Jax maintained his appearance of ease, but inside, the tension returned.
Until Amanusa, he'd never noticed his tension, because until Amanusa, it had never entirely left him.
He'd never relaxed completely because he'd never
known how Yvaine would react to anything, or what
she might demand of him.

Yvaine might have rescued him from the Inquisition, as Amanusa had. But she might as easily have
considered his sacrifice her due and escaped without
him. Amanusa never would. Jax was as certain of
that as he was of the sun's rise every morning. He belonged to her. She would never abandon him care-
lessly, like one might leave behind a pair of boots
that had outlasted their usefulness. He was her servant. Her responsibility.

During their passage through the dead zone, his
belief in how she thought of him had been strained
almost to breaking. She seemed to value him more
highly than most would value a servant. One did not

allow a servant such close contact—wrapped around her skin-to-skin, as near to naked as made no difference. He was her pet, he'd decided. A faithful hound whose head she had held when he was so ill.

But one did not introduce a pet as one's fiancé. Why had she done it? Surely she couldn't still intend— She had tried out her name with his. But she'd been joking. Hadn't she?

He hadn't laid claim to the Greyson name in order to have a name to present her with when they married. Had he? No. He'd just wanted a name. A whole name. A man's name.

So she would think of him as a man and not a pet.

Dear God, he was falling in love with her. Why else would he be wanting to reclaim his manhood?

And he was still a blood servant. Not a man. Not an ordinary servant who could leave a bad master and seek another. Not even a pet. He was a tool. A magical instrument.

Instruments did not fall in love.

He already had. *Bloody hell.*

Amanusa licked her spoon clean and laid it in her empty bowl. "Jax? Didn't you like it?"

He realized he'd taken only one bite of his dessert. "It's excellent." He laid his spoon down. "But I'm afraid I consumed too much at dinner to do it justice. Would you like it?"

She looked covetously at his nearly untouched dish. "I shouldn't. I'm sure I've eaten quite as much as you, and I'm not nearly so large. Though I shall be twice as large as I am now if I keep eating this way."

Jax chuckled. She had no ability to dissemble. It was a wonder they'd survived the outlaws' camp, given her propensity for blurting out the truth. Fortunately, Szabo thought her threats amusing. He pushed the dish of crème brûlée toward her. "We'll walk back to the hotel to make up. It's only fair. I did finish your beef."

Amanusa bit her lip as she watched the dish slide toward her. "It is very good."

"Exactly." He nudged it a fraction closer. "Indulge while you can. Crème brûlée can be difficult to find in the wilds of Scotland."

She didn't reply. Her spoon was in her mouth. Her eyes fluttered closed as she savored the sweet dessert and when they opened, her thoughtful mood had returned. Jax braced himself for whatever it might mean.

"The gentlemen at the laboratory were most enthusiastic," she said as she spooned up another tiny bite. She seemed to be of the "make it last as long as possible" school of dessert-eaters, rather than the "gobble it down" faction, though she did appear to belong to the "and then look for more" subset.

She took the bite, savored it a moment before she swallowed, then spoke again. "Some of the magicians at the conclave were pleased by the reappearance of my magic. But not all of them. I think not even most of them."

"You are probably correct." Jax curled his palm over the heavy silvered head of his new walking stick where it leaned against their table. He'd refused to give it in to the coat closet at the door to the restaurant. "Ignorance and fear flourish where there is no one to avert it with truth."

"You said that you would marry me, if I asked

again when we reached Paris." She watched the spoon stirring the molded dessert into a tumble for another moment before laying it aside. She looked up at him. "I am asking. If you absolutely can't bear the idea, I won't insist, but Jax—I'm so afraid that we'll need the magic. The—the—" Her eyes flicked to the diners around them lingering over their demitasse cups. "You know."

"Amanusa." He was reaching for her hand before he realized it, and stopped himself, his hand resting awkwardly in the middle of the table. He lowered his voice so the murmur of conversation and clinking silver around them would cloak his words from all but Amanusa. "I am your servant. I—"

"You're an earl," she interrupted. Her hand met his in the center of the table, gripped it tight.

"Not anymore. Not for three hundred years. I'm a servant. I don't know how to be anything else. You deserve better than being tied to me. Let me—"

"But I'm already tied to you." Amanusa shook her head. "And I don't want anyone else. I don't trust anyone else. Jax, you *promised*."

Abruptly, she let go of him. She stood, her voice utterly cold, calm and un-Amanusa-like. "I won't force myself where I'm not wanted. We'll go straightaway to Scotland and look for the spells to break your binding." She whirled and wove her way through the tables toward the exit, as if desperate to get away, to hide from him. So it wasn't anger that gripped her. When she was angry, she didn't run away, she shouted.

"Amanusa—" What was wrong? The only time she hid from him . . . was when she was hurt. Upset.

Was she upset? Why? Didn't she understand? It wasn't proper, what she proposed. Jax threw a fistful of francs on the table and hurried after her, remembering at the last minute to grab his stick.

He caught up with her in time to hold the door for her departure. "Amanusa," he began again, striding down the street beside her. "It's not that I don't— *Amanusa*." He caught her arm and pulled her round to face him. "Stop. I can't talk to your bonnet. I can't talk to you when you're racing away from me."

"I don't see that there's anything to talk about." She jerked away from him and started off again in her ground-covering peasant's stride. It made her skirts rustle and bounce. "Just leave me alone."

Jax caught her by the waist this time, spun her in a left-face maneuver, and pointed her across the street. "I can't. Our hotel is in that direction." Why wouldn't she listen? He hadn't said anything for her to be upset about. She couldn't be upset.

He gave her a little nudge off the curb, then captured her hand and wound it through the crook of his arm, holding tight when she would have pulled away. Angry with himself for saying whatever it was he said, Jax lost the last frayed edge of his patience. "Stop it," he said. "You're acting like a child."

She fought harder to pull free and when Jax refused to let go, she kicked him in the ankle. Utter shock that she would do such a thing made him loosen his grip and she jerked free, breaking into a run, darting down an unlit alleyway.

With a curse, Jax was after her. She couldn't run well in those skirts. "Amanusa!" He dropped his stick as he hauled her into his arms, wrapping her up so she couldn't hit him with those flying fists, not any more than she already had. "Amanusa, what is wrong with you?"

· "I'm a child. Isn't that what you said?" she retorted. "Of course anyone would be, compared to you. Not everyone can live to be three hundred and what? Thirty-seven? Three hundred forty-three?"

"I don't know." He tried for levity. "Once one gets past two hundred fifty, birthdays lose a bit of relevance."

Amanusa growled and fought harder to break free, obviously not amused. Jax had to be quick to grab a fresh hold every time she managed to break it. She was not a small, easily subdued sort of female. "Will you stop fighting and just listen to me?" he gasped out.

"Why?" She wriggled one of her pinned arms up between their bodies and got her hand under his jaw, pushing his head back hard enough he thought she might take it off. "What are you going to say I haven't heard a dozen times already?"

"I might already have said it," he snarled through his forced-shut jaw, "but you didn't listen."

In a flash, he let go with one hand, grabbed her wrist at his chin, and spun her around, pulling her back against his front, her arms crossed and pulled tight to either side in a sort of straitjacket, with himself as the jacket. She struggled futilely to escape, kicking at his shins and stomping at his feet. He had to step lively to keep unstomped and relatively unkicked until finally she subsided.

"I listened," she growled at him. "You don't want

to marry me. Fine. Don't. I said I wouldn't force you and I won't. You want my permission to have sex with every woman in Paris? You have it. Feel free. But don't you dare tell me you're doing it for my own good. *Don't you dare.*"

Each word flayed another piece from Jax's hide.

"Maybe I didn't listen." Her voice was softer now. "Maybe I didn't understand how strongly you feel about this, about not wanting to marry me—but you didn't listen either. I told you, Jax. I told you why I asked."

He had heard every word, had ached for the things she'd endured. But to tie herself in marriage to one such as him?

"You promised." She stopped struggling, stood motionless in his grasp. Now he heard her tears and was flayed anew. He felt raw. Exposed.

"If I don't marry you, I won't ever marry," she whispered. "You're the only man I trust enough to marry, the only one I've ever trusted. But if you can't bear it . . ." She used his grip on her wrists to pull his arms forward, wrapping them around her in place of her own. "I'd never ever force you."

More of his thick, self-protective hide sloughed away and Jax shuddered. Yvaine would have forced him. She had forced him to do so many things, sometimes on mere whim. Amanusa wasn't Yvaine. He knew that, but it was still hard to remember.

It wasn't her trust at issue here. It was his own. On an instinctive level, he did trust her. His body knew she would never use magic to harm him, never retaliate unfairly, or he would never have dared to lay hands on her this way. He never, in the hundred years he'd served her, would have taken physical hold of Yvaine this way.

But his mind kept whispering to him, telling him what he was, what Yvaine had made him, asking why this sorceress would want him, a man who had nothing of worth to offer save for what she already had. It was all he had to offer her. Himself.

Something he'd long ago learned had no value.

Amanusa valued him. She saw him as protector, as partner. As more than just a magical thing. She saw him as a man.

A man worthy of her complete trust. Amanusa trusted him, a woman who had no reason to trust men and every reason to fear the harm a man could do. She trusted him so completely that she allowed him to imprison her like this without once calling on the weapons she possessed. She could have stopped him, could have rendered him helpless with less than a word. And she hadn't.

Yvaine would have. Yvaine would never have allowed the first touch. Yvaine had never, ever trusted him. And he'd never trusted her, because she'd betrayed him from the very beginning.

So did that mean Amanusa trusted him because she was a person who could be trusted?

Jax held Amanusa with his arms where she'd placed them around her, his mind flashing from raw shock to understanding. Yvaine had bound him so tightly because she feared him. She'd never trusted him—because she herself could not be trusted. People always feared in others the sins they possessed themselves.

Jax groaned, letting his head fall forward until his

cheek brushed along hers. He shivered at the touch against his exposed nerves. He felt odd, as if his chest were too small, his throat too tight. He'd been learning to love her all along, but he had clung to his fear and his mistrust, unable to give them up. Unable to love her as she deserved.

He did have something else to offer her, he realized. She claimed she didn't know what love was, but it was a small step beyond trust. Since she trusted him, perhaps if he loved her enough, he could teach her about love. Perhaps they could learn together.

His memories still weren't what they should be, but he didn't remember feeling this way ever before, even before Yvaine. He thought perhaps this was new to him too. It didn't matter. The only thing that did was this love he felt. And if he loved her—

Jax turned his head the fraction necessary to murmur in her ear. "I am an idiot. Forgive me?"

She gave a tiny start at his words, turned her face toward his. "What?"

"I—" He began again, carefully enunciating every word. "Am an idiot. A great, bloody fool. And I humbly beg your forgiveness."

She twisted, as if to pull out of his arms, and his grip tightened, reflexively.

He didn't want to let her go. "You won't run away again, will you?"

"Jax—"

"Our thanks, monsieur, for capturing the witch for us."

The guttural French was so unexpected, Jax blinked for far too long at the roughly dressed man with the knife in his hand, and the others spread out behind him. Only when the man lunged, did Jax thrust Amanusa behind him and dive for his dropped stick, whacking it across the man's shins hard enough to knock him howling back.

Amanusa screamed. Jax whirled around, stick out to fend off the other thugs, but no one had circled around to attack her. No one came at her, yet. He hit the trigger that released the rapier inside its wooden sheath, drawing out the long, sharp length of steel, retaining the hollow staff in his other hand. Not as good as a dagger, but better than nothing.

"Ooo, the English pig has a pig sticker," one of the men mocked. There were five of them, all roughly dressed, all armed with sharp knives glittering in the distant lamplight. They had the air of men who knew how to use them and had, often.

"Works well on French curs." Jax moved the rapier's point in a tiny circle. "Run along before I run you through."

"Five of us. Only one of you." The man in the lead, the one who'd lunged first, served as spokesman.

"Not the best odds. But then, I've faced worse, and here I am, facing you. How many of you do you think I'll kill before you can kill me?"

Amanusa stifled her cry of alarm. She didn't want to draw Jax's attention away from the attackers, not again. They wouldn't kill him. She wouldn't let them.

"We only want the witch, monsieur. Give her to us and we'll kill you quickly."

Jax laughed, a dark ominous sound that sent shivers skating through Amanusa. "You know what she

is, and still you dare? You who have spilled enough
innocent blood to overflow the gutters of the streets
you prowl?"

Some of the men glanced uneasily at each other,
but the leader attacked with a snarl and a feint, and
the others followed his lead. They spread out, like a
wolf pack attacking a stag at bay. One would leap in
with a slashing attack and while Jax fended him off,
another would dart in from behind with glinting
steel to slice and stab. They were trying to encircle
him, to get at Amanusa. But she was no doe without
antlers.

Jax was a blur of motion, spinning from one side to
the other, sword flashing through the air in a bright,
deadly counterpoint to the whir and crash of the staff
in his other hand. He fought with a skill Amanusa
never imagined possible, knocking the men back
again and again. He was magnificent. Powerful and
swift, dangerous, glorious, and all hers.

But he was still one man against five, and when one
of them caught Jax's skin with his knife, Amanusa felt
it. It was a shallow cut across his back. Not enough to
slow him, not enough to keep him from smashing his
stick across the other's arm, but the cut bled. Magic
rose. And Amanusa gathered it in.

She tried to wrap it around Jax, hide him from
their attackers, but in the midst of a fight, it wouldn't
stick. Or perhaps—yes—the men had spells laid on
them. True sight, she thought. And shields against
magic.

While Jax fought off two men, two others circled
around and this time, one of them lunged at
Amanusa while the other went for Jax. She jumped

back, slower than she could have. The knife sliced through her sleeve, along her upper arm, and magic flared.

Jax shouted. He'd been cut again, across his forearm this time, and as he attacked, driving the thugs back, blood flew. Amanusa hissed with pain as she touched her bleeding arm. The cut was deeper than she'd hoped, blood soaking her jacket, her blouse. She caught it in her hand and threw it out, splattering it across their attackers.

The instant it touched them, their magic shields flared and died. None of the men was unbloodied, and with their shielding gone, Amanusa's blood and Jax's blood mingled with theirs. She sent her magic rushing into them, invoking the call of innocent blood for justice. She forbade the magic to kill or maim, but otherwise let it do as it willed.

The attack stopped, the men shuddering as memory hit them, this time from the victim's side, the suffering they'd inflicted now visited upon them. They dropped their weapons. They screamed and fell to the ground in convulsions. Amanusa looked away.

Jax put his arm around her, tucking her face into his chest, his wooden staff bumping awkwardly against her back as if he feared setting it aside. "Justice can be harsh," he murmured, "when there is no remorse to call forth mercy."

Amanusa leaned into him, trembling arising from somewhere until she shook so violently she feared she couldn't stand. She didn't want to need his comfort, not when he didn't want her. Her arms burrowed beneath his frock coat and went around him anyway. She clung tightly to him as the magic raged. She tried to block the awful images from her mind, the sins committed with such casual carelessness by these men, but she was the sorceress. It was her magic and her blood that invoked it.

Whistles sounded at a distance. Footsteps thudded against pavement, rushing toward them. *What now?*

Amanusa clutched at Jax, then set him free, in case they needed to fight again.

"Witch!" The accusation came in English, in a vaguely familiar voice. "This woman attacked these men with black magic. Sorcery. Arrest her!"

"Shut yer gob, Nigel, or I'll shut it for you." Harry's familiar voice came ringing over the whimpers of the fallen men.

They were safe. Amanusa turned her face into Jax's bloodied shirt again, clinging to him for strength. "Blood of my blood," she whispered into it. "Send the power back to those who granted it. Give them the rest they so richly deserve."

The magic seemed to swirl threateningly once more over the thugs, before it rose into the air and dissipated on the breeze.

"What has happened here?" a new voice demanded, in French. Harry's stone translated for her, but she could still tell the original language.

"Sorcery," Mr. Cranshaw intoned, for it was the English wizard Harry had threatened to shut up. *"Sorcellerie."*

"I saw it." A woman's voice now, older, cultured sounding. "We did, didn't we, Louis-Baptiste?"

Amanusa loosened her grip on Jax, and when she wobbled only a little, dared let him go almost entirely, clinging only to his forearm. How would she manage without Jax to rely on? She turned to see an outraged matron and her equally outraged spouse talking to a man in a policeman's uniform with a great deal of gold braid on it. A whole troop of other, less gaudy policemen stood behind him.

"Those men—" The woman gestured at the thugs collapsed on the paving. "They attacked the gentleman and the lady."

"Look at them. They are lying unconscious on the street!" Cranshaw shouted. "With blood all over them! It is black magic, I tell you!"

He must not have one of Harry's translation stones, Amanusa decided, or the police superior would pay more attention to him.

"Oui," Louis-Baptiste agreed with his wife. "We were on our way home after the theater, walking to the corner there to catch a cab, and we heard this lady scream. I came ahead to see what was happening, and saw the gentleman protecting the lady from those men with his stick-sword. He is quite a fighter, that one."

"Is this so?" The officer looked at Jax, who nodded. "Then why are they on the ground and you are not?"

"Blood magic." Cranshaw was shaking with outrage, his face dark. The light was bad in this narrow alley, but Amanusa was certain he'd gone red with fury. *"Sorcellerie du sang,"* he hissed.

The policeman gave him a quick glance, while the matron's eyes widened and she stepped a pace back. "So?" he asked. "Explain."

"The lady is a member of the British National Council of Magicians," Harry said, stepping forward.

She'd heard him before. Of course he was here. And Elinor too, smiling worriedly at Amanusa from behind the alchemist.

"And therefore Miss Whitcomb is recognized as a magician by the International Conclave currently meeting in Paris," Harry went on. "Would you deny her the right to defend herself?"

"No one is denying anyone anything," the officer said. "I am merely trying to discover the truth."

19

AMANUSA TUCKED HER hand in her pocket and closed it around the translation stone, wishing it gave clarity and persuasiveness to one's words as well. "Innocent blood demands justice," she said yet again. She was getting almighty tired of having to explain this.

"We are not the only innocents these men have attacked over the years, and when our blood was spilled—" She showed the cut on her arm and that along Jax's forearm. "I called magic on behalf of ourselves and all the other innocents whose blood these men have shed.

"This man—Rene Boulanger—murdered the grocer and his family in Faubourg St. Jacques last week. Only his most recent crime. That one is Georges Cie. You have been looking for him, I think. He did commit the crime you suspect him of, and many others. He likes little girls far too well." Amanusa went on, identifying the other three unconscious men and labeling them with the crimes they'd committed.

"They were hired to attack us," she said, weariness piling on top of exhaustion. "But they did not know who hired them, nor did they see his face. It was a man, but he wore a cloak and hat, and kept to the shadows."

"How do you know these things?" the French police captain demanded.

"The magic exposes their crimes. It shows them to me. Innocent blood does not want anything hidden." A wave of horror swept over her and her knees crumpled. Jax caught her, held her steady, the sword's sheath bumping against her side.

"I have seen every last detail. More than anyone should have to see. But for them, for M. Villet and his wife and their three little boys, for Lily Charbonne and Jeanne-Anne Duval and Marie-Claire Beauvais and all of the others, I will do whatever is needed to give them their justice. They experienced the horror. I can bear to merely see it."

She hadn't quite learned yet how to limit the magic only to vision, but it was better this time than the last. Surely next time would be easier still, less reliving the horror and more like watching a terrible, tragic play?

Was that what had made Yvaine into the cold creature she was? Years of cutting off her emotions while watching visions of depravity and cruelty? Or had she been unable to block the experiences and been filled with hate and the icy thirst for revenge? Amanusa wanted, needed to know. She did not want to become a copy of Yvaine, whose callous manner surely had contributed much to the world's opinion of blood sorcery.

The police captain called his men and had them cart away the criminals, who began to revive with the rough handling.

"What about her?" Cranshaw flung an accusatory hand toward Amanusa. "Why aren't you arresting that foul creature? She is a witch. A *sorcire du sang*. A temptress and a worker of black magic, enslaving men with her wiles."

The Frenchman turned, raising a single eyebrow as he looked at the apoplectic wizard. "If it were a crime for a woman to tempt men," he said in heavily accented English, "every woman in Paris would be in prison. To be a temptress, a woman has only to exist. It is the fault of the man for falling to temptation."

He lifted a finger to abort another outburst from Cranshaw. "Nor," he said, "is it a crime to defend oneself from attack, using the weapons one might have. Far from committing a crime, this lady has done a very great service. I too have heard the cry of innocent blood demanding justice. And if it is black magic that hears the cry and is able to answer it, then I say—*give me more black magic*."

The policeman turned his back on a sputtering Cranshaw and bowed deeply to Amanusa. "Captain Louis Vaillon at your service, mademoiselle."

Amanusa introduced herself and Jax, who finally put his sword back in its case to shake hands with the captain. The blood smeared over his hand reminded everyone of their injuries, and they were hustled into a hastily summoned hansom cab and taken to the hotel only a few blocks away.

Alone with Jax in the small cab, Amanusa slumped against the high back wall. She ached all over, her arm burned where the villain had cut it, and her clothes were stuck to her skin with blood, both hers and Jax's. Maybe if she got some of it back inside her, she wouldn't feel so tired. No one could see her barbaric behavior beneath the hood of the cab. Amanusa brought her blood-streaked hand to her mouth and began to lick it clean.

It wasn't all her own blood. On her right hand, the bloodiest, it mostly belonged to Jax, for she'd had her arm around him, under his coat, where the cut on his back had bled. It tasted the same, but it . . . *felt* different. Stripped down to basics, and yet with a bright complexity that promised . . . But she wouldn't have years for exploring Jax's complications. She needed to set him free of her as soon as possible.

The thought twisted her stomach, churning it more than the horrors committed by those criminals. But she refused to keep him where he didn't want to be.

"Amanusa?" His weary voice came from the shadows beside her. His hand fumbled from his lap into hers until he found her hand—the one she wasn't licking clean—and clasped it. Her stomach relaxed its twist.

"Yes, Jax?" She cleaned a thick pool of his blood from her palm, savoring its differences.

"Will you marry me?"

"What?" Shock thrilled through her, from her suddenly racing heart out to her tingling extremities and up into her head where it rendered her mind inoperable.

"Will you please do me the honor of becoming my wife?" He turned in the seat and brought her hand up to his mouth where he kissed her blood-smeared fingers.

"B-but—"

"I had just realized what a great, hulking idiot I am when those creatures attacked. I understood finally just how much you trust me, and that you hold me at greater value than I hold myself—than I have held myself in a very long time. Yvaine taught me that I am worth nothing—less than nothing—"

"That's not true!" Amanusa couldn't keep the words from bursting out, though she'd had no intention of interrupting him. His speech began to heal the aching hollow in her gut. He'd asked her for marriage this time.

She saw his smile in the light of a passing gas lamp. He brushed his fingers along her temple, down her cheek, leaving a cool dampness behind.

"You are the first to think so in a very long time. But because you believe it, I begin to believe it as well. And if you have enough faith in me to think I am worth marrying, then I will do my damnedest to live up to that faith. Because of you, I am no longer just a magical construct. For you, I can be a man again. And this man humbly begs you to grant his plea for your hand in marriage."

"You have to take all of me, not just my hand." Amanusa wanted to smack herself for the stupid quip, but her hands were both holding tight to both of Jax's and her mind still wasn't working quite right.

"Every wonderful inch," he agreed. "And you have to forgive me my idiocy."

"What idiocy? Jax, do you mean it?" She could scarcely believe it.

"We can marry tomorrow, if you like. I did promise, and a Greyson always keeps his promises. At least, I do now. I just couldn't believe you truly meant for me to keep it."

Joy flooded Amanusa so swiftly she had no time to wonder at its cause or source. She stretched up toward Jax, her eyes locked on the rough-carved planes of his familiar, comforting face. His eyes flicked from hers, to her lips, and his mouth met hers in a kiss.

Had she meant for him to kiss her? She didn't know, could only react, with her brain out of commission, and kiss him back. His mouth opened, his tongue licked across her lips and she gave him entry, tasting her blood and his mingling from what had been deposited on his lips and hers.

A new flavor—not a literal, physical taste, but something that wasn't magic and yet registered with the same magic sense—slid across her magic sensor. Something that was partly Jax and partly Amanusa and wholly new. Magic shivered into being from that new thing. Powerful magic that whispered gently through Amanusa. Warm, without the acid burn. She whispered back, sending it to shield and to heal. She could sense the pain in Jax's back and forearm fade, and she reveled in the delicious feel of this new magic.

It buzzed over her skin, sensitizing it to every touch, making her yearn for more. More touch, more sensation, more everything.

The horse came to a halt and Jax broke the kiss,

staring at her in shock as his tongue swiped across his lips, licking up the last of the stains. "What have you done?" he gasped out, voice harsh. "That wasn't just your blood. Much of it was mine."

Amanusa shrugged, not sure why he sounded so frantic. "I know."

"Yvaine never tasted my blood. Ever. She went to great lengths to avoid it."

"Why?" She frowned at him. It hadn't felt danger- ous, tasting his blood. It felt good. To both of them. His pain had abated as his wounds began to heal, and she felt energized, her veins fizzing with the new, mellow-feeling magic.

Jax shook his head. "I don't know—"

"Are you all right?" Elinor Tavis hovered beside their cab.

"Better than before," Amanusa said as Jax alit and helped her out. "I was able to start the healing on Jax's injuries."

She hissed and jerked away when Harry Tomlin- son took her injured arm to help her into the hotel. She had to speak out to be heard over his apologies. "It's too bad I can't work healing magic on myself."

"Wizardry will have to do, then." Elinor hustled them across the hotel to the stairs. "Come along with you, now."

"I don't suppose either of you would know whether it's possible to arrange for a wedding by tomorrow," Jax said diffidently.

Elinor squealed. "Tomorrow? Truly?"

"We put it off until we got to Paris. There were . . . complications in crossing Hungary and Austria. But now that we are here—" Jax smiled down at

Amanusa. "I find myself unwilling to wait any longer."

Amanusa felt her face burn in one of those blasted blushes. Fair as she was, the blush showed clear to the part in her nearly transparent hair. But she'd have been even more embarrassed if Jax hadn't taken the lead in asking. He truly did want to marry her. Soon.

Worry rose off him in waves. Tasting his blood had so sensitized her to his moods that she could tell what worried him. Besides his worry about her taking in his blood, he worried about her injury, that she'd lost too much blood too quickly. She did feel a trifle light-headed.

With a curse, Jax swung her up into his arms. "She's bleeding too much. Where?" And he strode up the stairs and down the hallway, following Elinor's rapid scurry.

They reached Elinor's hotel room where Amanusa insisted Jax remain for the healing. She didn't want him out of her sight. Bad things happened, and worse happened when they were separated.

Besides, the lessons from Yvaine warned over and over again about the care that had to be taken with disposal of the sorceress's blood and Amanusa's had spattered everywhere. That in the street and on the cobbles was used up in the justice magic, but her skin and clothing held more. She needed Jax to help her with it.

While Jax rinsed blood from the rag used to wash her clean, Elinor stitched up the spell-numbed cut in Amanusa's arm. The stitching didn't hurt, but she found the tug at her skin a bit unnerving, and distracted herself by calling the blood together in the water basin so Jax could soak it up with one of his rice-paper squares. She gathered up the rest of the ambient coppery-tasting magic, leaving behind the green-grass-smelling magic—and then didn't know what to do with it.

"Give it to me," Jax said.

Elinor looked up for a moment from her stitching, at Jax and then Amanusa. Then she turned back to her work, whispering a spell as she sewed. Amanusa could feel it working, could hear the wizardly melody floating in the room, and knew she could never create such delicately beautiful magic.

Her own magic was rich and earthy and . . . sensuous. It held the pounding rhythm of a heartbeat and the hot rush of desire. No wonder people feared its power.

"Give me the magic," Jax said again. "It's why I was bound. It's what I'm for."

Elinor faded from Amanusa's awareness as she looked up at Jax, there beside her, holding her up. Her fingers slid between his, pressing their palms tight together. "If that is what Yvaine believed, then she was a fool, because you are so much more than she ever allowed you to be."

"Give it to me." He whispered it this time, bringing their clasped hands to his lips to press a kiss to her fingertips. "Elinor stores magic in her ointments and amulets. Harry stores his in his pebbles. Blood magic can only be stored in blood and bone. You've done it before. You know it won't harm me. It may be what has kept me alive so long."

Amanusa brushed the back of her hand along his

whiskery jaw. His beard was redder than the hair on his head. She cupped his face, then closed her eyes to look for the magic storage spaces inside him. But she couldn't get in.

Something held her at bay, held her outside of Jax's body, apart from his thoughts. She could still feel her magic, her blood sliding through his veins, and it warmed her, kept her from panic when she bumped up against the—the skin, the barrier that kept her out.

Elinor had gone. Amanusa was vaguely aware of that. She'd gone out the door after responding to Harry's knock. There was only Jax, only Amanusa here now. She leaned toward him, close and closer still as she sensed something layering over Jax's continuing worry—his awareness of her as a woman and of her semiclothed state.

"Jax?" Amanusa's lips brushed his as she murmured his name, utterly unafraid. "Take the magic."

"Yes, of course."

The barrier between them vanished as he somehow reached out and took the excess magic from her. There, along his bones, she saw the places made to hold the magic and laid it in gently. Not like the last time, during the attack in Budapest when she'd had to pour it clumsily into him, desperate to rid herself of it without ever having done it before.

Jax gasped and pressed his cheek tight against hers. "I'd forgotten," he whispered. "The glorious burn of magic in my bones."

"It hurts you?" Amanusa grabbed hold of it again, ready to haul it out and send it . . . somewhere. To the victims of those criminals.

"No, no." He caught her hands, kissed them both,

distracting her. "I'm fine. Grand. It feels good. But it's like using a muscle after you haven't in a long time. There's a bit of an adjustment. A tiny strain until you're used to it again."

She studied his face, watched inside him as the magic settled in, ready to act if he didn't tell the absolute truth. After a moment, he relaxed, smiled at her, and she found herself eased out of his body as if she'd been politely ushered to the door. What if she needed the magic? Would she be able to get it? How was he able to keep her out when he never had before?

Jax fetched the clean blouse Elinor had hung from the doorknob before she stepped out for her corridor conference with Harry. As soon as Amanusa was buttoned into it, she ordered Jax out of his shirt and frock coat and went to fetch Elinor to work her magic on him. Harry and Grey Carteret came in with her.

"I thought you were staying at the laboratory," Amanusa said as she rinsed the cloth to wash Jax's arm while Elinor began work on his back.

"Something's come up," Harry said. "Alvaro— he's near as smart as Pyotr—thinks they might 'ave learnt something an' I thought you might want to 'ave a look with your magic and see if you agree, so we came to ask. Good thing we came back when we did, or we'd've missed all the excitement. We 'eard a scream and saw Cranshaw run, an' followed 'im. And there you were, at the end of the scream."

He plucked a chair from the desk across the room and set it near the bench where Amanusa and Elinor worked over Jax before sitting in it backward. Grey sprawled across the bed, ignoring scowls from Harry and Elinor.

"What is it they've discovered?" Amanusa asked through a yawn.

"Rather not say." Harry folded his arms on the top rail of the chair's back. "Better if you wait an' see for yourself. Reach your own conclusion, like."

He sat up straight, making a fist to bounce on the chair rail. "While I was waitin' for Elinor to finish here, I had Grey send a message to a bloke I know with the French government. Dalcourt says you can get married tomorrow at the registry, but there's a heap of paperwork to be done first. He'll get it all arranged. So that's done. You'll have to be at the Faubourg St. Michel registry building by nine tomorrow morning to sign things."

"Thank you." Jax nodded at the two men, dignified despite the woman muttering spells at his naked back. Amanusa let Jax's thanks stand for them both.

After another moment, Elinor finished with Jax's back. She stood and lifted his injured arm to inspect it. "Nice clean slice. No need for stitching here." She probed it lightly. "Already healing, like your back, thanks to Amanusa's sorcery. We'll just numb it, clean it, and dress it."

Amanusa's heart felt full. These people owed them nothing, yet they'd helped when she and Jax needed them. They did want something from her—but it was no more than she expected from herself. She wanted to help with the deadly magic-free zones.

Jax shrugged back into his ruined frock coat. "My sorceress is beyond exhausted. I am taking her back to her room and sending her to bed."

"Don't forget," Harry said. "Nine o'clock sharp at the St. Michel registry building."

"Will you come?" Amanusa gave in to sudden impulse. "You and Elinor. As witnesses."

Elinor scrambled up from her chair to hug Amanusa. "Of course we'll be there. We wouldn't miss it for anything."

"Should I be feeling unwanted?" Grey put in.

"You *are* unwanted," Harry retorted. "It's 'cause you're useless."

"I am useful for a great many things." Grey paused, as if considering. "Of course, a great majority of those things are useless . . ."

Amanusa couldn't help laughing. "Come, if you like. If you're awake at that hour."

Grey struggled to escape the pillows and the fluffy featherbed, making a show of it, extending her laughter. Once on his feet, he bowed. "Gentle lady, for you, I will force myself."

"Good evening, then." Jax bowed, and steered Amanusa out of the room.

There was something she'd wanted to ask him when they were alone, and now that they were, she couldn't remember what it was. She scoured her mind from one end to the other, turning out all the corners—if minds had ends. Or corners. They had trails and paths, she was certain, for her thoughts often raced along them like frightened rabbits. And she'd gone wandering down one of them now. She was too tired to remember, and her arm hurt. She was just barely aware of Jax tucking her into bed.

THE MORNING OF her wedding day—a day she never thought she would see—Amanusa dressed in another of the white dresses Jax had insisted on. After last night, she understood clearly why a sorceress wore white. The dark blue of last night's dress hid the blood, made it that much harder to retrieve it and its magic. The magic released by the burning was much less than magic collected by recovering the blood. She would be wearing more white in the future, even if it did make her look pale.

This dress had frills, but not so many she looked silly in it. Made of thin muslin, it was cool in Paris's late August heat. In the usual way, she had no right to wear white to a wedding. But as a sorceress—she had every right.

Jax wore white too, a white linen summer coat that made him look very man-of-the-world. After three hundred–plus years of living in the world, she supposed he was. He'd risen early, dressed quickly in the suite's dressing room, and vanished.

Elinor walked down to their suite on the floor below hers, looking fresh and lovely in a bell-skirted dress of pale green muslin. Together they descended to the lobby where Jax waited with a bouquet of roses that took Amanusa's breath away. White, with every petal edged in crimson, they were sorcerer's roses. They still had their thorns.

He had a little posy of pinks in the same colors for Elinor, who was touched by the gesture. Harry, waiting with Jax, looked both bewildered by Elinor's reaction, and as if he wished he'd thought of the posy himself. They were on their way out when Grey clattered down the stairs, skidded across the lobby's polished marble floor, and pulled up with quickly assumed dignity at the back of their party.

20

AT THE REGISTRY building, the paperwork was assembled and waiting for them, including a paper from the English embassy that had to be signed and sealed by the local magistrate. Once everything was filled out in multiple copies, and signed in a dozen places, and stamped and sealed by three or four officials—or so it seemed—the wedding itself was anticlimactic.

The magistrate spoke a few simple lines, got the agreement of John Christian Alvanleigh Greyson to marry Amanusa Maria Whitcomb, and her consent to marry him. Then he said a few more official-sounding sentences. Everyone—Harry, Elinor, and Grey included—had to sign yet another document, and it was done. Amanusa was Mrs. John Greyson.

They all went together to an elegant restaurant to celebrate at their wedding breakfast with *coquilles* and *omelettes* and *éclairs* and *framboises* and a great deal of champagne. Amanusa laughed until tears ran down her face, though when Jax asked, she couldn't tell him what amused her so.

"It's only a bit after noon," Harry said, leaning back in his chair, an arm draped over the back of Jax's chair beside him. "Conclave meeting's not until five, when some of the conjury spirits start waking up."

"Mine don't." Grey yawned. "Mine are proper slugs. Refuse to wake 'til the moon's risen. Or midnight, depending."

"Moonrise today is at four-seventeen."

Grey paid Harry's announcement no attention, other than raising a single eyebrow.

"I know a conclave meeting ain't—isn't exactly anybody's idea of wedding day fun," Harry said. "But I think you ought to go, after last night's adventure. I think we ought to make sure the governors know what happened, an' I think we ought to make it as public as we can. The more as knows what's goin' on, the 'arder it will be for 'em to do it again."

"Reluctant as I am to be separated from my new bride for any length of time," Jax said with a gallant little bow toward Amanusa, "I believe you're right. I think Amanusa should go to the afternoon's meeting. I'll keep Elinor company in the lobby."

"So then." Harry sat up straight and slapped his hands on his knees. "Since there's hours to fill between now an' time for the meeting to start, I think we should all go see what the lads 'ave learned about the machines after workin' all night—'cause you know they did—an' what the new Mrs. Greyson's magic thinks about it."

When they arrived at the conclave's laboratory, proof of the all-night labors showed in the unshaven faces, disheveled clothing, and abandoned coffee cups scattered about the room. The machine lay cracked in two, its intestines rusting green and orange and black in the daylight glaring down from the skylights overhead. Other bits of the machine lay on nearby tables. Amanusa couldn't tell whether the separate pieces had been broken off, or had simply fallen off in the process of opening the thing up.

"Matteo Alvaro." A lanky black-haired man with a beaky nose and pale skin under dark-bristled cheeks shook Amanusa's hand. "Alchemist. Portugal. Met yesterday, but I'm sure you don't remember."

He didn't give her time to respond before he turned away to drag her closer to the table with the machine. "What do you see?"

Amanusa blinked. "A machine. Broken open. Rust and corrosion and copper patina." She copied his abrupt speech pattern without intending to.

"Yes, yes, but what else? Look with your magic."

How? She looked a question at Jax, who shrugged, seeming as bewildered as she. "I am a sorcerer," she said. "My magic doesn't work very well with things that don't bleed. What do you see?"

"But machines do bleed." That came from one of the very young men, an apprentice. "The machines that we make do. They bleed oil."

"Oil is alchemy." Alvaro poked at the machine's insides with a metal rod, frowning. "I will tell you what I do not see. I do not see any nuts or bolts or screws. Not performing their usual tasks, that is."

"Then, what's holding it together?" Amanusa leaned over the table and peered into the machine's depths.

A jumble of metal bits and pieces formed a busy-looking tangle. She had no idea what purpose they might serve, but she had no doubt they worked toward a purpose of some sort. It *looked* like they did. She recognized small tools—pliers and hammer-heads and half a scissor—turned from their original purpose and stuck together by some glue, some force she didn't know. A long bolt seemed to serve as a support, but it wasn't threaded through or screwed down to anything. Just stuck on.

"Is that a stone?" She scraped away a flake of rust

to expose a gray rock with shiny bits. Why would anyone put a rock in a machine?

"Quartz crystals," Alvaro said. "Rather large ones, if you'll look on that side of it." He pointed with his metal stick at a number of square clear crystals protruding into a nest of coppery-green wire.

"What does it all mean?" She looked up at him, bewildered. "How are all of those things stuck together? How do they work? What do they do?"

"We do not know how they work or what their purpose is." Alvaro tapped his pointer in the open palm of his other hand. "We have only guesses. Theories. These will, however, give us a place to begin in sorting out what it all means. We surmise—"

"Not all of us," someone called from the back of the room. "Some of us think you're cracked in the head."

"Be quiet, Hansen. We're tired of you." Someone else Amanusa couldn't see.

"The machine was not built by human hands," Alvaro said in a rush, as if to get it out before any more interruptions.

That didn't make sense. Amanusa frowned, looking from the machine to the alchemist and back again. "Who else could have?"

"The machine itself, perhaps." Alvaro tugged her toward the other half of the machine. "Look there. A tiny bit of a thing. A few wires and a nail, a wheel from a child's toy. I think that is the beginning, and these other pieces were added on as it grew."

"Added on how? Why do you think someone didn't make it?" The idea seemed extremely farfetched to Amanusa.

"Don't you see?" Pyotr Strelitsky, seeming mostly

recovered from yesterday's trauma, chimed in. "It is precisely because we cannot define, describe, or duplicate the process that makes it unlikely to be human built. We do not have the ability to fasten things so securely together. Not like this."

"Welding." Hansen, the debater, was a stocky wizard with a thick shock of wheat-colored hair.

"Welds don't hold like this," Alvaro retorted. "It's stronger than welds."

"Besides, we cannot tell what this machine's purpose is." Strelitsky had a long ivory letter opener to poke at the jumbled insides. "Humans construct machines to *do* something, for a specific purpose. The machines have an efficiency about them, an order. They are not so higgledy-piggledy inside. Things are used for their proper purposes, not stuck on any old way. Our machines are bolted together, because it's easier. More efficient."

"But—" Hansen began.

Alvaro overrode him. "How could a man build it? The machines cannot live outside the dead zones, and men cannot live inside them."

"We don't know that for certain, and men can survive for a time in the zones."

"It is easily tested and proved, and it is reasonable to assume, given their behavior as we have observed them, and the condition of this specimen," Alvaro said. "Magic damages them. And there is a limit to the amount of time even a head-blind man can spend in the dead zones. No one could remain long enough to build something so sophisticated as this."

"He could go in and out. He wouldn't have to remain in the dead zone from beginning to end of the construction." Hansen glowered just as fiercely at Alvaro as Alvaro glared back at him. "And as for *why*— a man could use these machines to do things for him in the dead zones. Loot the buildings of abandoned valuables."

"Apart from the fact that this machine has no discernable purpose, no human-built machine will work without the operator controlling it," Alvaro retorted, then waved his hands to forestall the other man. "We have been arguing these same theories all night. You bring nothing new to the table."

"I simply wish to ensure that our sorceress—" Hansen tipped his head in a weary bow "—is fully aware of all possibilities and not simply given the opinion of the majority."

"Is it the majority opinion?" Amanusa asked. "That the machines . . . built themselves?"

"By a very small majority." Alvaro shrugged. "We were hoping that sorcery would be able to tip our information one way or the other."

"What does your magic show?"

"Conjury detects no human aura," one of the conjurers said.

"Hasn't been touched by humans since this lady put it in her box," Strelitsky added. "Alchemy can read the materials that were used in its construction, but the deterioration has made most other information impossible to read."

"What about wizardry?" Amanusa looked to the wizard Hansen.

He shrugged. "Wizardry does not work very well on nonliving things."

"Are you sure there is no sorcery you can perform

to determine whether this machine was built or, or birthed?" Alvaro asked. "Whether human hands constructed it, or it constructed itself?"

"There might be something in the spellbooks in Yvaine's tower." She wanted to help. She just didn't know how. "But I would think this machine is too damaged for me to learn anything now."

"We could get another one." Harry spoke for the first time since they arrived. "You'll need to run more tests anyway. A fresh machine'll give fresh information."

No one spoke when he paused, so he went on. "Besides, I've been wanting to see what Mrs. Greyson's magic can do with the dead zones. Her first working of major sorcery knocked the borders back across most of Europe. Maybe she can do more."

A babble of voices responded, excited by the idea, which made Amanusa nervous. She did not want the pressure of attempting brand new, never-done-before-by-anyone magic with an audience. She feared her look to Jax was close to desperate.

Harry must have seen it. "You lads 'ave been workin' all night. Mrs. Greyson don't need a bunch o' rubber-neckers spyin' over 'er shoulder. We'll give a full report at the conclave session this evenin'. And we'll see wot we can do about gettin' you another machine to work on. They're gettin' more aggressive about folk goin' into the zones, so maybe it won't be hard to grab one."

He paused, his mind obviously ticking something over. "That's why I think they built themselves. They're startin' to act like, like ants protecting their nest. I don't know any machine that'll do that. I don't know any man smart enough to build somethin' that'll do that."

The babble started up again and escalated quickly as old arguments arose. Harry seemed to take this as farewell, for he tipped his head toward the door in signal, and the English party filed out.

Just before the door shut on the noise, Amanusa heard a deep voice cry, "Data! We need more data before any hypothesis."

The cab ride to the dead zone near the *Chambre de Conseil* was long enough Amanusa fell into a doze. When they arrived, she looked around her with great curiosity. Though they had passed through the magical vacuum of a dead zone, Amanusa had been on a train at the time, traveling at great speed. She wasn't able to inspect it closely. Now, holding tight to Jax's hand, she ventured past the line of demarcation into the barren section of the street, watching him closely for any sign of distress.

She stretched all her senses, especially the one that detected magic. Jax was a blazing bonfire of magic, but other than his bright glow, she could sense nothing at all. The vacuum sucked at their magic, trying to break the loop that fed it from Amanusa to Jax and back again, endlessly. It wasn't a vicious, purposeful attack. More like the magic had died and the land—the stones and air and plants—everything in the zone needed magic so desperately to replenish what was lost that it tried to steal it from those who had it.

"*Oi!*" Harry called from halfway down the block, beyond the magic's boundary. "You all right?"

Amanusa looked the question up at Jax.

"I'm fine." He took in a deep breath to demonstrate. "Where do you suppose we might find a machine for the lads in the laboratory?"

A buzzing, clicking sound made Amanusa turn around. On the steps of one of the doorless, derelict houses stood a mechanical creature. The body was vaguely cylindrical, for it was made of a series of once-hollow tubes—pipes or stove flues, perhaps—sealed together in a bunch about the length of her forearm in diameter. It was about twice that in length. Down the sides of this body ran a series of scalloped wheels that appeared to be made of spoon handles welded together like flower petals. Amanusa didn't know where the bowls of the spoons might be.

The thing seemed to Amanusa more a curiosity than a threat. Until it rattled forward and pitched down the steps of the abandoned house in a controlled tumble to the street. A metallic clatter behind them had Jax jerking her around to see another machine—this one squat and flat, apparently made of tea trays with insectlike legs of narrow pipe—scuttling down another set of stairs.

"No need to search, I see." He pushed her behind him, toward the zone's boundary. "Seems the machines have come to find us."

"Maybe they'll follow and we can capture one at our leisure." Amanusa dragged Jax with her toward the boundary, entirely certain she did not want to be outnumbered by them. The first two machines had been joined by half a dozen comrades, all apparently armed in some fashion. They gave chase, some faster than others. The ones with wheels seemed to have more trouble with the round cobbles than the ones with legs.

"They're rather like soldier ants, don't you think?" Amanusa walked backward, watching the creatures. "Designated and equipped to protect the nest. I wonder if there's a queen machine, like a queen ant."

"Stop observing them and run." Jax shoved her ahead of him with his grip on her upper arm.

The tea tray creature caught up to him and sliced at his ankles with whirling blades.

"*Run.*" Jax let go of Amanusa to dance out of its range.

She ran. A few more paces put her safely across the magic line. She turned back to shout at Jax, and her heart nearly stopped to see him dart back in, snatch the tea tray thing by its edges, and fling it over the heads of the watching magicians to clatter on the street beyond.

"There," he said, when he was safely on the living side of the line, not even breathing hard. "You've got a local machine to study."

Amanusa snatched up his hands to examine them. As expected, white blisters formed where he'd grabbed the machine. "You could have waited for help."

"I saw the opportunity," Jax said, white-lipped. "And I took it. I was afraid it would get at you."

Harry and Grey stood a few paces away, observing and guarding the machine Jax had tossed. It crawled feebly toward the dead zone boundary, pipestem legs collapsing at every step. It flung its whirling blades out at the men to keep them back.

Elinor joined Amanusa in examining Jax's injuries.

"I have an ointment for blisters like this, but it's in my room."

Amanusa reached in Jax's inner coat pocket for his silver flask. "Pour this over his hands. It will sting, but it was spelled just last night. It's still potent."

As Elinor poured, Amanusa cast a glance toward the machine again, just as Grey lashed out with a foot and flipped the thing onto its broad, shiny back, where its legs twitched in midair and its sharp blades clattered against the cobblestones.

"Do you know how galling it is," Grey said, voice bored and elegant as always, "to have to stand aside when someone is in danger because any attempt to assist would only make things worse?"

"I do indeed." Harry nodded. "I never make it past that first set of steps there without collapsin'. If I'd gone in, I'd have to be dragged out by my heels."

"Quite. Doubt if the ladies could drag our unconscious carcasses to safety without slicing away large chunks to lighten the load." Grey sighed as he prodded the dying machine with a toe. "Still, it is extremely galling."

Amanusa turned her attention back to Jax's palms, healing rapidly under their coating of bespelled liquor. She slipped into the magic of her blood inside him to ease the pain and hasten the healing more.

When she returned from the magic, Harry and Grey had joined them, leaving the machine lying dead in the gutter. Harry was the most obvious in his staring, but Elinor and Grey stared too.

"How are you feeling?" Elinor took her hands, studied Amanusa's face.

"Fine." She looked at each of the others in turn.

"Why?" Harry said. "Why do the dead zones bother a sorcerer less than they bother us?"

"Because Amanusa carries the source of her magic within herself," Jax said. "Sorcery is *blood* magic. Internal and self-contained."

"There was magic in the room when I was stitching Amanusa," Elinor said. "I could sense it, but I couldn't manipulate it. I don't have the right tools. Blood magic, wasn't it? From all the blood that was spilled."

"Yes." Amanusa wondered how much Elinor had deduced, and if any of what she'd deduced were sorcerer's guild secrets.

"Jax said to give it to him, because sorcery must be stored in blood and bone and flesh, not in plants or rocks or spirits. So by holding onto Jax, you are holding onto a store of your magic."

"Alchemy's in the rocks and air and water—but there's no magic in those things inside the dead zones," Harry mused. "Maybe if I carried something with me—a stone I powered up, maybe—"

"I could wrap a spirit round my head." Grey leaned on his cane, his expression of ennui a thinning mask over intense interest. "Like a magic tank, instead of a fish tank for transporting fishes through air." He paused. "Hate to put the poor things through that. They're already dead. The dead zones make them more so."

"Why would you want to?" Amanusa asked. "What would be the purpose of wrapping a spirit around yourself or powering up a stone and going in? Just to prove that you could?"

"To learn what the zones are so we can learn how

to stop 'em," Harry retorted. "You can't cure a disease until you know what disease you're treating. We got to know what this is."

"It's a dead zone. It's a place where the magic has died." Was that what she'd felt? "Or maybe—the magic has been all used up. When we were in there, I felt something sucking—no, that's not right—" She worked her way through, thinking out loud.

"There was a vacuum. No magic. And the magic we had—it wanted to spread out and fill up the vacuum, but we didn't have enough to refill what was empty. It would have taken all the magic we had until we had nothing left, and we would have been empty, and the dead zone still wouldn't have enough magic to fill itself up again—and the magic it took would die too."

"The earth," Harry said. "The earth and the stones are empty. Earth is the most basic of magics, an' the most vulnerable, because it don't move. Air, water, fire—they move. They change and change back, but the earth, it just sits there. Other things pull magic from it. Plants grow in it. Spirits rise from it. People live on it. But maybe when it's empty, it reaches out to pull magic back, enough to stay alive. As alive as earth can be."

"And when the magic isn't enough," Elinor said. "It pulls more and more and more, making the dead zones grow larger."

"But why is it in *spots*?" Grey demanded. "If that is what is happening, why isn't the level of magic shrinking uniformly worldwide? Or even continent-wide?"

Amanusa shook her head. She had no idea, and

she was sure no one else did. "Perhaps we should concentrate first on a way to keep the zones from growing any larger," she said tentatively. "And let the men in the laboratory try to find answers to the machines and all the other questions."

"Trust a woman to keep us focused on practical matters." Grey's eyes twinkled as he swept off his top hat and bowed to her.

"I been thinkin'," Harry said.

"Dangerous behavior," Grey put in when the silence stretched.

"Stifle it, conjurer." Harry didn't bother to look at him, just glowered at the dead zone and the machines. "I been thinkin' it for a long time, that we needed all four magics to deal with these things, all four workin' together, and it worried me, 'cause we didn't 'ave but three. Till now."

"But what kind of spell would work?" Amanusa couldn't imagine.

"We shouldn't simply make something up." Elinor sounded less alarmed than she likely was. "We need to study the matter, look at possibilities, see what's been tried before."

"I know what's been tried before," Harry said. "I've kept track of every spell in every country across Europe. I've done 'alf of 'em. An' nothing's worked. Not until Mrs. Greyson here worked that justice magic that made the dead zones shrink."

He bent and picked up a handful of dust and gravel from between the cobblestones. "Amanusa's right, though. We need to start with keepin' the zones from growing. All the magics 'ave protective warding spells. Let's try buildin' one. We got magicians here from all the four guilds. Let's each of us put up our own sort of seal an' figure a way to tie 'em together."

"If everyone contributes a little blood," Amanusa offered, "I believe I can do that."

"Wot do we put it in?" Harry cast about for a container. "An' I'll need water, as well as earth. Earth with magic in it."

"This dead zone stretches for five city blocks," Grey said. "Just how much blood are we talking about?"

Five blocks. Amanusa blinked. She hadn't thought there would be so much ground to cover. She should have, given the size of the dead zone they'd passed through in the Grand Duchy of Baden. "More than a few drops. Less than the average doctor's bloodletting. But if you're that opposed to it, Mr. Carteret, I don't want your blood. It must be *willingly* offered. Otherwise, it's no use to me."

"I didn't say I wasn't willing," Grey protested. "I simply reserve the right to moan and whinge about it. I'm perfectly willing." He thrust his arm at Amanusa, exposing the veins on his wrist, covering his eyes with his other arm. "There it is. Take it."

"Let's wait 'til Harry's found us a bucket." Amanusa glanced at Jax, who rolled his eyes, and she sputtered with laughter.

"Now you're laughing at me?" Grey lowered his arm and glared at her over it, before dropping his mock-cower. "I am hurt. Deeply hurt."

Harry returned from his search. "Found a lad who'll sell us a bucket and fill it with water—from a fountain, not the Seine—for a few francs."

"Why not the Seine?" Amanusa asked.

"Clean water's got more power. An' I think the river runs too close to the dead zone here. I think it's leaching magic out o' the river."

"The river doesn't flow *into* the dead zone, does it?" Elinor touched Harry's arm, concerned.

"Nah. No river does, that we've found. Probably part o' the reason the zones are in spots." Harry looked at Elinor. "You got what you need for the spell?"

"Oh. No." She looked sheepish. "I'd better busy myself with my gathering, hadn't I?" She glided to one of the living chestnut trees lining the streets and stared up into its branches. "Though as usual, I seem to be in need of more stature. I need twigs. Green branches to build my wall. And I can't reach them."

"I can." Harry grabbed the nearest branch and paused before wrenching it free of its parent. "Is there some particular way I need to take it? Or can I just break it off?"

"Just break. I'll tend to the particular matters. But no branches thicker than that one."

Amanusa removed the lancet from her pocket as Elinor began to murmur while Harry broke off slender branches. She slid her finger into the silver ring and Grey shuddered ostentatiously as he watched her.

"What about you?" she asked him. "Do you have what you need for the spell?"

He looked at the sky, then he pulled a large watch from his waistcoat pocket and consulted it. "If our Harry is correct about moonrise at four-seventeen, then in twenty more minutes—by the time all the components of our five-block spell are assembled—I will. Until then—"

He looked about, spotted a bench against the wall of one of the houses, and strolled in its direction. "I believe I shall rest for my labors."

Grey flipped up his coattails and sat on the wood slats of the iron bench seat. Then he pivoted, lifting his feet as he lay down, tilting his hat forward over his eyes, all in one smooth motion. He seemed to be quite practiced at resting.

Amanusa sighed, trying to relax her shoulders by force as she exhaled. She'd slept wrong last night, or perhaps the tensions of the last few days had tied her shoulders and neck into the aching knots they seemed to be made of today.

"All right?" Jax moved close behind her, his head dipping as he spoke quietly near her ear. It felt as if he wrapped himself around her, made himself into her shelter. She'd had so little shelter in her life.

She couldn't stop herself from leaning back into him, taking advantage of his strength. "Mmm."

"Mrs. Greyson." He brushed his knuckles along her cheek.

She looked up at him, feeling peculiar. She wasn't used to the name, though it had been used several times already. "Mmm?"

"I just wanted to say it. Mrs. Amanusa Whitcomb Greyson. My wife." He slid an arm around her waist, nuzzled her ear. "I like the sound of that."

She leaned back harder, letting him hold her up. She liked the way he said it. Possessive, but in a good way. Not the way one would say "my house" or "my jewelry," but the way one might say "my son," or "my beloved."

Not that they were in love. They weren't. But there was that same pride in the other, the enjoyment in being together. Would she say it the same way? "Jax Greyson. My husband."

It felt different from saying "my servant." It had much the same feeling as when she'd laid claim to him on the boat to Vienna, declaring *mine.* So she said it again. "Mine."

"Yours," he agreed.

And tonight, he would take possession of her, with more than just words. She wasn't afraid, she realized. Nervous. Jittery. Not exactly aglow with eager anticipation. But she wasn't afraid.

"Don't think about it," he murmured into her ear.

"About what?" But she knew, and she knew he knew. "I'm not."

"Liar." He closed his lips on her earlobe and rubbed his tongue over it before suckling gently.

Amanusa shivered, able to give herself up to the sensation because they were standing in broad daylight in the middle of a public street. Nothing too intimate would happen here.

"You know you have nothing to worry about tonight." Jax's words came out muffled, because he still held her earlobe gently between his teeth. He released it to press a kiss just beneath the ear he'd teased so sweetly. "You know I will never do anything you don't want. If kisses are all you can bear, then kisses are what you shall have."

He laid another kiss along her jaw, just over the bone, and it skittered through her, making her breasts feel heavy and her nipples pucker as if from cold. But it wasn't cold she felt. She burned, as if magic raced along behind his kiss. Perhaps it did. Was this desire? He'd said kisses could raise magic if backed by desire.

She tried to think like a magician. "Jax—" She tilted her head to give him access to more of her neck. "This is protective magic we'll be working here, correct?"

"Aye." He slid his lips along the skin she offered.

"So, wouldn't the magic from a few kisses seal off the zone even better, if we add it? I sealed the machine in the box with just blood, but wouldn't . . . well, blood *and* sex make a better protective seal for five city blocks?"

He paused in his progress along her neck, lifting his head, but only a small distance. "Possibly."

His breath whispering over the damp left by his trail of kisses made her shiver. Again, not with cold.

"Probably." He raised his head more and scanned the street. "Not much privacy here."

"Jax." She whipped around to glare at him, pulling out of his embrace. "I didn't mean *sex* sex—"

"I know." He caught her hands, kissed them. "I know. But it is so very public here. Too public for the kind of kisses this magic would need. Too public for you."

"But if it's for the magic—" She let go one of his hands to turn and examine the street. "What about there? In the corner by the stairs up to that door."

"It's not very sheltered." Jax sounded dubious.

"It is from the live end of the street." Amanusa gestured at the dead zone. "There's nothing living in that direction to see us, except for machines. And Grey, and he's got his hat over his eyes."

"Are you sure? Not about Grey, but about—" Jax searched her face. Then, apparently finding what he sought, he strode toward the sheltering stairway, towing Amanusa after him with the hand she'd kept in his.

Amanusa was still laughing when he spun to set his back into the corner where stairs met building, using the momentum of stride and spin to impel her into his embrace. She collided with his chest with a tiny "oof" and looked up at him, her laughter fading at the intensity of his gaze.

"Jax?" Her voice trembled and she hated it. She wasn't afraid. Just . . . shaky.

"Amanusa." His intensity didn't fade. Somehow, it increased as he lifted his hand to trace his fingertips across her forehead and down her cheek. He smoothed over her eyebrows and down the length of her too-prominent nose. She'd never liked her nose, but if Jax did . . .

He slid a finger—bare like hers, for he was as likely to need lancing as she—across her lips, parting them slightly. She didn't feel blisters. Had they healed so much already? Must have. She wanted him to kiss her now. Her lips quivered in anticipation. But he didn't. He brought his fingertips to her eyes, closing them, teasing across her pale lashes.

Then he kissed her. Tiny touches of his lips to her eyelids. "Amanusa," he murmured when he kissed the first one.

"Mrs. Greyson," he said, after he kissed the other.

Eyes still closed, lips parted as he'd left them, Amanusa turned her face up to him, waiting for the kiss he'd—he hadn't promised it, not in words. But he was here, in this sheltered corner, with her. Surely he meant to—

His mouth brushed butterfly-soft across hers, and he spoke against her lips, into her mouth. "My *wife*."

Amanusa's eyes flew open and she saw Jax staring back at her, his eyes clear green-blue, without a speck or smudge of brown anywhere. "*My* wife," he said, and he kissed her.

21

JAX HAD KISSED her before. On the train. In a carriage. On the boat. They had all been very nice kisses. But this kiss made those kisses dry up and blow away like leaves past their time. Those kisses were puppies playing on the lawn. This kiss was the wolf at the door, ravenous and demanding to be fed.

Jax spun again, trapping Amanusa in the corner, shielding her from the street. With the arm around her back, he pulled her hard against him, so her skirt was forced into the wall behind them, driving them a little way out of their little shelter and threatening to snap another hoop. Amanusa didn't care.

She was in a corner, a man taller and stronger than she between her and the open air. And she didn't care. He held her so tight she couldn't get away, her breasts crushed into his chest, his mouth taking possession of her own, and not only did she not care, she liked it. Because the man was Jax, and Jax would never, not in another three hundred years, do anything to hurt her.

Because she knew it wouldn't hurt, she could let herself notice that it actually felt rather nice to be held this way, to be kissed this way, as if he needed to kiss her more than he needed to breathe. The press of his hard, male chest against her breasts made them feel full and . . . and eager? Anxious?

How could breasts be anxious? She didn't know, but they were. Or she was. She wanted—wanted—

"Oi." Harry's sardonic hail broke through the veil of sensation wrapped around Amanusa.

Jax broke the kiss, but other than tucking his cheek against Amanusa's to gasp in her ear, he didn't move. Amanusa was reasonably certain that she couldn't. Her knees seemed to have dissolved.

"I know you're newlyweds an' all," Harry said. "But we do 'ave a bit o' work to be doin' 'ere."

Amanusa peered past Jax's shoulder to see Harry standing with his back turned pointedly toward them. Elinor hovered just beyond, staring at the ground while she blushed a fiery red. And past Jax's other shoulder, Amanusa could see Grey Carteret sitting up with his feet still propped on the bench, his arms looped around his upthrust knees, watching them with an intent, utterly absorbed expression on his face.

As her blush burned up her skin, Amanusa hid her face in Jax's jacket. How long had Grey been watching? What had he seen? Surely very little, with her hidden behind Jax's broad shoulders.

"At least we didn't break another hoop," she muttered.

Jax pulled back and looked at her, a peculiar expression on his face. "You're not angry."

She blinked up at him. "Why would I be? I'm the one who suggested it."

"But I—" He took a deep breath, then took a step back, drawing Amanusa with him so her compressed hoops wouldn't suddenly spring up in front of her. "My control doesn't seem to be what it ought."

"I didn't notice anything wrong with it." She smiled at him. He seemed to need the reassurance. She adjusted the lancet still on her finger and took a deep breath, preparing to go forth and work magic.

"Amanusa." Jax touched a strand of pale hair escaping from her bonnet. "When it's time—tonight, when we're alone—we can begin with kisses and simply see where they lead."

He didn't need to reassure her again. That kiss was all the assurance she needed. "If we begin with kisses like that one, I have no doubt they'll take us anywhere we want to go."

She led him back to where Elinor and Harry peered into their bucket. Half full of water, mucky from the earth mixed into it, Elinor's twigs stuck up out of the concoction, most of them still bearing their leaves, creating a bizarre bouquet. Amanusa could sense the magic pooling inside. Like Elinor with blood magic, Amanusa could only poke at it, make it squawk rather than sing. But with her magic added . . .

Grey strolled up from his bench, tucking his pocket watch away. "Shall I go last, or shall you?" he asked Amanusa. "If you, we have a few more minutes yet to wait. My familiar spirits prefer that the moon be a full handsbreadth above the horizon when the moon insists on rising in daylight. It took me ages to convince them they could rise with the moon."

As she spoke, Amanusa watched Jax, wanting his confirmation that her guesses were reasonable. "I can go ahead now and do the warding part of the spell, then when your spirits answer, I can see about binding the magics together."

She raised her little fingertip lancet. "Your wrist, sir."

With a mournful sigh, Grey extended his arm and covered his eyes with the other. Amanusa took hold of his hand to steady him, and stopped. She shook her head and let go. "No good."

Grey jerked his arm from his eyes and glared at her. "What do you mean, my blood is no good? I'll have you know it's the best blue English aristocratic blood available—"

Amanusa laughed. "I meant, your shirt's in the way. And your jacket. You need to take off your jacket and roll up your sleeve so you don't get blood on your clothes. The blood itself is perfectly fine, I'm sure."

"Oh." Grey adjusted his shoulders beneath his frock coat, then he shrugged the garment off. "Quite."

He unfastened the gold cuff link and rolled up his sleeve exposing a sinewy, tanned forearm. Mr. Carteret wasn't as languid as he seemed to wish everyone to believe. Again, he presented his bare wrist, but this time he didn't cover his eyes.

He watched intently as Amanusa gripped his wrist with one hand to steady it. She studied the pale blue lines of his veins, rippling over muscle and tendon, selecting the most prominent. She posed the lancet over it and spoke just louder than a whisper. "Steady."

She plunged the point through his skin, holding tight against his reflexive jerk. Jax was immediately there with the embossed silver vial to catch the blood that flowed out. Four seconds. Five, and she pressed her thumb hard over the opening, holding it there until she sensed the blood beginning to clot. She licked her other thumb and substituted it over the little wound, whispering a "quick-heal" spell.

"That's it?" Grey asked when she released him. "That's all of it?"

"That's all of the collecting-your-blood bit." Amanusa cleaned the lancet on a bit of rice paper she dropped into the potion bucket. "There will be more when I actually work the spell."

"It hardly hurt at all. It did a bit, of course, but very little. Less than I expected. You didn't take very much." Grey examined his already healing wrist. "Are you sure you took enough?"

"I'm sure."

Harry already had his jacket off and his sleeve rolled up, Elinor holding the jacket like a proper apprentice. He didn't flinch when the lancet struck, staring stoically off into the distance while Amanusa drew five seconds' worth of his blood. She could feel the magic stir when his blood joined Grey's in the vial.

Elinor was next. Her hiss at the stab of the lancet made Harry recoil and Grey flinch, and they both insisted on inspecting the tiny puncture when it was done. Elinor appeared quite flustered at all the attention.

While the others were thus occupied, Jax handed Amanusa the silver vial and proceeded to shrug out of his white frock coat.

"I don't need your blood." Amanusa frowned at him as she pulled the disguise spell around her to veil guild secrets.

"I think you do. I think you should." Jax laid his jacket on the nearby steps and unbuttoned his shirt-sleeve. "It's *five blocks,* Amanusa. Use some of my blood so you don't have to use so much of yours. I know mine carries less power than yours, but it has more than theirs. And now that we're husband and wife, I am even more blood of your blood, even though we haven't yet— It might add that much more power."

He held out his wrist, demand in his eyes. "My blood is yours, Amanusa. Use it."

She couldn't deny him, not when he looked at her like that, all masculine power and—and something else in his eyes that made her feel as if he held up some great iron shield for her to huddle behind. She looked away just in time to pinpoint his vein as the lancet plunged home.

He took the vial back from her numbed fingers and caught his own blood, letting it flow past five seconds. Ten. Fifteen. When she would have sealed the wound, he moved away, out of her reach, until twenty seconds had ticked by. Then he held his wrist out to her again and Amanusa slapped her damp thumb across the wound.

"Do not—" she hissed.

"*Half,*" he growled back. "I put in half of what is needed for this. And I will do so any other time so much of your blood is required from your veins. I am not just servant anymore, Amanusa. Yes, you are still the sorceress, but I am your husband now, and I will not stand by and watch you bleed yourself dry when I have more than enough to spare."

Shaken, trembling at his words and their vehemence, Amanusa glanced from the blazing blue of his eyes to the still-oozing wound at his wrist. He bled for her. He'd insisted on it. So she wouldn't have to. To lessen her burden.

Raising her eyes to his again, she held his gaze as she lifted his wrist to her mouth and suckled gently at the little opening, tasting once more the lovely difference in his blood. She licked her tongue across the cut and spoke the "quick-heal" spell with her lips brushing over his skin. It made Jax shudder.

She licked the last taste of his blood from her lips, defying his scowl. "I already have your blood in my veins. A little more won't make any difference."

"We'll discuss it later." He turned away, rolling down his sleeve.

"Is it my turn yet?" Grey popped up to ask. "To work magic? Though I haven't actually seen much sorcery besides blood-letting. Are you through?"

Amanusa shed half her shawl, thanking Elinor when she lifted it away and folded it in her arms. "Just one more bloodletting to go, and I can work the first spell. Then you, then me again to tie them all together." She reinforced her disguise spell, encouraging the others to look away, to focus on their own magic.

Jax took the lancet from her, opening her vein before she could argue. He had to move her hand with the vial into place, to catch the blood, so quickly did he act. "This deep," he murmured, "it's easier if I do the lancing."

He counted off twenty seconds and fastened her thumb over her cut, then brought her wrist to his mouth in an echo of her action. The sensual slide of his tongue across her skin made her nipples tighten and her breasts anxious all over again.

Could they be wanting him to lick her *there*? The picture of it bloomed in her head and made her squirm. A whisper of magic floated across her skin, scented with desire. She caught it, swirled it into the magic riding the blood in the vial.

Dragging her gaze from Jax, Amanusa turned and poured the blood all at once into the bucket. She pushed Elinor's sticks aside to swish the vial in the water and rinse all the blood from it, then she used the sticks to stir the mixture thoroughly.

She held her hand out to Jax. "I want that other magic from you now."

He took her hand as ordered and seemed to *open* himself. The sex magic their kiss had made flowed toward her, sliding from between bone and muscle, from the spaces between his organs and around his blood vessels. She poured it into the blood in the bucket, whispering the words of protection Jax had taught her and adding a few of her own.

Amanusa let go Elinor's twigs and straightened to look at Grey, who took it as his signal to act. He withdrew what appeared to be a cigarette case from his pocket, but when opened, it turned out to be a pencil case. He selected a thick bar of graphite and crouched in the middle of the street at the edge of the intersection to write a sigil on a cobblestone, muttering in rapid Latin.

The air cooled and Amanusa felt a breeze whisper past. Except it wasn't a breeze, for the leaves of the trees didn't stir, nor did her fallen wisps of hair. Grey's spirits had come to call.

His Latin came faster, and a bit louder, almost as if he argued with the spirit. He marked other symbols on the stones around his first and the Latin changed into something else. Not German, but something like it.

"I don't believe Grey's spirits want to cooperate," Harry said quietly.

"Maybe I should bind the magic together so they can't get away." Amanusa plucked one of Elinor's leafy twigs from the bucket and dunked the leafy end in the earth-water-blood mixture. "Whatever you need to do as I mark the barrier, do it."

Elinor took out another twig. Harry picked up the bucket and carried it to where Grey shouted at his spirits in something that might be Polish now.

"Don't blot out my sigils, for God's sake." Grey was sweating as he kept marking more and more stones. "I haven't got them sealed yet so they'll still wash away."

"We'll be careful. Is this a good place?" Amanusa indicated a nearby cobble with a toe.

"Yes, fine." Grey squeezed the words out between bursts of angry near-German, Polish, and probably Spanish, before going back to Latin.

Amanusa swished her leaf-brush in the solution again and let it drip onto the stone. Elinor wedged her twig into the gap between the stones, for all the world like a tiny green picket. All of them spoke, invoking their own warding spells—Harry in Latin, Amanusa in English, and Elinor in a language utterly unrecognizable to Amanusa.

Amanusa spoke again, reaching for the donated blood, reaching *through* it to Grey's spirits, Harry's mud, Elinor's twigs. She used the magic in their blood to tie all the magics together. It felt right as she did it, the magics blending into a smooth whole.

"Here. Come here," Grey ordered, springing to his feet and beckoning. "Drip a bit of that just there." He pointed at his original sigil, glowing a faint blue.

Harry and Amanusa hurried over with bucket and brush and she carefully let a droplet fall where Grey indicated. She felt the magic solidify.

"Now Elinor, one of your twigs . . . there." Grey's hands twitched, as if he wanted to snatch the little stick from her and thrust it home himself. Elinor anchored the twig firmly between Grey's marked stones.

Amanusa could almost see him wrap his spirits around the twig and cement them down with the sorcery-alchemy solution. He spoke one more sentence in a firm declarative tone, and the magics locked tight, swelling suddenly into a high, solid, invisible wall a few feet long.

Grey snatched off his top hat and sent it sailing high into the air as he whooped in victory. He snatched Amanusa into his arms, sweeping her off her feet into a giddy whirl, before planting a smacking kiss on her mouth. He let go before Jax could protest and did the same with Elinor, whirling her higher because she was smaller. Then he grabbed Jax and kissed him too, catching him off guard. Jax, being larger than Grey, did not whirl.

Grey turned to Harry, who was as tall and thicker than Jax, and the celebration stopped when Harry looked at Grey and said, "Don't even fink about it."

Instantly the giddy delight vanished from Grey's face and he looked around for his hat. It had fallen near the curb. He retrieved it, replaced it on his head, and returned to the others, adjusting his cuffs. "I'm sure Harry knows that conjurers have tried countless times to work magic on or around the dead zones and always the spirits have refused. But when Amanusa bound the four magics together, they lost their fear. It's as if—" He looked from Amanusa to Jax and back. "Could the sorcery protect them from the ill effects of the dead zones?"

Amanusa shook her head at Jax. She did not want to be consulting Yvaine here, especially when Yvaine likely had no answers about this. "I don't know. It's possible no one knows, since these dead zones are so new. When we get back to London, I can look in the sorcery books in the council library to see what they say."

"A few feet of warding don't ward much," Harry said. "We still have five blocks to cover, an' not much time before the meeting starts. We'll be late enough as it is."

"Right." Grey strode to the corner and went to one knee to mark his sigil on the sidewalk, right against the corner of the abandoned house. Amanusa dribbled a bit of the solution on it and Elinor wedged her stick between the cobblestones there.

As they moved on around the dead zone's perime-

ter, Jax took over the solution painting from
Amanusa. She didn't know how he could tell she
needed to concentrate on holding and binding the
strands of magic together, but he knew. With every
sigil Grey drew, every twig Elinor planted, each drop
of bloody mud painted, the wall stretched and solidified, becoming that much stronger.

The machines moved with them, peering out of
broken windows, clanking to each other in the
streets, becoming noisier and more threatening with
their claws and blades with every stretch of wall that
was built. The twigs and sigils and splotches created
anchors for Amanusa to tie the blended magic to, but
she had to hold it all in her hands—her will—
whatever her magic-using appendages were—until
the spell was complete.

Five o'clock had come and gone by the time they
got back around to Grey's mass of glowing symbols
where they'd begun. A small crowd had gathered,
standing at a distance to stare at the glow and at the
scurrying scores of machines. Those who'd followed
them on their circling route—children mostly—
joined up with the people waiting.

"*Monsieur Invoquer*," a man called out. *Mr. Conjurer,* Amanusa's translation told her. "What are you
doing there?" he asked.

"Building a wall," Harry told them. "Now stay
back so we can get it closed up."

Elinor's twigs were gone, but there was still a layer
of slurry in the bottom of the bucket, thick with
magic. All five of them stared into the bucket at it.
Amanusa tugged at the heavy weight of magic she
hauled behind her. Jax handed Elinor the paintbrush

twig he'd been using, its leaves tattered and mostly gone, and took Amanusa's hand. When he did, though she could still feel the weight of the magic, it became easier to move it.

"Pour the rest of that between the cracks," she said. "There's blood in it. We can't leave any behind."

"Pour it over the stones," Grey said. "Over the sigils. It won't harm them now, might even power them up more." He paused, and when he spoke again, his voice was thoughtful. "I've never seen them glow this bright before. Not in daylight."

Without a word, Harry upended the bucket and let the muddy liquid splash out over Grey's glowing symbols. The sigils seemed to shudder, then glow brighter, as if soaking in the magic that poured over them and slid down to seep into the earth beneath the stones. Elinor used her battered twig-brush to sweep the last clinging bits of bloody soil from the bucket, and planted the twig on the opposite side of the central stone from her first.

Amanusa tied the magic to that twig, led it somehow through that central stone with its bold sigil, and tied it to the first twig. "Blood of my blood," she murmured. "Blood of alchemist and conjurer and wizard, bones and blood of the earth, broken flesh of green life, animating spirit, join now in protection. Hold back what would do harm. Hold fast your magic against what would steal it away. Hold strong in your guardianship. *Hold.*"

The other voices, of Harry and Elinor and Grey once more invoking their spells of protection, fell silent when she did. For a moment, nothing happened. The world seemed to hold its breath with her, the magic burning through her, pulling at her, crushing her.

Then, a visceral *thunk* boomed through her, as if a gigantic lock clicked shut, and the magic thumped into place around the dead zone. The sigils glowed yet brighter, for just an instant, then faded to a dull gray. The air where the wall rose shimmered faintly, almost opalescent in peripheral vision, invisible when observed straight on.

"Why do you build a wall?" a woman's shrill voice demanded. "Why do you not destroy what is killing us, so that we can return to our homes?"

"We're workin' on it," Harry shouted, turning to face the crowd. "So far we ain't been able to touch these patches at all, much less stop 'em from growin'. But if this wall works like I think it will, then we've got that figured. An' if we can stop 'em from growin' any bigger, we'll 'ave time to work out 'ow to destroy 'em."

"Why should we believe you? *Magicians.*" Another woman, narrow-faced and dressed all in black, spit on the ground. "It is you who have caused these abominations."

"No, it's you." Harry advanced on the woman.

The small crowd faded back behind the woman, until she realized her exposed position and tried to lose herself in its midst again. She didn't succeed, standing pressed against the leading edge of the group.

"You're the ones brought this on." Harry stabbed a finger at the woman, then at the crowd. "With your rules against magic and turnin' your nose up at it.

That place in there is like it is 'cause all its magic's been killed. There is no magic there. None.

"An' when the magic dies, plants start dyin' and animals an' people. Even the stones themselves die. So think about that, why don't ya, every time you sneer at a magician, or punish your kid for usin' a study spell to 'elp 'im understand 'is lessons.

"Tomlinson." Grey got Harry's attention. "Lovely speech, but it might be more suited to the conclave chamber. Where a meeting is going on this very minute."

"Right." Harry looked back at the crowd, glowering. "Don't pass that wall. It's not safe beyond it, an' we don't know what passing through all that magic might do to a body. Nothing, maybe. But I wouldn't want to be the one to test it, would you?"

22

JAX WENT TO the next street and collected a cab large enough for all of them, including the ladies' hoops. Amanusa let him hand her in and collapsed in the corner, feeling as if she'd just built the Great Wall of China single-handedly. She'd seen pictures of it, when she was a little girl in Vienna. Elinor sat opposite, and this time, Grey squeezed in next to Jax. Harry climbed in last, after supervising the cabbie stowing the machine in the boot.

"I know you meant for Amanusa to attend the meeting this afternoon," Jax said, "but I am taking her back to the hotel. After that spell, she's in no shape to handle the strain of a meeting where half those present will think it a pity the criminals didn't slaughter her."

"She may be your bride," Elinor said, "but she is a woman grown, not a child, and a magician as well. You cannot make decisions for her without at least soliciting her opinion."

A slight snore from Amanusa's corner announced her thoughts on the matter. Jax smiled and slid his arm around her, tipping her head onto his shoulder, reveling in the knowledge that she'd given him the right. "Even adults can push themselves beyond their limits. And when they do, it's the responsibility of those who care for them to see that they take the rest they need. Harry can report what happens."

"I don't suppose as it'd be too effective if she fell asleep in the meeting and slid off 'er chair," Harry conceded.

Amanusa woke enough to walk into the hotel under her own power—mostly—when the carriage paused to let her and Jax off. Elinor stayed with the cab. She could wait in the chamber lobby, she said, and hear the news all the sooner. Amanusa fell asleep while Jax was getting her out of her corset and hoops. She slept until she heard voices, and the light sliding through the gap in the curtains was a mellow, late-summer-evening gold.

She found her new dressing gown—white, but with pink-embroidered ruffles down the front—and slipped into the parlor to see what was afoot. Her head ached horribly, but not enough to dim her need to hear their news.

The three English magicians—or two magicians

and an apprentice—had returned. Amanusa hid her yawn as she padded into their little parlor and curled up next to Jax on the sofa, tucking her bare feet beneath the skirts of her dressing gown.

Elinor turned to her, eyes alight. "The most wonderful thing, Amanusa. You won't believe what has happened." She sat on the settee opposite, Grey beside her, leaning on his walking stick.

"Let's tell it in order, a'right?" Harry sat perched on an ornately carved chair upholstered in blue-and-gold striped satin, looking as if he feared it might collapse under him. His derby hat perched on his knee, which jiggled nervously. What did he have to be nervous about?

"We got to the meeting," he said. "Late, but not too late. Maybe five-thirty. Gathmann recognizes us right away from the podium an' wants to know where you are. So I told 'im.

"I told 'im about the attack last night, an' about the warding spell this afternoon—an' about the wedding this mornin' too. They understood as how you might be a bit tired."

"And then Harry asked that you be recognized as a master magician," Elinor blurted out.

Amanusa looked from one magician to the other. "What does that mean? Won't it complicate things?"

"I 'ope it clears 'em up." Harry set his hat on the floor and propped his elbows on his knees as he leaned forward to explain. "Your status in the conclave right now is based on your membership in the English council. Which is based on you bein' apprentice to Yvaine. It's provisional, an' it's an apprenticeship. Which Sir Billy din't bother to explain to the conclave governors, an' I don't blame 'im for it. But that's what is. Or was. Apprentices don't generally get to attend meetings, unless they're ready for th' journeyman's test."

"So, again, what does that mean? What was decided? What's going to happen?" Amanusa twined her fingers through Jax's, seeking his touch as always when she was uncertain. Master magician's status sounded good, but she had a feeling there was a catch.

"The governors, an' whoever else wants to go along, are goin' out to inspect that warding wall we built, an' if they're satisfied it's master-level work—"

"When," Elinor said. "When they're bowled over by it."

Harry's mouth twitched, as if Elinor's excitement amused him. "*When* that 'appens," he amended, "they'll set a test."

"What kind of test?" Amanusa's hand tightened on Jax's. Her whole existence sometimes felt as if it had been nothing but test after test. She was tired of tests.

"An attack, usually. Magic assault. Can you defend yourself against dark magic? Can you stand on your own? Master magicians got to be able to protect themselves. They got no right to be protected like an apprentice does. An' yes, Elinor, I got protections around you. Though after today, I ain't—I'm not so sure you need 'em. They'll be plenty impressed with your work on that wall, too."

"Will we have warning?" Jax asked.

"No. But it won't 'appen 'til after they decide about the magic—the wall."

"If they abide by the rules." Elinor sounded bitter. "If I were you, I'd be prepared for anything, at any time."

Amanusa looked at the men, to see whether they agreed with Elinor's assessment. Not that she had to. Frightened, ignorant people seldom followed rules. They acted on their fear, either running away to hide, or attacking. Amanusa had lived that way herself for too many years. Oddly, she wasn't afraid now.

Or maybe it wasn't so odd. After all, she had magic now. And she had Jax.

"Let them come," she said. "We can handle anything they throw at us."

Harry returned her gaze for a long, considering moment. "I sincerely 'ope you can."

"Well." Elinor's cheeks bloomed with a sudden blush and she popped to her feet. All three gentlemen rose with her. "I daresay we have taken up quite enough of your wedding day. But we felt you should know the news straightaway."

Grey paused as they left and marked a sigil on the back of the door. "So that only those who wish you well may pass," he said with a smile and a bow.

Amanusa didn't tell him Jax had already warded the rooms with a spell that did the same. She merely smiled and waved her thanks as they departed, leaving her alone with her husband.

Amanusa and Jax had been alone together for the whole of their journey to Paris. But they hadn't been married then.

She'd been alone with Jax today, after the magic at the dead zone, but she'd been so exhausted, she was scarcely aware of his presence, save as comforting, efficient hands undressing her and tucking her into bed. This was different.

Jax put a glass of water in her hand. "Drink it."

Amanusa obeyed.

"I'm ordering supper," he said, ringing for a servant. "You slept through tea, and now you've had some sleep, you need to eat."

She nodded carefully. Her headache had grown steadily since she woke until now each hammer blow threatened to crack her skull. She stretched a hand toward him and when he took it, the headache faded slightly.

"Poor lamb." He slid onto the settee beside her and kissed her temple. That helped even more. "Dragging all that great lot of magic halfway around the city. It's more work than you should be attempting so soon. You've only been studying sorcery since—was it only May when I found you?"

"In-depth study." She sighed, leaning into him. "But that's not what's worrying you, is it?"

A quiet rap came at the door. Jax kissed her temple again before going to answer. He spoke quietly to the servant there, then returned.

He sat at the far end of the settee, which made Amanusa frown. Why didn't he want to touch her? Her head still hurt. She turned on the settee, putting her feet up on the cushion and sliding them forward until her toes, still covered by the voluminous raw silk dressing gown, touched his leg. "What's worrying you?" She asked it point blank this time.

"What makes you think anything is worrying me?" Jax gave her a smile without meeting her eyes. His hand drifted down to settle atop her silk-covered toes.

Amanusa scowled at him. "It's all over you. Worry. I can hear it in every word you say. I see it in your face. I can smell it, taste it—and if you weren't sitting way over there, I'm sure I could touch it, too. You're worried. Why?"

"After last night? After the news you just heard, you have to wonder?" Jax shot her a glance before denying her his eyes again.

His hand wrapped all the way around her ankle, over the silk, away from her skin. Her head was pounding again. She wanted his touch. But not if he didn't want to touch her.

"*Jax.*" She poked him with her toes. "I know you're worried. Talk to me. I am the sorceress, after all."

"And I'm the husband." He shot her another quick look, his jaw going hard and stubborn. "You put me in this position. You gave me the right to worry."

"But not alone, Jax. Share your worry with me. A wife is supposed to be a helpmeet, not a burden." She reached past her upthrust knees to touch him. "We're still partners. Aren't we?"

Finally, at last, he met her gaze, looked into her eyes. "If you haven't figured it out yet on your own, I suppose I will have to tell you. You veiled how much of your blood you put into that bucket, but still, it came perilously close to revealing sorcery guild secrets, the truth about the source of a sorceress's power, in her own blood. More than that—" Jax gripped both her ankles as he turned his body toward her, intensity in every line. "If that warding works as well as I think it will, the conclave will be after you to work the same magic around every dead zone in

Europe. This one was only a few blocks around, and look how tired it left you.

"How big was the one we passed through in Germany? And it was growing. I'm told that the bigger they are, the faster they grow. I will not let you drain yourself dry for them."

Oh my. His fervent words warmed Amanusa all the way through. "I don't want that either." Not now that . . . She grabbed for ways to prevent it. "I need apprentices. I need a whole classroom full of them."

Jax shook his head, a crooked smile twisting his full, kissable lips. "It's not easy to find a classroom full of young ladies willing to spill their own blood for humanity's sake."

"Do they have to be young?" Amanusa shrugged. "Or ladies? We look for those like me. The ones who have nothing left to lose. And the ones who understand the difference between justice and revenge."

She cocked her head as she looked at him then, sorting through all the worries she saw written across him. "But that isn't all of it. It's a great deal of it, but—"

"How do you know?" he burst out. "How can you look at me and just know that I am worried? How can you tell this worry from that worry, when a week ago you could not?"

"I could sense—"

"Physical. You could sense the physical from me, when I was injured, when I touched the machine, when I fell ill in the vacuum—but you've never been able to sense my emotions." He looked uneasy.

As well he ought. She'd never meant to trespass so far into his heart and mind. "I'm sorry. I won't—"

"Amanusa, I don't mind you being able to sense how I'm feeling. It's the why of it that worries me. You tasted my blood. You have my blood flowing through your veins. In the more than one hundred years that I served her, Yvaine never took my blood. *Ever.*"

"But—why not?" Amanusa took a moment to inventory all her parts. "I feel perfectly fine. A little tired—or maybe more than a little—but that's due to this afternoon's spell-crafting, I'm sure. Other than that, I feel no different than I did yesterday morning. What difference could taking your blood possibly make?"

"I don't know." The strain in Jax's voice came through clearly. "And that's what worries me. Ask Yvaine."

"Jax, no."

"Ask her. We're inside a fully warded set of rooms. No harm can come to you, even if I fall unconscious."

"We were married today. Maybe I don't want you unconscious." Amanusa pulled her feet from Jax's grip and dropped them to the carpet. "I don't understand why you're raising such a fuss about this. It's nothing. Less than nothing."

"You don't know that." Jax captured one of her hands. "We don't know anything about it, except that Yvaine was so careful not to let it happen. Which in itself indicates that it's dangerous. Amanusa, I am serious about this. If you do not ask Yvaine, I will."

"You can't. I've bound her mouth shut."

"She's inside me. I think I can."

"Jax—" Amanusa caught his other hand, held tight to both of them, pleading with him.

"Amanusa," he said sternly. "I don't want to quarrel with you, but about this, I must insist. If I were only your servant still, perhaps I would not. But you married me. And as your husband, it is my duty to look after you. To protect you, even from yourself. We must know."

"Who will protect you from yourself?" she cried, unable to stop herself. Why did she feel so frantic? It wasn't Jax's worry influencing her. His worry was about her. This sense of panic was all about Jax.

"You will, of course." His smile was gentle. He brushed her tumbled hair back from her face. "But think, Amanusa. Eventually, I'll need to rid myself of the rest of the magic Yvaine stuffed into my head. And the unconsciousness hasn't lasted nearly so long, these last few times. This is as good an opportunity as any. Better than most, because we do very much need to know what Yvaine can tell us about this."

Amanusa bit her lip, clinging to his hands, needing that skin-to-skin reassurance as she thought. She puffed out a disgruntled breath. "All right. We'll ask her. But if you're unconscious all night, I will . . . I will beat you. With a stick."

"I will lay it in your hands myself." He did his old servant bow, pressing his forehead to her hands. But he was smiling when he did it.

She squeezed her hands tight around his with an exasperated growl. "You know I could never actually beat you. But I'd want to. Badly."

He looked up at her from his bow, not bothering even to attempt to suppress his grin, and winked. "I know. Now ask."

Amanusa took a deep breath and blew it out again, sorting her disordered emotions and calming them. Jax would be all right. And they did need to get rid of the rest of Yvaine's blood. She just wished it didn't have to be now.

"Yvaine of Braedun." She reached for her magic inside Jax, taking hold after a brief hesitation. "Tell me about tasting the blood of my servant. What happens when the sorceress tastes the servant's blood?"

The blue faded from Jax's eyes, brown blooming in them. Amanusa shuddered. She would never get used to that. She wanted the woman out.

"The sorceress rides through the veins of others," Yvaine said with Jax's voice. "The sorceress does not take into herself the blood of others. Especially do not, under any circumstances taste the blood of your servant. It will make you weak and unable to use your servant as needful. Keep your blood pure and untainted."

"What about—?" Amanusa didn't get her question out before Jax's eyes rolled back in his head and he toppled backward on the settee.

"Is that it?" she demanded. "Yvaine! Is that all you have to say?"

She shook Jax's hands, patted his cheek. His eyelids fluttered, but he didn't rouse.

"Yvaine, tell me what it does. Tell why it's important?" If Amanusa could reach inside Jax and snatch hold of Yvaine, she would shake her until her eyes rattled in their sockets, until she coughed up the information Amanusa wanted so badly. But Yvaine was dead, and Jax did not deserve the abuse.

A knock sounded at the door. Supper already? But this was an excellent hotel and things happened quickly. Amanusa ran for the coins in her purse, trying to remember how much she'd seen Jax give the servant the last time. She opened the door and waited for the footman to roll the cart in. No one who meant harm could pass the door's layered warding.

The footman set the cart near the table by the window and began to lay the dishes out, casting curious glances at Amanusa's unconscious husband. Oh Lord, Jax's nose was bleeding. Another drop of Yvaine's blood. Amanusa thrust the whole handful of coins at the servant and hurried him out the door.

She found a slip of the rice paper, blotted up the old, dark blood, and held it to the gaslight, until the flame burnt her fingers and the magic whispered off to join Yvaine in her distant grave. Jax looked horribly uncomfortable on the settee, so she adjusted the angle of his neck, stuffing a pillow under his head, and rearranged his limbs so that he at least looked better. She couldn't help stroking a hand down his dear, kind face. He was a handsome man, but it was his kindness that made him so attractive to her.

She couldn't stand and stare at Jax until he woke. Well, actually, she could, but she wouldn't. Why should she? He was her husband, but that didn't mean she was in love with him, or anything of the sort. They were rather literally attached to each other. But she could give him the room he requested.

The delicious aromas rising from the table drew her. Amanusa peeped under the covers. Jax had ordered a hearty dinner. Salmon patties, sliced beef, and crusty bread to soak up the juices—enough food to fill two shelves on the cart. Who did he think would be eating all of this? Her stomach rumbled ominously.

"Have you eaten?" The words rode out of Jax on a groan and Amanusa rushed to help him sit up.

"No, I haven't. The footman just brought it not two minutes ago."

"Don't wait on me." He brought a hand to his forehead, rubbing it. "You need to eat. Magic drains your energy. Food and rest put it back."

"Food and rest put it back." Amanusa repeated the words in unison with him. "Yes, I know. But I'd rather eat with you. Come sit at the table. Let me serve you this time."

Jax let her help him stand and leaned on her as they walked the short distance to the table. "How long—?"

"Not long at all. Maybe five minutes." Amanusa scowled. "Probably because Yvaine didn't tell me anything."

"Nothing at all?" Jax stopped and stared at her in shock.

"Nothing useful. Nothing I needed to know." She shrugged. "She just said, 'The sorceress rides the blood of others, she does not allow others' blood into her.'" Amanusa made her voice sound pompous and eerie both at once, quoting the old harridan. "But she didn't say why, and she didn't say what would happen if the sorceress did taste someone else's blood."

Amanusa decided in that moment to keep the part about her servant's blood making her "weak and unable to use her servant," to herself. She didn't feel weak in the least, and she had no intention of using Jax. Not the way Yvaine had used him.

"Perhaps she feared me locating the information and using it against you," Jax mused.

"You never would." Amanusa pulled out her chair and Jax seated her before going around to his own chair. He never neglected the little courtesies, no matter how many times she told him they weren't necessary. They made her feel . . . cared for.

"Against you? No, never." His smile warmed her. "But against someone like Yvaine? Probably."

"What was she like, Yvaine? You've never really told me."

"I shouldn't tell you now. Do you honestly want her present on our wedding night?" Jax served the soup, despite Amanusa's intention to serve him. He was sneaky like that.

"She's already here. At your insistence. I think we should drag her into the open so we can exorcise her. Yvaine the woman, not the magic she left in your head."

Jax sighed. "She's been in her grave two hundred years. We should leave her there."

Amanusa reached across the table to clasp his hand briefly before letting him eat his soup. "But she's not in her grave, Jax. She still haunts you. How did you meet her? Can you remember?"

23

More than I'd like. I met Yvaine in York. Leaford—the earldom—is in the North of England, and Henry—Henry VIII—was king then. Henry had just beheaded Anne and George Boleyn, and married poor Jane Seymour that summer. A year or two before that, he'd shut down all the little monasteries, which upset no end of folk, and there was a big uprising in York that fall. Pilgrimage of Grace, they called it. Being the arrogant earl I was then, I went along with the Duke of Norfolk when he led the king's armies out to deal with the rebel riffraff.

"In the end, there wasn't a battle—not that year. Norfolk negotiated a truce and everyone went home. But I wasn't ready to leave. I'd come for some fun, and by God, I was going to have it. So a gang of us— some who'd already succeeded to our titles and some who hadn't any title to succeed to, unless several uncles, brothers, and cousins died—rode from Doncaster, where the negotiations took place, to York. To see the sights. Or to drink and carouse and . . . whatnot."

Amanusa set the soup plates on the cart and served the fish course. "And did you see the sights?"

A sardonic chuckle escaped him. "Mostly, we saw 'whatnot.' Alehouses and brothels. But I also visited all the magicians in York. I was thirty-four then. I'd married, produced an heir and a spare—poor Margaret, having to put up with me for a husband—" His voice trailed off as he vanished into his memories. Not pleasant ones, from the look on his face.

"I think you are a very fine husband," Amanusa announced.

Jax gave her a skeptical look. "Your opinion of a marriage lasting an entire, endless day. Wait a few years and I'll ask again." He looked at his salmon patty and drizzled hollandaise sauce over it. "I'm not the same man I was then. Margaret suffered with the original version of me, full of self-importance and ignorant cruelty."

He paused to stare blackly into the past again. "I would almost rather not have some of those memories returned to me. They shame me."

Amanusa touched his hand again in silent support.

He looked up at her and smiled. "But they serve to remind me that I do not care to become that man again."

She smiled back and took a bite of her salmon patty. It was good and she was hungry, but she was more interested in Jax's tale. "Why were you visiting magicians in York? How many did you visit? Was Yvaine based in York then?"

"No, she'd been called in to serve in the courts after the rebellion. Her master—the sorceress who'd taught her—was still living then, but Morwen was getting old, the magic close to burning her up, and she'd sent Yvaine to handle the session." Jax began to eat, but didn't seem to taste it.

"And I was visiting magicians to learn magic," he said. "I suppose I must have visited a half dozen or better. York was the second city in England then, and had more magicians than most. I'd always been fascinated with the power to be attained through magic, and I had studied it with my tutors, of course. Then, as now, actually working the magic was seen as coarse. Something peasants did, or the merchant class. Not the nobility. A nobleman hires magicians. He does not practice magic himself.

"But even though I was essentially tone deaf—magic blind—I was fascinated with magic. Probably because, try as I might, I couldn't perform the least little spell."

"And then you met Yvaine." Amanusa watched him closely, trying to read his moods, but he'd closed in on himself.

He smiled at her, sad, wistful. "Then I met Yvaine. It was at a dinner, hosted I think by the local goldsmith's guild. The dinner was over. I'd drunk far, far too much wine, and I wasn't in the mood for dancing. I was practicing a simple alchemy spell, determined to get it right at least once, to make the candlewick smoke if not burst into flame.

"And Yvaine walked up to me. She was a beautiful woman. Tiny, with lush curves and rosy satin skin and long brown curls that tumbled down her back, the color of the caramel over the crème brûlée you like so much."

Amanusa concentrated on eating. She looked nothing like that, with her tall, angular frame and straight, white-blond hair. But maybe that was a good thing.

Jax went on, lost in his memories. "She asked if I wanted to learn magic, and I laughed. Drunk as I was, she still frightened me a bit. Powerful magicians can do that. You carry that power around with you like a cloak, like armor and weapons bristling from you."

"Do I frighten you?" Amanusa had to ask.

He swam back up from the past and looked at her, *saw* her. And he smiled. "I'm part of your armor."

The smile faded a bit and he reached out to her this time, clasped her hand. "There's an element of—not fear, but—respect. Maybe a bit of awe. Respect for what you can do and the power you can wield. It's there. But because I am a part of that power and because you are who you are, no, you don't frighten me."

"Good." Amanusa smiled at him, content to hold his hand until he freed her.

"Eat." He took away her empty plate and replaced it with a plate of beef and delicate dumplings. "Your strength still isn't where it should be."

And how did he know that? From experience? Or something else? Amanusa cut into the tender beef, but before she ate it, she asked, "So what did you say to Yvaine?"

"I told her that I would love to learn magic, but I was head-blind. If she could teach me, despite my handicap, it would make her the greatest magician in all England. And she said she could do it. So I went with her, eager to learn everything she could teach me."

Jax paused, his fork in midair. "I don't remember much of that next week. I've never been able to, even before she filled my head up with this posthumous presence of hers."

He took the bite, chewed pensively a moment, then swallowed. "I remember—I think—pain. Bleeding.

And sex. A lot of sex. And magic. For the first time in my life, I could sense magic. I could work magic. I remember being giddy with delight. Absolutely thrilled that the magic would obey me."

He took another bite. "Of course, it was Yvaine's talent working the magic, not mine. And when the week was done and I came back to myself again, I was bound. Yvaine's servant."

"I thought you said you were willing." Amanusa burned with righteous indignation on his behalf.

"I was. I remember that much clearly. Every step of the way, every time one portion of the binding was completed and another lay ahead, she asked me 'Do you want this?' And every time, I answered 'Yes.' Because I did want it. I wanted every bit of the magic she offered.

"But I didn't understand what it ultimately meant. I thought, when it was done, I'd be able to take what she'd done, what she'd taught me, and go back to being Earl Leaford. But when it was done, John Greyson, Earl Leaford, was dead. Jax lived on."

"What did you do?" Amanusa reached for his hand again, but he didn't seem to see it.

"What could I do? I was bound. I couldn't even protest, for she'd bound my voice to silence until she needed it. I didn't speak for most of the next five years."

"How horrible!" Amanusa wanted to do violence to the woman. Since she couldn't, she struggled not to release the violence storming through her by throwing cutlery around the room.

"She wasn't actively cruel. Not deliberately. And while Morwen was alive, it wasn't so bad. Morwen kept Yvaine from her worst impulses, and she was kind to me. She tried to convince Yvaine to release me, or to loosen the binding. But apparently, a blood servant must be completely head-blind, and folk like me were difficult to find. At least at that time, in that place. Yvaine always refused to change anything. And by the time Morwen died, about ten years later, I'd learned how to survive it."

"How?" Amanusa tried to clear the tightness in her throat, but it wouldn't go away.

"By accepting what I had become—a servant— and becoming the best possible example of a servant that I could manage." His mouth twisted in a sour grin. "Sometimes I didn't manage very well, but I tried. It was hardest when my sons died. The younger took the title after his brother died at thirteen. William, though, he lived to seventy-three. And I was still as you see me now. Yvaine did let me attend the funeral."

"If she wasn't deliberately cruel, what was she like?" Amanusa didn't understand and she wanted to, if only to know how to comfort Jax and what pitfalls to avoid. She did not want to become Yvaine.

"Righteous," Jax answered without hesitation. "She cared far more about the idea of justice and about humanity as a whole than she did for individuals. If a few persons got ground up in her wheels of justice, that was unfortunate but unavoidable."

"Too bad, so sad," Amanusa whispered. She recognized the attitude, knew it all too well.

"Exactly." A gentle smile rose on his face. "I was a tool in her quest for justice. Something to hold the magic needed for greater spells, something to raise magic when she didn't have the time or inclination. If it caused me pain—well, pain can raise magic too, when it's willingly endured, and my will was hers. Only afterward, when she loosened her grip, did I regret."

"Oh, Jax—"

His smile became tender, personal. All for her. "But it's because of that, because of the people Yvaine gave me over to, the things she sent me into, that I understand your past. Mine is much like it."

"But you served Yvaine for . . . for—"

"One hundred and six years."

Horror swept through Amanusa. She sprang to her feet, stumbling over the cart in her rush to reach Jax, to hold him, comfort him. Fortunately nothing fell, not even Amanusa, for Jax caught her and swept her into his lap. She took full advantage and wrapped her arms tight around him.

"It was a very long time ago," Jax said into the ruffles of her dressing gown. His arms were around her, but carefully, as if he feared she might shatter. "More than two hundred years."

"But for most of that time, your memory of it was clouded. Now it isn't. It's fresh."

"Not so fresh." He nosed aside her ruffles so they didn't flutter in his face, and laid his head against her shoulder. "All that time, when I was searching, I knew I was also hiding. Just as I was both searching for something outside myself—you—and something inside myself—me—I was also hiding both from the witch hunters, and from things I didn't want to remember. The man I used to be, and the things that happened to me.

"Amanusa, I was far worse as Earl of Leaford than Yvaine ever thought about being. Her cruelties had a purpose. They aimed toward the greater good. Mine—" His sigh blew across her neck and he turned his face in toward her, his arms tightening around her. Amanusa stroked a hand through his thick hair, twined her fingers through the ruddy waves.

"I was cruel for my own amusement," he said. "Or in a fit of reckless temper. Or simply because I could. Yvaine rarely acted on a whim. I rarely acted on anything else." He went still for a moment, the warmth of his breath coming through the silk of her dressing gown as he pressed his face into her shoulder.

Finally he spoke again. "I came to believe—and I still do—that what happened to me was divine justice. Payment for my sins. A lesson in humility. I begin to think now, that what I was had to be utterly destroyed so that I could be made over into what I always should have been. The task isn't done, of course, but—"

"Is it ever done? Do we ever become what we should be on this side of heaven?" Amanusa laid her cheek atop his head as she spoke. "Yvaine caught you, and she bound you, and she left you for me. The knowledge still in your head is just knowledge, and we'll rid you of the last of it soon enough. Yvaine is dead. We may have to lay her ghost more than once, but for tonight . . ."

She sat back, tugged at Jax until he lifted his head and looked at her.

"Tonight," he said, "Yvaine is in her grave. Amanusa is my sorceress now."

A hesitant smile crawled onto her lips. "Amanusa is your wife."

He stared at her a moment, before an answering smile appeared. "So she is."

His hand rose to cup the back of her head and bring her down to meet his kiss.

They had kissed before. Amanusa liked Jax's kisses. She'd been surrounded by his strong body before, both of them clad in far less than they wore now, and it hadn't frightened her. Of course, they'd both been deathly ill from the lack of magic, too weak to stir. She wasn't afraid now. Or not exactly.

She wasn't afraid of Jax, either fully clothed as he was now or nearly naked as he'd been on the train coming through Baden. It was the act itself she feared, and suddenly there it was, looming over her.

"Shhh." Jax kissed his way across her cheek to nuzzle her ear. "Don't think about it. Nothing will happen that you don't want. Nothing *can* happen without your permission. Let's make tonight about you, shall we?"

He drew back then and looked at her. Amanusa stifled a whimper. She just wanted to get it over with.

"Don't you want your dessert?" He gestured at the cart. "Crème brûlée and éclairs, both."

She attacked his necktie, tugging it loose. "If I ate anything else, I'd be sitting in my chair thinking. Worrying about what was to come, and it would build up bigger and scarier in my mind and I'd never get through it."

She stopped, in the middle of unbuttoning his collar, and looked him in the eye. "It's not you that scares me, Jax. You do know that, don't you?" She laid her hand along his rugged jaw. "It's just— How do you do it? After what she did to you? How could you even think about offering to have sex with that red-painted harpy on the boat? And then do it?"

"I didn't do it, if you'll recall." He took her hand from his jaw and kissed the palm, then put it back, though it landed more on his neck than his face this time. He stretched one of his long arms to the cart and brought back the platter with the éclairs. "And I wouldn't dream of banishing you to that distant chair for your dessert."

He picked up one of the chocolate-covered, crème-filled pastries and took an enormous bite. He had a wide mouth to go with those full, mobile lips. Then he held the remainder to her mouth, the gleam in his eyes saying, *Go on. Bite.*

Amanusa tried to take a dainty bite, but Jax wouldn't let her. Still it was smaller than his. She swallowed, and he was still chewing.

"I mean it, Jax." She licked her lips and froze as he scooped an errant dollop of cream filling from her lip and slid it into her mouth on his finger. It tasted sweeter than licking her blood from his fingers, but made her feel just as peculiar.

She pushed his hand away. "Don't distract me. I really want to know. Did you endure the same things I did? I know it can happen to men. Were you—?" She couldn't say the word.

Jax could. "Raped." He said it gently, using the napkin on his hands and her face. "Yes."

"Then how did you— How do you—?" She gave up and looked at him helplessly.

He tucked her against him and fed her another bite

of éclair. "I was older, if you'll recall. That in itself gave me a better perspective on things. You were just a child. Rape was your introduction to sex."

"The outlaws didn't capture us 'til I was fourteen."

"Like I said, a child. And I got to go back to Yvaine, afterward. She did tend me, care for me."

"Until the next time she needed to use you."

"Well, yes. But it wasn't every day. Wasn't even all that often. She did usually let me choose my partners, which helps a great deal." He picked up another éclair. He'd finished off the first.

This time he offered her the first bite. Amanusa shook her head. "You first. I like the cream best."

He grinned at her and complied, feeding her the entire middle of the éclair.

"Are you trying to fatten me up?" Amanusa asked when she could speak politely again.

"Just trying to keep you from becoming skin and bones." Jax gave her a quick squeeze. "I like a well-padded wife."

Amanusa's mind circled back around again. "So, since I've chosen you, you think it will be easier for me to have sex—"

He stopped her with a finger laid briefly across her lips. "We are husband and wife. We will not 'have sex.' We will make love."

"But we don't love each other," she said in a small voice.

"Doesn't matter. We are fond of each other. We trust each other. That makes it more than just intercourse. We will make love."

"Shouldn't I give you permission—"

Jax put his finger over her mouth again. "No. Not

yet. I don't want you worrying about what might happen. Tonight is just for you."

She pulled his hand away. "But don't you want . . . ?"

"Of course I do. But I'm used to wanting and not having. And it will happen soon enough. Until it does, until you're ready—truly ready, not just wanting to 'get it over with,' I don't want you releasing any bindings. All right?"

Amanusa nodded, eyes wide as she gazed into his. How did he know what she'd been thinking? How had such good luck found her after so much of the other sort, to stumble across a man like this? But then, he had stumbled across her, hadn't he?

Jax drew her back into a kiss, gentle this time, sweet with cream and chocolate and the slide of his tongue over hers. Amanusa spread her hands flat across his shoulder blades buried beneath layers of jacket and waistcoat and shirt. Big men had always frightened her, but she liked Jax's broad shoulders. She liked his lean height. He didn't try to knock her down to size like other men often did. Jax's height made her feel protected, not threatened.

Abruptly, Jax broke the kiss and stood, lifting Amanusa in his arms. Her squeak was almost lost in the clatter of the chair falling over, but Jax froze. He'd heard it.

Amanusa leaned in to murmur in his ear. "I was only startled. Nothing more."

His grin was feral. "Good." It found an answering wildness deep within Amanusa that shivered in response. "Then I don't have to set you down."

He kicked the fallen chair out of his way and

strode into her bedroom with her in his arms. He placed her on the bed and Amanusa immediately popped up to a sitting position. She didn't want to wait passively for this lovemaking. Inaction made it too much like before, when she'd simply endured what was done to her. This time, she wanted to participate.

Jax lifted an eyebrow as he sat beside her on the bed. "Nervous? It's all right if you are. We don't have to . . ."

She put her hand over his mouth. "Will you stop going on about it? I know I don't have to, but I *have* to. I'm tired of being afraid. I wasn't afraid this afternoon when you kissed me."

"We were on the street. It couldn't go any further. Of course you weren't afraid." His smile was kind and understanding and it made her want to smack him.

"Will you stop being so damn noble?" Amanusa lurched to her knees in the crinkly featherbed and pushed his frock coat off his shoulders. "You're going to make me think you're the one who's afraid."

"I am." He pulled his coat the rest of the way off and tossed it at a chair. He missed, but paid no notice. "I'm bloody terrified of frightening you, or hurting you, or—or somehow botching this beyond repair. I used to think initiating a virgin was the most difficult sexual act to perform properly, but this . . . Making love to a woman—a woman I-I am fond of—who was so cruelly treated as a child—"

"It's not a performance, Jax. I'm not going to be judging you or giving marks afterward like some schoolmaster."

He rolled his eyes at her. "No, you'll just be huddled in a corner, weeping."

"I won't."

"How do you know that?"

"Because I never have before. Not even the first time. Trust me. I am stronger than that."

He looked at her then. Came out from whatever memories haunted him, and looked at her. And he smiled. "That's right. You are."

Amanusa slid from the bed to pull off his half-boots. "And this afternoon, when you kissed me—" She felt the stupid blush rising, but ignored it. They had to at least be honest with each other. Honest with the important things, anyway. He'd admitted to his fear, so she could admit her own truth.

"I liked it. I liked how you kissed me. I liked that you weren't quite in control, and I wanted . . . You made me . . . I . . ." She stumbled to a halt, staring at his long narrow feet inside their black stockings.

"What did you want, Amanusa?" Jax pulled his feet up and reclined on an elbow to look at her. He held his hand out and she took it, let him draw her back onto the bed beside him.

The blasted blush would not actually burn her head into nothing but smoking ash, much as it might feel that way. And if she didn't tell him what she felt, what she wanted—how would he know?

"More," she said. "I wanted more. I felt—My-my breasts were anxious. I know that sounds silly, because breasts can't actually have emotions on their own, and what a silly thing for them to feel, if they did have them, and why should a bosom—"

Jax stopped her babble with his mouth. With a kiss.

A ravening wolf of a kiss like the one this afternoon. He tumbled her back on the bed and tucked her half beneath his chest as he kissed her, devoured her whole. But she was not so consumed by the kiss that she did not notice his hand slide up and over her ribs to wrap gently around her breast. She whimpered.

"Is this what they were anxious to have?" His quiet words in her ear were muffled, for he'd closed his teeth gently on her earlobe as he spoke.

"Or was it this?" He slid his thumb over the hardened tip of her breast, and Amanusa jerked with the pleasure of it. That was exactly what she wanted, without knowing it. She could feel his smile against her cheek.

"Like that, do you?" he murmured with a lick of his tongue beneath her ear. That made her quiver too.

He lifted himself, looking down her body for the tie to her dressing gown. Amanusa collected enough of her sense and her strength to go after the buttons on his waistcoat. He unknotted her sash and returned to the kiss as if he never left it, but he held his body up as if giving her permission to continue unbuttoning his clothing. So when she finished with the waistcoat, she started in on his shirt.

Jax flipped her ruffles to either side and laid his hand on her breast, only the thin linen of her gown between his skin and hers. Her whole body shook, and she popped two buttons off his shirt to bound across the floor when her hand jerked along with the rest of her. "Ohhhhh—" breathed out of her in a moany sigh.

She didn't know one could smile and kiss at the same time, but Jax was. He seemed far too pleased with himself, but since she was rather pleased with him too, she couldn't object. She loved the heat of his hand soaking into her through the thin, soft fabric. He didn't pinch or grab, just held her. Felt her, squeezing, but gently. Not as if he'd like to squeeze and twist it right off her chest.

Jax sat up, lifting her along with him. "Let's get this off, shall we?"

24

HE REMOVED HER dressing gown. She took the chance to push his waistcoat off his shoulders. While he shrugged out of it, she unbuttoned the last few buttons of his shirt and, in a quick nerve-wracking decision, dragged it off him as well. He'd been more unclothed than this on the train.

Jax caught hold of his shirt before she could toss it to the floor and looked at her warily. Amanusa met his gaze, smiling a little. "Your skin doesn't frighten me."

She laid a hand on his naked chest to prove it. She slid her hand over the firm muscle to press her finger over his nipple. It made a hard little bump pushing back against her. "This afternoon," she whispered, "when you bled my wrist, when you licked it closed—" Could she say it out loud? Without her head poofing to smoke from the dratted blush?

"Tell me, Amanusa." Jax lifted her wrist to his mouth, the same one as before, and he did it again. His tongue licked over the tender flesh, the blue veins just beneath the skin, and throbbed against it in rhythm with her pulse.

She reacted in the same way. "I wanted—my breasts wanted—"

His eyes darkened. They were the same green-blue, but darker somehow. Or maybe it was the way he looked at her with them.

He didn't look very long before bearing her down to the bed again with yet another kiss, the heat of his naked chest searing through her flimsy gown. This kiss didn't stay at her mouth for long. He kissed her cheek, her jaw, then nibbled a moist trail of kisses down her neck.

He paused there, kissing—making love to her neck—as his fingers found the little buttons at the neck of her nightdress. She could see lights in the mirror over the dresser. Streetlights? Or maybe lights from the building across the way.

"Amanusa," Jax whispered.

It took her a moment to realize he waited for a reply. "What?"

"Are you here? Are you with me?"

That was a silly question. "Where else would I be?"

He smiled. He wasn't angry. He tapped her temple with a finger. "Gone away inside here. If this is going to work, love, you have to stay with me. You can't leave your body behind."

"I—" She had. She'd been lying there, motionless, thinking about the lights in the mirror. "I didn't mean to."

"I know. Sometimes it's the only way you can endure. But I don't want you merely to endure this. It's not making love if it's something you have to endure." Jax stroked his hand up her side. "You were doing all right for a while. What changed it?"

Frustration stormed through her and she threw herself upright, arms and legs flailing in a useless battle against herself. "I hate this! I *hate* it. I think we're getting somewhere, that we've moved past my past, past yours—and then something else pops up to throw a spoke in the wheels and we're slinging around in the mud again."

Jax was sitting up too, wrapping his arms around her, chuckling through his shushing attempts to calm her. "If it's not a performance, love, neither is it a race. No one is timing us. There's no hurry. We've all the time in the world."

He was behind her, a warm, solid, comforting presence. He pressed a kiss to the angle where her shoulder rose into her neck and she shivered. He opened his mouth on her skin, sucked lightly, and licked his tongue over it, like what he'd done to her wrist this afternoon. She shook harder.

"Better?" His lips brushed her ear.

She nodded. She was better, but not "fine." Not even quite all the way to "all right."

"Mihai didn't like me to move," she said, before she knew the words were there. "He liked to undress me and look at me before he—you know. And he didn't like me to move. Mihai was second to Szabo before Teo. He took me, after the—the first . . . He—I—if I was with him, the others didn't bother me." She shrugged. "He was all right. He didn't hit unless he was drunk, and he didn't get drunk very often. And he was old."

She didn't try to keep the bitterness from her bark of laughter. "Probably not any older than you. Than you appear. Mid-thirties, maybe. But I was fourteen. He seemed ancient to me." She rubbed her cheek along Jax's where he leaned over her, wrapped around her, and she pulled his arms tighter. His warmth helped chase away the cold inside her.

"How long were you with him?" Jax asked when the silence stretched so long it made even her uncomfortable.

"Three years. Almost four. I was—I didn't grow much bosom until I was almost eighteen." She laughed again, a breath of sound this time. "Still don't have much. But I wasn't young-enough looking for Mihai anymore. He protected me though, sometimes, after that. Wouldn't let anyone beat me too hard, that sort of thing."

"What happened to him?"

"Bullet from an Imperial soldier's rifle. They brought Ilinca up to try to save him, but he was gut-shot, like Costel, and Ilinca didn't have much wizardry. I cried when the bastard died. Can you believe it?"

"He showed you a little kindness in a place where no one else showed any at all." Jax kissed her temple. He smoothed her hair out of the way and kissed her cheek.

"Szabo let me go back with Ilinca to learn herb lore and healing. That was a kindness, though his intention was to acquire a resident healer for his camp." Amanusa turned sideways in his—it wasn't his lap, for she sat between his legs rather than atop them. She turned so she could put her arms around him in return. There was as much comfort in holding him as in being held, and she needed the double dose.

"I did go back for a while, after I learned what Ilinca could teach me. But when she died—that was when I put the purgative in the soup and made everyone sick, and worked my bargain with Szabo."

She leaned against his broad, strong shoulder, his skin warm beneath her cheek. "Was it justice, Jax?" she asked in a small voice. "That they all died? Or was it bloody vengeance?" She hadn't realized it bothered her until this moment.

"First off," Jax said firmly. "You don't know that they all died. You don't know how many died, or if any of them did. All you have is what that hellhound Kazaryk said, and I doubt he'd know the truth if it bit him on the arse."

Amanusa acknowledged Jax's logic with a sort of nod. It was hard to nod properly whilst leaning on a shoulder.

"And second, it was justice. If anyone died, it was because he needed to. You can't tell me Teo didn't deserve it. Blood magic—even wild, out-of-control magic—doesn't execute anyone who doesn't deserve it. Especially when you call for justice, which you did. All right?"

"All right."

"Now." Jax lifted her head enough to kiss her forehead, then lifted it more to look her in the eye. "Have we dealt with that nonsense well enough that we can go back and deal with the things that aren't nonsense?"

Amanusa gave him a puzzled look. "Isn't it all nonsense?"

"Absolutely not. What those men did to you was a crime. They injured you, Amanusa. Physically and—" He tapped her temple. "In here. They taught you bad habits. They used you for their pleasure and you've no idea how to find your own. You've been taught that you have no right to it, to what might please you. You didn't know it was possible for you to find pleasure in sex. I'm not sure you believe it yet. Do you?"

She shrugged. "For other people, maybe. I think . . . I must be made wrong. Or they broke something inside me that made me wrong. I'm barren, you know. I've never been pregnant. I can't give you sons. They broke that. I'm sure it wasn't the only thing they broke."

"I don't need any more sons. I've got descendants by the trainload—Carteret, for one, and all his relations. I am certain that you are neither made wrong nor broken. Not physically—at least not other than the barrenness. That can happen when a child is abused as you were. But that has nothing to do with this." Jax slid from the bed, taking Amanusa with him.

He led her to the mirror and stood behind her. "Did this Mihai undress you, or did he have you undress yourself?"

"He did it." Amanusa watched Jax in the mirror, watched his eyes as he watched her. His hands, crushing the fullness of her nightdress where they rested at her waist, were brown against the white linen, but his body was fair, his skin almost as pale as

Amanusa's. "Mihai didn't like me to move at all. Sometimes I think he wanted a doll, rather than a girl."

"I want you. Amanusa Whitcomb Greyson. My wife." The heat in his eyes made her shiver, brought that wildness inside her back out from hiding again.

He brushed his hands along her arms and returned them to her waist. "In that case, I think you should unbutton your gown. I think it may have been when I undid that first button that you left me." He paused. "You truly do not mind me being without my shirt? It doesn't remind you of bad—"

Amanusa shook her head. "It reminds me of you and me together on the train through the vacuum zone. They were all hairy as bears, and mostly, they just unfastened their trousers and—" She flipped her hand to indicate what she still couldn't make herself say.

"Then I'll keep my trousers safely on, all right?" His eyes crinkled at the corners as he smiled. With his wide, full mouth, even a small smile stretched a long way, especially when it reached his eyes enough to crinkle them. He was a dear, darling man. And he was hers.

Buttons. She had buttons to deal with if she wanted . . . this. Wanted to work sex magic. If she wanted to get over what those horrible men did to her. Wanted to be whole. Wanted—wanted to make love to her husband and have a real, normal, ordinary life.

Or as ordinary a life as a woman could have who worked blood magic and had a three-hundred-seventy-something-year-old blood-bound familiar for a husband.

She did want it. With an urgency that surprised her. She was tired of being broken. She wanted to be fixed, or as fixed as she and Jax between them could manage. And if that meant unbuttoning her nightgown and baring her angular, unfeminine body to view for the first time in six or seven years, she would do it. Whatever it took.

She thrust buttons out of buttonholes with brisk, efficient, determined motions, staring at her flying fingers as she did.

"Look at me, Amanusa." Jax eased a fraction closer to her, hands somehow heavier on her waist. "You don't have to look at your buttons to undo them. I want you to look at me. I want you to be absolutely certain that it's Jax Greyson here with you, not Mihai or Teo or some other bloody dead bastard. It's me."

Her eyes met his in the mirror the instant he spoke. Blue eyes, but darker, greener than the blue-sky shade of her own. Not brown like Teo's, or the muddled hazel of Mihai's. Blue. A deep, dark forest lake to pull her in. Not to drown, but to float away without care.

"That's my girl." His voice was warm, but his eyes held heat. Though how a lake could burn, Amanusa didn't know. Maybe it wasn't heat, but wildness. A lake hidden deep in the forest couldn't be tamed.

She'd run out of buttons, she realized, and stood motionless, gripping the bottom of the placket, staring at Jax while he stared at her. He wasn't watching her eyes anymore. His gaze was fixed on the strip of skin visible between the unfastened sides of her nightgown. And on the shadowed peaks of her breasts that showed through the thin fabric.

Mihai had stared, but his stare never made her feel like this, all fuzzy and anxious. Mihai's stare had frightened her. Until it just made her go numb. She didn't want to go numb now.

The wildness inside her stirred. It came from that part of her that touched magic. The part of her untouched self that had never been broken, the part of her soul she'd hidden from the thieves who had invaded her body to steal all the bits of her they'd shattered. It was the part of her that had stood up to Szabo and made her bargain. And now it wanted Jax. It wanted to tangle in that wildness she saw in his eyes.

That part of her was strong—and yet so infinitely fragile. She wanted to wrap it up and hide it away again, safe.

But this was *Jax*. Jax, who watched her with untamed eyes, freed from his own brokenness, with depths she might never reach, but wanted, suddenly, to explore. This was Jax, who would never hurt her, whose hands trembled where they rested at her waist. Jax, who—though wounded himself in much the same way—fought to heal the damage those others had done to her.

He was watching her face again, his expression neutral, perhaps even cautious. Amanusa was sick to death of caution. "Look at me," she said, and opened her unbuttoned nightgown. She shrugged it off her shoulders, peeled her arms from the sleeves.

Jax looked. His mouth opened and his tongue took a quick trip across his lush lower lip before he cleared his throat. "You're beautiful." His voice held a delicious roughness.

"I'm not." The damned blush started at her waist, where the nightgown pooled over Jax's hands. Or did it go all the way down? Amanusa didn't want to know.

"You are," Jax insisted. "Is a lily any less beautiful because it isn't a rose?"

"I'm too tall and broad-shouldered, and my breasts are too small."

"Stop arguing with me." Amusement danced in Jax's voice, sparkled in his eyes. "You're just the right size to match me. Any shorter, and we'd both get terrible cramps in our necks. And if you're the proper height, then your shoulders cannot be any less broad or they wouldn't match the rest of you."

He moved closer, touching his chest to her bare back, matching himself to her. "I'm still taller. My shoulders are broader. And as for your breasts . . ."

Amanusa held her breath as he shook his hands free of her piled-up gown. It hung there at her hips as, with great care, he closed his big, long-fingered hands over her naked breasts.

"Look there," he whispered in her ear. "A perfect fit."

Breath sighed out of her as she stared at his hands so gently cradling her breasts. It made her whole body feel . . . anxious. As anxious as her breasts had felt before, as they still did. No—more anxious than they felt, because now Jax touched her breasts, eased some of their anxiety. But not all of it. She still wanted *more*.

Amanusa slid her hands over Jax's, pressing them

more firmly against her eager flesh. She leaned back into him, needing the support for her jelly knees. Jax caught his breath, then brushed aside her hair with his nose to open his mouth over the column of her neck and suck lightly. Amanusa cried out as sensation flashed lightning-fast from Jax's mouth to her breasts to that place between her legs.

"Look," he whispered. "See how beautiful you are. See how magnificent you are. See yourself with my eyes."

Magic stirred, and suddenly—she didn't look through his eyes, but she could sense Jax. She could tell how good her breasts felt to his hands, how her hair brushed his shoulders and caressed his stomach, how even her smell intoxicated him. She felt beautiful to Jax.

He groaned, his head falling forward. He opened his mouth over her shoulder, licking it first, then suckling once more. He flattened his palms over her breasts, rubbing them in little circles that made her nipples tingle and the lightning spark again. Amanusa felt her nipples pucker against her hands, but her hands were over Jax's. His hands were on her breasts.

She tried to pull back, to give Jax the privacy of his mind, but he . . . grabbed hold. Shared the sensations with her. For half a moment, she wondered if he should be able to do that, but the sensations swelled in a wild raging flood and swept her thoughts away like so much rubbish.

He moved to the other shoulder, licking, sucking, kissing. Amanusa shook with the pleasure of it. Then, carrying her hand along, he slid one hand down her stomach. The other plucked lightly at her nipples, making her want to hurry his downward journey. But he seemed determined to prove this was no race, for he took his leisurely time, stroking his fingers over every inch of her skin, capturing her fingers when they slid down to twine with his, circling her navel before delving in.

Her body screaming with anxiety, Amanusa twisted her head and bit down on Jax's ear. Just a quick, sharp nip before licking over the bite. He jumped, which she expected, but she didn't expect his hips to surge against her bottom, or his passion to surge into her through the magic of her blood in his veins. She burned, hotter, wilder than before, and she bit him again, sharper.

He moved his ear out of reach. "Easy, love." His amusement made her want to bite his other ear. "Patience is a virtue."

"Jax," she moaned. Or was it a whimper? She *wanted*.

She tightened her grip on his hand and tried to shove it lower, to that oh-so-anxious part of her. For a moment, he resisted, then gave in to her urging.

"Whatever you want, you know I'll give it to you," he said into her ear.

"I don't know what I want, exactly. I just, I—"

"Shhh—" He slid his hand lower and lower, toward that part of her that . . . Why would it be anxious? Why would she be damp there when she'd never been before, except after—after—

Jax shushed her again. He caught her ear in his teeth, catching her attention with the gentle nip. "Look at me, Amanusa. *At me*. Think about me. Think about us, here together. It's me touching you. You have hold of my hands. You can stop them. You can move them where you like. Whatever you want, love."

Love. He'd called her that more than once tonight. It was just a word, the way he used it, like Mihai had called her "dearest." But she liked hearing it anyway.

"All right?" He kissed beneath her ear.

She nodded, and Jax slipped their hands beneath the precariously balanced edge of her nightgown to touch the pale curls hiding her sex. The gown slipped, caught briefly on her bottom, then on his wrist, before it slid slowly down to crumple around her feet.

"Beautiful," he whispered. "Magnificent."

He combed his fingers through the crisp blond hair over her mound until she relaxed again—as much as the anxiety would let her. This was Jax. He wouldn't grab. Wouldn't gouge or pinch or twist. He would— oh heavens—he would make her feel good. She didn't know how, but he said it was possible for her to find pleasure in the act and she trusted him to show her.

The gentle stroke of his fingers felt good already and he hadn't gone beyond the surface. Slowly, gradually, he pressed harder, just where she felt the most anxious, and it felt even better. Better than she'd thought possible, and yet the anxiety still gripped her, still feared—no, wanted. It wanted and she didn't know what it wanted, except *more*.

She saw herself in the mirror, head thrown back, body arched against Jax, her breasts thrust high as she strained for *something*. She let go of Jax's hand on her breast and reached up to grab a handful of his hair, but she didn't tug on it. She needed his face where it was, where she could see it in the mirror, for it was his face she focused on.

She needed to see his face—his green-blue forest-lake eyes and his wide, mobile, full-lipped mouth. His rough-carved features and hard-set jaw. Jax. *Her* Jax.

His finger slipped, plunged between her netherlips and touched something, a nubbin that sent pleasure vibrating through her. She cried out, Jax's cry echoing hers. He stroked over the nubbin—a thing she'd never known existed though the body was her own—and it happened again. Intense pleasure built higher and higher, drawing her up onto her toes as she reached for it.

"Jax." Her hand convulsed in his hair, her eyes wild and frantic.

Another stroke and another, and time froze for an endless, ecstatic moment. Then the pleasure exploded, cascading through her in astonishing waves.

"Amanusa!" Jax's body echoed the arc of hers and he pulled her tight against him as his hips thrust into her bottom.

She could feel his cock throbbing inside his trousers as he spent, but more importantly, she could feel his pleasure, feel that same explosive peak as it blasted through him. It made her cry out again.

He staggered. He caught himself, then caught hold of her, swinging her around and out of her crumpled nightdress to collapse together on the big wingback chair to one side. They gasped for breath, Amanusa sprawled as much over the chair as over Jax. After a while, he stirred, lifted her more properly onto his lap and settled straight in the chair rather than twisted to one side. He tipped his head forward so Amanusa could put her arm behind it, across his shoulders. She nestled in, her naked breasts plumped against his bare torso.

"What just happened?" Amanusa leaned her head against the wing of the chair to look to him. "I could feel you, feel what you felt. Was I supposed to do that?"

"I have heard of it being possible." Jax struggled to assemble his shattered reality. Too many impossible things, things that should never have happened, had. He owed her information, explanations, but he had none, not even for himself. He did have truth, however, and that was the least of what he owed her. "I could feel what you felt as well, however. And that has never happened. Ever."

But that wasn't the worst of it. The greatest impossibility— "Amanusa, when you reached climax, I—"

"I know. You climaxed too. I felt it." She frowned at him. "I thought you couldn't do that, if I didn't—"

"I can't. Or—I couldn't. I shouldn't have been able to." He hid his face in her shoulder, unable to look at her, to see the suspicion rise in her eyes. "I lied to you, Amanusa, when I said that I was a eunuch. I can be aroused. Yvaine allowed me that much, to rise and harden. I should have told you, I know, but—"

"You didn't want to frighten me." She stroked his hair, pressed her lips to his head. She wasn't angry over the lie? "I understand."

Jax held her tighter. Could a woman be any more

perfect? No wonder he loved her. "But I should not have been able to spend. I don't know how that happened. I swear I did not lie about—"

Amanusa put her hands on both sides of his head and lifted it, until he couldn't avoid her crystalline gaze. "It's all right, Jax. I'm not angry. I'm not going to punish you. I'm not Yvaine, I'm your wife. Not your owner." She searched his face for a long moment. "Do you believe me?"

"Dear God, we are a pitiful pair." He felt the smile in his depths, thought it reached his eyes, but couldn't bring it as far as his lips. "If you're not stumbling over your past, I'm crashing into mine. It's a wonder we're both whole and sane."

"I'm not so sure we are." Amanusa wrapped her arms around him and kissed his forehead as she pulled him in again for a cuddle. "Either whole or sane. But we're broken together, and we're mending what was broken, even if it might take us the rest of our lives together."

He brushed his lips over her collarbone and let his breath sigh out, reaching for contentment. It stayed just beyond his grasp, all the unanswered questions niggling at him.

"Actually," Amanusa said before he could ask any of them. "I'm glad it happened, that you could spend without me having to unbind anything. Even when I was still a little afraid of you—and I was never very afraid, because I never sensed any cruelty or meanness in you, even at the first. But even then, I thought it was a terrible thing to do to a man, though it was a relief to me. So I'm glad you were able to free yourself."

"Yes, but how?" Jax sorted through his various worries, now the gears in his mind began to fit themselves together again. They all boiled down to one. "Are the bonds between us raveling? Am I—?"

Losing you? He couldn't say it aloud, couldn't let his desperation show. Not because she would be angry or annoyed, but she might laugh. Or worse, pity him. And if they were coming apart— "Can you still use me as your servant? What will happen if you can't, if they come against you in this test and you can't access the magic we just called?"

"I won't use you, Jax. Not like Yvaine did. Never like that." She held him tighter.

So tight, he had to turn his head to breathe. That put her rosy pink nipple right before his lips, and the temptation to put his tongue out and taste it was too great to resist. Amanusa's gasp had him tasting again, and from there, it was only a fraction's shift to pull it between his lips and—

25

Jax stood and set Amanusa on her feet. "You are far too distracting for conversation when you are without clothing, and we need to know what has happened. It could be dangerous. It could indicate that the magic is coming unraveled, or worse. Put something on so I can think, and—" He looked ruefully down at his probably ruined trousers. "I'll go clean up."

He left the room without looking back, before he

could get distracted again. He left the trousers for the hotel valet and pulled on a fresh pair of knee-length drawers, but he couldn't make himself dress further. It was still his wedding night.

He shrugged on his dressing gown—Amanusa had insisted he be fitted out with a wardrobe when they'd ordered hers—and hurried back to find Amanusa swathed again in her layers of raw silk ruffles. He hoped she'd put her nightdress on underneath it. The more layers, the more likely he'd be able to think. He'd already spent himself once, but it didn't seem to matter. It had been a very, very long time, after all.

"I think I know what's happening," Amanusa said, sitting cross-legged in the middle of the bed.

Jax sat on the chair, where it was safe. Somewhat. "Go on."

"I think, because I've tasted your blood, it has given you back some of the things Yvaine took when she bound you. It's given you the ability to choose."

He shook his head. "I could choose before."

"Not very much. You couldn't choose to leave me, to go somewhere else. You couldn't choose to—to spend." She turned an adorable pink. He hoped she never stopped blushing when she talked about sex.

"But now—" She snapped her fingers at him. "Jax, are you listening to me?"

"Yes." He dragged his attention away from her blush, away from remembering just where it began.

She gave him a skeptical look, then dragged the coverlet up to wrap around her. He hoped it would work, but he didn't think so. She could be covered up so that only her face, only the tip of her nose showed—covered so that nothing showed—and the sound of her voice would arouse him.

"This afternoon," she said, "when we were building that warding wall, and I reached for the sex magic we called, it seemed as if you had to—to open yourself and let me gather it. And last night, when you wanted me to give you the blood magic from the fight, I couldn't get in. I couldn't get inside you until I told you to take the magic. And you said yes, and that's when I could give it to you.

"I think, when I tasted your blood, you gained the ability to lock me out. I think it made us more truly partners, in every way, because now we have to work together to accomplish what we have to. You have to be willing every time."

Jax stared at her, unable to wrap his mind around the concept. "But—we're still bound? Sorceress and servant?"

"Sorceress and familiar. And I think we're bound closer than before. You're bound to me, but I'm now bound to you in return. The power isn't all on one side anymore."

"That *bitch*." Jax threw himself from his chair and stalked to the window to stare out at the night, hands clenching into fists over and over again as he fought down his rage.

"She's dead." Amanusa spoke from close behind him, letting him know she was there before she laid a hand on his shoulder. She treated him like an angry man who needed soothing to be safe.

He liked it. He would never, in another three hundred years, do anything to harm this sorceress—his sorceress—but he liked, after so long, being treated like a man. Someone with the right to be angry. Someone with the power to act on that anger.

"She's dead," Amanusa said again, "and I'm glad she is, because if she wasn't, you wouldn't be mine. But I wish, just for an instant, she wasn't. So I could kill her."

Jax spun around and hauled Amanusa into his arms, needing to hold her, to know she was real, and here. And his.

He held her tight. Too tight, likely, but she didn't object, so he didn't let go. The anger seeped away with the ticking of the mantel clock. He took a deep breath. "It required my time with Yvaine to make me worthy of Amanusa. You wouldn't have wanted the man I was."

"I want the man you are now. I need you."

For the magic. He heard the words, even if she didn't say them. She couldn't need him for anything else. Not the way he needed her. Not like his next breath.

But it was all right. She'd married him. She'd given him back his manhood, made him into a man rather than a thing. She'd bound them closer than ever. He wouldn't lose her with his neediness.

"Take the magic." He loosened his grip and lifted his head to see her strong, beautiful face. "Build your shields."

This time, he somehow sensed Amanusa *reaching* toward him, and just as she arrived, he thought *yes,* and the channels inside him, the ones where the magic hid, opened up and began to flow. He could feel it pouring out of him into her, a fiery cascade that felt as good as it hurt.

She gasped when the magic hit her, turning it into the whispered spell, building armor plating around them both, solid, protective, light as air.

"Jax?" Her voice quavered.

"What is it, love?"

"Was there supposed to be so much?"

"I don't know." He shook his head, wishing he did know. "I've never been much good at reading magic, even after I was bound. Head-blind, remember? Why?"

"It feels like more." She tilted her head and her fingers twitched, as if feeling something. "Or maybe it's simply that it's stronger. A difference in quality, rather than quantity. It's definitely different."

"How can you tell? We've only raised sex magic by kissing before." He wanted to believe in a difference, but feared to.

"Still the same magic." Amanusa gave him a teasing look. "Who's the sorceress, and who's head-blind?"

He laughed, joy bubbling up from the blood they shared. He was himself again, or more himself than he had been in a long time. He could say yes, or no, and mean it. He could choose.

"Amanusa—" Did he dare ask?

"Mmm?" She seemed to still be playing with the magic.

"Do you think I really can keep you out? If you want in?"

She looked up at him, eyes sharp. "Try it."

"Are you sure? I don't—" He sensed her *reaching* again, angry this time, predatory. So much like Yvaine that he braced for the pain, jaw tight and hard, while his mind cried, *No!*

And nothing happened. He was alone inside his head, inside his body. He felt cold. There was no warm presence snuggled in beside him. His vague awareness of magic was utterly gone, and he missed it. "Amanusa?"

"You did it." She smiled at him. "You've shut me out."

"I don't like it."

Her smile wobbled. "I don't either. I can't feel you." Her hand closed into a fist, touched her heart. "Here. I can't feel you here, inside me."

Jax's hands tightened on the arms of the chair to keep from lunging across the room at her. He wanted to be inside her, in every way possible.

Yes, he thought, and the warmth seeped back in. He could sense the magic in the air and inside himself. One more answer and he would be done with asking for tonight at least. "When you reached for the magic that time, it felt like Yvaine."

"I meant to. I tried to think like her, that I was entitled to the magic and you were only a tool, a thing." She bit her lip. "I didn't like it."

"Because that's not who you are."

"I could be. The power is tempting. That's why I didn't like it, because the magic doesn't care. It just wants to be used. Maybe Yvaine didn't start out the way she was. Maybe the magic made her like that. I wanted to be sure—I wanted you to be sure that if I ever become like Yvaine, like Szabo—so devoted to a cause or an ideal that I don't care who I hurt—I wanted to know that you could stop me. Keep me away from the magic."

He was out of the chair and moving toward her

while she still talked. "You could never be like Yvaine."

"I could." She wouldn't look at him.

Jax crawled onto the bed and pushed her flat onto her back as he moved up over her. "Never. Not even before you tasted my blood. Your past wouldn't let you become what you hate. But if my blood in you does what you say, I'll be better able to watch over you, to help you. Give you what you need."

He let his weight settle over her. Her eyes went frantic, began to dart this way and that, as if hunting escape. "Look at me, Amanusa," he said then. "Look at *me*."

He waited until she looked, until she began to relax beneath him. It thrilled him that she would react that way to him, to his face. He lifted just enough to drag the coverlet down and untie her dressing gown again. She hadn't put her nightdress back on, and a tremor shook his whole body when he realized it. Thank God he hadn't known before.

In a near frenzy, he rose to his knees and wrestled his way out of his dressing gown and drawers. Laughing, Amanusa sat up and shed her ruffles. She laughed. Who would ever have thought it? Jax couldn't laugh. Not yet. Not when he still hadn't found his way inside her.

He fell to hands and knees over her, able at last to indulge himself with the sight of her glorious nakedness—her high, proud breasts, the endless stretch of sleek legs, the flare of her hips, the little mound of her stomach. "You are so beautiful."

"You are the first to ever say so." She held her

arms out to him, smiling. "The first to make me be-lieve it."

His arms shook with the effort of holding himself up. He was afraid to take her offer, afraid of forget-ting himself in her embrace. "I want you so much, I'm afraid of hurting you, or frightening you."

"You won't. You can't." She ran her hands up his arms to his shoulders. "Jax, you gave me what I needed. You showed me there was beauty and pleas-ure and joy in making love. Let me give you what you need. Let this be your turn. Come and take what you want."

It couldn't be that simple. Could it? She tugged at his shoulders and his elbows collapsed. Somehow he kept his weight from crashing into her, but though he fell slowly, he still fell, and her body cushioned his fall.

Take what you want, she said. He scarcely knew what that was, it had been so long since he'd been able to have it. He wanted . . . wanted just to take her, like those bastards in the mountains, to plunge inside her and hammer at her until—

"Do it, Jax." Her fingers roamed into his hair, play-ing in the too-long waves. "Whatever you want, do it. Take it. It's not like in the camp. It can't be. You're my husband. I chose you. We've shared blood. You can't hurt me because you would feel it."

It sounded logical, but he wanted it so much, he couldn't help looking for the viper in the nest. Some-thing had to be wrong with it.

"Jax." Amanusa squeezed her hand between their bodies and touched his cock where it pressed into the softness of her stomach. He caught his breath. She

wrapped her hand around his rigid flesh and he groaned, his hips twitching. She squirmed, trying to maneuver her body, to bring him where he wanted so badly to go.

"Do you mean it?" The words grated out of him, his voice gone harsh.

"Whatever you want, Jax. You did as much for me. Please. Let me do this for you."

He pulled back to search her face, not quite yet able to believe. He pushed himself into her hand and she didn't retreat, didn't look away. Her eyes returned his hungry stare with a wild hunger of their own. Still watching her face, Jax tugged her hand away and took hold himself. He probed her folds, sucking in a quick gasp when he found her as slick and wet as before.

He would take what he wanted, but he would make it good for her too, because that was part of what he wanted. He wanted to feel her come apart in his arms, screaming his name. He rubbed his tip over her sweet spot until she moaned, until he couldn't bear any more and brought himself to her entrance.

He stopped then, poised just outside. "Look at me, Amanusa. See me."

He wanted her eyes on him not only because he didn't want her frightened, but because he wanted her focused on him and nothing else. Her eyes fluttered open, and when he knew his image registered in her mind, he thrust home. The wet, slick heat of her body enfolding him almost brought him to climax right then. He laced his fingers through hers, pressing them hard into the mattress, and held on, his cheek against hers as he fought for control. He wanted more from this. More for himself and much more for her.

"It was easier," he rasped, "when I wasn't the one in control."

"But it's better now?" Amanusa sounded uncertain.

Jax lifted his head to see her. "Oh yes. Much better. More difficult, but better." He withdrew almost all the way and drove back home again, sliding his hands down to her hips to lift them so he could rub across that place inside her, the one that had taken him so long to learn.

Amanusa gasped. Jax grinned, a fierce, predatory grin. He was going to make her scream.

He didn't hold back. When he tried, Amanusa clawed at him, drove her hips up into him. So he let go that much control and pounded into her. He could feel her reactions, know how *that* thrilled her, and *this* thrilled her more, and he gave himself over to it. The sensations built higher and tighter until he cried out with every thrust, every breath. Wild, barbaric sounds that harmonized with Amanusa's moans and whimpers.

Her body went taut, paralyzed with pleasure, and he shouted, giving one more hard, perfect stroke, so that they exploded together, throbbing and pulsing around and into each other, captured by the perfection of the moment. A moment that lasted forever and not nearly long enough.

"Oh my." Amanusa combed Jax's hair out of her face.

Jax turned his head to press a kiss on her temple. It

was nice that she was tall. "Is that a good or a bad 'oh my'?"

She poked his arm with a forefinger. "You felt everything I felt. What do you think?"

"You know men and our frail self-esteem. I want to hear it in words." He lifted his weight off her, but couldn't bring himself to leave her altogether. He nuzzled along her cheek, unable to stop kissing her.

Amanusa nuzzled back. "If I tell you that I want you to take whatever you want any time you want, will that satisfy your need for words?"

He chuckled, content. "I am going to be so bloated with magic, you'll have to give spells away for free to keep me from waddling with it."

She pulled back abruptly, worry in her eyes. "Will too much magic hurt you?"

Jax gave her a hearty kiss and slid to one side, propping himself on an elbow. Her worry warmed him. "I haven't carried huge loads of magic very often. Yvaine almost never f—" He edited his language. "Never had sex with me herself, which raised the most magic. She sent me to parties—orgies—"

He watched Amanusa through his lashes for her reaction, fearing her disgust, but now able to believe she might not condemn him for it. "When she had a great spell she wanted to work, I would sometimes carry the magic for weeks. It did me no harm to carry so much magic, didn't affect my physical self at all, but I felt bloated. Because I felt it, I moved differently. It made me walk like a fat man, or a pregnant woman."

"I am not sending you to any orgies, so you can get that idea right out of your head this instant."

Her snappishness, her obvious jealousy, had Jax laughing with delight. He scooped her into his arms, rolling onto his back with her atop him. "With you as my wife, how can I even see other women? I shall be that most boring of creatures, a faithful husband."

"Good." She gave a brisk, satisfied nod and folded her hands on his chest. "Now what?"

He laughed again. He'd never ended lovemaking with so much laughter. "Now, you reinforce our magic shields, and then I suppose it will be time to begin the 'happily ever after' part of our lives?"

"Oh, Jax, do you think it's possible?"

"What? 'Happily ever after'? No, I suppose not. Not the 'ever after' bit. But I think we ought to be able to manage 'Happily some of the time.' Perhaps even 'Happily most of the time.' " He brushed back a cascade of pale blond hair so he could see her face. "I'm happy now. Are you?"

Her smile made his heart turn over. "Yes," she said. "I am."

She reached for magic, Jax gave it, and she added another, brighter layer of protection to that they already wore. Then, tired by the effort, they slept.

Jax woke her once more in the morning's small hours to make love again, needing to know if she'd really meant it—whenever, whatever he wanted. She did. How could he love her any more?

The attack struck just before dawn, crashing past the wards around their hotel room as if they were walls made of paper, shrieking across the personal shields built with so much pleasure in the night. Amanusa screamed as the attack pierced the shielding, pain slicing through her. She grabbed for the magic Jax thrust at her. Shouting the shielding spell, she built up their defenses from the inside out.

"Must we just endure the bombardment?" she gasped between waves of attack. "Can't we attack in return?"

"Sorcery doesn't have much offensive magic without innocent blood being shed."

Amanusa thought frantically as she spoke another spell, built another shield. She didn't know enough. She needed more spells in her repertoire.

"The attack is fading," Jax said. "I've still got plenty of magic. What if we turn it back on them? Reflect the spell back at them with your magic in it."

"Can we do that?"

From the nightstand, Jax pulled one of the notebooks she'd filled on the train and flipped through it. "Yes, here. I thought I remembered it."

Amanusa finished yet another defensive spell. "I didn't think you could remember what Yvaine said when she spoke with your voice."

"I can't. But I always looked over what you'd written when I woke." He climbed back onto the bed, unaware of his nudity, his finger marking the spell in the notebook.

She spoke it as she read, pouring magic into the conclave's testing spell, turning the attack back on its source, confining it to pain and forbidding death or physical injury. Then she let it go and felt it slingshot back across the city.

Only then did they hear the shouts and pounding at the suite's door. "It's Harry," Amanusa said, recognizing the voice as Jax found his dressing gown on the floor and pulled it on.

"They must have felt the warding shatter. I'll tell them to come back later." He closed the door to the bedroom as he padded out to the parlor.

Amanusa decided she could take time for undergarments beneath her dressing gown before emerging to consult with their friends.

Friends? The word brought her up short. She'd never had friends. Not since her family left Vienna. Did she now?

She rather thought so. Harry and Elinor and even Grey, for all his nonsense. They seemed to like her and care what happened to her, and she liked them. Amanusa smiled as she tied the ribbon on her chemise. She had a husband—an excellent one—and she had friends. Life was suddenly very good.

But why were they all shouting? Amanusa threw her dressing gown over her unmentionables and tied it hurriedly shut before snatching open the bedroom door to see what was going on.

Jax stood in the doorway, arms braced on either side of the frame, barring the way. Harry and Grey, also in dressing gowns, stood just in front of him, and Amanusa thought she saw Elinor in a shabby green wrapper in front of them. Beyond her friends were several gentlemen in morning coats and suits. Amanusa could barely see them past all the bodies in her way.

"Mademoiselle Whitcomb?" A heavily accented voice floated over the heads of her friends and husband, speaking a few more sentences in French.

"Oh, wait. I don't have my translation stone." Amanusa turned back into the bedroom and rummaged through yesterday's dress for the stone in her pocket. The dressing gown didn't have pockets so she held it in her hand.

"There is no Mademoiselle Whitcomb," Jax was saying in his fluent French. "There is only Madame Greyson."

"My apologies." The other man's accent had vanished. Magic. "And my congratulations on your marriage. I am desolated to be disturbing you so early—"

"Just get on with it."

Amanusa recognized that voice. It was the English wizard, Cranshaw. The one who feared and hated sorcery—and women—so much. Her stomach began to churn.

She rose onto her tiptoes to see, a hand on Jax's shoulder for balance. The man at the forefront of the group had turned around to look at Cranshaw, who stood with a cluster of four—no, five other scowling magicians. Behind them, at the door to the suite, she saw uniformed policemen.

Cranshaw flushed under the man's stare, and after another long moment the man turned back around. What was Captain Vaillon doing in her hotel suite? Amanusa's head went light and fuzzy.

"Madame Greyson." Vaillon met her eyes over Elinor's sleep-touseled head. "I have been asked by the International Magician's Conclave to execute a warrant of arrest for the investigation of a magical crime. These men—" His disdain showed clearly in his voice. Probably too clearly. "They have been sent to ensure that you do not use your magic to escape."

Amanusa gripped Jax's shoulder, needing the support as her head threatened to float entirely away, and she lost track of the whereabouts of her knees. Dear

God, what was wrong with these people? Why couldn't they just leave her alone? "What crime am I supposed to have committed this time?"

Jax glanced over his shoulder at her and immediately abandoned his role as gate to wrap his arms protectively around her. Vaillon stepped forward and held out a folded paper. Amanusa reached between Harry and Grey to take it, but before she could open and read it, a little man all in black, save for the red cockade on his top hat and the red badge on his frock coat, came in. He marched across the parlor, the occupants parting before him, until he stopped just behind Vaillon. *Kazaryk.* He had pursued her even to Paris.

Amanusa's knees gave way, only Jax's hold keeping her upright. How long had the Inquisitor Plenipotentiary been here? The thought of Kazaryk's greedy cruelty working with Cranshaw's rabid hatred of sorcery terrified her.

"You are charged with the magic assault on an officer of a duly constituted national council," Inquisitor Kazaryk spat.

Actual spittle flew from his lips. She had forced him to confront his own crimes, and he hated her for it. Amanusa saw the promise of her death in his eyes.

Another man had come in with Kazaryk and stood beside him, glaring at Amanusa. She hadn't noticed him beside the Inquisitor's blazing threat. She glanced at him now, wondering what it was about him that seemed so familiar.

"You are also charged with the murder-by-magic of twenty-three innocent men," Kazaryk said.

Amanusa gasped. She might have cried out. The other man was *Szabo*.

Dragos Szabo, with his gray-laced black hair slicked back and his bristly chin clean-shaven between his bushy side whiskers, dressed up in a fancy suit. No wonder she hadn't recognized him.

"You betrayed my trust," he snarled.

"Your trust? What about my trust?" Anger—absolute fury—drove out her fear. "What about what your men did to me? What about my murdered mother? My little brother? Where was the justice for that? Did you give me justice? No. So I took it."

"You have heard it from her own lips," Kazaryk crowed, triumphant. "She confesses to her crime."

"This is a hotel room." Vaillon's voice rang out. "Not a court of law. Proper procedure will be followed."

"Then arrest her, by God," Cranshaw shouted. "Do your duty. Or has sorcery enslaved you as well?"

Vaillon turned to glare at him again. "It is *my* duty, monsieur. I am the one who knows what my duty demands. I do not take orders from you. You have satisfied yourselves that I am free of magical influence. Now, if you do not shut your mouth, I will arrest you as well for interference in my duty. Do you understand?"

Cranshaw subsided, muttering. In centuries past, magicians had defied civil authority. It was one of the things, according to Jax's returning memories, that had sparked the witch-burnings. A great many more people had small talents than had great enough talent to become master magicians. Their numbers made a difference when the council magicians abused their power.

The masters had agreed to abide by civil law in order to obtain the protection of that law from angry and fearful mobs. Even Cranshaw did not dare defy the law and risk a return to those days, much as he might wish to instigate a mob against Amanusa and her sorcery.

"Surely you cannot mean to take her into custody in her dressing gown," Elinor protested.

"Of course not. Madame may dress. I will remain here in the parlor with my policemen, and these . . ." He sneered, as only the French can sneer. "These 'gentlemen' may go into the corridor, if they insist on waiting."

"How do we know you won't let her go?" someone demanded.

"Because unlike you," Vaillon said, "I have honor. This lady has honor. She will not run. But if she did, I would stop her."

"You didn't expect to find us alive, did you?" Jax said then, looking at Kazaryk, at the magicians. "Did you launch the magic attack on us yourselves?"

"No." Amanusa shook her head. Her fist closed around the satin shawl collar of Jax's robe as realization hit her. "They wouldn't be here if they had. They would be trying to cope with the results of their own spell. These cowards persuaded the conclave to authorize the attack as my master magician's test. They manipulated them into timing it just before dawn. Just before Captain Vaillon was to arrive with his arrest warrant and discover our bodies. That attack was meant to kill. Is that how you test all your journeymen?"

Harry looked shocked. The magicians behind Vaillon looked defiant. But they hadn't been the ones attacking.

"I reflected the spell used against us back at those who attacked, but I barred the reflected magic from killing," Amanusa said quietly. "Who are the barbarians in this room?"

26

"OUT." VAILLON TURNED to eject the magicians from the parlor, grabbing Kazaryk by the shoulder to turn him forcibly around and propel him out the door.

"You destroyed the revolution," Szabo growled.

"No." Amanusa was suddenly too tired to growl back. "*You* destroyed it, Szabo, when you let criminals and thugs join your revolution. They turned it into nothing more than a rabble."

Vaillon shoved the outlaw chief backward, handing him over to one of the policemen.

"Amanusa, I am so sorry." Elinor squeezed between Harry and Grey and pulled her into a fragrant hug.

"I can give you only so much time, madame, monsieur," Vaillon said, returning from the closed suite door. "Time for dressing, but not time for consulting with your friends."

"Thank you, Captain." Amanusa smiled at him. More gratitude would be offensive to his dignity before his men. She hugged Elinor again, squeezed Harry's and Grey's hands. "And thank you all for your support. It means a great deal to me."

"We're not the only support you got," Harry said with a little salute. "So we'll be off now to rally it. We'll meet you at the conclave chamber. That is where you're takin' 'er, right?" he asked Vaillon.

"*Oui.*" With a little bow to Amanusa, Vaillon escorted her friends to the exit and Jax swept her into the bedroom.

With the expertise of the servant he was for so long, Jax helped her dress. Before he retreated to his own dressing room, he bent for a quick kiss. The instant their lips touched, desire flared. Amanusa clutched at his lapels, terrified that all she had gained would be lost, desperate for more time, more kisses, more everything.

Gently, Jax pulled away. "It will be all right. You are in the right here. Vaillon and his men will ensure that the law is followed. And he will not give us more time than we actually need. I must dress."

"I know." She turned to face the mirror, took hold of her new silver-backed brush to keep from clinging to Jax. He touched her cheek, a lingering caress, then he fled.

When he returned, Amanusa had her hair braided and coiled on her head, a jaunty, military-styled hat atop the coil to match her white, braid-trimmed dress. Jax picked up his sword stick, settled his top hat on his head, and offered his arm to Amanusa for escort. Vaillon and his policemen waited in the parlor.

She hid the trembling of her hands in Jax's sleeve and the terror that spawned it behind the mask she had learned to wear in the outlaw camp. *Never let them see your fear.* It might make them think her less feminine, but men like this did not respect the feminine. They respected strength. She had to be strong. This trouble could yet end in the spilling of innocent blood, and with so many arrayed against her, she did not yet know how they would get out of it. But one way or another, get out of it they would.

"You are not named in the warrant, monsieur," the captain said. "You are not under arrest."

"I am her husband, Captain, and her familiar. Where else would I be, but by her side?"

Vaillon's eyes glinted with approval. He gave a tiny, heel-clicking bow and gestured toward the suite's door.

Whole hordes might be lined up to destroy her, but at least she did not stand alone. Her eyes filled with tears and she blinked them furiously back. Having Jax at her side almost made it worse, because now the outcome mattered.

MAGICIANS ALREADY FLOODED into the grand chamber when Amanusa arrived with her police escort. Elinor met them in the lobby to clasp Amanusa's hands and stare worriedly at her with tear-filled eyes.

"It will be all right, Elinor," Amanusa said.

"I'm supposed to be saying that to you." Elinor swiped the tears away with her gloved fingers. "Harry and Grey are rousting out the progressives. The traditionalists—though they deny the true, *old* traditions—they've been busy all night. They're already all here, but it's not enough for a quorum. Not yet."

Men waited at the multiple sets of double doors into the chamber, members of whatever the French called their Inquisition, according to the striped sashes and cockades they wore. The stripes were four colors—black, white, red, and green—to represent the four great magics. The white stripe in cockade and sash made Amanusa feel minutely better. Sorcery was acknowledged at least in that small way.

Vaillon escorted Amanusa and Jax to the doors, but before they entered, one of the guards stopped them. Massilean Guard they were called, after the old Roman name for Marseilles, as if claiming the guard had been around since then. Perhaps it had.

"Only magicians inside," the guard said, looking at Jax.

"He is my husband." Amanusa hoped it would get him in, but it was a feeble hope, and in the end, a disappointed one.

Jax kissed her cheek. "I'll wait out here with Elinor," he murmured. "It will be all right. You have committed no crimes."

"That's hardly the same as being innocent," she whispered back. But she couldn't cling. She didn't dare appear weak. These men might be better dressed than the outlaws in Szabo's camp, but they were no less dangerous. And she was out of practice in standing against their hate.

"Here." Jax thrust magic at her. "Build your shields higher. Make them thicker. If you need me, I'll get to you one way or another. No matter what, I will find you."

"Yes, all right." Amanusa let herself be drawn away from him. She focused on whispering the words of the "shield-building" spell to keep the threatening tears away. When the magic was layered thick, she expanded her awareness and realized Vaillon was escorting her down the aisle toward the dais. "I thought only magicians were allowed into these hallowed halls."

Vaillon's lips twitched in an invisible smile. "Magicians, and the duly appointed representative of the civil government during the investigation of a crime. *Moi*."

"Good." Amanusa smiled. If she were guilty of the crimes with which she'd been accused, she had no doubt that Vaillon would see her punished. But since she wasn't guilty, she was glad of his presence. He was a fair, open-minded, and honest man, and she'd found far too many of the other sort lately.

Men flooded into the chamber, some of them wearing dressing gowns over their trousers, with slippers on their feet. Harry and Grey were apparently rousting the progressives from their beds. Amanusa watched Cranshaw's scowl grow darker as more and more magicians rushed in.

The English wizard paced in the space before the dais on the other side of the great hall from her, the seats behind him almost completely full. Elinor was right. They had been plotting. Probably since before Kazaryk and Szabo reached Paris. Had they been plotting other things besides this?

Amanusa let none of her worry show. She could still feel Jax's presence in the back of her mind. Or perhaps it was at the bottom of her heart. He flowed through her blood, just as she flowed through his. She would never be alone again.

Finally, the governing board trod ponderously up the steps to the dais and Herr Gathmann hammered the gathering into session. Magicians continued to file in, but no sign of Harry or Grey yet. Amanusa caught occasional glimpses of Jax and Elinor in the lobby when the doors opened and closed. She could hide her trembling, mask her face with calm, but she couldn't stop looking back at the doors to see where her two main supporters might be.

Gathmann called Captain Vaillon to the podium to read out the arrest warrant and the charges against Amanusa. She turned to face the conclave as well as the governors from her corner at the front of the room. She did her best to appear confidently innocent as Vaillon read the outrageous accusations. The ominous mutter of voices made it difficult, as they rose and fell with each charge, like a mob working itself up to attack.

When he was done, the captain came back down the steps and took up his post by her side. "Courage, brave lady," he murmured.

"I ask to be recognized by the president." One of the men on the dais stood and shouted over the rising mutter of conversation.

Gathmann gave his recognition and the man who approached the podium was no one Amanusa had seen before, tall and dark with large features that assembled into an attractive whole. Not as attractive as Jax, of course.

"I am Nicos Archaios," the man announced as the noise subsided. "One of those charged with finding a solution to the dead zones that have been plaguing all of Europe. I led a party to the zone in the St. Germaine district to investigate the warding spell built around it in hopes of stopping its growth.

"What we found, gentlemen, was no mere curtain

struggling to hold back the bleeding away of magic, which is more than we have ever been able to construct. No, we found a wall. A solid prison wall entrapping the deadly zone."

Amanusa began to hope. She feared it—hope had been too often dashed in the past—but it sprang up anyway. Might he convince them of sorcery's good qualities?

"This wall contained the magic of alchemy—of water and earth, and of wizardry—the bones of trees. But those alone—bah!" He threw up a hand, the sudden shout startling Amanusa.

"We have tried this before, and never did it work, but this wall—this wall also held the magic of conjury. Spirits bound their magic into the wall. Never have we been able to use spirit magic against the death sectors, because the spirits would not stay— but bound they were. Bound by sorcery. By *blood*."

A clamor arose, drowning out Archaios's words. Men shouted against sorcery. Others shouted in favor of it and against those who disagreed with them. Others, Amanusa thought, shouted just to be shouting. Or perhaps to quiet the rest. Her trembling started up again. Would the conclave break down in riot?

The Massileans spread out into the crowd. Gathmann pounded his gavel on the podium—it had to be making dents—and slowly the uproar subsided.

"Goin' well, I see," Harry said into Amanusa's ear.

She startled, then couldn't help laughing, though it was a feeble laugh. She was too nervous. This kind of passion on the mere issue of sorcery couldn't help her cause.

Gathmann recognized one of the magicians in the audience, and he stood, asking, "Where did this blood come from, eh? What innocent lies dead, drained of blood?"

"No innocent at all. Nor is anyone dead." Grey Carteret sauntered toward the podium steps, swinging his walking stick idly, as if on a stroll through the park. "If I might, Herr Gathmann? I was there. I am the conjurer whose spirit magic helped build that wall."

Gathmann gestured in invitation and Grey climbed the stairs, taking his time, letting the anticipation build.

Harry tipped his head toward Amanusa to mutter from the side of his mouth. "We decided Grey should tell about makin' the spell. They been 'earing too much from me. I get carried away, talkin' about how we need to fight the dead zones. They ain't 'eard from Grey at all before this. An' the fact his dad's a duke don't 'urt any, even if he is third or fourth son down."

Grey reached the podium and laid his silver-headed walking stick across it. Then he looked out at the crowd, waiting until all noise hushed and all eyes turned his direction. "I was there, gentlemen. I saw Amanusa Whitcomb Greyson spill the blood required to build this spell. I gave up my own blood for it."

Dramatically, he held up his arm. The wrong arm. She'd drawn Grey's blood from his left. "Voluntarily, gentlemen. I gave my blood willingly. If not, she didn't want it, was on the verge of refusing it until I convinced her that yes, I wanted to spill a few drops of my blood to stop the horrors of this dead zone from spreading any farther. We all spilled blood, all of us who participated in the building of this wall. And this sorceress took less than any physic ever bled from me for fever.

"I am a conjurer. My spirits, my familiars have always refused to remain in the vicinity of a dead zone, or to work magic nearby. But the instant the blood—shared from wizard, alchemist, conjurer, and sorcerer, and mixed into the water and earth of alchemy—the instant it was dripped onto the stones where I drew my sigils, the fear left the spirits.

"It was as if the blood protected them. Strengthened them. Enabled them to do what I asked of them." Grey's voice grew stronger, louder, filled with passion and power. "And you have the stupidity to want to destroy this magic? You are madmen!"

At Grey's accusation, the shouting began again. Amanusa realized her hands were twisted together and forced them to relax, to lower to waist level. She couldn't make them let go completely, but she could stop twisting them.

Archaios, the investigator, jumped to his feet. "I propose—" he shouted, and half the mob quieted instantly. Cranshaw's group kept shouting for her head.

Gathmann's hammering and a subtle reordering of the Massileans got them quiet. Archaios stepped up to the podium as Grey gave graceful way.

"I propose that Mrs. Greyson be pardoned for any and all crimes that she may be accused of on the grounds that sorcery cannot be lost to us again," Archaios cried.

What? What were they doing?

"I second," someone shouted from the heart of the chamber.

"What about my men?" Szabo jumped to his feet from a chair in the center of the front row. "What about the men she murdered? Left lying in the dirt with blood running from their mouths, their noses, their eyes. Twenty-three men with blood on their fingernails and their privates! What about them?"

"Vote!" Harry shouted. Others took it up.

"No." Amanusa whirled on Harry. "You think I did it, don't you? You think I murdered those men."

She ran for the dais and began to climb. "I demand an investigation," she cried. "I murdered no one. *Justice is not murder.*"

The hall fell silent again as everyone stared at her, bewildered. Those in front told those behind, who hadn't heard, what was happening.

"She has the right." Vaillon stepped forward from where he'd followed her onto the platform. "She has the right to insist on a hearing. A proper investigation."

"And who will testify to the truth?" Kazaryk said. "The only ones still living who were present are this woman and her cicisbeo. They will not give us the truth."

Amanusa mounted the last few steps to the top of the dais and stalked to the edge of the platform. "Blood never lies." She stared out at the crowd, at Kazaryk and Szabo. "Even you, who have forgotten like the rest of the world what sorcery truly is, even you know this. *Blood never lies.*"

She looked down at her accusers on the floor before her. "And innocent blood will cry out for justice.

These men accuse me. Very well." She looked out at the conclave. "Let us see what the blood says. Let it tell us the truth."

"You are the only sorceress," Cranshaw shouted. "What guarantee do we have that you will tell us the truth of what the blood shows you? That you won't just use your magic to murder these men like you did the others, or enslave them for your evil purposes?"

"I have murdered no one. I have enslaved no one." Amanusa looked at the Hungarians again. "Can you say the same?"

Szabo fidgeted, unable to meet her eye. Who would have believed the man still had a conscience? Kazaryk only glared.

Once more she looked out at the gathered magicians. "I can bring neutral witnesses into the magic to observe. It will not require any of the witnesses' blood, and only a drop from those who claim to be innocent victims."

"Who would volunteer for such black magic?" Cranshaw cried.

"I." Louis Vaillon stepped forward on the dais. "I will volunteer. As representative of the Emperor Louis Napoleon of France, I will stand as witness."

"Accepted." Gathmann pounded the gavel down, trying to take back control. "Two witnesses are required. The other must be a magician, to represent the conclave."

"I'll volunteer." Harry's offer and Grey's came simultaneously.

"They worked magic with her yesterday." Cranshaw was turning several unattractive colors in his outrage. "Who's to say she didn't bind more than the wall? They're her allies. They'd say anything."

"Cranshaw has a point," Gathmann said. He looked over the crowd. "Do we have any other volunteers?"

Archaios, standing a few steps away from Amanusa, tensed, as if debating the issue, but before he could make his decision, someone called from the floor.

"I will do it." Antonio Rosato, the Italian wizard, stepped into the aisle and made his way forward. "I saw this lady risk her own life yesterday to save the life of a man she did not know. I do not believe she has murdered anyone. She will not harm me. I will join in this magic."

"I demand that this unholy ceremony be performed right here in this chamber," Cranshaw said. "In full view of the members of the conclave where we can stop her before she kills or enslaves anyone else! Let nothing be hidden from us."

Amanusa hid her worry. How could she preserve guild secrets and still get her blood into the cup? Would this even work? If they were so opposed to sorcery itself, would they care about the truth? She wished she had Jax's skill at sleight-of-hand. But she would do whatever she had to do to clear her name. "Agreed. We can do it here on the dais. There won't be much to see, however."

"What do you need?" Gathmann laid his gavel on the podium as the rumble of noise rose on the chamber floor.

"A little furniture rearranging." She surveyed the dais, thinking about the mundane to divert her mind from the panic hovering, waiting to pounce. "Podium over there out of the way, I think. Five chairs—the large ones—in a half circle in the center. It would probably be best if the governors watched from below. Then I need a pot of tea, Inquisitor Kazaryk, Monsieur Szabo, the witnesses, and this." She drew her lancet from her pocket and slipped it onto her forefinger.

She also wanted Jax, but she wanted him safe more than she wanted the comfort of his presence. If he remained in the lobby, surely "out of sight, out of mind" would hold true. "It might be a good idea to arrange some of your Massileans on the floor around the dais, in case someone panics."

"As you request." Gathmann inclined his head and beckoned the nearest Massilean guard.

The dais was cleared of extraneous people, Grey giving her a look as he descended. Amanusa wasn't sure what he meant by it. *Good luck? Be careful? I hope you know what you're doing?* All of those probably.

One of the Massileans arranged furniture while two others escorted the suddenly reluctant Kazaryk and Szabo to the platform. Dr. Rosato mounted under his own power. The Massilean escorts remained on the dais, behind the chairs.

Amanusa arranged the men; Rosato and Vaillon in the two outside chairs, Kazaryk and Szabo to either side of her place in the center. Her white dress with its scarlet trim made her shockingly visible among the men in their somber colors.

The tea was brought in on a little footed tray, with five cups rattling in their saucers around the fat white teapot. Amanusa had the apprentice set it off to the side and poured a single cup of tea. One would make it easier to disguise the fact that she didn't take any of the tea, and the men needed to take only a swallow for the magic to take effect.

Then she walked to the center of the semicircle and faced her accusers. She held up her hand with the lancet around her finger, let the light glitter along its sharp silver point. The light flashed with the trembling of her hand, but hard as she tried, she could not stop the trembling.

"Dragos Szabo. Anton Kazaryk. You claim yourselves victims, that your blood is innocent. Do you offer your blood to prove your claim?"

"Yes." Kazaryk looked as if he wanted to spit at her, but refrained. Perhaps because of the Massilean alchemist standing just behind him.

Szabo couldn't meet her gaze, but the stubborn old goat firmed his jaw, glaring at the magicians in the chamber behind her, and nodded.

"Say it aloud." Amanusa gestured at the crowd of observers. "So they can hear you."

"Yes," he muttered, then flicked an angry glance at Amanusa. *"Yes."*

"Give me your hand." Amanusa held out her left hand, palm up, her right poised with the lancet.

Szabo extended his hand, squinching his face up and turning away.

She isolated his longest finger and, with a quick stab and a squeeze, drew out a fat droplet of blood. She let the others—the witnesses and the two Massileans on the dais—see how small the drop was, then she scooped it up with the side of the lancet and strode to the tea tray, her skirts swaying with every step.

She stirred Szabo's blood into the tea, and with her wide skirts hiding her actions, quickly lanced her own finger and squeezed a few drops of blood into the cup. She sent magic with it, praying that the spell would work as she intended. As she hoped. If it did not—she thrust away that fear.

When she returned for Kazaryk's blood, he didn't hesitate, holding up a finger in a rude gesture. How childish. She enjoyed his wince when the lancet drove home. Perhaps that was childish too. She didn't care. Again, she collected a drop of blood and stirred it into the tea, along with a spoonful of sugar to hide any metallic taste.

Amanusa picked up the cup and turned to face the audience as she brought it to her lips and pretended to drink. "One swallow," she said, handing the cup to Szabo. "You need to leave enough that everyone gets some, but you need to take a good mouthful."

Szabo sipped warily.

"A mouthful, Szabo."

The Massilean behind him shifted position, nothing more. Szabo took a larger drink. The others drank in turn—Kazaryk, Vaillon, Rosato. More than a swallow was left when the cup came to Rosato, but he tossed it all down.

"It would have been better with a nice Chianti," he said, handing her the empty cup with a smile. "Magic always goes down better with wine."

"Really? I've found vodka to work quite well." She had to force the feeble quip past her frozen face, astonished she could make one, no matter how inane. Everything depended on this.

Rosato burst out with a laugh, but smothered it

quickly at the hum of disturbance from the watching crowd. Apparently they did not approve of levity at such moments. For herself, she was grateful someone could laugh.

Amanusa set the cup back on the tray and moved the tray beside the podium in the corner, for something to do while she waited for the magic to settle into their respective bloodstreams. She returned to her chair and sat, folding her hands in her lap.

Her hoops didn't do well in the throne-like chair. Exchanging it for one of the small armless chairs on the chamber floor gave her another few endless minutes that she could occupy her mind with something besides worry.

"What are we waiting for?" Cranshaw demanded from the floor.

"I told you there wouldn't be much to see," Amanusa retorted, then regretted it. Those on the floor were watching, not participating. She did not owe them answers. Not until the spell was done.

She sat again in her chair. "Catch me if I fall," she murmured to the Massileans behind her. One of them inclined his head in assent.

"We are waiting . . ." Amanusa offered her explanation to Vaillon, the nonmagician in the room. "Because it takes a little time for the magic to reach the bloodstream. I believe we are ready now. I will bring you and Dr. Rosato into the magic first, then we will inquire of M. Szabo, and then Inquisitor Kazaryk." The Inquisitor was the mind she dreaded visiting most, so she would put him last. He'd killed his conscience long ago.

"If you will relax into your chairs?" she said. "You

will probably be more comfortable if you close your eyes."

Amanusa spread her feet a little more for stability, and settled firmly into her chair as she closed her own eyes. This was the moment of proof. More even than the spell binding the dead zone, this spell would demonstrate the power and the value of sorcery and her ability as a magician.

Justice magic was one of the foundations of sorcery, the magic that no other guild could perform. If she could not do this right, she did not deserve the name of sorceress. Moreover, if she did not do this right, she would lose everything in the world that mattered to her—both Jax and the magic. Therefore, she could not fail.

She took a deep breath, and her lips moved without sound as she invoked *Blood of my blood*.

27

AMANUSA *REACHED* FIRST to touch Jax pacing in the lobby and worrying. She couldn't speak to him, could only touch and hold him somehow, and assure him she was well.

She let him go reluctantly and followed the fresh magic into Vaillon. Without much magic of his own, he might need more help from her and more time to adjust to the spell.

She checked his mental shields. Vaillon had a right to his privacy while they went rummaging through Kazaryk and Szabo. They were strong. He had a decent magic sense, though somewhat thready, and his years as a policeman had helped build solid shields. Without blood magic, no one would know what Vaillon thought if he didn't want them to.

The captain's shielding secure, Amanusa gently opened his inner vision, adding to it until he ought to be able to see whatever she did, then she . . . glued it to her own. Or perhaps she put her vision over his like a pair of spectacles.

Amanusa reached for her blood, her magic inside Dr. Rosato. His shields were pristine, his mind bright with curiosity. He felt warm and—green—when she showed him how to open his inner vision. When both men seemed comfortable to her inside the magic, she *reached* for the magic inside Kazaryk, then it was time to ride Szabo's blood.

Dr. Rosato exclaimed as they rushed into Szabo's bloodstream and halted near his heart. It pounded furiously, clearly demonstrating his anxiety. She invoked her own blood in its role as innocent, as victim of Szabo's heartless leadership. She opened her memories and Szabo's and let them see the past.

Vaillon actually snarled as the brutal deaths of Amanusa's mother and her little brother flowed past. Szabo's guilt and regret registered. So did his joking about "breaking eggs to make an omelet." Then Amanusa unveiled her own pain, her "deflowering" at the hands of the entire outlaw gang, and the years with Mihai, while Szabo looked the other way, telling her when she wept that she would get used to it. She let them feel everything she had experienced, made them experience it with her. Her bargain, allowing her to live apart from the camp and Szabo's determination to bring her back, unfolded for them.

Then Szabo threw up a shield. Or he tried. Amanusa's magic shattered it with a thought. Nothing would be hidden. Memory bloomed, and the watchers saw Szabo meeting with Teo while in the background, Amanusa worked over Costel's wounds.

"We need her here at the camp," Szabo growled. "This having to go and fetch her is no good. I have had enough of her defiance."

"I could make her stay," Teo said, his voice dark as he watched her in the hospital shelter.

Szabo gave Teo a wary look. "Without her striking back at us? We can't afford another episode like the last one."

"When I break a woman, she stays broken. She won't dare do anything but what I tell her."

"She still needs to be able to heal my men. It'll do us no good to have her in camp if she's too damaged to work."

"I won't break her wits." Teo's grin made Szabo shudder. "Only her will."

"Her pet idiot might object."

"Then he's a dead man. He might be a dead man anyway. Depends on if I can train him to serve you and me as well as he serves her. Or if he annoys me enough."

Szabo stared at the flames of the campfire a long moment. The watchers could hear him thinking. *The revolution truly did need a healer. It was Amanusa's own stubborn defiance bringing this upon her. It wasn't like she was an innocent virgin, anyway. She was older now, not a child. It wouldn't be so bad this time. Besides, they needed her. The cause demanded it.*

"I'll take a party down to the river to trade tomorrow," Szabo said. "Wait 'til I'm gone." That way he could deny knowing anything about Teo's plans. And he wouldn't have to hear the screams.

In a flash, Amanusa shared the events of that morning, the working of the justice magic, and the crimes committed by the men who died, not only against her and her family, but against other innocents. They saw Szabo's outrage when he returned to the decimated camp, and his awareness of just which men had died, and which ones remained alive. And they saw him plotting with Kazaryk for revenge against her for destroying his cause.

Then she followed her blood into Kazaryk, bringing the others along. Shields barred her way, better-built shielding than Szabo had attempted to throw up. But her blood was inside the man. He could not keep her out because she had already breached his deepest barrier.

The Inquisitor's mind was a darker place than Szabo's, full of self-righteousness, self-importance, and self-interest. Whatever Kazaryk wanted was right and virtuous. Whatever got in the way of that was wrong and wicked. He was zealous in the performance of his duties because that way led to promotion, and the greater possibility for power and for enrichment.

Finding a witch powerful enough to kill so many men at once would garner promotion, possibly over the heads of several of his rivals. If torturing one crack-brained Englishman would get him this witch—

or any other profitable information—then the Englishman deserved torture. Anyone who thwarted his goal
by snatching the man out of his grip committed a
crime. And anyone who thought to make him suffer
for anything he had done deserved to die.

"I have seen enough," Rosato announced as
Amanusa brought them up from the depths of
Kazaryk's sludge pit mind. "And if this is an example
of the standard operation of the Hungarian Inquisition, I believe the conclave should investigate."

"Are you satisfied with the investigation, *Herr*
Vaillon?" Gathmann drew near the dais to ask.

"Oui." The Frenchman came to attention, seated
in his chair. Amanusa thought he might still be a bit
disoriented.

"Then, I break this spell and release the witnesses."
Amanusa let go of the magic, murmuring the words
that would send each man back into his own mind.

Gathmann mounted the dais again. "What is your
report, Wizard Rosato?"

The Italian drew himself slowly to his feet. "If I
were to tell you the horrors I witnessed, horrors suffered by this innocent woman when she was a mere
child, you would weep in sympathy. Terrible crimes
were committed against her with the willing collabo-
ration of these men. And she received no justice."

Rosato flung his hand toward her accusers on the
stage, and Amanusa noticed tears flowing down Szabo's face, crumpled in remorse. Kazaryk stared
straight ahead, expressionless, almost as if his mind
was not at home in his body. Quickly, Amanusa
checked the magic. Her blood still flowed through
him, but the magic was quiescent, as it should be.

"The men who died committed torture, rape, and murder," Rosato was saying. "They deserved their punishment. It was justice, delivered at the impartial hands of magic."

"You lie!" The shout came from the traditionalist side of the chamber.

Rosato drew himself up in outrage. "Do you dare to insult my honor? Do you wish me to describe in detail every crime? Every blow? Do you wish me to describe the faces of the men who forced themselves on an innocent girl of fourteen? On a little boy, eight years old? Do you truly wish to fill your ears with such degradation, as I have just filled my mind?"

"Lies," someone else cried half-heartedly.

"No," Szabo whispered, shaking his head back and forth, back and forth. "No."

He lifted his head, still shaking it. "It is true, all of it. I did not watch it. I could not bear to watch it, but I heard their screams and I did nothing to stop it. I heard the men joking afterward, and I joked with them."

He broke into loud, broken sobs. "God forgive me, *I joked with them.*"

"And what happened to the men who died was justice, was it not?" Rosato demanded.

"Yes," Szabo sobbed. "Yes."

"What about the assault against the Inquisitor?" Cranshaw demanded. "What about that?"

"Self-defense," Rosato said. "*Signora* Greyson's fiancé, now her husband, was illegally arrested and tortured by the Inquisition for being a foreigner in an unexpected place, and having had a spell worked upon him. *Signora* Greyson used the innocent blood of her fiancé to free him. A magician is permitted to use magic to prevent harm to oneself or others. *Signore* Greyson still bears marks from this ill treatment. Self-defense."

"The government of France concurs with this report," Vaillon said. "No crimes were committed by this woman. But if this man, this Inquisitor, were in my police force, I would have him in irons for corruption and abuse of power."

"The conclave has oversight of enforcement of conclave law governing magicians," Gathmann said. "Two reliable witnesses have charged Inquisitor Kazaryk with crimes. These charges will be investigated."

The Austrian and Hungarian councils immediately protested, arguing that the conclave had no jurisdiction to investigate events inside Hungary. Amanusa feared the session would disintegrate into political wrangling without resolving her situation.

Harry climbed the first few steps of the dais to shout, "I propose that all accusations against Madame Greyson be dismissed as unfounded."

Archaios started the huzzahs. It was some time after Gathmann climbed onto the dais to beat his gavel on the podium, but it was not until the battered podium was carried back to the center of the platform, that the chamber began to quiet. It took considerably more time before the vote could be determined, because each side tried to shout the other down.

Finally Gathmann and the governors declared that Amanusa was free to go. She had done nothing wrong. She sagged back into her chair in sudden relief. It was over.

The chamber erupted in a violent uproar as those on Amanusa's side celebrated, and those on the other attacked. Vaillon leaped to the floor to take command of his policemen in the lobby. The Massileans around the dais swept up everyone on it and hustled them into the maze of offices behind the chamber.

When they reached the safety of the governor's meeting room, the governors noticed that Amanusa and Szabo had both been spirited away along with themselves.

"What about this man? What is to be done with him?" Gathmann asked, looking to Amanusa more than the governors. "He is no magician, so we have no role in his fate. We could turn him over to the Austrian authorities . . ." He watched Amanusa now, without any pretense that he consulted anyone else.

"You cannot say that you've done nothing wrong," Amanusa said to her old nemesis. "When you look the other way and do nothing to stop what you know is a crime, you have that crime on your own hands. Especially when you conspire with someone and encourage him to do it. You are guilty of everything done by the men under your leadership."

Szabo groaned and curled into a smaller ball.

Amanusa sighed. "Let him go. His revolution has been destroyed by his own blind eye. He will never forget what he has done, or be free of the guilt that chokes him—at least until he finds some way to make amends for what he has done. It may be impossible. I do not know yet if I am capable of forgiveness myself. Perhaps someday. But until someone forgives—" She felt the visceral click of a spell locking into place. "He will find no peace."

With a jerk of his head, Gathmann signaled to the Massilean guard captain who hauled Szabo to his feet and propelled him out the door.

"What will you do now, madame?" Gathmann still watched Amanusa with an intensity that felt a bit predatory.

"Find my husband." Her smile flickered. "I am sure he has the news of my vindication already, but I am also sure he won't truly believe it until he sees me." It wouldn't seem real to her either, until she found Jax.

She sighed. "And then, depending on what you gentlemen decide about my master magician's status, I suppose I will go lay claim to the sorcerer's tower I have inherited in Scotland, and begin taking apprentices."

"Conclave law states that a magician must take apprentices—"

"Whatever likely candidates the national councils send me—or any woman who asks—I'll be happy to test for her affinity to sorcery and her talent for magic. If she passes the test, and has a good heart, I will teach her, whatever her status in society."

"A good heart?" The Egyptian governor frowned. "What does that have to do with—"

"Everything. Magic without morality, without heart, is too dangerous." She summoned up a smile. "Now. If you gentlemen will excuse me?"

Gathmann signaled for the Massileans to provide her an escort, though the noise from the chamber seemed to be dying down. The Massilean leading the way opened a door onto chaos filling the lobby. Magicians shouted at each other, occasionally degenerating into shoving matches, but no further due to the swift intervention of Massileans or Vaillon's policemen.

"Were you to meet M. Greyson in a particular place?" the guardsman escorting her asked, a concerned expression on his previously stony face.

"No, just—outside the door I went in, I suppose. He and Elinor—Miss Tavis—Harry Tomlinson's apprentice—were waiting there."

The nearest magicians noticed them and surged forward. The Massilean escort stepped forward, invoking warding spells against ill intent, and the men swept right past. These were her supporters.

"Here's our heroine!" They tried to pick her up, apparently to carry her on their shoulders, but her skirts and crinoline foiled that idea, as well as a belated sense of propriety. Instead, they swarmed her, sweeping her into the lobby in a relentless flood of enthusiasm, congratulating her, shaking her hand and kissing it, introducing themselves in a blur of faces.

Amanusa lost her guard escort, lost track of Archaios and very nearly lost her footing before she spotted Harry's bright red waistcoat through the crowd and shouted at him. It took four tries and a helpful alchemist tapping his shoulder before he responded and squeezed through the crowd to her side. Grey and Elinor came with him.

"You did it!" Harry scooped her into a bear hug. "I never doubted it an instant."

"Then why did you ask for a pardon rather than outright dismissal?" Amanusa raised an eyebrow at him. "Where's Jax?"

"Isn't he with you?" Elinor leaned to one side to look past Amanusa, as if she might be hiding Jax in her skirts.

"No." Amanusa frowned. She could sense him through the magic—he seemed all right physically, not worried about anything. But she couldn't tell where he was. "I haven't seen him since I left you both here to go inside. Except for glimpses when the doors opened. Where did he go?"

"To meet you." Elinor's hands clutched at each other, twisted together. "When the fighting broke out inside, at the end, one of the men with the striped sashes—a Massilean—he said you had left the building for your safety and Jax should meet you back at the hotel."

"No, they just took us to a back room to wait 'til things calmed down—maybe the guardsman didn't know. Or maybe he thought things never would calm down." Amanusa shook her head. "It doesn't matter. Let's go back to the hotel and find him. I want to tell him what happened."

"He knows." Elinor's smile was a little misty. "One of the journeymen passed the word when everything was dismissed. But he knew you were working magic. He seems to have quite a sensitivity to it."

"Jax is head-blind." Amanusa headed through the crowd toward the nearest exit. If she waited for the others to move, she might be waiting all day. "He has a sensitivity to me. And I want to tell him anyway. I need to see him."

"Ah, true love . . ." Grey's cynicism shone through.

"He's my familiar as well as my husband," Amanusa retorted. "Love is immaterial."

"Love always matters," Elinor said as she settled into the cab Harry flagged down. "It's obvious you two love each other."

"How?" Amanusa sat opposite Elinor who looked puzzled so Amanusa expanded her question. "How is it obvious? What is it you see that makes you think we're in love?"

"I don't know about 'in love,' but loving each other— You worry more about Jax's well-being than your own. Jax worries more about you than himself. You look after each other, protect each other, care for each other. That's love, and it's there between you. 'In love' is another level, adding passion to the rest. It may be there too, but it's more difficult for an outsider to see." Elinor gave a little unconcerned shrug. "But you and your Jax? A blind man could see the love there."

Amanusa looked at Harry, who nodded.

Even Grey agreed. "It's quite tiresome, frankly. It's simply not done to wear one's heart on one's sleeve."

"Be quiet, Grey. I find it quite lovely." Elinor smiled at Amanusa.

Did she love Jax? How could she not know if she loved someone? Granted, it had been a dozen years or better since she'd had anyone to love. She was utterly out of practice. And if she loved him, was she in love with him?

Was this need to see him, to take his hand and tell him everything he'd missed—was it merely the blood bond of familiar and sorceress? Or was it something else? And was the uneasiness she felt trickling through her due to her confusion about love, or was something truly wrong?

They reached the hotel and Amanusa hurried up to their rooms and Jax. But he wasn't there.

Not in the parlor, in either bedroom, or the bathing room. The others followed behind her, searching the same ground again. She flew back down the stairs, to the concierge by the front door, her unease rising to worry.

"Excuse me. Have you seen M. Greyson? My husband? He's so tall—" She measured with her hand. "And he has ruddy-brown hair and—"

"I know M. Greyson. He married the lady magician. You. Everyone knows the Greysons." The concierge gave a tiny heel-clicking bow. "And I have not seen your husband. I am told you and he departed the hotel together before I came on duty."

"Yes. Thank you." Amanusa tossed him a distracted smile before pushing her way out the hotel doors onto the street, where she came to a frustrated halt. She checked her sense of *Jax* in the magic, through the blood that bound them. Physically, he was still unharmed, but something began to worry him. What?

"Amanusa." Elinor caught her hands, stopped her frantic pacing. Amanusa hadn't realized she was pacing until Elinor stopped her. "It will be all right. I'm sure he's simply been delayed. He'll be here soon. The traffic was terrible outside the conclave chamber, early on."

"I don't think so." Amanusa shook her head, clinging to Elinor's hands. "I don't think that's it. Something's upsetting him, something . . . I don't know what, but he's worried. Something's not right."

"How do you know?" Harry was curious, not dismissive.

"He is my familiar. There is a blood bond between us. I know." A horrible thought skittered into her head, and all her blood left it, dizzying her. She grabbed hold of Grey for support. "What if—since they failed in their direct attack on me, what if they've decided to get at me through Jax?"

Harry swore, long, colorfully, and almost indecipherably as his accent thickened to pure Cockney.

Amanusa led them back inside and found a lobby chair. Where could he have gone? She sat, closed her eyes and *reached* for her magic inside Jax, invoking the full spell to ride his blood. The distance made it difficult. He wasn't anywhere near the hotel in St. Germaine. The double layer to their bond—he wasn't walling her out, but she could only slip through cracks around his edges. He was asleep, she realized. Or unconscious, rather. She could smell herbs and magic, but couldn't identify which ones.

He was dreaming. Frightening dreams where an armored Jax fought with sword and flail against an army of bowler-hatted bureaucrats, who rose and fought again with missing limbs. He fought to reach Amanusa, to rescue her from the swarming hordes.

Amanusa inserted herself in his dream, at his side with her own bloody sword. *Together,* she thought at him. *Always together. Never alone again.*

"He's waking up," a strange male voice said.

"It's magic. The witch is getting through to him." Someone else spoke. *"Send him deeper."*

The scent of herbs rose, became almost overpowering, and Jax's dream began to crumble around her. *Never alone,* she cried before it was gone and she was inside her own head. But Jax's presence rested near her heart. She wasn't alone, nor was he.

"Well?" Harry demanded.

"He's unconscious." Unable to remain still any longer, Amanusa popped out of her chair. "They're using some kind of wizard magic to render him unconscious, but he's not hurt. We have to find him."

"I agree, but 'ow?" Harry caught and stopped her before she started pacing again.

"Call Vaillon." Amanusa's mind spun, grasping and discarding plans and possibilities. "He likes me. He'll help."

"The conclave will help as well," Grey said. "Some of them, anyway. Gathmann will. It's illegal to interfere between a magician and his—or her—familiar. Whatever form that familiar might take."

"Does that blood bond o' yours tell us where we might begin this hunt?" Harry asked.

"Not in St. Germaine. He's farther away." Amanusa bit her lip, nerves and worry getting the best of her. "I might be able to tell which direction to search if I try a few directions, see if any feels more right."

"Do it. I'll send word to Vaillon an' Gathmann—"

Grey interrupted Harry. "Let me or your apprentice write the messages. Your handwriting is so execrable, they might think you were confessing to some crime."

"All right. Elinor, you write. I'll organize messengers. Amanusa, you see if you can pick a direction. Grey, go wif 'er. Best she not be alone, I think."

Grey raised an eyebrow. "You trust me to accompany her?"

Harry raised one back. "You try anything out o' line with that one an' you'll be wearin' your balls as watch fobs."

"Likely." Grey gave a delicate, ostentatious shudder, then held his elbow out to Amanusa. "Shall we, madame?"

She barely took time to lay her hand on his arm before starting for the door. She needed to find Jax. *Now.*

28

OUTSIDE ON THE street, Amanusa called up her sense of *Jax*. Was it stronger than before, or weaker? The hotel faced east on a bustling street with spindly saplings in the boxes along the paving. Amanusa walked straight ahead, toward the street, without sensing any real change. She turned left, north, away from Grey, and walked a few paces. The sense of Jax grew stronger. Maybe. She wasn't sure.

Amanusa turned on her heel and walked south, back toward Grey, and her Jax-sense faded. "North," she said, spinning to face that direction. "Maybe as far as the other side of the river."

She started walking. This time Grey caught her arm and stopped her. She barely refrained from striking out.

Grey didn't flinch. "Wait until Vaillon and Gathmann come, or send envoys. We'll call out the progressives to search as well. We'll find him for you."

He dragged her back inside the hotel just as messengers hurried out the door. Elinor made her go into the café and eat the breakfast they'd missed with all the early morning excitement. Amanusa ate to fuel the magic, the buttery croissants tasting exactly like the awful food in the outlaw camp due to the same kind of fear.

Fear for someone else, not herself. Someone who meant as much to her as her mother and her brother had meant to the child she'd been. She did love him.

Vaillon arrived in person. Gathmann sent the captain of the Massilean Guard. Grey and Harry explained the situation and the officers agreed to send their men out in pairs, one policeman and one Massilean together, beginning with the area north of the hotel. The Massilean would use his magic to search and the policeman would lend authority.

Amanusa refused to stay in the hotel and wait, so Vaillon and Harry accompanied her. Elinor did as well, to return to the hotel with Amanusa in case she collapsed.

She wouldn't collapse. They didn't know her. She had already survived the worst the world could throw at her. She would survive this, and she would find Jax.

Clinging to her sense of him, she led the searchers to the Pont Royal crossing the river from Faubourg St. Germaine to the Tuileries Palace. The squared-off dome centered on the vast palace of Louis Napoleon Bonaparte—Emperor Napoleon III—shone copper-green in the afternoon sun, sneering at her. Halfway across the bridge, she stumbled. Something was wrong.

Pain ripped through her from the center out, and she fell, screaming. It didn't last long, no more than a few seconds. It felt as if someone had tried to rip out her heart. Harry was there, helping when she fought to stand, the pain ebbing quickly. Save for her throat. She'd screamed it raw.

"What happened?" Elinor asked.

Amanusa shook her head, shook Harry off. "Pain. Not mine. It wasn't an attack on me. They attacked Jax. They hurt him, and I felt it."

"I didn't know you could do that," Harry said.

"You should go back." Elinor took her hand, tried to lead her back toward the hotel.

Amanusa planted her feet. "They're hurting him. I have to find him."

"But . . . M. Vaillon, surely you agree this is no place for a woman." Elinor appealed to the police captain.

"I might agree perhaps, if she were any other woman. But I have seen how strong she is. If she wishes to come, I will not stop her."

Amanusa continued across the bridge to the Quai de Tuileries. Crows gathered in the trees and along the wharf, along the roof of the Tuileries to either side of the dome. Was their Crow among them? Did he gather reinforcements? Could he do anything here?

If Crow could help, he should hurry up and do it. If not, he didn't matter. Only finding Jax did.

JAX GROANED AS he woke again, this time in a dingy, windowless garret room. Hadn't he been in a comfortable parlor the last time he woke? Or had that been some sort of drug-and-magic-induced dream? He shut his eyes again as he probed inside himself for Amanusa. Yes. There. She was still with him. The blood bond was safe. She was safe.

"You might as well open your eyes, friend," an unfamiliar voice said in an unfamiliar accent. "I know you are awake."

Jax did as the voice suggested and saw a well-dressed man with black hair brilliantined flat to his skull and an enormous waxed and curled mustache. He sat in a wooden chair across from the narrow iron-framed bed where Jax lay. A battered three-drawer chest was the only other furnishing. An oil lamp on the chest provided light. Jax turned over to face the man, feeling at a disadvantage in his shirt-sleeves. Where was his jacket?

"Over the years," Jax said, "I've found it best to spend a few moments taking stock of a situation when one wakes up in an unfamiliar place, particularly after one has been kidnapped and bespelled."

"Just so, the caged bird wishes to return to its cage. You may think you have been kidnapped, my friend, but in the end, you will be free."

"I am not your friend." Jax sat up, holding the other man's gaze. "Nor are you mine."

The other man shrugged. "I do not doubt you believe this. But when we are done, you will thank us. I am Yuri Mikoyan, and you are Jax Greyson."

Jax didn't bother answering. Silence often brought information. Besides, his head was pounding from whatever they'd done to him. He didn't feel much like talking. He leaned his head against the wall behind him and waited.

"You will be asking yourself, 'What do they want with me? What are they going to do?' " Mikoyan went on when Jax was so disobliging as to fail to ask the questions. "We—myself and other like-minded magicians—will be freeing you from your slavery to the witch."

"I am not her slave. I am her husband." He had been Yvaine's slave, but Amanusa wasn't Yvaine. Amanusa had tasted his blood. She had given him the ability to choose. A man who could choose was no slave.

Mikoyan shook his head sadly. "You see how she has twisted your mind? Until you believe that captivity is freedom. It is against nature for a man to be subordinate to a woman."

"I am not subordinate. We are partners. Equals."

"She claims you as her familiar!" Mikoyan slammed his hand on the top of the chest beside him, making the lamp rattle, the flame shudder. "A familiar is a thing, a tool. It is always subordinate."

"How would you know? You're an alchemist. Alchemists don't have familiars. A wizard can only have an animal familiar, which does not have a human mind and is, of course, subordinate. Conjurer's familiars are spirits. I have heard conjurers speak of their familiars as if they were more powerful than the magician, not less. If a magician is afraid of his familiar—if he must force it to do his will—then he will of course enslave it and make it subordinate. My sorceress does not fear me. I choose to assist in my wife's magic. There is no coercion. We are equals."

Mikoyan's sad head-shaking returned, and it infuriated Jax. Why wouldn't the man listen?

"Your mind is so filled with lies," the alchemist

said, "you cannot know the truth. We had hoped you would be willing to tell us how to break the spell binding you to the witch. Our first attempt caused you considerable pain. But I see you are too blind to her evil to help yourself."

"Amanusa is not evil." Jax rose from his cot as Mikoyan stood to depart. If he charged the Russian, perhaps he could knock him down, get out the door, and at least know how many he faced. He might even get away, if the plot had only a few coconspirators.

Mikoyan paused at the door to shake his head again. "Poor, blind fool."

The door opened, Jax lunged. With a flick of his fingers and a single word, Mikoyan used the air to knock Jax flat.

"You will see," Mikoyan said as the guard at the door let him out. "When you are free, you will thank me."

The air sat on Jax's chest while the door was re-locked and footsteps thumped down the stairs. The spell released, perhaps when Mikoyan was too far away to maintain it, or perhaps when the man decided to let it go. Jax didn't know.

He sat back on the bed and held his pounding head in his hands. They hadn't been able to harm the spell binding him to Amanusa, but it had hurt like bloody, stinking hell when they tried. More pain was inevitable.

He and Amanusa were bound together by blood. As long as her blood flowed through his veins—and his through hers—the bond could not be broken. And the only way to get Amanusa's blood out of his bloodstream was for her to call it out. Their blood was so thoroughly mixed together, even after so little time, these men would have to bleed him dry to rid him of hers.

His stomach hurt, like everything else, but it took time to realize some of the pangs were hunger. He'd missed breakfast, and hadn't eaten much supper last night. He'd been too focused on making sure Amanusa ate to replenish what the magic had taken from her. Who would do that now he'd been kidnapped?

Jax went to the door and rapped. "I'm hungry. Do you intend to starve me too?" He asked it again in French.

"Best if your stomach is empty." The answering voice sounded young, sympathetic, and spoke English. An apprentice? Or journeyman, maybe.

"Can I at least have some water? My head's pounding and my mouth's gone to dust with the damned magic you've thrown at me."

"I'll ask." Footsteps clomped away again.

Jax tried the door. It didn't even rattle in the frame. Likely they'd added locks and bolts when they hatched their plot.

More footsteps returned than had left. Must mean he was getting the water. A young man, over twenty but not by much, opened the door and handed Jax a mug with perhaps an inch of water in the bottom. Another man stood behind him in the shadows.

"It's best if your stomach is empty," the guard said again when Jax stared incredulously at the scant swallow of water. "Given how you reacted to the first attempt."

"Did it occur to anyone that you might kill me, trying to break the familiar's bond?" Jax held the water in his mouth a moment before swallowing it. He handed the cup back when the young man gestured for it. "What's your name?"

"Esteban." The young man—a conjurer, according to Jax's borrowed magic sense—gave him a pitying look much like that of Mikoyan. "Wouldn't you rather be dead than a slave?"

"No, actually I wouldn't. Particularly since I'm—"

The door shut in the middle of Jax's protest, but he finished anyway. "—*not a slave!*"

Damn and blast. They wouldn't hear anything he had to say. The next hours promised to be very bad.

His stomach was growling again when the door opened to admit Mikoyan, Esteban, and two other magicians, one blond, one dark like Esteban. Another man stood in the corridor outside, in the shadows where his face could not clearly be seen.

"Will you come peaceably, or must we carry you out?" the Russian asked.

Jax weighed his options. Four, or presumably five against one were not the best odds, especially since they were every one of them magicians. The two new faces were as young as Esteban, so might not have reached Mikoyan's master level, but he had no way of knowing. Why start the pain before absolutely necessary?

He stood. "I'll come."

Then Esteban and the big blond man produced leather restraints.

No. Oh no. He'd been restrained before. He had never liked what happened after. Esteban reached for his wrist and Jax exploded into motion, shoving one man into the next, fighting toward the door. He couldn't do it, couldn't be bound helpless like that. Mikoyan's air spell tripped him, knocked him flat.

"No!" he shouted, lost in the panic. "No— Amanusa! *Amanusa!*"

He continued to struggle, despite the weight bearing down on his chest, his arms. He couldn't let them do it, had to fight, even though the fight was hopeless. His vision went black, the weight crushing the air from his lungs—and she was there. Amanusa, warm and wonderful in his mind.

Breathe, she whispered, her magic filling his veins, making breath possible. *What's wrong? Why are you—?*

The memories were already exploding through his mind, reaction to the leather cuffs that had triggered his panic. Metal shackles, ropes could be borne. They meant only pain. But leather—that meant worse. That meant Yvaine was giving him away to someone for sexual purposes, someone whose tastes he didn't share. It had been too long. He'd lost the way of it, of enduring. He couldn't do it.

She flowed through him, embraced him. *I'm with you. I won't leave you. Where are you?*

"Don't know," he gasped, and realized he'd spoken aloud. *Unconscious,* he thought. *When they brought me here. Didn't see.*

"What did he say?" someone asked.

"Get him downstairs." This voice spoke English, but with a different accent. Not Russian, not French— but familiar. It had the flavor of a translation stone. Who? "Before the witch can animate him."

Jax bellowed when buckles pulled leather tight around his wrists and ankles.

Peace. Amanusa held him tight. *I'm coming.*

They hauled him to his feet and propelled him out the door, the air spell still tangling his limbs, weighing them down.

Not alone, Jax thought at her. *They are too many— five of them, at least. They want to set me free. To break the binding spell.*

So that's what— Amanusa cut off her thought.

"What?" Jax demanded aloud.

"Did you have to make him so heavy?" the darker man complained.

"Would you rather fight him all the way, Paolo?" Mikoyan retorted. "Just move."

You felt it. Jax went still with horror when he understood. *You felt what they did to me.* He couldn't bear it, knowing his pain had reached her, that the bastards had hurt her too. He reached for his "no."

Jax, don't shut me out. Amanusa's own panic flared through him. *I need the connection. I need it to find you. I can bear the pain. I've borne it before. Worse.*

All the more reason you shouldn't have to bear this. He paused. "I love you, Amanusa."

He said it in his heart and his mind, and aloud. He wanted them all to know, even if none would believe him. Then he pushed her out and locked down the connection, Amanusa's anguished cry echoing in his head. The bond was still there, but she couldn't reach him through it. She was protected.

The kidnappers hauled Jax down three flights of stairs and into a parlor cleared of everything but a polished dining table moved into the center of the room, sofa and chairs pushed against the wall, apparently for resting in when they tired of their labors. Jax was lifted atop the table and placed on his back, thankfully with his clothing in place.

He was fastened down, arms stretched over his head, and when he was pinned helpless to the well-waxed walnut, Paolo began placing candles, while Esteban marked sigils on the table around Jax's body. Jax assumed the blond man—Oleg, they called him—was a wizard. He hadn't confirmed it before locking away the magic-sense Amanusa shared with him.

Jax tried once more to reason with them. "You say you're doing this to free me from slavery."

"We do not say," Mikoyan replied. "We do. We set you free."

"A slave is a slave because he has no choice. You are taking my choices away from me." He yanked on the wrist restraints, trying to pull his arms down, bring them in for protection. He knew he couldn't, but he couldn't stop himself from trying. He hated this.

"We are giving you your freedom," Mikoyan said.

God, they were stubborn. "Even if it kills me." Even if it killed *her*. Would it? Jax didn't know.

"If you are dead, you will be free." Mikoyan seemed to have appointed himself their spokesman.

"I will be dead! Just because that is your choice doesn't mean it is mine. Damn it, I don't want to die!" Not now, when he'd discovered so much to live for. Amanusa didn't love him, but she was fond of him. It could grow into love, if he had time.

"We will take every precaution to ensure that does not happen." Mikoyan stepped to the foot of the table where Jax could see him without having to crane his neck. "You have been so ensnared in the witch's spells you do not know your own mind. You do not know how to choose. We will break the spell, then you will be free to choose as you wish."

"And if I choose my wife? Will you break the bonds again? Or must I choose as you want me to in order for you to leave me in peace?"

Mikoyan exchanged a glance with the man in the shadows, at the opposite end of the long table, beyond Jax's outstretched hands, where Jax couldn't see him. Paolo began lighting the candles as Mikoyan went on.

"When the spell is broken, you will be free to choose as you wish. But when it is broken, you will see the evil for what it is. You will understand what has been done to you, and you will not wish to return to your chains. Instead, you will demand recompense for your servitude."

Jax wanted to tear his hair in frustration. Fortunately for his hair, he couldn't reach it. "Did it occur to you that I am three-hundred-seventy-something years old? If you break the spell, you may have nothing but a mouldering corpse on your dining table."

"Then you will have the satisfaction of having lived a long life." Mikoyan nodded at Oleg the wizard, who blew an herbal mixture into the flames of Paolo's candles.

Jax banged his head on the table. "Is that it? You're jealous that I've lived so long? God, if you only knew—"

The magicians ignored him as they began to chant a Latin formula. If someone had tried this when he was bound to Yvaine, would he be fighting it? In the early years, before he'd outlived his family, probably not. Even later, he likely would have welcomed the attempt to free him of Yvaine. But Amanusa had already done it. She'd set him free.

There was a tremendous difference in being tied to someone without understanding what you'd agreed to, and tying yourself because you loved them and couldn't bear living without them. With Amanusa, with the double blood-bond, he was free to be the man he always should have been.

Pain jolted through him and he let it out with a bellow of sound. He'd learned that a long time ago. Pain was stronger than he was and he proved nothing by keeping silent. Shouting helped. Maybe the pain didn't actually ride out of him on the shout, but it seemed as if it did. And the noise always seemed to gratify those causing the pain.

The agony intensified. He yelled louder, straining against the hated restraints. And he felt Amanusa probing at the edges of his mind. Grimly, he shut her out.

"Get the gag," Mikoyan said as the pain faded for a moment. "If he keeps screaming like this, he will disturb the neighbors and we do not want a visit from authorities, or anyone."

Esteban's face hove into view, his eyes filled with pity. As he pushed the rolled leather gag between Jax's teeth, Jax pleaded silently for help. Esteban flushed and looked away, focusing on getting the gag snugly buckled. "Where did you find these things?" he asked. "The restraints and all?"

"At a mental asylum," Mikoyan said. "They are used to restrain the inmates in a manic state, to prevent them injuring themselves. They will do the same for Mr. Greyson."

Jax pulled deep inside himself, using defenses he'd long ago learned, removing himself from his body. The pain would still hurt, but it would flow through his body and out his mouth in a scream. The gag muffled screams. It didn't stop him from screaming.

He found his blood bond with Amanusa, there at his core, and curled himself around it; making sure her awareness was safely barred from entry, all his permissions retracted. He would endure. Or he would die. But Amanusa would be safe.

The pain lashed through him, inside to out. Endlessly.

AMANUSA SEARCHED FOR Jax the rest of the day, keeping to herself that she'd lost her sense of him, that he'd cut her off. The bond was still there. That couldn't be severed. He was still hers, she was his. But she couldn't find him.

She watched the crows, hunting for some sign of *their* Crow. But they all looked alike, all acted the same. It seemed that more of them gathered as the search progressed through the city toward the hill of Montmartre, but she couldn't be sure, and she had to be. Jax's life depended on it. No one could bear that much pain and live. The heart would simply give out. Give up.

And she couldn't help him. Couldn't send magic to sustain and soothe him. Jax had cut her off.

I love you, Amanusa. He said that, and then he had shoved her out and barred her way back in.

If he loved her, how could he do that to her? How could he push her away and leave her frantic with worry? He was the one who'd called out to her to begin with. He'd called. He'd *reached.* And she came. She would always come, just as he would always answer her need. Except now, when he thought he was protecting her, the idiot man.

"Amanusa. *Amanusa.*" Elinor had hold of her arm. "That's it. I'm taking you home, back to the hotel."

"No, I have to find Jax." She pulled out of Elinor's grasp, and stumbled into Vaillon.

"I must agree, madame. You should rest." Vaillon handed her back to Elinor, and Harry.

"I can't. I have to find him." Didn't they understand? But how could they? They weren't the ones bound heart-deep.

"Amanusa." Elinor took her arm in a firmer grip and walked her toward the hired carriage waiting at the corner. "You are so tired you can scarcely keep walking. You're so tired, you can't use your magic to locate him. You've hesitated at every turn for the last hour. It's dark. You've been awake since dawn when you fought off a terrible magic assault and—"

Elinor blushed. "And I doubt you got much sleep last night. You've been running yourself into the ground all day, literally, and with all the magic you've used. You cannot find Jax until you get some rest."

"Grey's arrived," Harry said. "An' the rest o' the conjurers, now their spirits are awake. Most of 'em, anyway. They'll keep searching. Spirits are good at findin' things that are lost. Especially people."

"Captain Vaillon . . ." Amanusa appealed to the policeman again. He'd been supporting her need to search.

This time, he failed her. "Your friends are correct. You can do nothing more if you do not rest. Return to your hotel. Try to sleep. The conjurers will search during the spirit hours. In the morning, if your man has not been found, we will begin again with fresh energy."

Amanusa tried to break free as Harry led her to the carriage. He simply swept her into his arms and dumped her inside.

Elinor gave him a look as she climbed in after. "You'd better come along," she said. "In case she gives us trouble at the hotel. You've been at it all day, like the rest of us. A rest wouldn't hurt you either."

Harry sighed. "Right. You're right." He climbed in too.

Amanusa fell asleep in the carriage. She woke enough to walk into the hotel and climb the stairs to her suite with Harry and Elinor guiding. She didn't remember anything after that.

She dreamed voices.

29

"IT'S NOT WORKING," someone said. "Why isn't it working?"

"I don't know." This voice sounded unutterably weary. "It's sorcery. Blood magic. We know nothing about how it works."

"We'll have to convince him to share what he knows."

"He may not know anything. Why would the witch tell him how to break the spell binding him to her as familiar? Everything we have tried has done nothing but cause him pain. We want to free him from his slavery, not torture him. If we keep this up, we will kill him."

"Then he will be a free man."

Alarm skittered through Amanusa. Was she dreaming truth? Or was this merely her fear?

The weary man sighed. "That is your choice, friend. Not his. He does not want to die."

"He doesn't know what he wants. His will has been corrupted."

"Even so, a man should know if he is willing to die or not."

"He cannot possibly know!" This man was shouting now, angry. Amanusa thought she ought to recognize his voice, but she didn't, quite. "One way or another, we will break the spell. John Greyson will be free of the witch. Or he will be dead."

Amanusa stifled her reflexive cry. She didn't want them to know she listened, even if this was only a dream. What if it wasn't?

"Perhaps we could find the witch, persuade her to break the spell . . ." the weary man suggested.

"You heard what Sergei reported, that police were everywhere, especially with the woman. She's never alone. We must keep trying. In the morning, after we've rested."

Another sigh. "I can't help feeling . . . if he dies with the spell still intact, she wins."

"No, we win. If we break the spell, we win. If he dies, we win, because we will have deprived her of her familiar, and that will weaken her."

Dear God, if this was real, they weren't doing this to "rescue" Jax. They didn't care about Jax at all. She *reached* out to him and the magic locked in, flowing between them almost as if they touched skin-to-skin. She soothed his hurts, eased the strain on his tortured heart, whispered her love to his locked-away thoughts.

A sharp rapping on the window brought Amanusa bolting upright in her bed, wide awake. Had it been real? Had she been able to reach Jax in dreams when he'd blockaded her out during wakefulness?

The attack on the window glass came again, this time accompanied by a harsh caw. Amanusa stumbled out of bed to raise the window and let Crow in. No wonder her dreams were so twisted up. With the window closed, it was stiflingly hot in the room.

No. Her dreams were tangled because Jax was missing. And if what she dreamed was true, he was in danger. She couldn't waste any more time.

Crow cocked his head and looked at her, seeming to say, *I can't leave you alone without you messing up, can I?*

"I know, I know. Have you found him?" Amanusa

hunted through the wardrobe for one of her simpler dresses, one she could put on herself, that didn't need too many petticoats. Crow stalked elegantly along the dressing table without answering.

"Then why have you come, if you don't know where he is?"

Crow hopped back onto the windowsill and looked at her with his beady little crow eyes.

"You do know?" Amanusa left off the last layer of petticoats and yanked her dress on. White. She might have to work magic and didn't need to lose track of any blood. When her head emerged again from the depths of the fabric, she spoke. "And you can lead me to him?"

Crow adjusted his wings as if settling to wait for her. Amanusa had to slow herself down as she buttoned up the front of the dress. She didn't want to button it crooked, didn't want to be rushing through the streets of Paris looking like a madwoman. Someone might stop her.

She made herself take the time to button up the blasted shoes and at least run a brush through her hair and tie it back with a ribbon. Dawn was lightening the sky behind Crow. Time was critical. She had to find Jax.

If it took setting Jax free of the blood bond to keep the kidnappers from killing him, then that's what she would do. That meant she had to allow the kidnappers to take her, and that meant she couldn't take any of her defenders along. But they could follow.

Amanusa scrawled a quick note, telling Elinor what she was doing. Then she offered her hand to

Crow, who cocked a beady eye at her and climbed daintily aboard to be lifted to her shoulder.

She didn't want to be separated from Crow for one second, for fear she wouldn't be able to distinguish him from all the other crows of Paris. In the hotel lobby, the few patrons and employees awake at this hour looked at her strangely when she crossed it with a crow on her shoulder. She didn't care. She was a sorceress. Sorceresses were supposed to be odd.

Outside, Crow took to the air and she cried out, afraid he'd fly off and leave her. But he only flew to a window box above a storefront at the street corner, where he perched and waited for her to catch up. Flight by short flight, Crow led her across Paris, returning to caw at her when she did not follow fast enough. Past the Palais Royale and the library to the Rue Montmartre and into the steep streets of the Faubourg itself.

Many of these streets had not yet been made over into Louis Napoleon's broad avenues, but they were not the narrow, crooked streets of the medieval city either. Crow led her to a tidy square of tree-shaded grass surrounded by neat houses, and perched on the pediment over a black-painted door. This time, as Amanusa neared, he didn't flutter away to another balcony railing or lamppost. He crouched where he was, watching her approach with one glittering eye, then the other.

"Is this it?" she asked. "Is this where the kidnappers have taken him?"

Crow opened his beak and let out a single raucous caw.

Amanusa lifted the brass knocker on the ominously

colored door and banged until someone came to open it. A young man answered, big, beefy, and blond, dressed in trousers and unbuttoned undershirt, with his braces dangling around his hips and a snarl on his round, ruddy face. As the moments ticked by, the snarl transformed into a goggling stare.

"Good morning," she said. "I am Mrs. John Greyson. I'm looking for my husband. Is he here?"

The wizard, for such he was, took one barefooted step out the door to scan the square suspiciously.

"I am quite alone. Is Jax here?" Amanusa hid her fears. She had plenty of practice at it.

With an oath her translation stone forbore to translate, the young wizard grabbed her by the arm and dragged her over the threshold, slamming the door behind her.

"Who is it, Oleg?" a man called from upstairs, footsteps drawing closer. "Who could be calling at this ungodly hour?"

"It is her, Mikoyan! The witch." Oleg gave her a little shake.

"What?" The man—alchemist—Mikoyan came flying down the stairs two and three at a time, dashing into the front parlor to peer out the windows as he pulled his braces up over his singlet.

"I came alone," Amanusa volunteered.

Oleg slapped her so hard her head bounced off the wall behind her and she tasted blood. Her lip split inside and out, on her teeth and the ring the wizard wore. "Do not speak," he growled. "A woman does not speak in the company of men."

Innocent blood already. Perhaps this would be easier than she thought.

"What are you doing?" Mikoyan, a mature man with dark hair falling in his face and an overlarge mustache, strode from the window in two steps to take custody of Amanusa from the younger man. "Are you mad? She is a sorceress. Her magic is based on innocent blood."

"Her blood is not innocent," another man said from the shadows beside the stairwell. "It is black with evil, tainted with the lives of those she has murdered."

Two more young men had appeared upstairs, peering over the railing, one of them still buttoning up his trousers. Five magicians, as Jax had said. She wished she could reach Jax, know more than simply that the bond between them still held.

"I would feel better if no blood at all is spilled," Mikoyan retorted. He gripped both her arms, his fingers digging in painfully. "What are you doing here? What is your game?"

"No game. I came to find my husband." Amanusa kept calm on the surface. There was already too much emotion clanging about for her to pour hers into the mix. "Is he here?"

"As if you do not already know." Mikoyan dragged her to the stairway. "Do you wish to inspect your property? See whether we have damaged him?"

"He is my husband, not my property." It was difficult to speak while the alchemist hauled her roughly up the stairs, but she managed. "Nor am I his property, but his wife."

"Lies," the voice from below hissed up at them.

She tried again, but feared it was useless. "Men and women were never made to be enemies, one subject to the other." She was having trouble catching her breath as they mounted the third staircase to the attics on the fourth level. Her shins and arms were bruised from all the stairs and walls and banisters they'd been banged into and from Mikoyan's grip.

At the top of the house, in a hallway with a ceiling so low the alchemist had to stoop and Amanusa almost did, they stopped in front of a door closed with an iron bolt and a padlock. One of the dark young men pulled a key from the watch pocket in his trousers, and opened the lock. Mikoyan shoved her through the door so hard she fell to her knees.

It didn't matter. Jax was there, asleep—or unconscious?—on the narrow bed.

"Where a woman should be," Oleg crowed. "On her knees before men."

Amanusa gathered her skirts, got them out from under her knees so she could crawl forward and reach Jax.

"Shut up, Oleg," one of the other young ones said. "You're a crude bastard."

"Jax?" Amanusa hovered her hands over his dear, beautiful face, afraid to touch him, though his face was still beautiful, still unbruised.

"I'm the one whose parents were married," Oleg retorted. "You want me to shut up, Esteban, you make me."

"Both of you shut up," Mikoyan snarled.

She had to know how badly hurt he was, even if it might hurt him when she touched him. "I'm sorry," she whispered. Sorry for hurting him with her touch. Sorry for losing him. Sorry for not loving him sooner.

She laid one hand feather soft on his cheek and slipped the other through the unbuttoned neck of his shirt to rest on his naked chest over his heart. Only then could she touch the magic inside him, slide in to spread through his bloodstream and see what they had done to him.

The contrast in his condition with her previous visits inside him was dramatic. His blood vessels leaked, blood beginning to pool in places it shouldn't—his abdomen, around his heart, in his brain. Crushing her dismay, Amanusa went to work, shooing the blood back where it belonged, sealing up the leaks and reinforcing the walls of his bloodstream with magic. Jax coughed, spraying his shirt and Amanusa's dress with blood—the blood she hadn't been able to put back.

"What are you doing to him?" Mikoyan threw her across the tiny room to slam into the corner of a chest she hadn't noticed.

"Repairing the damage you caused." Amanusa wiped her face with her sleeve. The white poplin was already bloody. A few more smears wouldn't hurt.

"Oleg." Mikoyan jerked his head toward Jax, who had coughed again and now lay collapsed on his side.

The wizard gave a quick nod and crossed the room to touch two fingers to Jax's neck. He used Jax's cleanish shirttail to wipe the blood from his bare chest and pressed his ear there to listen. "He is breathing better," Oleg said, sounding surprised.

"Of course," the whispery voice came spilling from the shadows. "He is her slave. She needs him healthy to serve her."

"He is my husband." Amanusa stayed on the floor,

on her knees, watching the magicians as she crept back to Jax. "I need him healthy because I love him." She couldn't stop the tears in her voice, hard as she tried. "He can't die before I tell him."

"How very touching, very romantic," the man in the hallways hissed. "How very false. You do not know the meaning of love."

"I didn't until he taught me."

"You love me?" The croak of his voice brought all heads snapping round to stare at Jax.

Amanusa's knees burned as she hurried across the last bit of space to her husband. She laid her hand along his face, now she knew it wouldn't hurt him. "I wasn't sure. Someone explained it to me. Love is caring more about the other person's welfare than your own. It's wanting to be with him and . . . and make love to him, and feeling as if your own heart will stop beating when you lose him."

He covered her hand with his and brought it to his lips. "You love me?" he whispered, his mouth brushing her fingers.

Amanusa shivered with sudden emotion as she nodded. "Oh, how I love you."

She leaned forward and touched her lips to his, stained with his blood, trying to convey all she felt with the kiss.

"This mawkishness will turn my stomach," the hidden man said, shattering the moment. "Particularly since it is nothing but a show and a sham, performed for our benefit."

"I love you too," Jax whispered when Amanusa ended the kiss.

"I know, darling." She trailed her fingers along his

cheek, savoring this last touch with her magic inside him.

She stood and faced the watching magicians. "I don't want you to kill him with your attempts to break our familiar's bond. I always intended to set him free, but that information was not included with the knowledge Yvaine of Braedun packed into his brain before her death. We planned to travel to her workshop to consult the volumes there and find a safe way to do it. I don't suppose you will allow us to continue with this plan."

"We do not trust you," Mikoyan said, before the man in the hallway could.

"Amanusa, no." Jax tugged at her skirts—her hands were out of his reach. "I don't want it broken."

She smiled at him. "I know that too, my darling. But even if the binding spell is broken, our love cannot break if it is truly love, and I believe it is. Love binds what magic cannot."

"I may retch," the shadow man growled.

She looked up at Mikoyan, resisting the urge to take Jax's hand. If she touched him, she would not be able to break what had to be broken. "You understand that I am new to the practice of sorcery. I do not know exactly how to do this. I believe I can do it without harming him further, but I am not certain.

"I will tell you, however, that none of your efforts, nothing you could try would break this binding between us, short of death."

"That is still possible," the alchemist said. "Your death, rather than his, since you have so foolishly placed yourself in our possession."

She inclined her head. "That is acceptable to me."

"No." Jax struggled to sit up, pulling on her skirts to assist him. He climbed up her body to stand, wrapping his arms around her. "No, Amanusa. It is not acceptable to me. I won't lose you."

She leaned her cheek against his. "Nor do I wish to lose you, Jax, darling, but it's not up to us, is it? They are the ones making the decisions here."

Amanusa drew back to gaze into the clear, bright, deep green-blue of his eyes, her hands cupping his face. Desire rose inside her to swirl with the love. He was injured, barely able to stand, but she could feel his arousal firming against her hip. He wanted her too, in this moment when death tried to catch their eyes and stare them down.

She forgot about their captors, forgot about magic, about anything but her love and desire, her need for this man in her arms. She kissed him. Her mouth opened under his as he kissed her back, hauling her tight against the hard ridge of his flesh. She kissed him as if she could drink him down, as if she needed him in order to breathe, to move, to live. Perhaps she did.

"Enough." Mikoyan grabbed her arm and jerked her away from Jax, who collapsed onto the cot.

Amanusa scooped up all the magic she could find and stuffed it inside her head.

"Bring him." The Russian gestured for the younger men. "This room is too crowded. We'll do this downstairs in the parlor."

Open to me. Amanusa hoped she could still speak in Jax's mind as she had yesterday. *As long as you are able, please open. I need the magic you just stored.*

Yes. And that quickly he was there, a warm presence inside her, more than just an anchor point. *Him.* Jax. Holding magic.

"Could we have tea?" Amanusa asked as she stumbled down the stairs in Mikoyan's wake, his hand tight around her arm, as the mystery man faded away ahead of them. "Perhaps some croissants or brioche? Something to break our night's fast? Or, if there is anything in the kitchen, I could cook something."

"Why should you lower yourself to a womanly task?" Mikoyan shook her as he spoke.

Amanusa sighed. "I did not realize reading a person's mind was a part of alchemical magic. If you already know everything about me, about what I think and how I truly feel, why don't you go ahead and break the bond yourself?"

Mikoyan growled and she remembered she didn't want to antagonize these men any worse. "My husband is in poor condition because of all you put him through. A little food will help him endure what lies ahead. And I haven't eaten since—"

She thought back. She'd eaten breakfast yesterday when Elinor insisted, but hadn't been able to choke down any of the food brought to her during the search. "It has been awhile. Food will help me properly perform the magic."

They reached the ground floor and she stumbled again from Mikoyan's jerking her about.

"Sorcery—blood magic—is more closely tied to the condition of one's body than other magics," Amanusa said. "If I am hungry, the magic is hungry."

She hadn't noticed so close a correlation, in truth, but she wanted Jax fed. It would help him.

"I'm starved," Jax said, sounding a bit more like his cheeky self. "This lot hasn't fed me since I got here."

"Then I'd say it was time." Amanusa scowled at Mikoyan. "Or did you intend to starve him, rather than magic him to death?"

The alchemist growled again, but he reached into his pocket for a handful of coins. "Paolo, go buy bread. And coffee with cream. Maybe some sausages. Go. And hurry back."

Paolo, the third young man, an alchemist like Mikoyan, took the coins and ran upstairs. Mikoyan shoved Amanusa roughly into a large chair while the others eased Jax down on the sofa pushed against the far wall. A few moments later, clad in jacket and a shirt he was still tucking in, Paolo dashed back downstairs and out the door.

"What instruments do you need to work this magic? To unbind him?" Mikoyan paced the room, stopping to peer out through the front window every time he passed it.

Amanusa reached into her pocket for the lancet, but it wasn't there. How could she have remembered the translation stone, but forgotten her lancet? "I will need a knife," she said. "Very sharp. The sharper the better."

"Will a razor do?" Esteban asked. The other magicians turned their horrified eyes from Amanusa to him, apparently appalled by the mere thought of bloodletting. Though the idea of killing one or both of them didn't seem to disturb.

"Do not trust her." The man still stood in the shadows of the hallway, keeping his face hidden. Because she might recognize him? Or because he wished to ensure she never would? "She is evil to the core."

"You know nothing about me," Amanusa said, "and a knife. With a razor, it is too easy to slip and cut too deep. And before you flap and moan about the evil, wicked sorceress getting her hands on a sharp object, Jax will use the knife on his own flesh. He knows how deep to cut. We will also need rags, to catch the blood, and a fire to burn them afterward."

She would call her blood from him, but would she be able to keep that part of him that flowed through her? She didn't want to give it up, but she would if it proved necessary to break the bond. Did it actually have to be broken? "How will you know the binding is gone?"

"We can tell," Mikoyan snarled.

"The binding is similar to that binding spirit or animal familiars," Esteban volunteered. "Any wizard or conjurer has spells to sense the familiars of others."

"Good." Amanusa nodded, satisfied. She settled back in her chair to watch Jax, who was watching her, silently pleading from across the room for her not to do this thing.

"Good, why?" Mikoyan stalked toward her, suspicion in every line of his body.

"Because you will know it is done and there will be an end to it. You won't keep trying and trying endlessly." Amanusa never took her eyes from Jax.

"Paolo is back." Oleg opened the door to admit the young alchemist. He carried café-au-lait in a thick stoneware carafe and brioche in a knotted napkin.

The sausages in their paper wrapping were stuffed in his pocket.

Esteban brought cups for the coffee and poured while Paolo passed around the food. Amanusa took only bread and coffee. *I will eat,* she whispered to Jax's thoughts, *if you will eat also.*

What if the breaking of the bond leaves me a three-hundred-seventy-year-old corpse? Jax took sausage and bread and coffee.

It won't. The condition of your body isn't tied to the magic. The magic has kept you young, but it has done it by sweeping the symptoms of age from your body. She'd looked, when she was inspecting what they had done to him. The breaking of their bond shouldn't in itself kill him, though he would begin to age normally again. The dead zones would still likely have their deadly affect on him, but outside the zones, he ought to be fine.

When we are free of them . . . His thoughts were fierce, insistent. *You must bind us again. I am your husband, and I will not be less than I am now.*

As you will it. It was easy to be the submissive wife when her wishes coincided with her husband's.

"Have you eaten enough?" Mikoyan's voice overflowed with sarcastic hospitality. "Are we finally ready?"

"I have a knife." Esteban came from the back of the house carrying a long, thin boning knife. "It was the sharpest in the kitchen. I sharpened it—"

"Take it to Jax." Amanusa waved him away as he brought it in her direction, perhaps for inspection. "He's the one who will use it." If she had to rid herself of his blood, she would use the cut on her already swollen lip. "You don't want me near the knife, nor do I wish to be."

Esteban and Mikoyan gave her an odd look. Oleg sneered. "She is afraid of it."

Amanusa ignored him, focusing all her attention on Jax. *As I pull my blood from you, I will withdraw all the magic and build shields around both of us. I'm afraid to leave any magic behind—magic bound you after Yvaine's death.*

Magic and Yvaine's blood.

Can I call her blood out as well?

I don't know. Jax took the knife from Esteban, Oleg and Paolo hovering, ready to grab him if he showed signs of aggression. Jax brushed his thumb across the edge. *It will cost you the knowledge that remains.*

He spoke aloud. "The blade will do."

There isn't much left. And we have her books, back in the tower. I'll try to call her blood.

Jax set the knife aside and looked up at her as he rolled up his left sleeve. The magicians hissed and recoiled as they saw the faint white lines of scars up his forearm.

"What?" the hidden man asked. "What is it?"

And when the shields are built, and I am no longer bound, then what? Jax held her gaze.

She felt his love and worry swell and flow toward her. *I don't know,* she replied honestly. The only way she could.

"His arm is scarred from elbow to wrist," Oleg croaked. "Scars of bloodletting."

I hadn't thought that far. Amanusa bit her lip, looking helplessly back at Jax. *All I could think about was getting you free, however I had to do it.*

Jax shook his head at her, a rueful smile on his lips. *So the rest of the plan is mine?*

Like when you carried me down the mountain. She smiled back at him. *I work the magic and mess things up. You get me out of it. We're a team.*

So we are.

30

"STOP GAWKING OVER old scars and free him so he suffers no more," Mikoyan snapped. "Are wards set and secure?"

"Yes, Master Mikoyan." Paolo dipped his head in a tiny bow.

Mikoyan and Paolo now moved close to Amanusa, leaving the others guarding Jax. "We will be monitoring the magic," the master alchemist said. "At the first sign you are turning it toward one of us, we will kill you."

Do not do anything foolish, Amanusa, Jax said. *If you live, I swear to live with you.*

Then I will have to be sure to survive this. She smiled at him as she sat up straight in the chair. "I am ready."

Jax took a deep breath. He picked up the knife, set it against the palm of his left hand, and caught Amanusa's gaze. "I love you," he said. "No matter what happens, I love you."

"I love you, too." She sent her love pouring into him and let his pour into her, marveling that there could be so much.

"This is my blood," he said. "Spilled by my will."
He took another breath, and as he let it out, he sliced
across his palm from one fleshy pad to the other.

At the same instant, Amanusa *reached* across the
room with her magic, her lips moving only slightly
as she repeated the words to call Yvaine's blood from
Jax's veins. Old blood first.

It welled up in a sullen line, thick and dark and reluctant to answer her call, oozing across his palm to
the little-finger side, where it dripped onto the pile of
napkins in Jax's lap. *Depart from my husband Jax,
you old besom,* Amanusa thought at the last remnants
of Yvaine. *We don't want you here. You are not our
blood.*

Finally, the dark, almost black droplets stopped
seeping from the cut in Jax's hand, and Amanusa
sagged in her chair. "Blot that, please, love." Her
voice was raspy with the strain.

"You're not done," the shadowed man hissed. "He
is not yet free."

"Old bonds have to be broken first," Jax said, wiping away the last of Yvaine's blood with the topmost
napkin. He tossed it over his shoulder, Oleg jumping
to get away without it touching him. "Get her a glass
of water."

Oleg sneered. He was so predictable. "She is only
a—"

"Get my wife some water, *now.*" The authority in
Jax's voice made Amanusa shiver. Not in fear, in . . .
pleasure? Desire? She didn't like it when other men
gave orders, demanded obedience. But when Jax did
it, it gave her a little thrill. Because he did it on her
behalf?

Esteban returned from somewhere with a glass of water, and Amanusa sipped, grateful. She smiled her thanks at him as he returned to guarding Jax. She set the glass on the floor beside her chair, since there were no side tables. Time to finish this.

Blood of my blood. She spoke the words to herself, to Jax, through the bonds that tied them together. *Return to me.* She caught up the magic with the blood, pulling it out of him and piling it around him in the thickest shield she could make.

Bright red blood, new blood, poured from the shallow slice across his palm, and dripped to the napkins below, staining them scarlet. Had he taken so much? She didn't know what she was doing. What if she bled him dry? What if she couldn't break the blood bond at all?

"Love you," Jax murmured. "Live." Was he so weak already?

She wouldn't live without him. She might survive— though that was in doubt—but she wouldn't actually live. They both had to get through this intact. Perhaps she couldn't pull only her own blood from Jax because she was holding on to his blood.

With a whimper, she hunted inside herself for those flavors of *Jax* and drove them out. Blood began to trickle down her chin from her split lip, out her nose.

Jax cried out, started up from the sofa, but Oleg shoved him back down. Esteban looked from Jax to Amanusa, then gently pulled a napkin from the bottom edge of Jax's pile, one not too stained, and tossed it to Paolo. "For the blood." Esteban gestured at his own nose and mouth, then at Amanusa.

Paolo dropped the napkin in Amanusa's lap, and she used it to blot away Jax's blood, feeling as if she wanted to weep. She hadn't taken much from him, but it had been enough. Now that she cast it away, the bleeding from the cut across his hand slowed.

Now what? She still felt a faint, ghostly bond between them. There was evidently something more that had to be done, though they no longer shared blood. A sob escaped her.

"I love you, Amanusa," Jax said. "That hasn't changed. I am still your husband. They cannot force us to divorce."

The faint bond throbbed, grew brighter with magic. *No.* That wasn't what had to happen. All ties had to be broken. There could be nothing between them in order for him to be safe.

Amanusa stood. "I cast you aside," she said, making her voice hard and cold, so it wouldn't choke halfway out. "John Greyson, I renounce you. You are no longer my servant. You are not my familiar. You are nothing to me. I do not have any part of you and you have no part of me. You are no longer blood of my blood. Your heart is not mine and mine does not beat with yours. All bonds between us are severed."

She reached out with her hands to grasp the faint ribbon of glorious magic shimmering between them, and she ripped it in two.

With a cry of anguish she collapsed onto the chair, Jax's shout echoing with hers. The pain of loss and loneliness ground through her. God, it hurt. How could it hurt so much? Not physically, though it seeped into the physical, making her chest ache along with her weeping heart, with the emotions that had been torn apart.

"*Amanusa*—" Jax's desperate groan made the anguish cut deeper. She could see the magic reaching toward her, groping, begging her to grab hold.

"I won't." She stuffed all the pain down deep inside, where she'd kept so much before, hiding it away where he couldn't see it, wouldn't suspect the truth. "I don't love you. The conjurer was right. I lied."

Jax recoiled as the hidden man cackled in delight. "You see?" he crowed. "The truth comes out. Now that she has no familiar, now that she cannot use him, she casts him aside."

She made herself sit up, stiffened her muscles, using the cold and the pain to lock them in place. If she was frozen, maybe it wouldn't hurt so much.

"Is it done then?" Mikoyan the alchemist asked. "Is the familiar bond broken?"

"It is." Esteban nodded, along with Oleg.

"Now, what will you do with us?" Amanusa didn't truly care. Jax was lost to her. Their blood bond was broken and she didn't know how to remake it. They might be married, but it wasn't the same. It couldn't be. How long before that fell apart too?

"Let them go," Esteban said. "That was the plan. We would set him free of her and let them go."

"What is to keep her from binding him to her again?" Oleg demanded.

"It was the plan to set them free," Mikoyan said. "That is what we all agreed to."

"But—" Oleg began.

"How can we set her free to work her foul magic on other unsuspecting innocents?" The hidden man came to the opening into the parlor. "We must kill her to keep her from undoing the good we have done."

"No," Esteban protested. "I did not sign on for murder. We would free him. That was all I agreed to."

"I can look after myself," Jax growled. He stood, ignoring the magicians behind him. "I am no longer her familiar. My mind and my will are my own. Do you doubt my ability to prevent what was done to me from happening again?"

Mikoyan looked sharply at him, then grinned and came to clasp Jax's wrist—the right one, not the one that had been bled. "Glad to have you back with us."

Jax gave him a brusque, cold nod. He looked down with distaste at his blood-spattered shirt and dragged it off, wiping his bare chest clean. "Do you have something I can wear, to get out of this filth?"

Footsteps sounded in the hall, and Inquisitor Kazaryk came into the room to hand Jax a fresh shirt. *Of course.* The man had dogged their steps too long to surrender without a whimper. Or a final attack. He was greedy for the power he thought sorcery could give him, and for the pleasure of the pain he thought sorcery caused.

Kazaryk smirked at Amanusa. "The empire has powerful friends within the conclave. They could not keep me." Then he turned to Jax.

"Perhaps you will be safe, my friend," Kazaryk said. "But too many others are not. She will still be free to work her evil." He watched Jax a moment. "My apologies for Nagy Szeben. I did not understand the situation at that time."

Jax slammed his fist into Kazaryk's jaw, sending

the smaller man to the floor. "Apology accepted." He shrugged into the shirt, covering up those lovely shoulders. "Sorcery is just magic," he said. "No more evil than conjury or alchemy."

"Agreed. As long as men are working it. Women are weak, easily corrupted by the power. A woman working magic is an abomination."

The man was mad. But then it had been apparent from their first meeting that the man had a twisted view of women. Amanusa couldn't bring herself to care too much. Jax was free. They would let him live. She had worked the magic and anything else was up to Jax. If he still wanted her.

"We must destroy her. John Greyson can be the new sorcerer." Kazaryk's head snapped around and he glared at Esteban. "Where do you think you're going?"

Esteban held up Jax's stained shirt, bundled with the bloody napkins. He'd even retrieved the one Amanusa had used. "To the kitchen. There is a fire there for burning these. Even I know it is not safe to leave so much blood about with a sorceress in her power."

"Don't be long," Kazaryk said.

"I will be as long as it takes. Linen does not burn easily and I do not wish to smother the fire." Esteban paused at the doorway to the dining room. "And if you are going to murder someone, I do not care to watch."

"Coward," Oleg sneered after him.

"Is it bravery to slay the helpless? Esteban is right," Mikoyan said as the young conjurer departed. "We did not agree to murder."

"Give her to me," Jax said. "You promised me payment for the years I served."

"What will you do with her?" Kazaryk asked, suspicious and eager both at once.

"Perhaps I will make her my familiar. What does it matter to you?"

Jax was head-blind. He couldn't touch magic. Could he? Whatever he wanted to do would be fine. If she was his familiar, she would still be with him.

"As long as she is under control—" Mikoyan began.

"Are you a sorcerer?" Kazaryk moved closer to Jax, intent on his face.

Jax refused to meet his eyes. He didn't know why the Inquisitor wanted to catch his gaze, but whatever Kazaryk wanted, Jax would be sure not to give it. "I could be," he lied.

Kazaryk almost capered in place. "Yes, bleed her dry. Drain away her life and take her power. We need sorcery. You can be our sorcerer."

Jax shuddered, wishing he could recall more of the intervening two hundred years. Even with Yvaine gone, much of that time was a blur. If this was how everyone thought of sorcery, no wonder it had been lost. Maybe so much secrecy had been a mistake. Perhaps if they knew the truth—but if they knew how much power her blood held, they might be all the more eager to drain her dry. He could discuss it with her later. Now, he needed to get her out of here. Alive.

She worried him, the way she sat in the big striped-velvet chair, staring at the vicinity of his chest, as if he weren't even there. Could she have truly meant what she said?

No. She had lied. Lied to the magicians and to the magic—but she couldn't lie to him. She loved him. She trusted him. He had to trust her. He had to carry out his part of the plan.

A decanter of spirits on a table shoved into the corner of the room caught his eye. These men—these bloodthirsty men—had no idea how sorcery truly worked. They believed one could steal magic by stealing blood. Therefore . . .

"Let us share her power among us all." Jax went to the table and splashed the whiskey into five glasses, then carried the tray to the center of the room. Kazaryk, almost slavering at the idea, fetched a spindly-legged table from the front hall and set it to hold the tray.

Jax took Amanusa's hands and lifted her to her feet. Kazaryk moved as if to grab her arm and Jax swept her out of his reach, into his own hold. "She is *mine,*" he snarled, hoping he sounded more possessive thug than protective mate.

Kazaryk spread his hands and backed away, his gloating smile still in place. "What will you do with her?"

"Spill her blood."

Jax didn't like how Kazaryk watched Amanusa, didn't like his eyes darting over her body and never her face, didn't like his tongue flicking out to touch his lip before vanishing again.

Jax held his hand out for the knife he'd used earlier. Oleg fetched it from the sofa. Kazaryk licked his lips again. Mikoyan and Paolo stood on either side of the chair where Amanusa had worked the blood magic, their arms folded, faces stolid. It was clear they believed he had changed sides, that he now wanted revenge against Amanusa. They didn't seem to disapprove of vengeance, but they didn't seem to want to participate.

Jax lifted the sharp boning knife and turned Amanusa's right hand palm up. He'd cut his own hand. They wouldn't suspect he had no intention of killing her if he cut her in the same place. He looked at her, waited until she looked back, drowned him in the blue of her eyes. Could she read the message in his eyes? *Trust me.*

He laid the knife against her palm and drew it across in the outflow of his breath. Immediately, crimson drops welled up and began to flow. Jax held her hand over each glass in turn, letting one or two fat drops fall before moving to the next. The blood plunged into the amber liquid, dispersing like smoke. He hoped Amanusa had charged the spell, but if she hadn't, he could speak the spell while she worked the magic.

With their blood bond broken, could they still work magic that way? He hoped so. It was the best he could come up with.

"Why her hand?" Kazaryk snatched up a glass, peering at the whiskey inside it. "Why not cut her wrist, bleed her out?"

"Because I'm not ready to do that yet. I don't want to waste any of it, and to let it puddle on the floor would be a mess as well as a waste." Jax clasped her hand in his, fingers twined, cut to cut, and willed his own wound to bleed more.

His bleeding had slowed, but not stopped completely. The wound was still raw. He wanted her blood inside him again and his inside her. He'd cut her right hand rather than the left for that reason. He could hide their entwined hands in her skirts and still drink with the others.

He held a glass out to Mikoyan, who didn't quite hide his distaste, but came to take it anyway. Kazaryk handed a glass to Paolo, and Oleg picked up his own.

"To success." Jax lifted the last glass in a toast. His success was not theirs, but they didn't know that.

"To victory." Kazaryk gloated a moment more, then tossed the whiskey and blood down his throat.

Everyone drank. Mikoyan and Paolo only sipped. Oleg tossed his back like Kazaryk. Jax did as well. He wanted as much of Amanusa's blood inside him as he could get. He would finish off the alchemists' whiskey if they set it aside.

Damn his stunted magic-sense. He couldn't tell if any magic was working. Was Amanusa gathering it up? It took time for the magic to work its way into a man's system, but his blood-to-blood contact with Amanusa ought to work more quickly.

"I don't feel any different," Kazaryk said after a few minutes.

"Give it a little time," Jax said.

"You were at the session yesterday. You were *in* the session. You should remember," Mikoyan said.

"That *farce*." The Inquisitor sneered and poured himself another drink.

Jax held tight to Amanusa's hand. Justice magic took only a few drops. More blood could change it to different magic. He wouldn't spike Kazaryk's drink again. But Kazaryk didn't ask for it. Maybe he wanted to see how the first dose hit him. He would learn soon. Surely.

Something whispered through the back of Jax's mind. *Amanusa?* he thought at her. No answer came.

Warmth bloomed. Love. *Amanusa.* She had returned to him. He hugged her close inside his mind, his heart. *Blood of my blood,* he thought fiercely. *Our blood, all of it,* one.

He *reached* for her, pushing his love at her. Amanusa whimpered. Kazaryk smirked. Silently, Jax pleaded for her to feel the magic, to take hold of his love and do what only she could do.

Without releasing her bleeding hand, he grabbed her shoulder and spun her roughly around to face him, giving her a sharp shake. Would she understand? "Thought you could get away with it, didn't you?"

He caught her face in a harsh grip, forcing it up to his, but she wouldn't look at him. He shook her again. "Look at me, woman. You belong to me now, do you understand?"

Her lashes flickered and she glanced up at him. Her eyes caught and held.

"You're mine," Jax growled at her, willing her to feel his love, accept it. "Until your life ends. *Mine.*"

She blinked at him. Her mouth dropped open in a gasp.

"We have all tasted your blood, taken in your power. It's in us now." Jax brought her injured hand to his mouth and ran his tongue across the still-oozing cut. She watched him do it, her tongue sliding over her lower lip in echo of his action, drawing his body tight despite the lingering pain.

"Your blood," he repeated. "Your power, inside all of us."

Amanusa's gaze flicked from his mouth to his eyes

as he prayed for her to understand his meaning and finish the spell. To bind him again, or at the very least, to deal with the men who'd kidnapped them, forced this brokenness upon them.

"You want my blood? To take my power?" Her voice held fear, but the touch across his mind held a fierce and powerful love.

"It's already mine." With one hand he gripped her shoulder and with the other, he licked up the blood that had pooled in the cup of her hand, holding her gaze as he did. "I'll take it all. I want it, and I will have it."

Yes, he thought, and *Please,* and *Hurry.*

The power slammed into him, a locomotive crashing through his veins. The blood bond of a familiar snapped back into place as if it had never left him, and he laughed aloud.

Kazaryk looked from Jax to Amanusa, a faint smile on his face. "Can you feel it? Is it the power you stole?"

"I stole nothing." Jax's grin felt feral. Vicious. Hungry. "She gave everything I asked."

"Oh, my God, it is back," Oleg cried. "The familiar bond is back."

"Kill her!" Kazaryk shouted.

Magic flared. Jax could see it again. It slid off the shields Amanusa had built around him, but she staggered.

"No!" He hauled her in close, hoping to wrap her in the shielding she'd given him. "You were supposed to save some for yourself."

"I love you," she whispered.

"I love you." He poured his love into her, pushed

and shoved so she would know how much he loved. "And if you get yourself killed, I will never forgive you. Now, stop them, damn it! They've tasted your blood."

She took the love he gave her and wrapped herself in it. The magic attacking them swirled around her, as if she'd vanished to its senses.

Amanusa turned to the four male magicians in the room, white with terror. Mikoyan stood firm, despite his fear, and Paolo stood quaking beside him. Oleg and Kazaryk scrambled to flee. With a flick of her wrist, they froze in place.

Jax stared. He cleared his throat. "Amanusa, love, what are you doing?"

"Stopping them. Isn't that what you wanted me to do?"

The fleeing magicians were frozen in midstep, eyes rolling in terror and fury. Jax had never seen such a thing. When Yvaine wanted to stop someone, she rendered them unconscious and they fell to the floor. She'd never turned anyone into conscious statuary.

"I didn't think you would do it like this." He walked around Oleg, studying his unbalanced posture.

"I didn't think so either, but Jax, there's so much power. You gave me so much when the bond reformed, I was—I just—I said *stop* and this is what they did."

Jax walked up to Mikoyan, who had refused to run. "This one—was he truly trying to rescue me from you?"

Amanusa's face got that absorbed look it got when she worked magic to probe thoughts. "Yes. He has a very poor opinion of women—" She came out of the spell to look at Mikoyan. "Some women are feather-brained idiots," she said to him. "But I think we can agree that a good many men are idiots as well, can't we?"

She linked her arm through Jax's. "He didn't want me killed, but he thought you should have your chance at revenge. He disapproved of what he thought you were trying to do." She smiled and patted Mikoyan's cheek with her clean hand. "He's the chivalrous sort who thinks women ought to be cosseted and protected and kept like pets, rather than allowing us to grow into our adult strength. He's a bit afraid of strong women."

"Any man with good sense is." Jax kissed her hand and smiled to let her know he was teasing. Mostly.

He looked at Mikoyan. "You broke the blood bond between us—or forced Amanusa to do it—so that I could choose. I have. I choose my wife, the woman I love with all my heart. Now, the bond is back—"

"Not exactly." Amanusa was apparently thinking again.

Jax's heart started to pound. "What do you mean, *not exactly?*"

"It's not the same bond. It doesn't feel the same. Does it feel the same to you?"

Suddenly frantic, Jax groped for the magic he'd never truly been able to sense. Amanusa caught his hand—except, she was already holding his hand. Had been since he'd laid their cuts together. He squinted—but it wasn't his eyes, exactly, that he used. He felt Amanusa's flesh-and-blood hand, and he felt another extra-physical hand holding his.

A hand that glowed, and as it glowed, somehow

transformed into a ribbon of light hovering between them. No—not light. Love. The light was love, and it tied them together and flowed between them.

"I can see it," he whispered. "I can actually see it, head-blind as I am. It's beautiful."

"It is, isn't it? I wish you could see it the way I do." Amanusa's eyes focused on Mikoyan as she leaned her head on Jax's shoulder. "I think I am actually grateful to you for forcing us to break Yvaine's bond. It was her magic that bound us, you know. And her spell was flawed. It was a one-way bond, tying Jax to Yvaine, but not Yvaine to Jax. He was Yvaine's servant, but not her familiar. It made the bond weak, and it made the magic weak. By breaking her bond, we were able to forge our own. A true familiar's bond. A heart bond."

"Built on love—" Jax breathed, understanding.

Amanusa looked up at him. "Yes. It wasn't magic you handed me when we reforged the bond. It was love."

"You could do so much better than bind yourself to me," he whispered, for her alone. "Than a headblind cripple who's lived too long past his time. You could have someone with more power, more magic. But I can't give you up."

"Someone else might have more magic," Amanusa whispered back. "But no one else could love me half so much as you do, nor could I love anyone else. You're the only one for me, the only one who could have taught me how to love. And love carries so much more power than magic."

Kazaryk made a strangled noise in his throat, drawing Amanusa's attention.

"Ah. Inquisitor Kazaryk is choking on our mawkish sentimentality again." She stretched up to give Jax a too-brief kiss. "We had better tend to our prisoners."

31

YOU'LL NEED TO blank their minds," Jax said. "Erase what they've learned about sorcery."

"Why?" Amanusa frowned. "Wouldn't it be safer if everyone knows sorcery can't be worked with stolen blood? Only with that willingly given?"

"That much is safe. But not that it's your blood that works the greatest magic. We'd never get it inside anyone again."

"You're right." She turned toward the two alchemists. "You two had better finish your drinks. You've taken too little blood to be safe. The less blood you've had, the harder it is for me to control the magic. So drink up, boys." She made a bottoms-up gesture and Mikoyan's arm jerked, sloshing some of his drink. "I've released you enough for that."

Mikoyan and Paolo gulped down the rest of their whiskey.

"What will you do with us?" Paolo licked the whiskey off his upper lip. "Kill us?"

Amanusa dropped her forehead onto Jax's shoulder and shook her head, sighing. "Why doesn't anyone ever listen to me?"

She lifted her head and looked Paolo in the eye. "*Listen.* Actually pay attention to what I say and let it soak through your ears into your tiny little brain, all right? Are you listening?" She looked at Mikoyan, at Kazaryk and Oleg.

"I am not a murderer," she said. "I have killed, yes. In self-defense. Because what those men in the outlaw camp wanted to do to me—I would rather they killed me. Should I have simply died? Do you deny me the right to fight with the weapons I have?"

Her hand closed around Jax's upper arm, fingers digging in hard enough to bruise. Jax reached across with the hand that had finally stopped bleeding, and pried her gently loose. She glanced at him and some of the tension slipped away, though the anger remained. He hoped it was her own anger, rather than his overwhelming her.

"Am I wrong to defend myself now?" She flicked her eyes toward Oleg and Kazaryk, as if afraid what her anger might do if she looked at them full on. "Inquisitor Kazaryk wanted to kill me. He has wanted to kill me for some time now. He would have allowed Jax to kill me, but he wants me dead. He still does. Look at the hate in his eyes. I stopped him. I could have killed you already, but I didn't. I won't. I don't want your not-so-innocent blood on my hands."

"Blank memory," Jax whispered. He didn't want her forgetting to do what had to be done.

"Do you think I could erase Kazaryk's madness as well?"

"I think that might take a bit more time than we have, even if it were possible."

Amanusa sighed. "Likely you're right. If you'd catch those two—I think they'll be more comfortable if they're unconscious."

Jax obliged. Oleg was a large and heavy young man. He thumped a bit when he hit the floor. Kazaryk wasn't nearly so large, so Jax thumped him on the way down.

"Jax." Amanusa's scold held amusement and affection. "That wasn't very sporting."

"It wasn't very sporting of them to tie me down and try to rip my heart out," he grumbled.

"How exactly do I do this 'blanking'?" She walked closer to look down at the unconscious men.

"I don't have Yvaine's library in my head anymore, but I believe you ride their thoughts to the memory you want and . . . smooth it over."

Amanusa blew out a breath of air. "All right. We'll start with Inquisitor Kazaryk for practice."

Jax nodded. "Might be a touch hard on Kazaryk, but given what he wanted to do to you . . ."

She took another deep breath, and as she let it out, she caught hold of her magic in the conjurer's blood and slid inside his mind. It was not a pretty place, but she was able to shut out the ugliness and concentrate on actual memory. Of course, his memory was shaded with his mania. Kazaryk saw her as a femme fatale with blood dripping from her mouth and coating her hands. She didn't bother correcting the memory. Who else would see it?

Quickly, she found the pieces she wanted, where Jax had to repeat himself so many times about her blood being inside the others. She was able to locate Kazaryk's horrified realization of what that meant, and all the other moments of understanding, and one at a time, she washed them away. She scrubbed a bit too hard to begin with, and erased a bit more than necessary, but they were bits he wouldn't miss. She thought.

After Inquisitor Kazaryk, she blanked out the pertinent parts of Oleg's memory, then turned to the still conscious alchemists. "You understand why I am doing this," she said, watching Mikoyan's reaction.

"Guild secrets." Mikoyan inclined his head. "I understand."

"I will touch no other part of your memory save for my time in this house."

Mikoyan gave his little bow again. He could move only his head and one arm, so could give only little bows. "Thank you," he said. "You are that rarest of creatures, an honorable woman."

"And isn't it a pity that honorable men are just as rare?" Her smile felt a little bleak.

"If I might request—I would prefer to remain conscious while you perform this magic. If I am to lose the memory of my children, I should like to hold them in my mind as long as possible."

"I won't touch your children, Mr. Mikoyan, but I don't object to your request." She raised an eyebrow. "Ready?"

He gave a brusque nod. The muscles under his control tensed, but while her blood flowed in his veins, no shield could keep her out. She slid in easily and found the memories, and the conclusions he'd reached because of them. On this third time, it was easier to precisely scrub away the necessary bits.

Then she called to her blood inside Mikoyan, breaking a tiny vessel inside his nose for it to escape. Jax caught it on a tissue and tossed it in the grate to burn with the blood from the others. She finished her spell with Paolo, and Jax had just set match to the papers when the front door rattled.

Jax leaped across the room to put himself between Amanusa and the door, bringing the fireplace poker up as weapon. Esteban burst in, followed closely by Harry, Grey, Vaillon, and a number of policemen. Their charge faltered, and they stared.

"Well." Harry propped his hands on his hips. "Looks like you rescued yourselves. Again."

"Sorry." Amanusa shifted her shoulders in a sort-of shrug. "But not truly. They were going to kill us."

"So this gentleman informed us." Vaillon indicated Esteban. "How did you . . . prevail?"

Amanusa sighed. "When people insist on believing that sorcery's power comes by stealing it, it's easy."

"Are they dead?" Esteban asked, eyes rolling toward Oleg and Kazaryk.

"Unconscious. They were the leaders of this plot." She didn't believe the alchemists deserved as much blame as the other two, but they shouldn't get off scot-free, either.

"Let's take 'em all back to the conclave and let the governors decide wot to do with 'em." Harry paused. "If that's all right with you, Captain. Your country, after all."

"Your magicians," Vaillon replied.

He gestured at his subordinates, who came to bear the unconscious men away. Amanusa released the magic on Mikoyan and Paolo, who staggered, but didn't fall. Not with the policemen gripping their arms. Amanusa stumbled as she followed, when the floor boards jumped up in front of her feet.

Jax caught her. "No more magic for you today."

Harry frowned. "What about the 'earing? Before the conclave, about all this?"

Grey urged Harry out of the way so Jax and Amanusa could pass. "I am sure Mrs. Greyson's wizardly admirers—Dr. Rosato, perhaps—would be happy to mix up a truth potion for the witnesses." Grey winked at Amanusa.

She couldn't make her eyes work well enough to wink back. "Truth serum would be good." She couldn't rest yet. But as Jax levered her masses of petticoats into the carriage, she couldn't quite recall why.

Amanusa slept through most of the hearing, on a cot that had been set up in a back room for the governing board's secretaries. All five kidnappers gave account of what they had done, according to French law, as did Jax. As darkness fell, they sent him to wake her and bring her in to tell what she had done, giving her time only to comb and tie back her hair and splash water on her face. She wore her same wrinkled, blood-spattered dress.

On the dais, Dr. Rosato handed her a cup of tea; which she drank. It had an odd aftertaste, but wasn't bad, with plenty of honey to sweeten it. After a moment, she began to feel light-headed, and one of the Massileans eased her into the chair that magically appeared behind her.

Under Vaillon's questioning, she told what had happened in the house in Montmartre, from the time she entered until the time she left, somehow managing to hold back sorcery guild secrets. When Vaillon was satisfied, Gathmann rose.

"Is there anything you would like to say to this conclave assembly?" he asked her.

Amanusa blinked. Was there? "Yes." She struggled to her feet and took Dr. Rosato's arm to walk to the podium. She stood there until the moment of dizziness retreated, looking out at the crowd.

"You lost sorcery," she said, "because of lies told about it. Sorcery has returned, and still you are afraid to give up the lies. None of the blood spilled in that house came from the kidnappers. Every bit of the blood you see on my dress belongs to my husband and to me, spilled by those who took us captive. Blood drawn by force, stolen blood, is innocent blood. It turns its power against those who shed it. Consider then, gentlemen. How can sorcery work by stealing the blood of innocents if that blood will turn against the sorcerer? It cannot."

A murmur rose in the crowd as they began to discuss her words.

"Blood magic comes from life, not death." Amanusa tried to hold the gaze of the crowd, and couldn't. But she tried. "Only blood willingly given, like that spilled in the miracle of birth, or like that donated by Mr. Carteret yesterday, can call up the magic to work spells. What you fear is nothing but a lie told for so long that the truth was suppressed.

"But it wasn't the supposed evil of sorcery that our kidnappers disliked. They would have been perfectly happy for my husband to steal my power by bleeding me dry and become the sorcerer. Because he is a man and I am a woman.

"Are you all so weak, so uncertain of your manhood that a strong woman can frighten you? It takes both men and women to create new life. Neither can usurp the role of the other. Why then is it so impossible to believe that not only is it good and proper for women to work magic just as men do, but that it might be necessary?

"What if suppressing sorcery and barring women from magic is the very thing that created these dead zones? What if the only way to drive them back is to admit more women to the ranks of master magicians? What will you do then?"

Harry leaped to his feet, shouting something that was drowned out by the din exploding across the chamber. Gathmann came to pound on the podium as Rosato eased Amanusa out of the way. Harry bounded up the steps onto the dais.

"Decide!" he shouted, audible once the noise began to subside. "I proposed two days ago that Amanusa Whitcomb Greyson be named master sorcerer and a full member of the International Magician's Conclave. She has produced a master-level work of magic in the wall around the dead zone—which still holds firm, I might add. And she has used magic to defend herself and others against deadly attack—of several varieties. This fulfills all the requirements of master's level. It is time to decide!"

"Vote!" Grey shouted. "Vote! Vote!" The assembly picked up the chant and it took several minutes of banging to quiet them.

"Show of hands," Gathmann ordered. "All in favor."

Hands sprang up all across the chamber, a sea of waving hands.

"Opposed," the president called.

The sea vanished. Other hands popped up, but they

were tiny schools of fish leaping from the vastness of the sea.

"Measure passes!" Gathmann slammed the gavel down in an echoing boom that expanded beyond physical hearing, with magic responding somehow. "Amanusa Whitcomb Greyson is accepted as master sorcerer by the Ancient and Noble Conclave of All Magic."

The chamber erupted into cacophony yet again. Cheering mostly. Amanusa smiled as Dr. Rosato shook her hand and Harry caught her up in a bear hug. Where was Jax? She wanted Jax.

And then he was there, sweeping her into a tight hug. "I knew you could do it."

"How did you get in?" Amanusa let him lead her down the steps to the front row where Grey had saved seats.

"Seems there's a rule about allowing familiars into the meetings. There are four cats, an owl, a crow, and two stoats presently attending the conclave. It took awhile to convince them a man could be a familiar, but Sir William finally got me in. He's not comfortable with the idea, but he'll tolerate us."

On the dais, Gathmann was continuing with the hearing, determining punishment for the kidnappers. Esteban the conjurer was sent back to apprentice level from journeyman for six months. Paolo would go back to apprentice for two years, under Gathmann rather than Yuri Mikoyan, who was barred from practicing magic for that same two years. Massileans led him away to put the bar in place that would render him head-blind. When the sentence was up, they would remove it.

Oleg and Anton Kazaryk were both barred for life from the practice of magic, as well as sentenced to prison in France. Kazaryk turned hate-filled eyes on Amanusa as he was led away, and she shivered. She knew there were others who hated blood magic whose minds hadn't been changed by her words, Nigel Cranshaw for one. She and Jax—and everyone who supported them—would have to remain on their guard.

"So," Harry leaned across Grey to whisper. "What're you goin' to do now?"

"I suppose we'll go to England," Amanusa said. "To Scotland, to take possession of my inheritance. Once Jax and I have sorted everything there, we'll begin taking apprentices, so we can do something about these dead zone things."

Harry nodded and clapped his hands on his thighs. "Sounds good. We'll see you in a couple o' weeks then."

Amanusa exchanged a laughing glance with Jax, who took over. "Let's make it a couple of months," he said. "We are newlyweds after all. And you've got a new apprentice to settle yourself."

"Oh, right." Harry stood and looked down at them. "So I do. It's goin' to be interestin', the next little while. There's new blood come into the council. I'm right eager to see what's goin' to 'appen."

"So am I." Amanusa leaned into Jax, her partner in magic and in life. "Good things. New things. I can't wait."

A few short months ago, she'd been powerless, isolated, living in fear. She had dreamed of justice for her family and of learning magic but never dared hope she might actually achieve either dream. And then Jax had appeared.

He handed her everything she had ever dreamed of—justice, yes, and powerful magic. Then he went on to give her more than she thought possible. She now had more money than she could spend in a lifetime, she who had once possessed only a single dress, but that was the least of his gifts. He brought her friends, the first in more than a decade. True friends, who would stand at her side in any fight. But the very best thing Jax had given her was himself.

His kindness, his steadfast loyalty, his bottomless love had healed the gaping wounds in her heart and soul. Challenges might lie ahead, but they didn't matter. With Jax at her side, challenges could be handled. With his blood flowing through her veins, the next hundred years would be better than she'd ever thought possible.

TOR
ROMANCE

Believe that love is magic

Please join us at the website below for more information about this author and other great romance selections, and to sign up for our monthly newsletter!